THE COMMON: PART I

KING OAK

THE COMMON: PART I

KING OAK

CATHERINE ARTHUR

For more information:

catherinearthur.com

Cover design Nell Wood

First edition June 2021

ISBN 978-3-033-08351-6 (paperback)
ISBN 978-3-033-08352-3 (ebook)

For Robin, my father

For Maureen, my mother

For Jack and Beth

In memory of Doris Arthur 1905–2001

The Running Horse, Leatherhead by Doris Arthur

Prologue

The Common is an ancient forest, where mighty oaks and other trees are teased to awkward shapes by pollard and persuasion. Stunted trunks yield long skinny branches which reach to the sky like fingers for a pie. Accessible, manageable, useful, invaluable. For homes, farms, and industries: firewood, charcoal, tanning.

It is a place where fallen logs, kindling twigs and sticks are gathered up and dried. The seasoned wood warms local hearths in the dead of winter, when frost or snow lie on the hard, ungiving ground. The fuel feeds the fires which cook the broths and stews of pea and barley, to bring a little satisfaction to the hungry bellies of those who live around the forest's edge.

Common people hunt and gather there. Under stunted oaks, or ones full grown, or trees of beech, ash, birch or hazel, and in amongst tall bracken, they graze their lean sheep, scraggy goats and greedy pigs, and here and there a cow or two. In good years, when the weather is their friend, they see their scrawny beasts grow heavy from The Common's land, perhaps even fat enough to add a little meat to their pots of paltry gruel.

At its fringes, an area of scrub where wise ones gather plants and herbs, and turn them into cures for common ailments. The Rye Brook wends through the landscape, lending reeds for rush-lights, to brighten for a moment, their dark and gloomy hovels.

The Common is a place where hunters chase their prey, where lovers meet and lovers love, and criminals conceal their crimes. Where children play and fight, find a fossil or a piece of ancient Roman tile, long buried in the earth. Some pretty treasure for their empty chests.

Common land it is.

Heavy, yellow clay lies atop a deep layer of sand, the soil acidic, barely fertile, waterlogged in places. Meagre, manorial waste, all but forgotten by local landlords and good for nothing except as bare bone, thrown to keep the common people peaceable.

And yet, The Common is invaluable.

A partnership of wood and earth, bird and beast, plant and pasture.

And, most of all, of common folk.

PART ONE

THURSDAY, JUNE 8

1780

Woodfield Lane

Late Evening

As the day fades, tiny points of light begin to decorate the early night sky and Molly Hogtrough is struggling homewards to the edge of The Common. The dilapidated cottage she shares with her husband George and their three year old son is actually her grandmother's. And by the grace of God, Eliza Greenfield has agreed to let them in.

A hefty sack of laundry and the wet London clay under Molly's tired old boots make the journey difficult. She cannot see where her feet fall under an enormous bump of shabby brown dress, and the ridges made by heavy carts give way easily under her weight, so down she slips into furrows of muck and sludge. One of her boots has almost come to the end of its patched-up life, its holey toe and paper thin sole flap together in a tuneless song and soft clay oozes between her toes. A sobering sensation, for there is no coin to buy another pair.

She hiccups, burps an acid bubble into the still evening air. 'Oh, do excuse and beg me pardon,' she says, in a put-on lah-di-dah voice, and giggles, turns to see if anyone is there to hear. Her husband, perchance? No. George promised he would catch her up, but her heart knows, *the bugger ain't coming,* and her giggle turns to grumble, 'Madame Geneva, you be repeating some this eve.'

Another burp, and second-hand gin comes up to greet her teeth. Her gullet is made raw as the harsh alcohol she drinks to numb her fears rises and falls like a spring tide. A tiny part of her wishes she had not drunk so much. But she likes what it does, it makes her free and fearless, forgetful of the work that lies ahead. However, as she stumbles along the lane, Madame is retreating and Molly Hogtrough will soon have to face her future once again.

The laundry seeps smells. Goose and tallow fat, sweat and urine, stale ale, spent tobacco and something equally unpleasant which she cannot place. She gags, and it is all she can do not to heave up the gin. Instead, she pulls the bag onto her back, away from her nose and becomes a snail. Father William comes immediately to mind, her wretched father-in-law, who walks bent double all the time now. *Not his choice, 'tis God's design,* she thinks. Punishment for what the old man inflicts on those who do their best to care for him.

Snail-walking does not help. Her heavy belly pulls and stretches her skin to its furthest limit. Discomfort is a reminder that what she has drunk to forget will not vanish, but must, in the end, be faced.

She stands up and the sack falls into the mud, splattering her already grimy skirt. She looks down at the dirty linen, cups her hands around her distended belly and her heart sinks. These loads weigh heavily on her conscience, her time, her spirits. When the laundry is done she will be eased for sure, but the outcome of childbirth is never certain. It will be a miracle if she survives it this time. She cannot be sure, cannot see, just as she cannot see past church on Sunday, but she believes there are two babies. Too many arms and legs are pushing against her skin and she hears their innocent souls in her heart. She crosses herself with a whispered prayer for a safe delivery, and smooths her hand over her skirt. *Don't burst.* ''Tis nearly time, God help me,' escapes her lips and her fear makes her belly queasy.

She looks back at her tracks in the mud. They lead to Ashted village, to The Leg of Mutton and Cauliflower Inn, where she left her husband. Or rather, where he remains. For she did not leave by choice. She was pushed. If he follows her tracks he will catch her up, like he said he would. But the chances are he will not, for Hal Archer has his attention now. *Damnded scoundrel! Bloody man.* Her curses flow like gin, and she is sure her husband and his friend are cooking up some crooked scheme. *Bloody man.* She is repeating as much as Madame Geneva.

The faint, up and down music of Moses King's pocket fiddle floats towards her, over the rise and fall of the land between the lane and The Leg. She peers and pushes her eyes into the gloom, wills the shape of her husband to appear. She can't see him, can't hear his footsteps, and neither can she hear him whistling, nor calling for her to wait. She can only hear his hollow promises.

If you go on ahead, I'll catch you, he promised. *Ten minutes at most, that's all I shall be.*

Liar. Bastard. She is ahead, but he hasn't caught her. His promises of late have been sorely empty, like his pockets. Unlike his tankard.

She revisits them, his promises. First, those he had no choice but to utter over five years ago, in front of the Rector and a whole congregation of witnesses, who will surely hold him to account. She travels along the strands of her memory, back to a misty morning in late October when he stood next to her in the cold and ancient parish church of St. Giles. How time crawls. It feels like forever. She is eighteen, her belly starting to swell and her husband to be is tall and warm and beardy beside her. He smells of man and straw and leather. His smile softens her heart, her fingers long to reach out, to stroke his cheek, to twist through his wiry beard. She remembers all his promises, as clear as a hunter's moon.

Love. Comfort. Honour.

Keep, in sickness and in health.

Keep only to me as long as we both shall live.

Have, hold, cherish, till death do us part.

Endow with all my worldly goods.

She leans her thoughts against each one to see how they have been kept. Or not.

Love. The way he strokes her, tickles his whiskers over her skin. Tingles her all over. His face, all smiles and never a frown when she puts supper before him. *Could be love. Or p'raps just cupboard love.*

Comfort. A helping hand, a glowing fire, a warm body to

snuggle up to in a soft, dry bed. A shoulder to cry on when a child is lost. But the roof leaks, the cupboards are nearly bare and the decaying firewood is dwindling. And where is he now? *With Hal Archer. Damn you, Hal-bloody-Archer.*

Honour. She pushes this aside, unsure of its meaning.

Keep, in sickness and in health. Being with child is surely not a sickness, but it is a stretch to say she is in health. Her whole body aches, the great weight she is carrying pulls her to the ground like a rusty iron anchor. He told her this evening that she waddles like a duck, but if she were a duck he would keep her. He would feed her stale bread, collect her eggs and protect her from foxes. And he doesn't keep her. He might even let her starve if he does not find work soon. And Hal-bloody-Archer is a fox if ever she saw one.

Keep only to me. This is worrying. His whiskers tickling another woman? *Good Lord!* It makes her squeamish and squirmy, sick to her heart. She shudders.

Have. He has her regularly, or used to, before her belly grew. Now her swelling is so monstrous she is scared it might burst if he stirs it. A dread surfaces and she returns momentarily to *Keep only to me.* Has her husband been getting his *have* elsewhere? She shakes her head to dispel the frightful thought, but it is a question she has asked herself too often recently.

Hold. He often holds her, wraps his arms around her, squeezes her. Too tight, sometimes, but only when they are away from certain eyes which might judge him too soft. Like Hal Archer, for instance. *Damn!* The man has invaded her thoughts again, that pillager of promises. That poacher of oaths. She pushes her husband's friend away to the shadows, but he keeps coming back like a fox in the night to steal whatever he can and leave misery in his wake.

Cherish. If this were a promise kept, her husband would surely be here with her, easing her heavy load of smelly smalls.

All his worldly goods. He has no worldly anything. He has nothing, except perhaps his whiskers. And his empty pockets. They live in Eliza Greenfield's cottage, where their bed has woodworm, the mattress stinks, and she cooks on a fire fed by rotten logs. He doesn't even have work. A few words burst out from between her pursed lips and she hears them fill the evening air. 'Damn you, George Hogtrough,' and she makes another cross.

As the gin fades she remembers too much of her precarious future and wishes she had drunk a gallon. Her husband's list of unkept promises grows.

See me safely home.
Help with the smelly sack.
Gather firewood.
Tend the strip.
Fetch water.
Find work!

Find work be most important. Without this we shall surely be lost, and she begins to scold her husband, but only in his absence, for Molly Hogtrough would never dare do it to his face. *If you just keep this one promise, everything would be better. I don't want to be lost, Georgie,* she tells him, silently. *I want to be kept.*

She looks up, and there is the dark shadow of the House across the fields, silhouetted against the darkening sky. That House is a place where no one wants to go and none escape. *The Workhouse. Once you get in there, you be well and truly lost,* she shivers and leans over, vomits onto the ground. Now there is a slick puddle of fear in the half-light at her feet and the yellow clay earth holds it fast, like it threatens to hold her boots.

Her throat is scratchy, for this evening's gin was particularly rough. The Darling of Dorking, the innkeeper called it. *Huh! Some darling.* But oh! How it banishes her frets and fears, and in their place come delicious fantasies. It keeps her. Holds her. It is like clay earth. But she's greedy, that Dorking bitch, needs frequent topping up. True, she promises nothing, but she leaves Molly's soul empty, a pain in her head and a sickness in her guts. George, on the other hand, promises much, but leaves the cupboards bare, an ache in her heart and another mouth to feed in her belly. And this time, there are probably two. She cannot win.

As she trips down the lane, she is more sober and tired by the minute. She stops to rest a moment at the side of the track, where meadowsweet rises tall, and honeysuckle and brambles clamber through the hedge, their scent masking the stench of body odours coming from the sack. Madame Geneva was holding back a tide of terror, like King Canute on a good day, and now, without her help, Molly's mind begins to churn. She slips into a reverie, re-spins her husband's promises, replays the evening and tries to imagine an easier, more secure future for them all.

For George and their boy, Little Joe. Her grandmother, Eliza.

For herself, if she survives the coming labours.

And perhaps, for her soon-to-be-born infants.

Rye Cottage

Earlier That Evening

She doesn't want to go to the Inn. Her body throbs, her eyes are drooping and the stool beside the fire beckons. And then her husband pulls her close.

'Come on, Moll, 'twill do you good to get out of this place, just for a bit.' His whiskers tickle her ear as he tries to tease her out of the cottage, 'I shall carry that laundry back home for you and I's sure Joshua Reynolds will offer a drink. Can't say no to that, now. What say you?'

The drink is a temptation indeed, although it is rather a long way to go when there is a flask of gin on the mantelpiece. As she sways in his arms, her jelly-legs lock into place and the room spins a little.

'If you's going up The Leg anyways,' her words come out in a stream, like the gin which has been tippling out of the flask all afternoon, 'you could bring back that washing and save me the trouble.'

'I could, but then I wouldn't have you by me side now, would I, eh? And 'tis about time you got away from here,' and under his ale breath, so the old woman, sitting crumpled in her chair by the fire cannot not hear, he adds, 'and that old bat.'

'Georgie, please,' she whispers back.

She wants to say, *Don't be so cruel to my grandmother, who's kindly provided a home for us under her very own roof,'* but she cannot be so forthright with her man. She holds her tongue, while she can.

''Tas been a while since you and I walked out a bit together, ain't it? Come with me, sweetheart,' and he pulls her closer, his tobacco-stained fingers stroke her chin, tip her head up and she feels his whiskers around her lips. ''Twill do you good, Wife, a stroll up the village.'

He is in a rare cheerful mood, no doubt fuelled by an earlier visit to the inn, and she does enjoy his company when he is in that half way place between sober and blind drunk.

'Alright, I'll come if you promise to carry the laundry.'

'I promise,' he says, and at that moment she believes him, wholeheartedly.

The old woman scowls as they leave the cottage, clicks her tongue on the roof of her mouth like she is geeing up an old nag. It is not a good omen.

'Won't be long, Gran,' Molly calls over her shoulder, and does not look back.

At the end of Common Lane, they cut across the fields, following the cinder path until they reach a wooden gate. George swings it open and bows low, like she is a lady, but she feels like Mother Goose as she patters through. A worn, grassy track leads them up a gentle hill towards their rented strip on the common field, where an abundance of vegetables should be well tended and flourishing at this time of year. God willing, if the weather comes good, a bountiful harvest will grace their table in the coming weeks and fill their stores for winter.

She glances over, and amid her neighbours' thriving plots she sees that theirs is overgrown, neglected. Her heart sinks. With Madame Geneva easing her troubles she looks the other way. In any case, it would not be advisable to remind her husband of his responsibilities and break his easy mood. As they continue towards the village, the early evening sunshine casts tall shadows and the sweet smells of summer grass, wild mint and marjoram, rise from the warmth of field and hedgerow. However, there is also an acrid smell in the air, something burning.

'What be that, Georgie?' she asks. 'Not The Common alight? Surely it be too early, ain't it?'

He laughs at her silliness. 'Come, 'tis only mid-summer. The forest ain't dry and cracked yet. 'Tis London Town, see? Mobs and rioters afoot this week.'

She stops, aghast. 'Good Lord! They ain't coming this way, is they?'

'No, they ain't. So don't you be fretting none. Redcoats went up today. Did you not see them marching across The Common?'

'Aye, I did, too. Joe's been copying them all day long, he has. Says he wants to be a soldier when he grows up.'

'Shall have to put a stop to that, then. Will have no son of mine dying for them toffs and their endless battles,' and he spits out the words, shaking his head.

'Come, 'tis only a game, Georgie. He be just a tot. Ain't serious, like,' she says, and wishes her husband could see the funny side of things.

'Yeah, well, I shall tell him, anyways. Start as we mean to go on with the little man, eh?'

They walk on in silence and stop before a rickety, criss-cross stile, which bars their way onto the Turnpike road. George stands behind his wife and crosses his arms over her swollen bosom.

Together they look back over the land. The hamlet of Woodfield is a huddle of cottages, nestled in the shallow valley along the line of a well-used track. An area of open scrub lies opposite. Further along the lane towards the forest, next to the Rye Brook, lies their home, Eliza Greenfield's old thatched cottage. A short distance over Rye Bridge is Caen Farm, where George once worked, and his childhood home – the tied property, Rose Cottage – stands opposite the Great Barn and the stables.

In the growing calmness of early evening, thin wisps of smoke from the chimneys reach straight up to the heavens. Beyond the tiny homes, a sea of trees, all dressed in their summer finery, stretches out to the horizon.

One tree stands above them all.

'Look! See the King Oak there, in the middle o' The Common? 'Tis where we courted all them years ago,' George says. He nuzzles his beard into her neck and she closes her eyes, remembering that free and easy time. His beard still smells the same, of ale and pipe tobacco, of leather and George.

'Weren't so long back, but it do seem like another lifetime. Afore Joe come along,' she says.

'Afore the old bat, ' George says.

She digs her elbows into his ribs, 'Georgie!' A hasty reaction. The gin has loosened her up, but here, alone, she can get away with it.

'What!?'

'She ain't that bad. You could be more kind.'

''Tis true she's old, though. As ancient as that King Oak, I reckon. Perhaps she ain't as worse as me own father, so I suppose we can be thankful we ain't living at Rose Cottage and looking after that old goat. I be pleased Jesse has the honour now. 'Tis one he be right deservin' of, too.'

'Why d'you say that now? What is it 'twixt you and your brother?' she asks, but does not expect an honest answer, for her husband rarely tells her anything about his life before their marriage.

'Ain't nothing, but you just stay away from the man, you hear me?' and he brushes a fly off her arm.

Jealous! she thinks.

'Anyways, I doesn't want to be thinking of none of them, not Father, nor the old bat, not our son even. 'Tis just you and me here, eh?'

He pushes his groin forward, begins to kiss her neck and fondle her breasts.

'Oh Lordie! George, you does pick your moments,' she laughs. 'But you knows it ain't happening husband. Just look at the size of me!' Now it is clear why he was so keen for her to come along.

'Come, Moll,' he urges, ''tas been ages. Look, we can lie under them trees there. None will see us. An husband got needs, ain't he?'

'Yes, he has. That I will agree on, but Georgie, I beg of you, please. Not now. I doesn't want to begin birthing here, of all places. So far from home and in the open air for all to see,' and she struggles to free herself from his desire.

He huffs and releases her, almost pushes her away. 'No, well, it won't be long now, and when you's all back to normal, like, I's taking you to that old King Oak, and I shall have you like I used to. What say you, Molly-Mary?'

He speaks as if she will survive the birth. She plays along, but perhaps she should let him have her here and now, for it may be the last chance they get.

'You think I shall have time for that, Husband? I shall have me hands full, as if they ain't already now. And will you not be busy at work by then? Lord knows we'll need the coin when these two come.'

The gin is making her ever braver and she has spoiled the moment with her harping on about his lack of work. Why can she not let herself go and have some fun, like she used to? He turns away and a cool breeze catches Molly's arms as his mood sours.

'Aye, well, I shall soon find work, you'll see! Our fortunes are changing. Soon everything will be better, I promise. I got plans, I has. Have faith.'

However, faith is not a virtue she can summon this evening. 'Changing fortunes sounds good alright, but God help us if them plans don't go the way you hope.' Molly's tongue is galloping, a loose horse. Her eyes close under her bonnet as the chill shifts into her heart. She has gone too far and waits for her husband's anger to erupt.

He withdraws further, moves six feet away. His eyes darken and his fists ball up. His wife's sixth sense is on form this evening, even with a skinful of gin to dull it, but he hopes she cannot see too much of the unlikely work he has agreed to. He must not let his wife get a sniff of his own fears, for if the dreadful scheme he is embroiled in does not go to plan, then God help them indeed.

Molly tries to focus on the King Oak in the distance, but her gin-eyes see two and she is not sure which one is real. The first time George laid her down beneath it, the tree loomed over them, watching with its enormous knot-eye. She lay on the moss in the gnarled rooty bed and above her, the King's once carefully pollarded branches stood tall, like thick strands of hair with an emerald crown. Just her luck, George planted an acorn there and then. At least he took her to the church when her belly began to show, alas, for nothing, for the babe did not survive to take a breath. Perhaps she should have resisted, listened to her wise grandmother's warning that the man was lazy and stubborn, a runagate. She could add sullen, moody and drunk to that. Perhaps he will cheer up again when they reach The Leg. *He will find work soon.* She repeats it. *Soon. Soon, soon.* And then the word is lost, as if she is hearing it for the first time.

Means nothing, she thinks.

George is already over the rickety stile. 'Need a hand?' he asks.

'I fear it ain't gonna take me weight. Look at that bottom step, 'tis all wonky and cricked,' and she frowns at the impossible obstacle.

'You's always a-feared of sommat these days. Try, or you can go back on your own, for I has need of an ale in me belly. Here,' and he grabs her outstretched hands and pulls her up, onto the step. 'There, weren't so bad, eh?'

She smiles at his already lightening mood, but as she lifts her foot onto the next step, a searing pain tears down her left side.

'Oh Lord! Sommat don't feel right,' she cries.

He is silent, and now it is he who is frowning. He grabs her arms to steady her.

'Let me wait here a moment, Georgie,' she says, and her voice wobbles with her legs.

'You cannot stay there, Wife. Your great weight will have the whole rotten lot over. Climb over quick , I'll see you down alright,' and now her fear has jumped to him.

'Can't do nothing quick, can I? Let me take it slow, I beg of you. Don't pull me.'

In a few moments, the pain subsides and with his help she has both feet on the Turnpike side of the stile.

'Shouldn't have come, Georgie. I knowed I should'a stayed home,' she shakes her head.

He does not speak, will never admit that he is thinking the same, but pulls her close, strokes her face. A tug of love, a momentary show of affection. A small piece of comfort.

As they turn towards the inn, she is startled by a movement at the side of the road. A tall man with dark red whiskers, wearing a dusty tricorn hat, is watching them from the shadows.

George whispers, 'Well, speak o' the old devil, and there he is in all his glory.'

Molly's cheeks turn rosy-red and she thanks the Lord she had not caved in to George's lust, for Jesse Hogtrough, her husband's older brother, is not ten yards from where they would have lain. *God forbid! I should'a died of shame.*

'Jesse, what brings you this way? Ain't our father keepin' you busy wiping his dribbly chin and his stinky arse?' George calls out, with a chuckle.

'George, Molly,' the man growls his greeting, tipping his faded hat towards them. 'I wonder you can find mirth in that, for you knows damnded well that Father's care falls on our sister's shoulders and she does bear it very well, indeed.'

'Aye, but if it should fall on yours I sees no better work for you.'

'And what would you know of work, eh?'

Molly steps forward and puts herself between the warring brothers.

'Come now, 'tis a right fine even', too good for a quarrel,' and she pulls her husband towards his ale. 'Good evenin', Jesse,' and she bobs politely at the man and catches his eye. *A kind eye, hard-working, sober. A good man is that Jesse Hogtrough.*

Jesse turns away, but it is not lost on him that his brother's wife is as drunk as a Lord.

They are like two peas in a pod.

The Leg of Mutton

Early Evening

As they draw closer to the gaggle and kerfuffle of the inn, George's mood lifts. This is his second home. Here, he finds drink and play and friends, deals cards and gossip, and may even find work. When he is not at the inn, he is at cricket in the field behind the old, oak-framed building, or so Emma Cobbett says. Emma, a maid at The Leg and a neighbour from Woodfield, is an invaluable ally. All her tales flow quite freely, for she loves to gossip and she loves her gin. She spills enough beans to keep Molly's larder full all winter.

George sharpens his pace and is several steps ahead, his wife's condition seemingly put out of mind.

She cannot keep up.

'You be waddling like a duck,' he says. 'Get a move on, Molly-Mary,' and as she draws level he pushes her arse with his thick fingers.

'Can't,' she says, resisting his hand, 'me load's too heavy. You carry it.'

'Can't,' he says, with a laugh, 'that be your job, ain't it?'

What be yours then? She wants to ask, but the words get stuck in her throat and all she can manage is, 'Quack, quack.'

The village green is a triangular patch of grass onto which the inn has spilled its patrons. In the centre stands the enormous Ashted Oak, perhaps a brother or a cousin to the King, its leafy branches offering protection against the sultry, early-evening sun and many are gathered under its shady cover. Her thoughts turn to the tree which offered them a bed of moss under its own branches, all those years ago. *That damnded King Oak has a lot to answer for,* she thinks and crosses herself. A cross for a curse, and he sees.

'Why d'you do that?' he asks.

'No reason.'

George tuts, shakes his head. 'I know not what goes on inside that pretty little head of yours.'

'That be a good job, too,' she replies.

George nods at folk, gives out greetings like pennies to the poor. As she looks around, she sees judgemental eyes, and mouths which gape at her gigantic lump, her heavy state. *'That woman should be at home in her condition,'* she hears, and her face begins to burn. The gin is wearing thin.

The innkeeper stands in his doorway, like a fish out of water, gasping for fresh air, for inside it is stuffy and smelly and hot. Joshua Reynolds is kind and generous, and rather round. His huge ginger beard is a foxtail, curled under his ruddy face. Upstairs, he is as bald as a turnip and rivers of sweat flow into an old 'kerchief tied around his neck. When he sees them coming, he pulls at the sodden, useless rag, leans over and stuffs it into an enormous dirty sack lying near the door. *Dear God. That's me laundry,* she thinks, with a heavy heart.

'Georgie,' Joshua Reynolds booms. ''Tis mighty good to see you, my man.' He has a big voice, a broad smile, and his teeth are good and white. 'And the lovely Mistress Hogtrough,' he says, grinning.

'How goes it, Josh? 'Tas been a while, eh?' George says, and winks at the innkeeper. Something unsaid passes between the men and they think she does not know its meaning. They are wrong. *Been a while! Who is he kidding?*

'Yep, that it has,' Joshua chuckles.

Kind and generous, and a liar, too, she thinks. Because George has already been here today and Emma Cobbett has already put his lies to bed. He was not looking for work like he promised. He was drinking and plotting something with Hal Archer, all morning. And he was at cricket, in the field behind the inn, all afternoon.

'Drink, George? And for your good wife?' Joshua Reynolds asks and turns to Molly. 'Gin, is it? Why, this evening 'tis on me, on account of you taking that there laundry,' he says and gestures to the sack, lounging by the door.

The size of it! Gracious Lord, 'tis capital George promised to carry that home.

Joshua Reynolds is babbling like a brook. 'Mistress Reynolds and I, well, we are right grateful you are able to take that load at such short notice.' On and on he goes, the words stream over her like water in the Rye Brook after a storm. Then he glances at her belly, and now his smile does not seem so genuine, for he must be asking himself how on earth she will manage his laundry with that enormous hump. 'So, an ale for yourself, Georgie? Gin for your good wife, yes? I have come by some good local stuff this week. The Darling of Dorking they calls it,' he says with a smile and a nod of his turnip-head.

'I might try that, too, if you don't mind,' George says.

The innkeeper calls to the maid, who is quick to hand him two small pewter cups, half full of clear liquid.

'Cheers, my friend and thank you, kindly,' and George takes a large swig. He shakes his head as the liquid sears his throat. His mouth opens and his pink tongue pokes out between beard and moustache, and he makes a loud *bbrrrrraaahhh*. He grins at Joshua and belches loudly. 'Ah yes! Goes down a treat.'

Joshua Reynolds laughs, but Molly is more than a little embarrassed at her husband's behaviour.

'Now Molly, you taste that and don't you tell me it ain't a true delight.'

She holds the dented pewter cup to her lips. The cold metal feels unfriendly against her warm skin, but the perfume of juniper and thyme is enticing. She takes a large swig, like George. The liquor scratches and burns, takes her breath quite away. She almost coughs it all back up, but blessedly, it stays down. She screws up her face and it goes as red as Joshua Reynolds' beard. For a moment she can't find any air. The men laugh and she sees another something go between them. *Bastards.*

'Go easy, Madam. You should not try to keep up with that husband of yours,' and Joshua winks again. At her, this time.

She recovers her breath and wheezes, 'You be right, Mister

Reynolds, 'tis a right pretty drink, that.' In truth, it is dastardly rough, but she plays along. No point looking more stupid than they already think she is.

And then, nothing matters, for the Darling of Dorking begins to dance through her veins.

'Tip top!' Joshua says and disappears into the gloom of his den.

George studies the noisy crowd. It seems to Molly that he is looking for someone. She contemplates his face while his attention is away. His nose is very straight. *Like Pebble Lane,* she thinks, a way they once walked, from Shepherd's Corner to Mickleham and back. The ancient track never turned until they reached an old farm gate. George told her the road was built by Romans more than a thousand years ago. It was the first time she had ever thought so far back. She wonders if his nose was built by Romans, too.

'Who you be missing this even, Georgie?'

'No one,' he says, dismissively.

'Huh,' she says, in disbelief. *Oops.*

He spins his head. 'What?' His heavy eyebrows come together and his dark eyes have a little glint of sharp in them.

'Nothing,' she says. 'Nothing.' No point upsetting his easy mood.

'I be looking for work, what else?' and he turns back to his search.

She studies his hair. Long and clean and lice-free, for she washed and groomed it this morning, and she noticed how the strands and wisps of silver woven through the brown are showing his age. He is six-and-thirty now, and twelve years her senior. She shudders to think he will be an old man soon, like his doubled-up father. Perhaps he will never find work again.

It is a sobering thought and she takes another sip to quell the surge of angst.

She looks at him again. He is hatless, says they harbour vermin. Perhaps he is right. Jesse always wears a dusty black one with three crooked corners. It suits him, for her husband's brother is a very different man, one who works hard on the land and does not spend time at the inn. Pious and God-fearing and teetotal and serious. *A good man.* And then she cannot stop thinking about her brother-in-law. She tries to concentrate on her husband, who wipes his hot brow and lets his fingers rest on his silvery-brown beard. He twists the ends of his wiry facial hair into stubby bits of string as he scans and peers into the chattering crowd.

His someone in particular has evidently not yet turned up.

He guides her to the edge of the green. There are a few bales of hay to sit on, or the warm grass if you can get down there. It's the getting up she cannot now do. There are smells among the noise of chatter and clank. Cider, gin, brandy, vinegar. Pipe and wood smoke. Roast mutton and cabbage. Sweat and sunshine. Cowpat and cut grass. And still there is that hint of London burning.

She looks around at the gathering. *'Tis like a congregation. The Church of St. Mutton.* Two people are standing near an old table, crying news from London Town and the crowd are eager for morsels, tidbits of terrible tales from the sprawling Metropolis. When it becomes stale they break away, form smaller congregations and talk about broken cartwheels, their hopes for a good run of dry weather, who is bedding whom, or who is the father of Jane's baby, or Eleanor's. And has the man yet been sworn in front of the magistrate? The mother and her child will surely be thrown out of the Parish, perhaps even offered a few pennies to go back to whence they came, for she does not belong here, that fallen woman, and those who are already taxed to the hilt must also pay the poor rates and support a costly war across the Great Pond. They will not want to keep her and her bastard, too. Let it go back to wherever it belongs. Let other men's coffers feed and clothe it.

George, however, is entranced by London talk. All this week it has been of mobs and riots, fires and attacks, on Catholic houses and prisons. Soldiers, shootings and murder by Redcoat. Mannews, to which she can hardly bear to listen. It seems so far away, but the smell of London burning brings it closer to home, to their quiet corner of Surry, which after all, is only two-and-twenty miles from the chaos. And although George has ears for the tales, he is still searching for his missing someone. She reluctantly turns her ears to the two would-be preachers.

'I come direct from Southwark this evening, and when I left the Borough it was very much in flames,' the shorter one says. 'The sky is red with bloody cinders, and after the distillery was broken open, streets boiled with burning gin. They are now blackened with the charred remains of Catholic chattels and Popish furniture, and even the bodies of some men.'

The congregation gasps and prattles at this dreadful image.

'What be the true cause of all this mayhem?' calls out a well-dressed gentleman. 'It cannot be attributed to anti-Catholic sentiment alone.'

'The no-popery mobs are certainly responsible in part,' the other mock-preacher says.

'Is it not Lord George Gordon who has stirred up this disorder? Perhaps he is intent only on political gain,' someone calls out.

She pokes George with a puffy finger, 'Who be that? Lord George Gordon.'

'How should I know? Some bigwig from Town. I only knows the names of them gentry round here, not those from abroad,' he shrugs.

She prays for someone in the congregation to ask about this mysterious man, who has conjured up mobs and rioters against the old religion. Her prayers are immediately answered.

'Tell us about this gentleman, this Gordon, if you will, Sir,' old Mister Piper demands, the man who used to blacksmith for the village when his now gnarled hands could hold the hammer straight, heave it up and strike it down on just the right spot. Now his tongue does the work instead.

'He is rather an eccentric character, descended from Scottish nobility by all accounts,' comes the answer. 'Some say he is a Puritan, others that he is a fanatical, religious madman. I believe the Earl of Guilford may have his work cut out against him.'

'Guilford,' she whispers, poking George again. 'That ain't so far abroad.' The Dorking Darling is making her brave.

'Do not try to be clever, Wife,' and her husband shoots her a dark look. 'And you ain't listenin' right. Guilford ain't Gordon, see?'

She has pushed him too far and retreats back to her almost empty pewter cup. He is an up and down man, her husband. His moods skylark. They may sing up high for a while, but they can also drop down in a flash, to the depths of his soul, and they peck at her heart as they dip past. As the talk drones on, she nudges him.

'Time to go?' she says, a question, not demand.

'Not yet,' he tells her, sharply. 'Wait a bit. I will hear more of what's afoot in the Metropolis,' he says and pulls up her hand

and brings it to his mouth, kisses it tenderly. *Skylark.*

She cannot tell him what to do, he is not that kind of man, and she has no *have* to bargain with at present, always a useful lever. She drains her cup, tips it back and forth, sees dark veins and scratches in the metal. The pewter holds onto things: coffee, brandy, tea, all trapped in its creases. Perhaps her future is caught there, too. She thinks she can make out a tree. *The King Oak?*

'Top-up?' he asks.

'Ain't we going?' she says, impatient to get moving. People are still talking about her size, whispering, '*Why is this woman not at home awaiting her increasement, instead of here, drinking gin like a trollop!? Tch, tch,*' she hears.

'Not yet, Moll!' he says and there is a touch of sour in his voice. A splash of ire. More than a hint of his wretched father William.

'Well then, yes, a top-up,' she says. *Might as well.*

He looks over to the maid and catches her eye. *Bring more,* he gestures. The girl nods, smiles.

Molly does not recognise her, she must be new here. *Is it her? Is he having her while he cannot have me?* She shudders. But would Emma Cobbett not have told her? Now the Darling of Dorking is making her suspicious.

The sun sinks and talk turns ever darker. War with America, disrupted trade, lower wages, rising prices, heavier taxes on tea and brandy, little work to be found. She does not listen, does not really understand how everything connects. Except the last bit. *Little work to be found. That's good. He don't need big work, little work be enough.* Something, anything. To keep the fox from the door, to stop Hal Archer from coming round and poaching him.

'You hear that, Husband? Little work to be found, that be good, ain't it?' Her eyes, with the ever darkening rings around them, glint playfully.

He laughs and whispers, 'No Moll, that ain't good at all. Little work means not much, silly.' He shakes his head and puts his arm around her shoulders, squeezes her tight and kisses the top of her head. How quickly he dips and rises.

It was not a mistake, she knows the meaning, but sometimes George is so deep in his dark he cannot see her light. Anyway, playing this way is safer than catching those dark dagger looks when she tries to be clever. She stares again at the bottom of her empty pewter cup. The veins are different. There is no tree now, just a mish-mash of lines and trapped drink. She can't read them like she can read tea leaves, and scratches cannot possibly tell her future. The maid arrives and covers them up with gin. Molly watches for any signs that there is something between the young woman and her husband, but George does not notice the girl, only the liquid she has poured into his cup, and her fear is quashed.

Lanterns are set on tables and hung from the lowest branches of the Ashted Oak, and lit before the light disappears. They are still droning on about impending doom, those quack-preachers. George is half listening, but still looking for that someone in particular.

'Lord North is responsible for this sorry state of affairs,' someone shouts. 'He has handled the war effort so terrible bad. We will suffer another civil war if he ain't more careful.'

She pokes his side again. 'Who's Lord North?' she mouths, the words hardly leaving her lips.

'That's your Guildford man, right there. He be the Prime

Minister. Once lived here in Ashted, that's how I knows, see? He be the top bigwig in Parly-ment now,' he whispers. 'Close to the King he is, God save him. The King, that is. Not North.'

'Civil war, though? That be bad,' she says. The gin has loosened her tongue some more and she must be careful things don't leak out that she wants kept in, or that will stir up dark looks indeed. That's the problem with Madame Geneva, she is so indiscriminate and sloppy.

'Sshh, Wife,' he says. 'Listen!'

She tries, but gets only half-meanings; soldiers, drafted, uprisings, quell, punishment. Some of these she understands, the rest are like the shadows of birds flying about her ears. She tries to make sense of them, but they remain awkward shapes in her mind and get more muddled as she repeats them.

Dratted, upsingings, quillishment.

Dratting, upsifted, quillment.

Dratment, upsinged, quilfted.

And then they are lost. Her legs are restless, her belly skin stretches and pulls. She puts one hand under her lump and tries to hold it up, nudges George to get his attention, but he shrugs her away.

'Ssshhh,' he hisses.

I uttered not, she wants to say. There was again a hint of Father William in that Sshiss. Now is not the time to push, but then, never is the time to push George Hogtrough.

The mood and the air has turned nippy. She pulls her shawl close around her shoulders, shivers, and her teeth begin to clatter without her permission. She spies old Moses King, sitting at a table near the door, gnome-like and round. In the light of the lanterns she can see his creased face, a halo of white beard circling underneath. He has a very un-Roman nose, squashed and veiny-red, and a twinkle in his eyes. He sees her looking and tugs at his cap. She dips him a little curtsey, smiles sweetly. *Music,* she thinks, and he hears her call. His pocket fiddle appears from goodness knows where and he begins to play. The melody breaks through the grim and the dark cloud of mob and riot is at once dispersed. *Thank God,* she thinks but stops herself from making a cross-in-thanks. This is not the place to show the old ways.

A shrill whistle comes from behind and George spins his head, owl-like. She follows his gaze.

And there stands that someone he has been searching for all evening.

Hal-bloody-Archer. She wants to scream it all over the village. *Hal BLOODY Archer, BLOODY HAL ARCHER is a POACHER. A poacher of promises.*

But she holds her words, bites her cheek until she tastes the metallic flavour of blood. She watches him approach.

He is tall, like her husband, although he is as blonde as George is dark. Thinner, too, and he always dresses well. This evening he sports a tidy hat, three corners, no dust. A long blue jacket with six silver buttons. *Silver!* No dust. Light brown breeches, black shoes. Silver buckles. *Silver!* No dust.

She wonders where he gets his clothes, his silver buckles, his fancy buttons, his no dust. *Where be his work?* She is immediately suspicious. It cannot be good. He is peasant born, like all the Woodfield folk, but Hal-bloody-Archer has raised himself to not-peasant, and now he even wears silver buttons on his clothes and silver buckles on his shoes. *Good Lord!* She is envious of his shiny things. Jealous of his lack of dust. Angry for the promises he steals.

Hal is striding towards them now, and eating up George's attention, the greedy fox that he is. Suddenly, she hears her husband's voice, all soft and loving. She dismays at his words and her heart sinks into her patched-up worn-out boots.

'Won't be long, Moll. I'll catch you along the lane. Just a few minutes be all, I promise,' he creeps the words out. 'You go on ahead. I just need to speak to Hal about that work I been lookin' for.'

'I can wait, Georgie, if you ain't goin' to be long,' she says, and her eyes plead with him. *Do not leave me to walk home alone, I beg of you.*

'No, no! You go on ahead. And did I not say I ain't gonna be long? You'll see. Just a few minutes, ten at most, that be all. Take that bag o' laundry with you, too, or likely I shall forget it. Run along, now. This ain't for your ears, this busyness.'

That hint of Father William has come about him again and he pats her on the arse. There is no more discussion, she is pushed away, and Hal-bloody-Archer has poached him from her. Again.

George does not see her angry eyes, nor feel her envious heart, for he has already turned to Hal, smiling, attentive, and they are walking away from the lanterns towards the shadows, while she collects the smelly bag. Old Moses King looks at her from under his hat and over his fiddle. She does not return his gaze, does not want to see his mischief nor hear his music.

She just wants to be safely home.

THE LEG OF MUTTON
LATE EVENING

The two men slink off to the other side of Ashted Green, to the shadow of a low, brick building. George looks back, watches the shape of his wife dragging the laundry behind her. He won't be long here and will surely catch her up, just like he promised. However, first he must fix that work which is sitting most uneasily on his chest and which he cannot allow Molly to even get a whiff of.

'So, Hal, what news?' he asks, in a low voice.

''Tis on! The meet set up for tomorrow, usual place. 'Twill be early, my friend, so you's got to be out of your bug pit prompt, like.'

'Right, and who we meeting, exactly?'

'Two from the river and two from the coast, that be all I

knows. Messenger would say no more,' Hal says. He leans up against the bricks, takes a silver snuff tin from his jacket pocket and pinches out a sniff.

George grunts. He does not like to be kept in the dark, especially when the risks are so high. And with this work, the risks are his life, his family, his everything.

'You ain't told no one, Hal? Ain't let on to one of your weepin' widows?'

Hal laughs, 'Georgie! I know not how you could even ask! You knows I value your life as highly as mine. Would be a sorry partnership if one of us were to blab, would it not?'

'Aye, true. Sorry, Hal. I's just got the willies in me. Sommat don't feel right. Can't put me finger on it. Perhaps 'tis only worry for Moll,' and he shivers at the thought of his wife's dangerous future as much as his own.

'She looks prodigious large. Must be near her time,' Hal says, wiping his nose with an embroidered handkerchief.

'Next few days, I reckon. But she's full o' fright. Can't say I ain't either. Drowning her fears in gin, too.'

'You wanna watch that, brother. Don't lead nowhere good.'

'Yeah, well, 'tis all what's gettin' her through the day, keeps her quiet, too. She don't badger me about where I's goin' when she's sloshing around in it.'

George shuffles his feet and looks at the scuffed boots he cannot afford to replace, and at Hal's jacket with its silver embellishments, the fancy buckles on his shiny boots. All paid for by his friend's attentiveness to lonely widows far better off than he. And rewarded most handsomely he is, too. Not a life George envies, for what Hal does for a living carries many risks.

But, *damn and shite!* The man dresses so fine. Sometimes he wishes he could swap places, just for a week.

'Lend us sixpence, Hal. I needs to get another flask for Moll,' George asks, and with this extra coin he will owe his friend almost five shillings. Five days' work, three if he finds some which pays well. *Damn.* And that is not his only debt.

'Sure, George. Come, I'll stand you an ale afore you go, too.'

George looks down the lane after Molly. 'Should really go after her, mate. Promised I'd catch her up.'

'Ah, come on, one won't hurt, will it? She'll be alright, tough little thing, ain't she?'

'Aye, suppose so. One more won't hurt.'

And just like that, Hal Archer has poached another promise.

KING OAK

MOLLY'S DREAM

The King Oak's thick branches and lanceolate leaves shade them from falling dew and starlight. Strong arms around Molly's tiny waist are warm against her skin and she breathes in his man smell, relishes the feel of his whiskers as they touch her lips. He lays her down on the soft spongy moss, a bed between two enormous roots. The perfect size, the perfect shape. The old King Oak must surely have grown this way over a hundred years or more, especially for this moment.

Their moment.

She should not be here, for they are not yet married, but he has courted and wooed, tickled his beard enticingly, won her heart completely. Now he gets to Have. Promises, whispered in her ear: a good home, strong children, food on the table and work aplenty.

Her belief in him is absolute and as he gives her his undying, whiskery love, she gives all of herself to him. It is new and unexplored, and these promises are for keeping.

Everything is to look forward to.

She feels the flicker of love in her heart, the touch of his fingers against her skin, a warm ache between her legs. A swell grows inside her, she reaches up and touches him gently on the cheek, where beard meets the smoothness of his skin. She finds his mouth, explores his taste, her eyes lost in his.

And then she stops and gasps.

Good Lord above!

She is shocked.

For the eyes she is staring into are not her husband's.

Woodfield Lane

Later That Evening

The sky has grown considerably darker since she drifted off at the side of the lane and into that dangerous dream. Molly shakes herself awake just as the clock of St Giles begins calling out the hours across the shadowy fields.

She counts the strikes. Ten!

'Have mercy on me!' she cries, grabbing the sack.

She has been away from home too long, for had she not heard the same bells ring seven as they left? God forbid her rascal son has gone wandering off, into the dark forest. Old Eliza Greenfield would not even try to hobble after him. She chastises herself for her weakness, curses her husband, the gin, Hal Archer, and forgets, perhaps refuses, to make a cross.

Each footfall stretches her already taught skin, which stings about her waist. She fights the wobble in her gait as she eases her way down the hill. At the Oxmoor Pond the earth beneath her levels out. A thin, silver mist, coiled around the gentle curves of the Rye Brook as it wends its way to the River Mole, has spread itself across the land. She cuts across the open meadow, following a well-trodden, grassy path, the shadows of low trees, bushes and scrub lining her way. Silky-leaved sallow, thorny hawthorn, and pollard oak, are scattered here and there, together with a myriad of wild herbs, which add to nature's larder.

A sudden noise comes out of the mist, an angry screech. She stops, holds her breath. A swoosh of wings above. *Only an owl, hunting.* She breathes again, but the damp hits her raw throat. She coughs and splutters, loses her balance. As she sticks a foot out behind her, another sharp pain tears into her swollen belly and a tightness pulls deep inside, a tugging at her groin. She cries out, smooths her fingers down her fragile skin, trying to reach into the depths of her body, to sooth and ease the pain. *Here? No, please, Jesus Christ almighty. Not here on The Common, all alone,* she prays. *What should I do? Not here. Hold on, hold on.* She hears a cry. At first she thinks it is again the owl, but it is her own voice, shaping her fear as it escapes her trembling lips, then loud and clear: 'Damn you George Hogtrough, damn you to hell.'

'You'll have he damnded, eh?' a man's voice, deep and gravelly, comes out of nowhere.

She freezes.

'And what will become of you and yer young 'un if your husband be damnded? And to hell of all places? May God forgive you, Molly Hogtrough.'

Then she smiles and her heart warms, for it is a familiar voice and she knows the depths of the dark eyes that grace the face from whence it comes. For they are the very same she was gazing into this evening, in her twilight dream of the King Oak.

It is her husband's older brother, Jesse Hogtrough, who for the second time this evening has been watching, unbeknownst to her. As he steps out of the mist from behind a dark tree, his long hair splays loose from under his dusty hat. While George would argue with this man till the ale runs dry, to Molly the sight of him is better than a cup of hot, sweet tea on a winter's evening, or perhaps a tipple of gin.

'Lord above, Jesse! What you doing here? Half frightended the living out of us, you did. Lurking about in the trees,' she lies, not at all scared, only surprised. For who would be on The Common at this time of night if they had no business here? None but those who belong, or so she believes. She has no fear of this place. It is her home. Her fears are of the future, whether she will have one, and if she does, how far into it she will be allowed to venture.

'On me way home,' he drawls. 'Seems I be just in time to save you from sinking in grime. Gimme that there bag o' rags, Sister,' and Jesse Hogtrough holds out his firm hand. She shoves the mucky sack towards him with a *thank you*.

And up it flies, with her spirits, as he balances it effortlessly on his shoulder.

'Phwoar, that be a bit ripe, ain't it?' he says with a grimace.

'Yes, 'tis truly so,' she answers, trying not to slur her words, to sound sober. 'Riper than a sow in sh..,' she stops, almost forgets it is not her husband with whom she is walking now. She is not allowed to say such words in the company of others.

Much she will say, though, for her tongue is freer, less fearful and she is more comfortable with this man than she is with her own. God forbid George Hogtrough should ever find that out, but why it should be so is quickly lost in the mist of gin befuddling her thoughts.

Jesse offers an arm, sleeves rolled up to his elbows, and her mood lightens further as she slips her tiny hand through the crook of his elbow and finds his bare skin. Her heart leaps as he squeezes. To keep her? *From falling down, of course.* She prays for strength to keep her imagination from falling to his comfortable bed. She is certainly feeling better now, looser, untied, and dangerously so.

He feels the peril and does not like the place to which it, and the obnoxious smell of alcohol on her breath, takes him. A tragic memory is brought to mind, a wound which scars his life with a disgust he cannot wash away. Lord knows he has tried. Seventeen long years he has worked to erase the past, but it will not leave him alone.

'Sometimes I be thinking I chosed the wrong brother to wed,' Molly laughs, but her tongue should have kept those words tightly bound, for now that devil is once again before Jesse as he was seventeen years back, at the King Oak. His loins are already stirring. He must banish it, this evil, and determines to weaken its hold when he gets home.

'Happen you didn't have no choice, Molly,' he scowls. 'Brother George had his eye on you since you was old enough to wed. You was his afore you weren't, if you get what I's saying.'

'I does, indeed. But I don't mean nothing by me curses on him. I loves him and with all me heart, truly I does,' she means to reassure him, but perhaps it is herself she is trying to convince.

'It's just that sometimes he do bewilder me so. He promised to help with that there blasted bundle o' trouble you's kindly carrying, then that rat Hal Archer went and turnded up at inn and here you found me, strugglin' on me own. Can't be right, can it? Perchance your brother should'a married Hal Archer, for he spends more time with that man than his own fam'ly.'

'Good Lord, Molly,' Jesse is shocked by her outburst. 'Now that ain't no way to be thinking, nor talking for that matter. For our Lord God will surely punish you for letting your thoughts stray to such evil. Ain't you got enough woes without calling on the wrath o' the Almighty to come a-visiting?'

She bites the inside of her cheek. 'Lord, you's right. I's not thinking straight.' A tear spills out of one eye, and she quickly wipes it away. As her stomach tightens with fear of God's anger, her belly begins to bubble like a stew as arms and legs kick and jostle inside their cramped home. A sudden pain jolts her.

Jesse frowns, 'You be looking fit to burst. How long now?'

'Any moment, I fear,' she replies, and he can certainly hear the angst in her voice. She breathes slowly, in and out, wills the pain away.

'Why on earth did you take on this work? Lord knows you'll never get it done.'

'Well, Gran ain't seeing so many people with her herby cures and Georgie ain't had no work for ages. I's worried they might impress him to the Navy if he don't find some soon. God Forbid,' she makes another cross, this time to protect her husband from the threat of sea thieves. She is treading dangerous ground, but cannot seem to stop ploughing it over. *Ain't clay earth,* she thinks. *'Tis quagmire.*

'I heared they did change the laws on impressment, not three or four weeks since, so you can stop all your worrying about them getting a hold of George. He be the wrong kind of man for the Navy anyhows. Fam'ly men ain't the kind they wants.'

Nor a lazy one, neither, he thinks. *Although it might lick him into shape.*

Jesse quickens his pace. He needs to be away. Her tongue is too fluid, her thoughts bordering on perilous, her fingers too close, too tight, too warm against his skin. It is a rare thing for him to feel the touch of a woman and the devil is working him loose, just like he did at the King Oak, all those years ago.

There is a part of her that wants to be home, too, but another which enjoys this man's company, his flesh under her fingers, his easy talk. She has forgotten that George might run up behind them at any moment, that his jealous eye might spy her arm in arm with his older brother, and one he shares no love for, at that. A most careless thing to forget.

They reach Common Lane, stony and rough, except where waggons have crushed stone to dust in the wheel ruts. Molly allows herself to dream all the way to the end of the lane, where Caen Farm lies, and into the tied cottage there. The place George grew up, where Jesse is now master since Father William took to his bed. Rose Cottage, where the hearth is roaring, the table laden with food. Up the narrow stairs lies a welcoming bed and she shakes her head. *No. 'Tis wrong. Go not there.* Her mind follows the lane past the farm and deep into the forest. The fern-lined path twists first this way, then that, ending at the ancient King Oak, where she finds herself again, and now asking whether her husband's brother would have been a better keeper of promises.

A cluster of higgledy-piggledy dwellings looms out of the mist to their left, the little hamlet of Woodfield, with orchards and chicken coops, pigpens and wood stores scattered all around the buildings. Past the huddle of homes is a small meadow where a few unseen sheep are grazing, their presence known only by the occasional tinkle of the bellwether and the odd bleat. A few steps further and a dim light appears up ahead, Eliza Greenfield's tiny cottage. A thin plume of smoke rises from the chimney, catches in the damp air and hangs over the building like a silken shroud. A most welcome sight.

'Thank the Lord Gran ain't let the fire go out,' she says, her mood much lifted by Jesse's company, his attention, and now the sight of home.

She smiles up at him as he opens the gate. She is such a pretty thing, but aging quickly, just like all the others he has seen much changed after wedlock, with the constant childbearing and loss which so often come along with it. The ravages of a hard, peasant existence etch scars into the pure smooth skin of young women's faces, if smallpox doesn't get there first. She will not escape the disfigurement of Father Time's touch. Already, dark circles surround her eyes and those twins will surely add their toll if she and they survive the birth. And that demon drink is fully about her, as it had been once in him.

'Come in for some supper, why don't you? Take that damp mist out your chest. Made a wholesome gruel today, I did. Will not take long to hot it,' and Molly pushes open the knotted, weathered door.

'Best not,' Jesse replies, surprised at the invitation. It would do none of them any good if he were found taking supper at his brother's table. It is the last place he wants to be. 'Early start the morrow and much to do in pre'pration afore I can get to me bed. 'Tis market day, see?'

'Ah! Yes, it is. Would that I could be there meself, but with these two knocking at the door I shall prob'ly not be abroad for a while. When them comes, there'll be a whole lot of trouble keepin' me busy.'

Aye, and trouble seems to follow this fam'ly, he thinks.

Rye Cottage

Late Evening

M olly's broken boot catches on the step as she trips across the uneven threshold of her grandmother's thatched home. Somehow, she manages not to fall headlong into the poorly lit, fire-warm room, but hears Jesse behind her, tutting at her drunkenness as he drops the filthy bundle on the floor. Sitting in the corner near the fireside, in a high-backed wooden chair, bolstered with threadbare cushions, is the ancient Eliza Greenfield, dressed in sour black and scrunched up like the sack of laundry. Through the gloom, Jesse can just make out her mob-capped head and dark, beady eyes.

He tips his dusty hat. 'Mistress Greenfield, good evening to you,' he says, raising his voice for the old woman's worn out ears.

'Who's that there, Moll? What've you bawt in now? A dawg or summat?' comes a dishevelled voice, crackly and weak with time, words muffled for lack of teeth. The old eyes strain and seem to Jesse to become sharper as she peers at him, and the reflection of the fire lights them up. To their owner, however, they are as dim and as dull as the sounds around her.

''Tis just brother Jesse, who kindly helped me home. Did me a right turn, he did.' Molly turns to Jesse with a softness in her eyes, and says more quietly, 'Thank you, Brother.'

'You be most welcome, Sister. Good evening and may God be with you,' but his voice is cold and stern.

She watches him scurry off into the evening, an unhealthy longing still stirring her. When he has disappeared from view she joins her grandmother by the fire.

'What you doin' bringing 'im here, Moll? Askin' fer trouble you is.'

'Ain't nothing wrong with Jesse Hogtrough, he be a good man. Goes to church reg'lar, like.'

'Jus' cause the man goes t' church, don't mean he be a good 'un. One Hawgtrough be enough, choild. Don't you go gettin' messed up with another. Ain't you got 'nough worries?'

Molly laughs, 'Don't be silly, Gran.'

'You thinks Oi's gawn soft in the head, all along of Oi's nearly eighty! Huh! Oi sees more'n you think, but not with these here eyes, see?' and she pokes a crooked finger at her head, then sniffs the air and wrinkles up her nose. 'What's that bleedin' awful stink?'

'Mister Reynolds' washing,' Molly sighs.

'Well, get it out of here, quick, loike. 'Tis makin' me feel roight quee-ar.'

Molly drags the stinking sack to the back door. It opens to a narrow lean-to, little more than a passage lined with shelves laden with bottles and jars of all shapes and sizes. They contain Eliza Greenfield's herbal remedies, her stock of dried plants, ointments and tinctures, a skill Molly has no passion for, and to her grandmother's dismay, no desire to learn.

Back inside, she hangs her bonnet on a hook slowly working its way free of the wood to which it is nailed. A reminder that George cannot even find the wherewithal to do his work around the home. Everywhere she looks his laziness is apparent.

'Did the child stir, while I been gone, like?'

'How should Oi know, can't hear a blessèd thing, can't see even less,' Eliza moans.

'Well, did he come down the steps?'

'Di'n't seen nothing,' she replies, snappy and bristly. The old woman lurches forward, points an accusing, gnarly finger at her granddaughter, 'And what you gawn and done with me poipe? Can't foind the blessèd thing anywheres.' She sinks back into the worn cushions and clicks her tongue sharply on the roof of her mouth.

Eliza's crabbiness can easily be remedied and once the pipe is found and loaded with baccy, the cure administered, Eliza Greenfield's mood quickly calms and she relaxes into her chair, puffing like an old charcoal pit.

'Where's that husband o' yours? Up to no good, Oi bet.' Eliza's eyes glint wickedly in the firelight.

'Had some busyness at The Leg. Back afore long, prob'ly,' Molly says, her muddy toes now free of her boots and warming by the fire.

'Runagate, he be. Runagate,' Eliza mutters, between puffs, 'Should'a passed him by. Stoopid gal. Will need a damnded miracle to get that lazy git t' do what's roight'n proper for his fam'ly. A good strong body he got now, ain't he? Won't last for long, no it won't. Only have to take a look at the father, all bent up and buckled.'

'Gran, I beg of you, don't talk about my husband so. Little Joe may hear and then we'll be done for, 'specially now he's taken to repeatin' everything.'

It is no mean feat to keep the old lady from antagonising her husband, and he in turn from throttling her. As Molly tries to get comfortable on the hard stool, soberness hits. Her head is throbbing, her belly hollow, sicky, and George and Hal are creeping about in her mind again, brewing their dark mischief.

Eliza stares at her through pipe and woodsmoke, and croaks, 'Have you thought how you will do when Oi's gone? Me, what's nigh on eighty and still bringin' in yer necessaries and that runagate not too far off o' forty, bringin' nothin' to the table. And don't you be looking at that bleedin' flask o' gin, for the answer ain't in it.'

Molly ignores the inquisition. She feeds the fire with a crumbly log and swings the blackened pot on its heavy iron arm above the flames. 'Me belly be gurgling prodigiously for lack. You want some?'

'P'raps just a small bowl, deary, warm me bones up.'

She stirs the pot, a thin gruel of oats, cabbage, turnip and peas, flavoured with herbs gathered from The Common. She drifts again to Jesse's home, where there is pork in his supper pot, not pathetic scraps. No Eliza, but instead, Father William and she shudders at the thought of cooking for the bitter old man, spiteful, twisted like his bones.

She stops her fantasy in its tracks and counts her lucky stars she is where she is. Just in time, for there is a shuffle of boots on the step and the door flies open. The dark silhouette of a man comes into the gloom and a golden dog shoots past him, dances and whines around Molly, demanding attention.

'You be home,' she says.

'Looks that way,' he says. 'You's surprised, eh? Thinkin' I weren't comin' back tonight, was you? Speak the truth now, wife,' and she sees a sparkle in his dark eyes.

Still in a good mood, then. Thank God.

He draws her close, wraps his thick arms around her, kisses her temples, her eyes, her nose. *This is love. This is cherish.* When he is like this she forgets, too easily, that he rarely keeps his promises.

'I do believe you has no faith in me, Wife. Did I not tell you I weren't gonna be long?' he whispers.

No faith? Happen he could be right. Although she is desperate for his love, her head is pounding and her eyes heavy. Cherish, keep and hold are tempting, but bed is calling louder. 'I weren't sure when you'd be back, 'cause you was with your friend and when you gets with him, well.' She stops, no need to stir up his dark looks again.

'Come,' he whispers. 'You surely cannot believe I'd leave you so soon to yer time?'

Like you did before, when little Rose was born, as still as a frozen pond?

She leans forward, nuzzling into his warmth where her curses and his brother are forgotten. 'Careful, or you'll be squashing them babes out. Got to get that laundry done afore they come, ain't I?' she says. She needs to tell him, because he can't see that he is hurting her. Can't see the danger he puts them in, does not know his own strength, and perhaps neither his weaknesses.

He loosens his grip. 'You's not to worry, Moll. They won't be coming afore next week, so Lucy Buttery reckons. Full moon will bring 'em, she says.'

But Lucy weren't at the inn this evening, and a cold shiver runs down her neck. *Is that slippery cow getting my Have?* and she forgets that it was she who was abroad this evening, not her husband. She who was in his brother's arms, if only in her dreams.

Molly leans close to Eliza who is watching and listening, but not really seeing or hearing. 'You hear that Gran? Lucy Buttery says the babes will come next week, with the full moon.'

Eliza peers out from under her lace cap, puffs on her pipe and blows rings of thin blue smoke towards George. 'Hawgwarsh, Hawgtrough. Full moon don't bring babbies, storms do. Ever'body knows that,' she cackles. 'You don't know nothin' boy, yer head's full of other people's nonsensicals'. Her eyes twinkle, but in an instant she becomes stern and shouts, 'Anyways, what you been doing wiv that scoundrel Hal Archer? He'll surely bring you trouble. You ought'a stay away from he.' Her parting shot is accompanied by an angry glare as her lips disappear into toothless gums.

George hisses at his wife, 'Lord above, Molly, what you been sayin'? Shouldn't go round gossipin' about yer very own husband.'

Skylark. His mood has dropped, and curdled as quick as milk in summer. He raises his voice for the benefit of Eliza, but continues to glare at his wife.

'Ain't nothing wrong with Hal Archer. Might've got me some work next week, on account of his good word on I. Other side of The Common, over near Epsum,' he says, confidently, with fingers crossed under the table, for it is a big fat lie. 'Could be a long run and all, ditching and that, for Farmer Trolter. So don't you go saying bad things about Hal. He be a good man,' and these last words are almost spat towards Molly.

'I never said nothing, George, I swear,' she whispers, but she is lying as much as George and will be in trouble deep should her husband ever find out how she has betrayed him to his brother.

'Who told you I's with Hal? Were it me wife here, with her gin-loose tongue a-wagging?'

Eliza sits back in her chair, her almost sightless eyes piercing the thick air between them. 'Naw, Moll di'n't say nothing. You think all along me eyes be bad Oi don't see. But Oi sees and hears more than you, son. More'n you ever will. And you heed my words,' her pointy, crooked finger stabs at him. 'Stay away from that man, or yer children will surely be growing up without a father and another man'll be beddin' yer woife instead o' you, boiy.' She lets out a piercing cackle, and then the room is eerily silent as her words cut through the smoke and slap George on the cheek.

A child's cry breaks into the room.

'Now you's gone and woke the little'un. I do wish you was more agreeable to one another,' Molly mumbles under her breath. She stands up and the room spins. She topples sideways and grabs the edge of the table just in time. George rushes to steady her, his anger forgotten. For a moment.

'You alright, Wife, you don't look so good,' he says.

Cherish, she thinks. *Comfort maybe. Hold, but only to stop me falling. Have? Lucy Buttery? Please, Lord! No!*

The child's grizzles tug at her, but she will never make the crude wooden stairs.

Even in the dim light she looks like a ghostly wretch, and George steers her to the bench. 'Sit down, woman,' he instructs, 'I'll go.'

She has no choice but to obey. That was her promise to him in the church. *The vows are skewed. He must not obey me, but I him. Church trickery.*

'Stay there,' he says, like she is a dog, and then demands the opposite. 'Put your Grandmother to bed, must be time, ain't it?' he hisses towards Eliza.

The words do not reach her ears, but the old woman holds up a gnarled hand in front of her face and catches his anger as it flies towards her. With a twist of her fingers she tosses it into the fire.

Hiss, fizzle, pop, crackle. Gone.

Eliza leans over and taps her pipe on the stone wall of the chimney. The spent contents shoot out, miss the dying fire and land at her stockinged feet on the dusty, cracked hearth. 'Moll dear, Oi's ready for me bed. Forgit supper.'

Molly manages to pull herself up and settles Eliza into her cot, built into an alcove on the back wall. A heavy drape – once a bedspread, a gift for one of Eliza's remedies and re-fashioned into a curtain – is drawn across the opening. The old woman will be out of sight till morning, God willing.

George soon reappears. 'The boy's settled. Had a nightmare he were lost on The Common.'

'That be my nightmare,' Molly says. 'I know not how I's going to keep him from running off when them babes come. I only has to take me eyes off him for a moment.'

She is surprised when George suggests making the backyard secure.

'Can you?' she asks.

'Aye, course I can.'

And cows milk gin, she thinks.

'This be tip top,' he says, supping the gruel like he has not eaten for a month.

She smiles, heart warm. *Skylark.* The mood he swings like a lamp in a storm is all calm and sweetness now, and she is all peace and joy. Until she remembers Lucy Buttery, *the slippery cow,* and the smelly sack outside the back door, *Lord God, help me.*

He sees the shadow cross her eyes, mis-reads her fears. 'Molly, don't you be worrying about my busyness with Hal. It be nothing, honest.'

She sighs. *Why's he telling me his work be nothing when 'tis everything?*

'Any more of that grub?'

She starts to get up, but he stops her.

'I'll fetch it,' he says. 'Two babes then,' he chuckles, as he sits back down, 'Twins, like me brothers, Ned and Jesse. You do look enormous fat, I do not rightly know how you can stand up.'

''Tis difficult,' she says. *How'd he think I could walk home with that laundry if he don't know how I can even stand?* The man is impossible. 'God willing they survive. I, too,' is all she says.

He reaches across and catches her tears on the tip of his finger. 'Don't worry so, Molly-Mary. 'Twill all be fine, see?' he says, but the waver in his voice betrays him. 'I knows you don't care much for Hal,' he begins, but she interrupts.

'It ain't Hal,' she says. 'And that bloody laundry's making me feel worser. I know not how I's going to bend over them tubs the morrow.'

The tears are rolling one after another now and the colour has rushed back to her face. Her half-finished supper is pushed away, 'Can't eat no more. Gives me such a burnin'.'

'I shall ask sister Annie to come by,' he says.

'Ain't she got enough to do? Your father won't like her to be away,' she says, but prays for his help. Another pair of eyes on Little Joe would be most welcome.

'She'll come. Eat up, you needs your strength.'

'I already sayed I can't eat no more,' she reminds him.

'Yeah, so you did,' he says, and she wonders if he ever hears a word.

Molly closes her eyes and drops her head awkwardly onto the table, wishing her chores were done. He takes her hand in his, and when she finally looks up, his eyes are fixed on her, but what he is thinking she cannot guess. If only she could, she would see his promises are not at all forgotten, but pressing hard on his conscience.

Ah, pretty Molly-Mary. If you only knew the work I's found. It'll pay handsome, like. Would that I could tell you, but that loose tongue of yours would spread it round The Common quicker than a dose of fever, and the hangman's noose would follow and be round me neck in a flash. Would that I could share me own fears, but you has yours and great they be. How I wish 'twere just you and me, for we had so little time afore life spread you thin, like November ice on the Oxmoor Pond. 'Tis going to get thinner, too. I gotta share you with our rascal Joe and that old bat in the corner, and them babes if they come good. You gotta trust me, though. I shall make it alright. I shall give you a good home, I shall. Just stay with me. Stay with us, Molly-Mary.

'And do not push me.' He whispers the last words so softly that

she does not hear. He kisses her hand gently, his wiry whiskers tickling at her fingers.

'Promise you'll get some work soon, George?'

'Promise. Now, you got those babies to be getting in the world, and safe at that. For I know not what I'd do if…' and his voice trails off, for he hardly dares to say aloud what she is also thinking.

CAEN FARM STABLES

LATE EVENING

The Common sleeps, except for night beasts on the prowl, hunting the shadowy undergrowth, skimming the silent skies. A breeze moves softly through the darkened greenery, the King Oak's crown sways and flutters lightly, the Wishing Tree reaches for the stars and the Flag Pond's limpid water slips silently around its rushes.

At the edge of the forest, Caen Farm is calm, the stables quiet until, stirred from their standing slumber, the horses shift and stomp. Someone has entered through the side door. They hear his heavy boots on the cobbled floor as he makes his way to the tiny tack room. They know him, for he is a regular visitor to their sleeping quarters.

Once inside, Jesse Hogtrough closes the door. One window, little more than a foot square, looks out onto an open meadow. He glances out into the moonlit dark. Nothing stirs. He does not want anyone to know he is here or what he will do, a thing done since Elizabeth left. Since he caused her to depart, after he broke her beautiful, innocent soul with a dreadful, drunken mistake which can never be undone.

A tool bench runs along the wall under the window. A simple wooden board fixed to the brickwork. He reaches underneath, feels into the corner, knows exactly where to find what he seeks. It is tucked away, hidden inside a little nook. He can just put his hand between the bench and the tight shelf nailed under it. His fingers squeeze into the hidey-hole, searching.

There!

If you didn't know, you would never find it. And no one must ever know.

Now he has it, his skin begins to shiver in anticipation.

He pulls it out by one of its nine tails, and his sordid ritual begins.

PART TWO

FRIDAY, JUNE 9

1780

Rose Cottage

Early Morning

Jesse Hogtrough likes to rise early, when morning is still a grey haze and before the blackbird heralds the break of day. As he looks out of the tiny latticed window of the room he shares with his younger brother, he sees the sun is already creeping above the trees. The cockerel made his first call long ago and the forest birds are in full song. He is late and he is uncomfortable.

He did not sleep well, spent most of the night pitching and tossing, troubled by the walk last evening with his sister-in-law. When he finally drifted off he dreamed he was a young man again, standing under the King Oak. And there was Elizabeth dressed all in white, with a crown of delicate pink flowers adorning her blonde hair. She held out her hands, they were as white as her clothes. Her face, her cheeks, her lips like chalk. But her eyes were the deepest blue he had ever seen, like the clear midday sky. She invited him to come close and as he stepped forward he felt her body against his, pulling him into her. Suddenly, he wanted her, needed her.

And then he was falling, spinning into her softness, tumbling into her bright eyes. But as he fell, a murky blackness enveloped him and he struggled to crawl back to beautiful Elizabeth. An unseen force was pulling him deeper into the darkness, squeezing him into an enclosed space, like the bottom of a dark sack. It was tight and full of something icky, red and spongy. He could not make it out, but the smell was awful, the stench overpowering, repugnant. He fought with all his strength until the sack ripped and out he tumbled.

He lay under an angry, swirling sky, looking up at the King Oak, its branches burned and blackened. And now, Molly stood where Elizabeth had been, her enormous pregnant body naked, caked in mud. She stepped over him, and then he saw it was not the ancient King Oak above him, but a man.

He shuddered as he recognised his long departed twin, Ned Hogtrough, and in his hands, the cat o' nine tails.

Now awake, his skin is clammy and he cannot shake off the uneasy dream. *Nightmare*, he tells himself. The wicked vice of lust had overtaken him when Elizabeth appeared, as it had once before, and the memory of Molly's fingers on his bare skin last evening makes him quiver. His disgusting lack of self control, his disgraceful fantasies – everything must be lashed away. He picks up the rough sackcloth vest, hanging over the chair beside his bed and slips it on. He cannot help but scratch at his chest as the fibres prick his raw skin. More penance will be needed to erase his dirty thoughts, but the cilice will have to suffice until he can get back to the tack room, and he quickly covers it with a thin linen shirt.

He tears his mind away from his sins and considers his work. Market day in Letherhed is the busiest of his week. He will need his wits about him to carry out Farmer Caen's instructions, the buying and the selling, the pushing and the pulling, dealing with all those tricksy characters, their sharp tongues and wily minds. There is a storm brewing, so his work at the farm must be completed before the heavens unleash their power and make the hay too wet to gather in and safely stack. Wet hay and warm weather is a recipe for disaster, as he is forever telling his younger brother. He looks over at the boy's bed and sees the lad is still asleep.

Jesse prods him with a sharp finger. 'Time to get going.'

Henry Hogtrough grunts. 'I be awake,' he mumbles and he rolls onto his back, his eyes blinking out sleep as he tries to focus on a dark crack running between the time-blackened beams.

Downstairs, last night's fire has already been rekindled. Apart from a yard or two around the hearth, the room is quite dark, the air woody. Jesse flings open the front door and stale air rushes out, escaping across the open scrub between the cottage and The Common.

At the table, he leans back against the wall. The cilice feels more coarse against his raw skin than ever. Before he has a chance to scratch, the door beside him creaks open and a tall, young woman appears.

'Mornin' Jesse. You sleep well?' she asks, as she puts down the earthenware jug she is carrying. The milk slops to the rim and she holds her breath lest it splash over. She dare not spill a drop of pearly liquid, for her brother cannot abide waste.

'Mornin', Sister. Like a river. Yourself?'

As she moves around the room, his gaze fixes on her.

'Don't seem to me like a river never sleeps, Brother. Was you tossing and turning, winding and a-wending for a reason?'

Jesse huffs and his sister is none the wiser. She cannot push, it will irk and she does not want to scratch his calm. There are many things she dare not do in this house.

He watches her in the fire glow as she prepares their simple breakfast. She shoves the heavy kettle towards the flames and it jerks back and forth against its chain, clanking out an off-key tune. She sets a tallow candle in front of him. It spits and stinks of rancid mutton, almost makes her gag. She turns away and brings her hand up to her mouth. *No. Not yet. Hold it.*

By flickers of firelight, Jesse can see her auburn hair is woven into a plait, curled around her neck and down over her breast. As she nears the table, the weak tallow flame highlights a worried expression.

She seems out of sorts, a little on edge. 'What tasks have you today, Sister?'

'Oh, you know, this and that,' she replies, with a shrug.

'Do enlighten me, Annie. What is the "this" of your "this and that", pray?'

''Tis only the same I do most every day, nothing special, nothing new,' she says, too quickly, with a hint of irritation. She has slipped. She is tired, in truth exasperated by this prodding to which she is subjected, the need to know her every move, her every breath. It stifles her. She is like a cat in a cage.

Jesse is a little taken aback at her uncharacteristically snappy reply. 'Something is amiss, Sister,' he replies calmly.

But she can read him like the rector reads the Good Book. His coolness belies an anger, an annoyance she will not stir.

'Sorry, Jesse. I di'n't mean to bite. I's just a little under the morning today,' she says, holding out her hand. 'Forgive me?' she pleads.

His eyes bore into her soul, hoping to unearth any secrets buried in its depths. He takes her small hand in his, gently grips her thin fingers with their nails bitten to the quick. 'Forgiven,' he says, and resolves to find out what is troubling her before the day is out. She is warm to the touch, perhaps too warm. 'Do not tell me you has the ague,' his gut tenses as he lets her fingers slip through his. Her hand is free, at least. Just her hand.

She shakes her head. 'No, no, Jesse. You got no need to worry. I's a little tired, 'tis all. Something and nothing. You know, Brother, do you not? What comes to a woman every month, reg'lar as the moon,' she lies, and moves away from him with a limp smile. He will not want to discuss a woman's intimate problems and she should get no further interrogation, at least not for a while. As she turns away, she wipes a tear from her eye with the corner of her apron, careful not to let him see her weeping, for fear of fiercer inquisition. She gathers herself and has plugged the leak before she returns to the table with four tin cups and a flagon of small ale.

'Mistress Caen asked if I might help in the kitchen this fore-noon. Lucy's tasked with baking a batch of pies, then bread after, while the oven's hot, like.' Not a pleasant prospect, a farmhouse bake oven, but at least in the company of Lucy Buttery she can breathe easily, share her troubles and speak her mind.

Rush outside to throw up when the nausea grips her.

'After dinner, I shall go to Rye Meadow, collect some rushes afore this weather breaks. Should have a tidy few rushlights to sell at market next week then,' she continues and sets four bowls around the table.

She does not tell Jesse she has employed young Billy Longhurst to dip the rushes she has already dried, a job which at present she cannot stomach, for the fat stinks and irritates, brings up her bile. Sharing her profits means less coin, but with Father lying upstairs and good for nothing and Henry not yet on a man's wage, they need every penny they can get to see them through the long winter.

Jesse nods slowly. His thoughts, however, are elsewhere.

'I cannot recall the last time Father took breakfast with us,' he says.

'True, an' he'll likely be in bed till dinner on account of his bones,' she whispers, in case William Hogtrough, lying awkwardly in his bed above, should hear and set his wooden stick a-flailing. She should have stopped there, but speaks on. 'Long gone are the days he went about like a man and not a dog, as he does now.'

She knows immediately, by the stiffening of her brother's body, that her choice of words has angered him.

Jesse straightens himself up. 'Now Sister, I will have no such talk at our table. He is our father and you will respect him no matter what,' he growls in a familiar tone, one which holds a seed of anger, an inherited skill.

He be his father's son alright, just without that flailing stick, she thinks. The son's flail is more supple, although just as dangerous. She knows the damage it does, for she spied him in the tack room once, through a knot in the old wood, and then there are the spots of blood on his linen shirts which she tries her best to wash away. Why he punishes himself so, she cannot say and is afraid to ask. She cannot even let him know she has seen his vicious lashings, lest they come her way, like Father's once did and sometimes still do.

'Oh Jesse, I di'n't mean no harm by saying he were like a … walked like a …,' she pauses, and continues without the offending word, to be safe, 'just that he be so crooked up now and it do give him such pain.'

'I see,' he says and relaxes a little. 'No harm done, I suppose.' The cilice prickles. He wants to scream, and scratch the self-in-flicted itch with which he lives, but does not flinch. After all, this punishment is to ensure he does not go the way of William Hogtrough, all buckled and bent and twisted and unrepentant. God knows these last years Father has been wicked indeed, espe-cially when the drink has a hold of him. However, his own sin is deeper and darker than anything the old man is capable of, and the memory of his immorality makes his heart sink and his balls shrink and wither.

'With respect, Brother, he ain't gettin' no better,' Annie says.

'No,' he says, and at present he has no solution to their father's worsening state.

''Tis easier now he stays so oft in bed,' she adds. Less able to hit her with his stick, a weapon which has replaced his weak-ening fists, and his mess is contained in one place. She can just about manage. It is a grim task, getting worse as he grows less able-bodied, less sober. Less human.

However, as she herself begins to grow and swell it will become impossible. She stifles another gag, turns away from the table, thinks of fresh flowers and clear running water to push the morning nausea away.

'He were complainin' last even of his eyes growin' dim,' Jesse says, shaking his head. 'I fear he will go headlong down them stairs one of these days.'

God willing, she thinks. 'God forbid,' is what Jesse hears, while Annie silently chastises herself. The unspoken notion of her father tumbling to his death down the dark narrow stairs scratches at her mind like her brother's coarse vest against his skin. *God forgive me. God give me strength to stop them wicked wishes.*

Jesse, oblivious to her treacherous thinking, adds, 'When Mother passed was the start of it. Lost his fear of God and turned to Devil and drink on that very same day. God rest her blessèd soul.'

However, Annie knows different. *You are mistaken, Brother. Your story has more holes than the bed of the River Mole. That wretch upstairs turned to drink when your twin disappeared, to sail on the high seas, or so we was told. And that was well before Mother died, for I remember her crying for Ned on her deathbed, after she give us Henry,* she thinks, but dare not correct him.

'I scarce have no memory of them days, when Mother were still alive. Seems so long ago,' she lies again, to put him off the scent. It is becoming a dreadful habit.

''T'ain't no surprise, you was only young.'

She was eleven when Ned left, remembers him as a kind and gentle brother, cheerful and true. His sudden disappearance left a gaping hole in every heart. Except perhaps Jesse's, and whatever truths have haunted her brother all these years he keeps close to his chest, with that cilice.

She changes the subject. 'I swear our Henry's growing an inch a week and bothered if I know where he puts all what he do eat.'

As she speaks, they hear heavy footfall on the stairs. A lanky, dark-haired lad lumbers into the room, rubbing sleep from his eyes. As he lollops across the worn, red tiles, his head almost skims the oak beams. Henry Hogtrough has a wide, smiling mouth, and the same thick, brown hair as his brother George. No bushy beard yet, but already a shadow above his top lip.

'Who be growing alarming? That not be I, you two's a-goss'ping about? And when I bain't here to offend me, an' all,' he asks, his voice dual-pitched and half-grown, being neither a boy's nor yet a man's.

'It certainly were you as was the concern of our talk,' Annie says, 'all along o' there ain't nothing else here growing like you, not even the barley in Farmer Caen's fields. You's looking like a rambling beanstalk. I swear, I ain't never before seen nothing grow so quick.'

Henry laughs, and Annie pours out three cups of stewed tea. With sunlight creeping quickly across the floor through the open door, she can finally snuff out the offensive candle, and leans forward to pinch the flame.

'Will you say the Grace, Jesse?' she asks, for they cannot begin to eat until her brother has spoken to his Almighty God.

He says his piece and all three finish with a solemn, 'Amen.'

Jesse looks over their bounty. 'Well now, tea, and bread and milk, and honey today even! What a blessèd feast and don't you be forgetting that Henry, lad. Don't you never forget.'

He reaches forward across the table, clasps his long-fingered hand around Henry's wrist and grips him tightly. 'The Lord, and

Farmer Caen, The Common and the land, why they do provide for us with food a-plenty and more, 'specially at this time o' year. And a roof over our heads an' all, a solid good one at that, see?'

Henry does not need to be reminded, for his older brother's words are repeated almost every morning.

The room grows ever lighter as they eat, each immersed in their own thoughts about what the day ahead will bring.

Annie is concerned about Henry's ill-fitting clothes. 'Jesse, that chest what Father guards upstairs. There must be summat in there of Ned's what would fit our Henry.'

Jesse rolls his eyes. The last thing he wants is to go rummaging through his twin's old clothes. He would rather forget the man existed. Some chance of that with all the dreams he has been having lately. *Nightmares.* 'Will see what I can do,' he says, less of a promise, more a put-off.

'And while you be at market Brothers, I beg you to return with an orange fruit, or two even. We can surely stretch the coin a little this week, it bein' summer and you two with work aplenty. Father could do with one, as a treat, like.'

As if his ears are being burned with a hot poker, there is a cry from the old man, accompanied by a loud thump as his walking stick thrashes the floor.

Annie turns her eyes to the ceiling. 'Regl'ar as the cock. He'll have to wait a bit, though. I ain't packed up your bevers yet,' she says.

As she is putting her brothers' mid morning snack into a small cloth sack, an excited bark comes from the farmyard. Jesse's scruffy black and white collie heralds the arrival of a visitor. Henry peers through the window and catches sight of the bulbous Farmer

Caen, toddling towards the cottage, with Hoppit dancing and yelping excitedly around his thick, bandy legs.

James Caen is an amiable fellow with a good reputation for being fair, although quick to temper when someone takes advantage of his generosity. His shaven head is usually hidden by a powdered wig, but this morning it is covered by an old-fashioned tall hat with a tarnished silver buckle. Barrel shaped, he looks like a deformed oak which has stumbled out of the forest. He announces his arrival, and without waiting for an answer or an invitation, ducks inside the cottage, hat narrowly missing the low lintel.

'Mister Caen, how goes it this fine morn?' Jesse asks.

A clammy hand grabs Jesse's. 'Tip top, thank 'ee. Gooin to be a roight foine day. Storm brewin' though.' Even the short walk from the farmhouse to Rose Cottage has made him out of breath, and his moon face holds his bulging eyes in their sockets by a whisker. Annie is afraid they will fall out.

He tips his hat towards her. 'Mornin', Miss Annie. And Henry, by God have you grown since Oi saw 'ee yes'erday?' he asks, eyes widening.

Annie holds her breath, lest they tumble.

'Well, you know what's to be done Jesse, as we discussed last evening?' Jim booms, his words bouncing off the ancient beams.

'Yes, Sir,' Jesse nods. 'I knows well enough.'

'Good, good. One more thing. We needs a couple of good strong rakes. Got the West Field to cut and gather in, wants doing quick loike, afore the weather turns agin. Them old rakes in the barn be roight middling ampery. Will snap as soon as look at 'em. See if you cannot get two more. For a pretty price, mind you,' he blares his orders around the room. 'We shall set to repairing them old 'uns when the rain comes on agin and we's not so pressed for toime.'

'Right you are, Mister Caen.'

Jim falls silent, scratching his grey-cloud beard, trying to find another order for his employee.

'Be that all, Sir? I be restless to get moving, afore them rogues in town take to drinking and scoundrelling, like,' Jesse says.

'Aye, can't never do a pretty business with 'em after they get the drink insoides of 'em, can 'ee? All goes crook'd.'

'True, that. I once brought a tidy sack of oats, for a good price, like. Tip top, I thought, but when I got home found 'twas real bad.' Jesse says. 'And the old devil had thrown in a fam'ly of meeces, an' all. Sad to say, 'twas only good for travish.'

Jim Caen laughs, and then asks, 'And how is your father? Shall I ask the good Doctor to call on 'im agin?'

Annie comes to William's rescue. 'Thank you kindly for askin', Mister Caen. He did take a turn for the worse last night after Doctor Scragg opened that issue on his back, but I believe he be feeling a little better this morn, so there be no need to trouble the good gentleman doctor.'

William will not appreciate another visit from the odious physician. For one, they have no money to pay his exorbitant costs, and the old man is far more troubled by the doctor's pernicious cures than by his own ailments. After yesterday's visit, he made Annie swear not to let the villain over the threshold again.

As if on cue, there comes another crack and a wailing groan from above.

'Well now, Father must be feeling *much* better this morn, for he be stamping for his breakfast like a fresh gelded horse what knows he's lost summat real important,' Annie says. 'Do ex'curse me, Mister Caen.'

She bobs a curtsey, then turns away to prepare William's food before she can be chastised by Jesse for her crude light-heartedness. It will come later, no doubt, but Jim is still chuckling as he leaves with the two Hogtrough brothers.

Annie watches them through the small window, and when she is sure they are busy and will not return, she nips quickly out of the front door, and throws up onto the rose bed.

COMMON LANE & RYE COTTAGE

EARLY MORNING

Once the cart is loaded with sacks of beans, peas and oats, and Jesse's head with Farmer Caen's instructions, the brothers are ready to leave for Letherhed.

The small market town is at the crossroads of two important routes. One from Kingston in the north, which continues on to meet the sea at Worthing, and the other from London Town goes in a south-westerly direction to the docks at Portsmouth. The two miles from Caen Farm could easily be covered in half an hour at a brisk pace. However, with Jim Caen's favourite old mare Lavender pulling the heavy cart, it will take an age.

They rumble out of the yard through half-dried puddles of wet dung. Bird song is their music as they walk either side of the horse, with Hoppit perched atop the sacks. Like a figurehead, the dog gazes into the distance, scans the horizon for enemy waggons, dips his head up and down as the wheels hit the waves of the rough old track.

Sheep and oxen graze on The Common scrub, and Jesse looks across the land to the farmer's livestock, sheltering under the canopy of a small copse, half way between the farm and the ancient woodland. Much of the grass has been cropped short, but a few swathes of wild flowers have escaped the animals' teeth. Patches of colour grace the scene: ox-eye white and foxglove pink, meadow vetchling yellow and forget-me-not blue. Brambles are decorated with tiny green baubles, which will swell and ripen into bunches of heavy black fruit in just a few short weeks. Some will appear on tables hereabouts, made into puddings or pies, but most will be sold at market, to fabric manufacturers or weavers, dye for their blue cloths and yarns.

Nothing wasted.

A network of worn paths criss-crosses the open land, skirting three or four small ponds, in summer little more than puddles which disappear during dry spells. It is an ancient, peaceful and beautiful place, and Jesse is more than content with life here, hard though it sometimes is, especially during the long winter months.

However, in spite of the growing warmth, he shivers, his nerves disturbed by the nagging feeling that change is coming. His dreams, *nightmares,* about his twin, make his wounds prickle and crawl. Everyone believes Ned to be dead, and what else can they think with no news to the contrary after seventeen years? But a gnawing knot is eating into Jesse's conscience, an increasing creep of nausea when he is in the tack room, and the lashes and welts, a reminder of past transgressions, have become more raw in recent weeks.

If his brother returns, then change will come for him, indeed, and Ned is nearby, of that Jesse is certain.

The brothers cross the Rye Brook by the wooden bridge and are soon in front of Eliza Greenfield's cottage, where their brother George resides. It is the first of the Woodfield hamlet properties, an oak-framed building which has stood since Elizabeth's time, with tiny bullseye-glazed windows looking towards The Common. The low thatch almost brushes the tops of Eliza's roses. The old woman's garden is her treasure, her worth, where she grows not only flowers, but a trove of herbs for her natural remedies. To outsiders, the cottage may look idyllic, a romantic scene of easy country living, but the picturesque betrays a desperate need for repair, certainly before the nights begin to draw in. Jesse spies several holes in the thatch and silently chastises George for not keeping his family's home properly maintained. Another winter with those leaks and cracks will be harsh and he shakes his head, the neglect reinforcing the only view of his brother he has.

Damnded lazy git.

Henry stops, 'Wait up! I forgot! George be goin' into town today for sommat or other, sayed he'd walk with us.'

Jesse groans. *That sommat is drink, most likely.* 'Whooa Lavender, wait now,' and he snaps at the reins. They wait a few seconds, but Jesse knows George too well. He will not appear until called, because the lazy bastard will still be snoring in his bed, will he not?

'Our brother needs a prod, it seems. Won't be long, lad,' he says and strides around the side of the tired cottage, with Hoppit at his heels.

He finds Molly hard at work in the backyard. The babes clearly did not arrive during the night, for she is preparing to do her laundry. She looks awkward, struggling to haul an enormous tub across the ground.

'Mornin' Molly. Here, let me do that,' and Jesse is by her side in a flash. 'Where's it going?'

'Jesse! You's always there when I needs help, ain't you? There would be good,' she says, pointing to a low table with two pails of water already filled beside it.

She has that dangerous look he saw yesterday evening and he recollects his dream, a naked, heavily pregnant, *dirty* Molly standing above him. *Nightmare.* 'George still in his bed, I e'spect.'

'Good grief, Brother! You has so little faith in him. He were up with the sun and already breakfasted. Fetchin' water from the brook, he be.'

Jesse huffs, 'Faith not got nothing to do with it. 'Tis early rising what ain't a virtue George holds dear.' In truth, he is a little disappointed at his brother's uncharacteristic activity.

'Sometimes he do surprise even hisself,' Molly laughs, but she is not feeling at all well. Her head is spinning from the remnants of yesterday's binge, her belly hollow and yet heavy, uncomfortable. And her fear has grown larger, not helped by the fact she must broach the uncomfortable subject of last evening's loose gin-talk before George returns.

'Jesse, what I sayed to you last even, I cannot remember all, but please, say nothing to my husband of it, would you?'

'Good Lord, Molly. Would not dream of it,' he replies and draws himself up, puffs out his chest with satisfaction at this secret. A bad move, for the sharp cilice scratches his sores. He releases his foolishness, lets out his breath.

Hoppit races over to Pudding, who is scampering beside George and his load, two large wooden pails hung from a yoke across his shoulders.

Molly smiles, waves and he smiles back through his beard. *He has good teeth,* she thinks. *'Tis a pity he lost that one at the front or they'd be perfect. Like Jesse's.* And then she looks back at the tall man by her side, who is not at all hers to look at in that way. As far as she knows, he belongs to no one and it has not even occurred to her the reason why he is not married. She will be dismayed if she ever finds out.

'Mornin' Brother,' George calls, as he approaches the yard. 'On yer way already?' and he sets the pails down near the tubs.

'Aye, day moves along quick like, with busy hands at work.' A nudge at George's laziness.

He receives a glare in response, but George has no desire to quarrel this morning and lets it wash over him. He claims his wife, crosses his arms protectively over her heart and their unborn children. She sways lightly from side to side and pushes her backside gently into his groin. George squeezes Molly tighter, feels close to her and she to him, in a way.

However, her eyes are still, dangerously, on his brother, who blushes at the show of affection between the couple, uneasy at Molly's unwanted attention. 'Looks like you ain't ready,' he says.

'One or two more pails and I'm done. I'll run and catch you along the road if you cannot wait,' George says, an anger in his voice he cannot hide.

Huh, thinks Molly, recalling his promise to catch *her* along the road. *He never did. Jesse caught me.* And again her gaze falls on her brother-in-law.

Jesse sees her looking and, disgusted, he turns to leave.

'Aye, would be best. That old horse be draggin' its feet, so like as it won't take you long,' he says.

'Wait up, I has an ask. Can Annie be spared an hour or two to help Moll?' George says.

Molly is a little surprised that her husband has remembered a promise, and Jesse likewise, at George's concern for his wife's troubles.

'Like as that be a capital idea. Loaned to Mistress Caen for the mornin' she be, but I's sure she'll be released.'

'Right, I'll nip to the farm an' grab her afore I catch you on the road,' George says, and he seems agitated.

Sommat troublin' brother George? Jesse assumes it is the dangerous threshold upon which his wife is teetering.

He is not altogether wrong.

However, there are also more pressing concerns on George's mind.

RYE COTTAGE

EARLY MORNING

Molly is left to traipse to-and-fro, filling the large cauldron hanging over the fire in the yard with water. Her back aches, her fingers sore, and she has not even begun. She pulls a stool into the shade and slumps down, but has hardly taken a breather when a croaky cry comes from inside the cottage.

'Molly! Moll!'

'Coming Gran,' she sighs and wobbles through the tiny narrow lean-to, past the old woman's jars, stuffed with herbs and remedies, teetering nervously on their cranky wooden boards. 'What be the matter, dear heart?'

'Well, dee-ar,' Eliza does not need to say more. As Molly's eyes adjust to the smoky room she can see the problem and it takes all her effort not to laugh out loud. Her grandmother begins to giggle like a child and Molly catches the mood easily, lets herself go. A rare moment of hilarity in the stern world she inhabits.

'Oi's in a bit of a pickle,' Eliza manages to blurt out.

She has clearly been trying to get herself ready for the day. Her night smock is lying on the floor, both arms are in her shift, but it is caught and bunched around her waist. Her heavy black dress is the wrong way round, upside down, inside out and she is bent over her crib, head stuck inside the partially drawn curtains. Eliza's lily white arse is protruding from amongst layers of garb, and that is all Molly can see.

'Oh!' she giggles. 'Your back end is as white as the full moon!'

'Get me out of this mess, choild. Oi can't stay 'ere all day! Quick afore the young 'un sees!'

However, Little Joe is already half way down the steps, a small grubby rag tucked under his nose, thumb in mouth.

'Too late,' Molly says and rushes to shield Eliza's behind from her boy's eyes. 'Come here, son.'

The child shuffles down the rest of the steps one by one on his bottom, holding onto the makeshift rope banister. He makes a beeline for his mother's skirt and wipes his nose on her apron. Under the hugeness of her bump, Molly loses sight of him, but steers Joe towards the table and sits him down.

'Wait here,' she says and hands him a piece of dry bread to suck. Before the little boy even puts it to his lips he has turned around and she hears his little giggle.

'Grammy skinny arse, Mama fat,' he says, cheekily.

'Joseph! You has your father's mischief, you does.'

When Eliza is straightened out, the daily demands begin.

'Fetch us me poipe, girl, there's a heart. Cuppa-tea brewin' is there? Oi must 'ave a cuppa-tea, sets ever'thing to roights, don't it?'

As Molly swings the arm over the fire her eyes catch the flask on the mantle. *Ain't too early for a cup of tea with a splash of sommat, is it?* she thinks. A perilous thought. But are these not perilous times? Her hand smooths over her apron, around the infants she is carrying under her tightly-stretched skin. Yes, a dangerous time, indeed, and surely a little tipple will not hurt.

However, her attention is disturbed by a knock at the door. The flask will have to wait.

It is Annie, looking thin and gaunt, eyes red. *What's up with her?* Molly asks herself. But when Annie speaks she sounds cheerful enough.

'Good day to you all. I come on Brother George's orders, to ease your load, Moll. And Jesse did say 'twas a right stinky one, too.'

''Tis so good of you to come, dear heart. I hope Father William will not mind to spare you today.'

'He will not know, Molly. So long as a flask of cider be at his hand, or gin be better nowadays, then all is as well in his world as it ever will be.'

Molly nods in understanding, her gaze drawn to her own supply of gin. She feels it calling, and impatient it is, too. She understands why Father William would choose it over cider, for it can put almost everything right.

'I feel bad about sayin' it, but I be glad when he stays in his bed. Anyway, it weren't Father what needed me this morn', 'twas Lucy and her pies. But Mistress Caen knows how close you is to your time, so she let me go. Says you should be resting up, like.'

'Ha ha! Would be a fine thing,' says Molly, and with one eye on that persuasive flask, she thinks, *would be a fine thing, too, to get a tipple of that in me tea*. 'Is everything well at home?' Molly says, and wonders whether she will get an honest answer.

'*Well* ain't the word I'd use, but you know how it is,' Annie answers, giving away nothing. 'And you, Moll? You reckon you's got two comin', then?'

'Aye, twice the work from start to finish and me skin be almost splitting. I keep thinking they'll fall out, all of a sudden, like. 'Tis very strange. Lord knows how I shall manage.'

Eliza shuffles closer. 'Havin' two is throice the work, an' Oi should know. Had ten. Well, eight what lived past babes, Oi did,' she mumbles.

'That must have been a struggle,' Annie says.

'Aye, but Oi had a good husband. Hardworking, he were. We always had food on the table, and we had a roof over us. Leaked a bit, still does, don't it? But that di'n't matter none, for he always got to repairin' it, he did. We was very happy, we was. Oi does miss him. Silly ol' thing he was, but Oi still misses him terrible, loike.'

Molly looks at the mantelpiece, to the drink which will help her forget her own husband's shortcomings, but it really is out of reach, for the moment.

Annie turns to her, 'So, what can I help you with, Sister?'

'Hot water afore anything, so I best go check that fire still burns. Help yourself to tea,' she answers, and Little Joe jumps down from his perch and follows his mother outside.

'You want a cuppa, Mistress Greenfield?'

'Just half a cup, dear heart. Can't stop pissing if Oi has too much,' Eliza says. 'Needs too much effort to get to the po, so Oi prefers to stay a bit droiy, loike.'

A shaft of light pierces through the tiny windows and the room is suddenly full of summer. Eliza can see far better now. However, the old woman does not always need a bright room, for there are some things she sees with eyes closed. She watches, as Annie attends to the tea.

'You be looking rather thinner since Oi sees you last, girl. Be ever'thin' alroight?'

It takes Annie a moment to decipher the toothless words, formed with gums and cheeks, and round at the edges. 'Why, perfectly alright Mistress Greenfield, but thank you for asking.'

Eliza clicks her tongue as the young woman sits down. 'And what about that?' The old lady pokes a crooked finger towards Annie's belly.

As she turns to meet the ancient eyes, Annie realises that what she has been hiding from the rest of her family cannot be hidden from this wise one, who has seen more of life than anyone she knows. She turns away, a little shocked.

'I don't,' she stammers and tries to pull herself together but her eyes are already brimming up. 'I don't know what you mean, Mistress Greenfield.'

'Yes you does, girl. And there ain't no use croyin' now. Too late fer that, ain't it? Now, if you needs help, loike, to make it disappear,' and Eliza twists her gnarled fingers in the air like smoke curling in the wind. 'Well, you just comes to me, see? Starving yourself moight do it, an' Oi guess that's what you been doin', cause you be roight skinny now, ain't ya? But then agin it moight not. And if you wants it gone, you must be quick, loike, and be sure that's truly what you wants. Can't make no mistake, for there ain't no goin' back, see? And ain't no cert'ity 'twill work neither, but can't leave it too long. What herbs Oi got should not be used a'ter a few early weeks. You understand me, girl?'

Annie turns and meets Eliza's black eyes. She understands all too well the dilemma she faces, but the decision is not hers alone to make. She has to give *him* a chance to rescue her first.

There is no time to say more, for Molly reappears in the doorway calling for Annie to come to the yard.

The water is boiling, and they can begin the long and heavy task at hand.

LETHERHED TOWN

EARLY MORNING

George soon catches up with his brothers. They idle into Letherhed, having spent most of the journey either deep in their own thoughts or making small chatter about the weather, crops, livestock and such like, for Henry's sake as much as anything. Without his presence, Jesse and George would likely remain silent. In fact, it is only due to Henry that they are even walking together.

The usually quiet and uneventful town is this morning astir with activity. The buzz and fuss of market always rouses the place into a frenzy, but due to the early hour, the transformation is still very much a work in progress. The Elizabethan Market House stands where the two main roads cross, and traders and merchants of all kinds are setting out their wares, in baskets and pails, on tables, hand drawn carts and stone slabs, anywhere a space can be found. The Market House is not big enough for all the sellers, and those who cannot find a place, or afford to pay the steep pitch fees, make do as best they can along the High Street. One can find here everything from string and rope, to candles and honey, braided hair pieces and lice-filled wigs, second hand crockery and cooking utensils, used clothes and shabby furniture. An aroma of herbs and spices, flowers and perfume, is starting to fill the air. It barely covers the stench of the open sewer kennels which run sordidly through the streets, only half dried after yesterday's rain and replenished this morning by freshly-emptied chamber pots.

Wood ovens across the town are baking bread and cakes and pies. Spit roasts in the taverns have begun to cook pork and mutton in anticipation of the extra trade which is sure to come their way. Long, low dogs, the Vernepator Curs, unable to flee the cooks' quick hands, are now trapped in their turnspits, perpetually running to escape the hot coals which chase and threaten to burn their paws should the meat stop turning, even for a moment. There is much profit to be made, for market-goers' appetites and insobriety grow large as the day wears on. The smell of baking and roasting joins the strange partnership of perfume and shite, increased by the heat of the day and unlikely to be dispersed by the gentle breeze.

The brothers part company when they reach the crossroads. Jesse and Henry go off to carry out Farmer Caen's instructions and George to arrange his work, although it is not quite the wholesome kind Molly believes him to be seeking.

His destination is The Running Horse, an ale house of some ill repute at the end of Bridge Street. The road leads from the crossroads all the way to Portsmouth, and just before the River Mole crossing the ancient building leans out into the road as if to pull its customers in. It is home to gamblers, drinkers, highway travellers, tea traders, brewers and all, and George is not disappointed to find Hal already before the open door. His friend's fine clothes of last evening have been replaced by a simple linen shirt and an old brown cloth jacket, slung over one shoulder. His blonde hair is tied behind his neck with a blue ribbon, his square chin clean-shaven, but even without his silver buttons and buckles, Hal Archer makes an unmistakeable and striking figure.

He smiles widely as George nears the inn. 'Georgie boy, up with the sun for a change, eh?' he chuckles.

'Hal, my good man, morning to you. And you's right, too early it be for me. Pretty surprised I be, too, at all this commotion and activity, the like of which I ain't never afore seen,' George grins.

The men have known each other many years. First, when they had no choice, directed as they were by their fathers, they worked the fields together. Later, they trapped and poached, drunk ale and gin and brandy, wooed and played, won and lost, gambled and plotted. Today's mischief involves persons from abroad, *furriners.*

'Only half the party be here, but shall we join them?' Hal asks. 'Ladies first,' he laughs and steps aside as George enters the gloom of the smoke-filled tavern.

Inside, a low fire is burning in the grate, a light for the many pipes. A group of shrivelled, white-bearded gentlemen, if they could be so called, sit at one of the few tables, playing at cards. Tobacco smoke hangs heavy under the twisted beams and the place has a familiar smell of stale ale, baccy, burnt coffee.

They nod to the innkeeper and Hal blows an empty kiss across the room to the man's daughter, Florie. He receives a tired, sarcastic smile back, for she is sure Hal Archer is mocking her. She has heard new whispers about him in the dark corners of the inn, which gossip that this one saves his love for those with something to offer in return. If true, it means that she and he work the same field, although at opposite ends of the plough.

George orders ale from Florie and the men disappear through a panelled door leading to a dimly lit passage. Half way along, Hal knocks sharply on a closed door. Behind it, furniture is scraped across the oak boards and then the door opens. A piggy eye appears in the crack and darts over Hal's face. Upon recognition, it is edged open just enough for the two men to squeeze through.

The room is little more than an antechamber leading nowhere, furnished with two rough benches, a few low stools and a long, sturdy table. There is no hearth, and yet it is uncomfortably warm. At one end, a large, ornately carved chair with threadbare red-cushioned arms is occupied by the Lord of some faraway manor, and Mister Barehenger is his name. Beside him sits his partner, known only to George and Hal as the Vice Admiral. They could be brothers, for they have the same look about them, but whether it is ties of blood or the life they have both led, George cannot rightly tell. The two other men in the room George does not know. They are clearly less than sober and are busy picking over the remaining crumbs of their simple breakfast of bread, cheese and boiled ham. Several empty jugs are scattered around the room and the tiny window, which looks out onto an alleyway running down the side of the building, is flung open. Even so, the room is filled with the stench of unwashed men and reeking breath, ale and smoke, sweaty feet and stale cheese. George wonders if they even made it to a bed last night, or if they have been here for the duration.

'Well now, here they are at last,' growls Barehenger from his throne, not getting up to greet them or offer a hand, but instead glaring with his piercing eyes.

'Mister Barehenger, Sir,' Hal says, nodding. 'And Mister Vice Admiral, how goes it?'

'Greetin's,' slurs the Vice Admiral, through the side of his mouth which does not hold his pipe. 'Goes good enough, s'pose. But we's out o' drink. Get that lazy fire ship to bring us more ale. She be slackin' pretty this morn, the wench,' and he clears his throat, spits on the floor.

Something troubles George about the Vice Admiral's words – *fire ship* – but he cannot fathom why.

'An' some more grub,' comes a small whine from the man with the piggy eyes.

'Shut it Crivins. Ye's 'ad enough fer now, always thinkin' of yer belly, ain't ya. Wait a while, till business is brewed,' the Vice Admiral snarls, and his lip curls like a deranged dog.

All eyes rest on George. As he is nearest the door, he has the job. He could just walk away, but this business is always lucrative when it comes about, so when he has ordered more ale from Florie, he drags himself back to the den and sits down as far away from the lions as he can. Not far enough, for the room is no more than ten foot by twelve.

He has met these two unsavoury characters once before and is surprised that they themselves have come to this meeting, rather than someone lower down the pecking order. The Vice Admiral brings out a pair of worn bone dice, fondles them like old familiars then casts them viciously onto the table in front of him, snatching them back and repeating his game over and over. His eyes are empty and glazed, his deeply lined face wears no beard, only a rough greyish stubble of one or two days' growth. The history of his life is written across his face in plentiful scars, which George reads like some strange hieroglyphed book. *Deep pockmarks, smallpox in childhood; broken nose, brawl at the Red Dragon Inn, ten years past; scar above left eye, heavy punch for taking a man's wife; crevice down right cheek, knifed for skimming the takings off a job.* He must be around forty, therefore, four or five years older than George, but it is clear from his scars and demeanour that he has seen a life which George cannot not possibly imagine and would not at all relish.

Next to him, Mister Barehenger is relaxing on his throne, one eye closed. *Looks asleep, but I reckon that man don't miss a trick,* thinks George. A little older than the Vice Admiral, his face has a similar map of scars, and his long, hooked nose has been broken many a time. His earlobes are garnished by two heavy gold earrings, almost hidden by his long and curly, thick grey hair.

George is not at all comfortable gazing at Barehenger and shifts his eyes away. They land on Crivins, a thin, ferret of a man, with small black eyes, too close together. His lank hair is matted on one side with what could be blood or Lord knows what and a cut above his eye is oozing pink liquid. He has almost passed into oblivion, his head leaning against the wall.

Suddenly, there is a clash and clamour as Barehenger kicks out at Crivins under the table, and a heavy-booted foot lands on his thin-skinned shin.

Crivins cries out, 'What the fuck did'cha do that fer?' and sniffs hard, wipes the back of his hand on his nose and transfers the thick green gunge onto his already grubby trousers.

'Who d'ya think yer talkin' too, yer scummy dog, eh?' Barehenger growls back, the words scarcely understandable. 'Dreamin' were 'ee? Ferget where you was, eh? In whose company you is?' And he laughs an evil chuckle, playing with the dreadful man like the devil plays with sinners.

Crivins avoids Barehenger's gaze, and although the kick had the desired effect of momentarily shaking him awake, the ale has too strong a hold, and the wretch cannot help but slip back into a hazy state.

'Useless shite, never could hold 'is ale,' Barehenger says, rolling his eyes and grinning a strange, crooked smile, showing two black teeth and one gold.

The other man in the room is younger and a little cleaner. He is sitting under the window opposite Crivins, awake and upright, but he has a stare about him as if he is watching something a hundred yards away. One eyeball is cocked sideways and George is unsure if he is looking at him or at Hal, or somewhere else entirely.

George shifts his eyes to the safety of the deep scratches in the table.

There is a gentle knock at the door, Florie with the ale. She plonks her bucket down and ladles beer liberally into fresh tankards, splashing it on her apron, the table, the floor. She looks worn out, perhaps up all night, too. The maid grimaces at him as she leaves the room and George notices a nasty pock mark on the side of her face which hadn't been there the last time he saw her, perhaps a month since. He realises now what troubled him about the Vice Admiral's earlier words. *Fire ship!*

Florie has the French Disease, which will eat into her bones and skin, and eventually deform the girl's face. It is said that even wise women like Eliza Greenfield cannot not cure that particular malady.

George looks at Hal, who grins back grimly. *Ah! Poor wench,* thinks George. *Comes with the work,* he supposes and as he wonders whether one of the men in the room has been fleeced by her for silver, or copper more likely, he looks around for suspects. Whoever it was will soon be carried afloat with her on that burning ship of certain doom.

As if reading George's mind, Barehenger nods at the condemned man, the unconscious Crivins. 'Captain Queernabs here, see? But 'ee'll likely be dead afore the year's out, anyways,' Barehenger hisses, out of the side of his mouth. 'Give 'im not a thought, 'tis the wasp what needs sympathy,' he adds, nodding towards the door, after Florie. 'If any's to give, that is. London Town's bleedin' rife with the poor dee-ar souls. Can't hardly find a clean whore nowadays.'

George struggles to understand the man and wonders if it is compassion or sarcasm he can hear. A surplus of ale is evidently not the cause of Barehenger's slurring, for he is not the type to be drunk on duty, nor let his guard down. George reckons him to be stone cold sober, or as near as can be when one only has ale to drink, for the water in London is said to be as putrid as the cesspits and not much better anywhere else these days. No, his drawl is likely a way of disguising what he is saying to all but those closest to him. Probably the habit of a lifetime.

There is another knock at the door, three sharp, slow raps. Hal jumps up and they are soon joined by two equally disturbing, men, whose presence fills the room to bursting.

However, now the party is complete, their business can begin.

Letherhed Market

Mid-Morning

Jim Caen's business is almost complete, and sooner than expected. However, the prices Jesse managed to negotiate for Mr Caen's produce are low and he will no doubt be none too pleased. It cannot be helped. There is much bewailing amongst the traders and farmers. Everyone is affected.

'All this talk of raised taxes, Henry, just ain't no good for trade,' Jesse grumbles. The coarse cilice cuts into his sweaty skin, making him grumpier than usual. ''Tis all very well them Lords in Parley-mint saying they needs more for their ec'scapades abroad, but they ain't got no inkling of the hardships.'

'Ain't it hurting their pockets more, Jesse? Them be the ones what pays most in taxes, ain't they?'

'Aye, Henry lad, you would think that. But I fear 'tis a far knottier problem. They's got all them troubles going on up in the Metrop'lis as well, the riots and the anti-popery stuff. 'Tis surely a protest aginst war. One after another, that be all this land knowed as far back as I can remember.'

Jesse is afraid that if old Jim Caen gets fed up, sells up and moves on, they could be out of home and employment. However, he does not wish to alarm Henry, for the lad *must* stay with the family, and he already has itchy feet, gripped by dreams of industry and far-away hives of activity. His feet are tapping the earth in tune to the march of the new iron machines and he longs to join the battle. His young brother brings the subject up at every opportunity. But if he leaves, they may never hear of him again. How will they let him know if they are forced from The Common to find work elsewhere? No one in the household can read or write, they have never so much as held a quill or a scrap of paper in their hands, or even formed the peculiar shapes in the dust of their back yards. The only mark they know is the cross they write in oak-gall ink in the church register when, or if, they marry. "This is me. Know me by my X". *Good Lord, the boy could be lost forever.*

As he gets hotter under the collar, worrying about their future, he wishes he could give himself permission to rip off the vest. However, he will not allow himself that luxury, for his nightmares of the King Oak, Elizabeth and brother Ned are a constant reminder that punishment for his wickedness must continue.

They stop at the blacksmith's and buy two solid rakes, and from the wheelwright next door, a spare wheel for the swing plough. They take their goods back to the Fair Field, where Hoppit is tied to the cart. Jesse is ready to return to Caen Farm.

'That were a quick mornin's work, lad,' he announces. 'Will be able to get back in good time, get that hay turned and dried, raked in, too, afore that storm what I feel rumbling breaks.'

'You be certain we's finished, Brother?' Henry asks, knowing full well that they have not.

Jesse winds his finger through his beard and scratches his chin. 'Aye, lad, that be all.'

'What about them turnip seeds what Farmer Caen asked for last even? Want drilling by the end o' the month, he sayed.'

'Lord above! Completely forgot, what with worry over Father and his decline.' Is it really Father William taking his attention, or the itches he cannot scratch which take his mind off his duties?

'Book learnin' Jesse, that's what you need. You could write a list, see? Won't forget nothing then.'

Good God, don't the boy ever let up. 'I read the land good enough, boy, and the weather, an' all. That'll do for me.' Something else forgotten is niggling at him as he strides back down the hill. *Annie's oranges!*

Henry skips after him. 'You could do both, could you not, Brother? I mean read the land and books, too. Could read the Good Book, an' all, without waiting for the Rector,' he reasons, appealing to Jesse's love of all things Godly.

'Look lad, that's as may be, but I have little time for such things. And neither do you,' Jesse says, poking his finger in Henry's face. 'So don't be letting no thoughts of fancy book learning settle down in that thick skull o' yours, right? Your place is on the farm, on the land what gives us all we needs. No need to go upsettin' things, see?'

Henry laughs inwardly at his brother's anger, more from nervousness than anything, for it could easily erupt into a strike or two. However, he will soon be a man, will he not? Then Jesse will have no say over his time or future. But he is not yet ready to make his move. Henry Hogtrough may not have had the life experiences his brother has had, after all, there are two-and-twenty years between them, but he is quick to learn, works hard and conscientiously, is always eager to do his best. *I can read the land, too,* he thinks. Not just the fields, or the soil which tumbles through his fingers as he works, but the nation, the island, the people. The mood in general. He listens to the gossip in the fields, and the town criers when he gets an opportunity to escape the farm. The changing times are racing towards them at enormous speed, and if they do not embrace the whirlwind they will be at the arse end of progress instead of at its head. The new world of machines, the buzz of busy industry, its whirring, clanking and clamour, is carried to Henry on the wind, and is pulling him towards it.

However, Jesse is determined to keep him on the land. 'I ain't getting no younger, and Father be on the way out o' this world. When I meself go, who's going to take on the farm work then? We has Annie to think of, see? I know not if she ever will marry. What if she don't find no husband, has no children? Chances are she'll live far longer than we. 'Tis our duty to provide for her or she'll end up in the blasted workhouse. God forbid! The shame! I would toss an' turn in me grave if it were so.'

Henry does not believe Annie would allow life to lead her to that particular door, but does not argue her case. Instead, he keeps picking away at Jesse, even though the threat of a fist is ever present. 'Brother, if I does book learning I can get me prenticed to one of them livery comp'nies, get a trade. Be able to give much more to our sister then, more 'an if I stays on the land, like. There be money to be made, but not here. London Town, that's where it's at,' and when Henry puts words to his dreams they become solid, real. Possible.

'You reckon 'tis easy to get in there, eh? And London Town ain't what you think. There be vice an' dis-ease, squalor. Varmints the like of what you cannot imagine. Rats as big as cats. The good Lord will not provide for you there, like what he do on The Common, where we belong. 'Tis in our bones, see?'

'London Town cannot be so bad as you say. You sees only the worsest stuff.'

Jesse shakes his head. 'Why boy, there be riots and fires burning there this very day, and them what's on the wrong side had their chattels torn out into the street and set alight, I heared. That be the true Metropolis, not the perfect place you imagine, with streets runnin' gold and gutters full o' silver. It just ain't like that.'

An uneasy silence falls between them as they finish up their purchases; the turnip seeds, then oranges. Next to the fruit stall, Mister Briars, the knife sharpener, is expertly skimming a metal blade, stealing away the nicks and gouges to create a shiny new, sharp edge. They watch his skill for a moment, then move out into the open square where the mid-morning sun is in full shine and small groups of market-goers are chatting in the warmth.

A preacher has raised himself above the crowd on a small grassy knoll near the market cross, shouting messages of salvation, repentance and redemption to anyone who will listen. A small crowd has gathered, but rather than gaining any ecumenical enlightenment they would prefer to see the man make a fool of himself. However, Jesse is always interested in the word of the Lord, eager for new stories, new teachings, and he stops before the man.

Henry looks around for some distraction. The Chitty girls are sitting in the shade of a tall building opposite, with enormous baskets of gingerbread spread out before them, and playing with two tiny puppies. Jane, the younger of the girls, calls Henry over, and he gladly leaves Jesse to his holiness.

Jesse studies the wild-eyed preacher, whose clothes are dull and dusty. His shirt and silk stockings once white, but now so grimy he might have rolled in yesterday's ashes. His buckles are tarnished, too, and Jesse shakes his head at the dishevelled appearance of a supposed holy man. The preacher punches out his message with a tattered Bible in a rhythm to rival the waltz, his hair as wild as his eyes. *Just another crazy fool.* The soldiers will be along soon to move the old man on, and Jesse's thoughts turn to the farm, where he has much to do. He really should be heading back.

He spins around, and crashes headlong into a well-dressed woman of about thirty, perched on tall wooden pattens. She is clothed in black, her wide, lacy hat streaming with ribbons. They find themselves almost nose to nose.

'Oh! I do beg your pardon Madam,' Jesse stammers an apology, stepping back to let the lady pass and doffing his battered cocked hat, not noticing at all that it is as dusty as the preacher's.

'Please, Sir. No need to apologise. The fault is entirely mine. I should have been attending to my feet and more conscious of where I was stepping, but instead I was trying to stop this kitten from absconding.'

A white kitten is struggling to escape a wicker basket hung

over her arm, and she is holding what he assumes is a bible, for there is a gilt cross imprinted onto the worn cover. He notes it is in far better condition than the wild-eyed preacher's.

But doesn't he know her from somewhere? He racks his brains but cannot recall from where.

Her memory is far better. 'Why I do believe it is Mister Hog-trough, is it not? Mister Jesse Hogtrough of Woodfield?' she says.

Jesse is surprised to hear his name spoken by such a lady. 'Why, yes, that be me, indeed,' he stutters. 'But do ex'curse me, for I knows your face, but for the life of me, Mistress, and to my very great shame, I know not your name. Please forgive me,' he says, wearing his best voice like a Sunday suit, smoothing out all the wrinkles and dressing it up with a sprig of polite. He can do nothing about his face, however, which is growing redder by the second.

The woman holds out a hand. Palm down and gloved in black silk, she proffers her long fingers for Jesse to grasp. 'Mathilda. Mathilda Richardson. I do believe we met at St Giles, where your brother married my cousin, Molly Greenfield who was.'

Now he has her! Molly's cousin, indeed! She looks different, older and more confident. The woman he remembers from St. Giles was far less forward, rather timid in fact. Jesse realises he should take the delicate hand he has been offered. He does so rather roughly and clumsily. He bends his head to kiss her fingers, as is expected of him. Then, he sees how dirty his hands are against the pristine glove. He only usually touches horses and oxen, pigs and sheep, scythes and rakes. He feels coarse and unclean in Mathilda's presence and wipes his hands on his breeches, as if it will make any difference, for now he sees they are as filthy as his fingers.

Mathilda does not seem to notice his discomfort and is all smiles.

He reclaims a little composure. 'Mistress Richardson, of course. I do beg your pardon.' He takes off his hat and holds it in front of him, and now sees that it is also tired and dirty. To his great embarrassment, he realises that he looks a lot like the dusty preacher, the only difference being the colour of his hair, which has not yet turned completely grey.

'Please, Mister Hogtrough, you must call me Mathilda.'

Jesse is a little shocked. The woman is too familiar, for she is clearly of a different class.

She sees his concern and adds, 'Well, we are almost cousins, after all, are we not?'

Her eyes are glinting green and bright beneath the fine lace of her hat, which she now lifts so that he can see her face in full. Jesse is mesmerised by the vivid colour of her eyes, the like of which he has never before seen, except in his dream of Elizabeth. But of course, hers are blue. *Were blue.* And this woman's face is so clear and fresh, her skin pale and smooth, unmarked by time or hard work, or a visit from the pox. He rests his eyes on hers for too long and she looks away, blushing, and attends to the kitten, still trying to make an escape. Jesse suddenly remembers his manners. He squirms, looks down at his feet, and his blushes keep coming.

'Well then, you must call me Jesse, Mistress Rich ... I mean, Cousin Mathilda,' he says, bowing lightly.

There is an uneasy pause and then they both begin to speak at once and laugh nervously together.

'Please, Cousin, do go on,' he mumbles.

'I only wanted to ask after my cousin. How is she? I heard news she was expecting again. Has the baby arrived?'

'Well, now. I sees her just this morn and they was still very much not arrived. But I do believe they are quite eminent,' he replies, his voice growing confident. He pulls himself up straight and puffs out his chest. Bad move. *Damn, bleedin' vest.* He tries to relax without Mathilda noticing his discomfort.

'Imminent, you mean? But you said 'they'?' Mathilda looks puzzled.

'Oh, aye! But you pro'bly ain't heared. Molly do believe she be having twins. And likely there be truth in that, for she be so very large.'

'Well! What a wonderful surprise. I do hope all goes well this time. Such a tragedy before …,' Mathilda trails her words away, not wanting to finish, to voice any details of the loss of her cousin's firstborn. 'But tell me, how exactly is my dear cousin faring? For it does pain me that we have so little to do with one another nowadays,' she continues, 'since we spent so much time together as children.'

Jesse is unsure what to say. He cannot divulge that he thinks Molly has made a grave mistake by marrying his lazy, stubborn brother, and that because of George's laziness she has been bending over her tubs this very morning trying to rid Mister Joshua Reynolds' undergarments of a most disagreeable stink, and so near to the dangerous travail she is facing. Or that he has seen black shadows growing large under her tired eyes, and that last evening she was sloshing about in gin. And, if he is not mistaken, she was looking at him in a way not conducive to being a woman married to his very own brother, but indeed, a lady of the night.

All of this he wants to say, as a cry of help, but cannot – or will not – as it is not his place to be so direct, and what a slur on her character it would be. He sticks to safe ground.

'Fair to middlin' I'd say,' is his response. And then something takes hold of him and he opens up far more than he means to. 'But she might do with a bit o' womanly support, what with her mother already passed, God rest her soul, and she don't have no sisters nearby to help, and her grandmother, the old Widow Greenfield, so decrepit now and such a burden, and their little 'un, I mean Little Joe, only three years old but goes too often abroad, and my sister, Annie, well, she do help on occasion, but she has her own hands full what with our ailing Father, now taken mostly to his bed, and with her tasks around the farm, too.' It all comes out in one long breath and Jesse is surprised at just how much he has given away.

'Oh dear, my poor cousin. It appears she could do with an extra pair of hands,' Mathilda says. 'I should come. I could be of some use, perhaps till the infants arrive and for a few days after. But of course, if she is going to have twins, then she really will be overstretched. Might she need my help a little longer?' Mathilda looks at Jesse demurely, and he realises that the lady had assumed he was soliciting her help. His expression turns to one of uncomfortable horror.

'Oh Lord! No, Mistress Rich …, I mean, Cousin Mathilda. Lord above, forgive me, for I did not mean to suggest that you should give up yer precious time to helping Molly,' he stammers.

'Not at all, Cousin! You certainly did not suggest anything of the sort, you merely gave an answer to my question. And I, upon hearing your answer and knowing that at present I am at such a loss to know how to pass my time, my own dear husband having departed this earth not five weeks ago, God rest his soul, well, I begin now to see how I may be of service to others rather than wallowing in my own grief. What do you think? Would it be at all appropriate for me to call on her, uninvited, so to speak? Or perhaps you might inform her, on my behalf, that I shall arrive? Let us say, tomorrow morning?'

Jesse had not heard of the death of Mathilda's husband. The wheelwright John Richardson was a skilled tradesman and will be missed by the townsfolk and those of the surrounding villages. 'I had no idea about your loss, Madam. God rest his good soul. I do not know how the sad news did not reach my hears. I do apologise, most professly.'

'Profusely, you mean?'

Jesse raises his eyebrows. Does he? He has no idea what he meant, but uncomfortable though he is, in his ignorance he can only stand corrected. He looks down at his hat. Thinking about the poor departed wheeler, he clasps the battered, dusty tricorn to his chest. Then he notices a stain on his leather jerkin, and that one of his boots is scuffed with a large scar gouged into it. More and more, he is beginning to see how shabby he looks compared to the well groomed, elegant lady standing next to him. His face reddens again, mortally embarrassed as to the state of his clothes, his lack of knowledge about local affairs and indeed, his very own language. Only then does he see she is dressed entirely in black. He should have known from her attire that she is in mourning. He feels extremely foolish.

'Well, anyway, thank you for your kind words. I am slowly becoming used to him being gone,' Mathilda says, a shadow crossing her fair face, 'but I know that the Good Lord has him, and that my beloved Mister Richardson will be an asset in death to those who are also no longer with us.'

Jesse nods in agreement and tries to shake off the awkwardness which persists. He wishes to extract himself from this troublesome conversation as soon as possible. 'Well now, back to the subject of Molly. I can't rightly say if it be alright. See, it ain't my household, so it would be inapprobate for me to say yay or nay.'

'Inappropriate, you mean?'

Jesse, corrected the third time by this woman, finds he is now becoming irritated by her. He continues on, hoping that this next suggestion will release him. 'My brother George, he do be in town this very day, so p'raps we might find him, ask on your behalf, like? I believe this would be the good and proper way to give an answer to your proposal.' This seems to Jesse as good a solution as any.

Mathilda agrees. 'That is indeed a very splendid idea. I am on my way at present to deliver this mischievous kitten to the Rectory, where I hope it shall find a quiet and loving home with the Reverend Russell's eldest daughter. I suppose you had also not heard that the Reverend's good wife passed away last week and left him with four young children. There is so much sickness in the world, I do declare we should thank the Lord for every day we wake up, and say another prayer when we find ourselves in good health.'

Mathilda had supposed right. The news about Mistress Russell's death is also new to Jesse, and embarrassment piles on top of embarrassment. 'Oh! Dear Lord, what a sad loss for the Reverend. God rest the poor woman's soul.' Jesse hangs his head.

They stand silent for a moment, and then Mathilda twists round on her pattens. She looks up at the clock tower, making calculations in her head. 'Well, it is presently ten o' the clock, so let us meet here in one hour. Do you think you might then have an answer for me?'

'Well, yes, I be sure we can find George in that time.'

Jesse had hoped to be getting home, but perhaps they can spare a bit longer in town, since their business for Jim Caen was conducted so swiftly. There is still the hay to gather in, and the vetches in the March Field need cockling, but he calculates that at least a quarter could be done by sunset if they put their backs into it. He watches Mathilda totter off towards the Rectory and looks around for Henry, who is still talking to the two giggling Chitty girls.

'Ladies,' he says, tipping his hat as he walks up to them. They curtsey in unison, their grubby skirts skimming the dusty street.

'Morning Mister Hogtrough,' Liza says. The eldest, a pretty girl of nearly seventeen, has a most dangerous look in her eye which betrays her as being far too forward. It reminds Jesse of Molly, yesterday evening. He shakes the memory away before he is stirred to something he should keep under control.

'Can I interest you in a piece of our delicious gingerbread?'

At the word *delicious*, Liza tips herself forward, bosom thrust towards prey as she offers him a round wooden platter with a few pieces of cake laid neatly across it. She smiles and her lips part slightly as she runs her tongue around them.

It is most enticing indeed.

He clears his throat as a shivery tingle runs around the top of his legs.

'No, thank you, Liza. 'Tis very kind of you to offer your lovely, erm, wares, but our sister did make us bevers and it would certainly be ingrateful to go home with it all uneated. How be your father now, after the accident with that pig?' Jesse asks.

'Father be mostly back to normal, minus half a finger and a chunk of pride. Don't guess it will teach him to stay off the drink, though. I be sure it wouldn't have happened if he'd been a bit more sober and remembered his wits. I mean, tryin' to teach a pig to sit like a dog!? Ain't goin' to work, is it?'

'Aye, I do believe it to be a pointless thing. Drink does have that effect, though, don't it? Makes a man do things he comes later to regret,' and the uncomfortable memory of Elizabeth at the King Oak so many years ago, stirs Jesse's cilice. It cuts a little deeper, the tiny fibres of the coarse shirt dig and hook into the raw crevices of his flayed shame. It becomes almost unbearable and he begins to hop from side to side, trying to shake the vest into a more comfortable position. Henry watches him. The man looks like he is dancing on hot coals and he stifles a laugh.

Liza has not noticed. 'Anyways, Father be round the back of the Lion Brewery, watching the fight with all them crowing cocks,' she says, lilting forward towards Jesse again at the last word.

'Well, I did not realise he lost a finger, poor chap,' and still agitated, he takes a step backwards, away from the dangerous thrust of Liza's bosom.

'Well, only half of one,' and Liza holds up her little finger and wiggles it at Jesse. 'Says he can still feel the missin' bit. That be right strange, ain't it? But serves him right, is what Mother says.'

Liza now turns her eyes, bosom and charms towards Henry, but continues speaking as if to Jesse. 'We do believe Henry should take one of these 'ere puppies home. 'Twould keep 'im right warm at night. What say you Mister Hogtrough? A capital idea, or what?'

It is Henry's turn to blush. He looks over at Jesse, who mulls it over for a few seconds, scratching at his beard, resisting the urge to run away to a dark corner and relieve his chest by ripping the sharp vest away from his sores.

A puppy, might hold the lad to the homestead for a few more years yet and curb his wanderin' feet. Why not? 'Well now, if Henry wants a pup, I sees no reason why he cannot. Now mind Henry, 'tis your 'sponsibility, you hears me?'

'Thank you, Brother,' Henry says and turns to Liza, now quite openly flirting with him, her eyes locked firmly on his, breasts puffed up and out. 'Which one do you thinks I should take?' He looks up and sees Liza's eyes begging, *'Me, me, take me'*, but those words do not slip by her rosebud lips.

'This one be the runt, 'tis so small compared the other, but now you decides,' Liza coos, brushing up against Henry's arm as she holds up the scrap of a puppy.

'Runts always makes the best dogs, so George says. Unless you girls wants it that is?'

'No Henry, 'tis yours,' Jane, the younger sister, says. 'What'll you call it?'

Jane is a year younger than Liza, a much quieter girl and to Henry, far more beautiful, with her clear skin, almond-shaped eyes and modest character. His legs go to jelly. 'Dorly will be his name,' he says, pulling himself up and smiling at Jane. 'Like the dorling of a pig's litter, but not that he looks any like a pig. He be a bit more prettier, don't you thinks?'

'Just a bit, Henry, just a bit,' Liza laughs, fluttering her eyelashes. 'And I be sure you can teach this little piglet to sit. But he be a she. 'Tis a bitch, look!'

Henry turns Dorly upside down. 'Well, so she is!'

Jesse wants to be away from Liza Chitty, with her provocative ways, and to get Henry away, too. *God forbid he ends up with a girl like her, she will make nobody a good wife, the man will end up a cuckold.*

'Henry, lad, we have some important business to attend to. Ladies, do ex'curse us,' and he tips his hat towards the girls.

Henry cannot take his eyes off Jane, who blushes as she catches his glance. When they are out of earshot, Jesse explains Mathilda's request.

'I did told her we must ask George first, if Molly would appropriate her visit. Now, where will George be?'

'Why that be easy,' Henry replies. 'An alehouse be my reckoning.'

THE RUNNING HORSE
MID-MORNING

The tiny den in which George and Hal are holed up, reeks like a slave galley. All that is missing is the pounding of waves against the wooden-framed walls. Instead, George can feel the hammering of his heart against his chest, unused as he is to being in such places, in front of such crooks. Next to him, Hal's knees are bobbing up and down under the table and he is shifting his arse this way and that, his fingers playing with a deep scar etched into the table. It is unlike either of them to be out of his depth, but here, in this hellhole, they are both floundering. Business is still not complete and only crawling to a conclusion.

For some reason, the late arrivals do not seem in a hurry to finish. The two men, Captain Will Oakheart, a swarthy sailor sporting an enormous beard, and Joseph 'Windy' Gusst, younger and cleaner, are no less scarred and marked than the other men. However, it is obvious these two spend their lives outside, most likely on open water. Sea dogs, fishermen, pirates, and probably more to boot, George guesses. Their skin is creased as much by the weather as by their battle scars, and tough, like tanned leather after years of sun, salty air, and more than a daily ration of rum. George swears he can see barnacles in Oakheart's beard, but maybe it was that last pint of purl he took, and on a very meagre breakfast at that.

Barehenger and the Vice Admiral on the other hand, are urban wolves from up near the river, where London Town is beginning to spill over the banks and creep south into Surry. Their skin is pale and pasty, for their business is done in the shadows, in gambling dens and brothels, seedy drinking holes, gloomy woods and moonless highways.

And revolting tavern back-rooms.

Both sides are equally menacing, and George cannot leave, he is in too deep, knows too much. *Get a damnded move on and we can get out of this stinkin' pit.* The words explode silently in his head and he does not realise he is scowling.

Barehenger's two drunken sidekicks have been sent outside to watch window and door for unwanted guests, although it is unlikely they will be of any use. The window has been shut tight and their boss is slouched back on his throne, his eyes bearing down on George. He speaks in his slurred and sideways manner without removing his clay pipe, the words slithering past his lips like a snake sneaking out of a woodpile. Everyone strains their ears to catch them as they slip across the putrid air, except the

Vice Admiral, who is completely uninterested and slumped back against a wall, fondling his dice and cradling a jug of warm ale.

'What's settled at present is that the goods'll be delivered by Captain Oakheart's people,' Barehenger pauses, tips a nod at Oakheart, 'to these two reprobates 'ere,' and grins at George. He is clearly amused, but George hardly catches the word and even less its meaning. He can only return the grin as politely as possible.

'Delivery will be tomorrow at midnight,' Barehenger continues, and as he shuffles the words out, his piercing gaze becomes fixed on George, whose skin crawls and creeps uneasily.

And then something jars him.

Wait! Tomorrow? Bleedin' hell, that weren't the plan! George kicks Hal under the table. Somehow, the skulduggery has been brought forward without any warning and now they have precious little time to prepare.

Hal sounds shocked. 'Why the change, Sir? If you don't mind me asking. We thought it planned for a week hence.'

Barehenger glares at Hal. 'You ain't heard what be occurring up Town these past days then? With the mobs and whatnot,' he grunts.

How could they not? It is on everyone's lips. George recalls last evening's stories at The Leg, descriptions and tales of riots and upheaval, discontent in so many quarters.

'Aye, we have, but what part do it play for us?'

Windy Gusst takes the helm. 'There is still a substantial amount of trouble on the streets of the Metropolis. The no-popery mobs and diverse others among them, I say, are causing mayhem. There are not nearly enough watchmen to control the crowds, and now the mob has done enough damage to cause the Redcoats to be brought in from all around the country. That leaves the highways reasonably clear for us to manoeuvre. It would be foolish of us not to take advantage of this fortuitous situation.' The man is well spoken and silver-tongued, no doubt from the spoon with which he was born, and unlike Barehenger, his words are easy to comprehend. George wonders how the hell, and why, he became involved in this treacherous game.

Gusst continues. 'Therefore, we will deliver the goods early. In fact, the waggons are already en route. We sent word to Mister Barehenger two days ago,' and he nods at Barehenger, who takes over the discussion.

'Aye, them no-Popery lot, they's certainly workin' for us, alright. The Vice Admiral here saw first hand how they destroyed Newgate Gaol. 'Tis a right colourful history at that.'

The Vice Admiral grins, showing the few teeth he has remaining, as black and as rotten as his soul. ''Tis true alright,' he slurs, his eyes alight at the memory. 'Colourful, Mister Barehenger, aye, and wonderful to behold. Them took to breakin' open prison doors with crows and climbed upon the walls to set in flames the rafters. Then the 'ole lot come a-tumblin' down.' The Vice Admiral lifts his hands and lets his fingers fall through the air like the burning beams, his eyes maniacal with glee. George imagines him in the midst of the flames, grinning like a devil.

'I sees them reb'llers atop the walls, flames lickin' at their boots. A wondrous spectacle, them boys was. And when all prisoners once in was let out, they fired the keeper's house and tooked all 'is chattels to the street. Burnt all to a cinder crisp, they did. And oh,' the Vice Admiral guffaws, then coughs, before regaining his breath, 'did he cry that he might send for the sheriff, but they would not allow it and all his shit burned complete to ashes.'

George is riveted to his seat by the scenes unfolding in his mind's eye, incredulous that the rioters were not stopped by Redcoats or the city's watchmen. It is one thing to protest against an unpopular law, but to fire a gaol and release its inmates, is another thing entirely. He recalls his old grandfather telling stories of the Diggers on St. George's Hill, not six miles from where they sit now. Did they not fight for common land, to plant crops and so feed their children? And yet, they were cut down like common animals, even though their cause was one of basic survival. So why no reaction from those in authority to these riots? It is a curious question and he finds his voice to ask.

'Where was the watch? Did none try to stop it?'

The Vice Admiral lets out a roar. 'You was not there, Mister Hogtrough, you did not see with your own daylights, what extra-hordinary fierce was in the h'air. Multitudes upon multitudes of 'em, all stoked with a cause pheno-meenal. What they desired none could prevent. Weren't 'nough watchmen, nor foot soldiers to stop 'em. Crowd was too great by far.'

'And it continues?' Hal asks, looking at Gusst.

'I heard from my associates that the Mob's path continued to other gaols. However, they stepped too far when they threatened to break open the doors of the Bank in Threadneedle Street. I perceive that was the last straw.'

'Aye,' says Barehenger, 'I mean, we cannot have no commoners gettin' a feel of all that precious bunce and runnin' it through their dirty mitts now, can we? Swells must be crawlin' in their sleep at the thought. Lord Almighty, an' what a fantastic thought it be.'

'Indeed, and therefore ten thousand military men for sixty miles around the Metropolis have been called to put an end to it,' Gusst adds.

'See how it helps our cause no end, gentlemen?' Captain Oakheart adds, in his broad West Country accent.

'Aye, while they's busy with trouble north of the river, there ain't so much of a sniff of them robin redbreasts on the south bank, see? We's able to move about with a little more ease in our manor. For the time bein' anyways,' Barehenger sidles out the words, his eyes for some reason still boring into George.

'Let us hope it continues longer and they's kept busy in the Metropolis. For Mister Barehenger is right, the fewer soldiers wanderin' hither and thither around the highways, the better,' Oakheart says, 'and, as Mister Gusst here has informed 'ee, the load's already movin' and will be here tomorrow. Midnight precisely, on that you can count.'

Barehenger continues, 'And we do not need to press upon you two gentlemen, that our precious cargo must be protected with your very own liveses, do we? From Redcoats or anything else what might like to get its filthy little mitts on it, see?'

The four leaders of this perilous pact turn to Hal and George, and the hair on the back of George's neck breaks into a run and heads down his back towards his bowels.

'For if any of our stock goes missing in the hours you has our precious goods in your possession, then rest assured, you – and yours mind, and yours – will be held accountable.'

Barehenger puts too much emphasis on these words, to George's great dismay.

And then the Vice Admiral leans forward and adds, 'And you

might find your daylights is darkened.' He breaks into a most undelightful chuckle.

It takes George a few seconds to understand the meaning of the words, but he soon gets it. *Daylights darkened, bleedin' hell! He means blinded!*

Hal seems completely unfazed, but then he has neither wife nor child to protect. And Barehenger isn't giving him a suspicious and evil eye, is he? George, on the other hand, has a head full of dark pictures, of coming home to find a petrified household, his wife raped, his home pillaged, and his three-year old son running naked from the burning shell of their meagre cottage. He shivers at the grim images. Lord God, when the babes arrive there will be five souls he should provide for, give shelter to, if he includes his own. *Lord, 'tis six with the old bat*, and he feels rather mean forgetting her, for it is only by her goodness that they have a roof over their heads. He tries to push his family out of his mind, away from this squalid room, where they may be spied, made vulnerable to the evil by which he is surrounded. Barehenger, once he catches sight of them, will know them, like a witch gazing into a crystal ball. *Damn! Why'd I agree to this?* The last time they did work for Barehenger it was easier, but the stakes were not so high. A test, perhaps. This time, their contribution has increased, and with the additional risk comes more wondrous rewards. It would take him at least six weeks to earn as much in the fields, but since he has fallen out with all the local farmers, this is where he now finds himself. Dealing with rogue wolves, sea monsters and the threat of the hangman's noose.

He tells himself that things must change, for his son, for Molly and the babes, if they live past the births. All of a sudden, he is awake and charging headlong into adulthood. Rather late, but better than never.

Oakheart is speaking, and although his accent is strong at least his words are clear. 'Gentlemen, I's sure Mister Barehenger wants to know what you plans on doin' with our valuable load, once 'tis delivered to your good selves.' The old sailor sits back, twisting an enormous Spanish doubloon coin-ring around a thick finger.

'And do leave nothing out. We want all the particulars, just to be clear that you understand exactly what is required of you,' Mister Gusst adds. He is a good ten years younger than George but with more authority than he could ever imagine possessing. George wonders what it is that gives a man such presence. The ability to strike fear into those around you? George does not have the stomach for that. And this is just not his game.

And the game? Tea. Lucrative, black market tea.

For a moment he wishes it were whisky. *Now that might be worth the risk. But then, nothing is worth a hanging.* Eliza Greenfield's words come back and slap him on the face again. Who will be bedding his wife, indeed, should he not survive this? He stifles a groan.

Hal has begun a monologue. Keeping his voice low he explains in detail what part they will play in this plan to outwit the tax extortionists, as Barehenger refers to them.

George and Hal will take charge of several large loads of tea from Oakheart's men and re-package the lot into small bags. Barehenger's gang will then collect the tea, which can be hidden, stored and distributed more easily as one pound packets than enormous sacks. Hal repeats the instructions, how much each new pack must weigh, and how every ounce must be accounted for, and how exactly the tea is to be packaged anew.

However, to George's great surprise, he hears for the first time that the packages are to be graded three different ways. From what he understood when first Hal told him of the work, they were to be provided with bags and some lengths of twine, and were only to fill and tie them. A simple task. However, it seems Hal has not been entirely honest with him, for they are also to be responsible for the grading. They must add quantities of different teas and sometimes not even tea at all but birch or hawthorn leaves to make up the weights, and each type must be tied a certain way, with a certain knot, to denote the different quality. And all this in a few short hours. Midnight to dawn.

When George realises he is staring at Hal with his mouth open, aghast at this dreadful revelation, he snaps it shut and looks away. His jaws clench and his fists ball up by his side. If he can refrain from striking Hal when they are out of this godforsaken place it will be a miracle. But Barehenger has seen him, and catches his eye, raises an eyebrow, as if asking, *Did you not know what you were letting yourself in for?* And the man's wicked eyes laugh.

George can feel the weight of responsibility around his neck, heavier even than a gallows rope.

Hal explains where they will meet Oakheart's men and passes a roughly sketched map of their meeting place, near the Oxmoor Pond. Windy Gusst takes it from Hal's long, slender hands, which have not dirtied themselves with the heavy clay earth of the fields around The Common for many months, years even. They have become skilled, instead, at caressing rich widows' needs, and one in particular has taken him to be her favourite, so why Hal wants to do this ungodly work when he has an easy source of income is another question which troubles George.

Hal explains further. 'Our meeting place be a mile or so distant from the Turnpike Road, like you said it should. We'll lead the waggons to the place where we plan to do the work. 'Tis deep in The Common forest. The path runs wide most of the way, then turns off and narrows. There we must stop and unhook the ponies. The beasts can carry all from there to an old barn we's found. Mister Gusst do know the exact whereabouts, 'ccording to the map what I give him. But I ain't drawed it on, for reasons I believe be clear.'

So far, no additional surprises, but George's fists are still clenched.

Barehenger questions Hal further. 'Pray do tell us about this place where you plans to carry out the work. How come you choosed it as the best place?' he growls out of his crooked mouth.

'Well that be easy like, on account of it being an old barn, hid deep in the woods, where not man nor horse will go this time of year. 'Tis not the season for hunting, nor for gathering too much firewood on account of the weather, and with everything in full bloom and leafy green you cannot hardly see the forest floor to collect kindling, see?' Hal says, with a confidence that George intends to shake from him when they escape this dreadful place.

'And to whom does this hidden barn belong?' Barehenger snarls again, in that way he has of making every sentence seem a threat.

'To Dukes Hall farm, and that be part of the Norton estate, near Epsum. An old palace house is Dukes Hall, lately fallen into much disrepair and the farm there be inhabited by some very unserious farmers. Two old brothers what took to drinkin' a while back. Them lazy sons o' bitches will not trouble us on account they don't hardly trouble themselves to do nothing, not even get out o' their bug pits of a morning, 'cept to reach for the bottle,' Hal explains, and he stares Barehenger straight in the eye. George is grateful that the man's gaze has fallen momentarily on his friend.

'So, describe this barn for us. 'Tis dry or do the roof let in rain?' Barehenger inquires.

''Tis mostly dry, and shingled, not thatched. It do have a hole here or there, but in general, pretty sound and there be enough dry space for us to work. 'Tis as good a place as any we could find. And it being so far in the woods, the trees having growed up all around mighty quick like, it be all but forgotten. There be a pond nearby, water for the pack animals, like.'

'And what, pray, be yer plan should any une'spected visitors arrive?' says Barehenger.

'There be an old well, what's now dried up. 'Tis very close to the place, should not be a trouble to ditch the stuff quick, like, if need be. No one will disturb us, though, 'tis right out of the way. Unless someone cackles, that is.' Hal looks at each face around the room, everyone a suspect, and has the audacity to grin at them.

George cringes, holds his breath, waiting for someone to erupt in fury at the merest suggestion that one of their own may possibly give the game away. Instead, Hal's cheek breaks the icy chill which has settled on the stuffy room.

After a moment's silence, Barehenger begins guffawing. 'Ain't no queer roosters in our house, mate!'

Hal has had a narrow escape. He finishes by showing that they know the weights of the packages they will have to make up and where they will meet Barehenger's men for the onward journey. It is a straight highway from The Common to Stockwell, where George believes Barehenger is based, but he guesses the men will cross the distance via farm tracks and little-used lanes. In any case, it isn't any of his concern. From there on, Hal and George's part in the plot will be over. They will get their money once the goods have been checked, and then they can put the whole thing behind them.

God forbid anything goes wrong, thinks George. *We'll surely not come out of this alive, from any side.* The regret he felt earlier about accepting the work is beginning to grow into a nauseating knot in his belly. However, there is no untangling it now. They know too much and it will be over when it is over, and not before.

The lords of very different manors, pirates and wolves, from sea and city, are finally in agreement. They can all now leave this revolting place.

However, George cannot quite heave a sigh of relief, as his part in the business has not yet begun.

LETHERHED BRIDGE

MID-MORNING

Jesse and Henry split up in search of George. Jesse goes to
The Bull, while Henry heads for The Running Horse, at the
bottom of Bridge Street. It lies just before the medieval toll
bridge which rises up from the gravelly road to cross the River
Mole, so named for its habit of disappearing into the earth and
re-emerging miles away.

The excitement of market is a welcome change to the monot-
onous routine of farm life and church on Sunday, and Henry
treasures memories of days like these. Jane Chitty's sweet face
is particularly clear and he smiles as he imagines long summer
evenings walking in The Common's forest, leading her to the King
Oak, a place where so many passions are sealed.

The puppy is alert and inquisitive, she wants to jump down and scamper, put her nose into the myriad of street smells in the semi-dried-up puddles of dirt. Henry holds her wrapped firmly in his jacket, fears losing her under the wheels of a waggon or the trample of the horses' heavy hooves, and there are many prancing up and down the streets today.

As Henry turns into Bridge Street, a tall black horse comes trotting past, its smartly dressed rider holding the reins short, slowing the beast's long gait.

'Step aside, step aside, make way for the Portsmouth Coach,' he hollers, his voice hoarse and strained. 'Portsmouth Coach, coming through. Make way, ladies and gentlemen. Make way!'

Henry arrives at the bottom of the hill near the inn, just as the heavy coach appears at the top and begins its precarious journey down the steep incline towards the bridge. People scatter to the side of the narrow street to let it teeter pass, and teeter it does, for it is loaded to the brim with passengers and luggage. Outside the inn, there are a few familiar faces making the most of the warm sunshine – farmers and tradesmen; the carpenter, shoemaker, chandler – but also many folk Henry does not know. Before he braves the stuffy tavern on his search for George, Henry goes down to the river beside the slippery ford stones and offers his pup a lap of muddy water. As he is walking back up towards the inn, he sees Hal Archer emerging from a side entrance, his tricorn pulled down to shade his eyes from the blinding sunlight. George appears behind, blinking away the indoor gloom, and then a very unsavoury character swaggers away from the door. As the man moves, his coat swings aside revealing a pistol hanging from his waist. Henry watches the three men cross the yard, followed by another man, looking very much like a storm cloud so dark is he. They stand near the stables in idle conversation, clearly acquainted and Henry wonders how his brother is connected to such interesting, if not diabolical, people.

However, he has no more time to ponder this, because the Portsmouth Coach has drawn up and is causing a disturbance to the still morning air. The elegant black and red carriage is pulled by four enormous chestnut horses, with their anxious driver sitting atop, gripping the reins. The crowd outside the inn and before the bridge are rowdy, the team of horses already excited on account of the hubbub and bustle of market. The coachman has so far managed to guide the beasts through the narrow roads and hordes of people without incident, but the scene before him he can do nothing about. A heavy wooden pole bars access to the bridge to all except those who pay the hefty toll, the Portsmouth Coach one of those. However, the parish clerk, who holds the key, is nowhere to be seen, even though he knows well what time they are due. The unhappy driver has no choice but to wait in the unrelenting heat and calls for water for the horses. A groom from the stables appears with some pails. Those passengers sitting on seats atop the coach aim to make the most of this unplanned stop, rather fortuitously outside a watering hole. Much to the driver's consternation, they are readying themselves to climb down.

'I beg of you, please rest where you are,' he calls out. 'We shall not be long here. The parish clerk will be along any minute. It is very unlike him to be late.' And under his breath he swears and mumbles to himself, 'Where on earth is that damned man. Two guineas a year we pay. Two Guineas! Damn him. Reparations will be due!'

A large, middle-aged widow sitting next to him, stands up and wobbles uneasily. She also seems determined to alight.

The coachman looks alarmed. 'Madam, do be careful, please,' he says and holds out an arm, barring her way.

'Thank you kindly, Sir, but would that I could stretch me legs,' she implores him. 'They are all a-pins and needles. I needs to get the life back in 'em, see?'

'Just a few minutes then, but be warned we shall leave as soon as the clerk arrives, with or without you,' the coachman says. *Damn, they will all want to get off now,* he thinks. And he is not wrong. Two young men in naval livery sitting just behind the woman, swing themselves over the edge of the coach with ease. The widow turns this way and that, unsure whether to climb down forwards or backwards until the two sailors offer to help.

'Why thank you kindly young gentlemen, I was quite certain I would not make it in one piece,' she says, but the sailors are already heading for the inn. The woman stretches her legs, one pace, two paces, and then follows them into the darkness of The Running Horse. Next off are six young gentlemen scholars on the basket seats, in a particularly jolly mood and equally keen to take advantage of this unforeseen halt.

With all the passengers from outside the coach now inside the inn, it looks a little less top heavy, although there is still a huge pile of luggage tied to the roof. The carriage door swings open. Nobody emerges, but a young lady's face appears. Seeing the area replete with half-drunken men, she shrinks back to her plush velvet seat. A chubby man, powdered and wigged then shows his face. He also decides to remain inside, even in the sweltering heat.

'Where on earth is the man with that key?' the coachman calls out to the crowd, becoming ever more fractious.

A large and important-looking gentleman with a silver topped ebony cane and a tall black hat comes forward. 'He's been sent for, but you may be in for a rather a wait. I do believe he was called away to attend to an urgent problem at the church.'

'What could be more urgent than the bridge being opened for the Portsmouth Coach, I ask you?' the driver huffs. 'We pay two Guineas a year to cross via this bridge, and make no mistake it shall be noted and reported to the parish overseers. It is a disgrace. Two Guineas!'

The chubby, wigged man sticks his head out of the door of the coach again. 'If anyone has a pistol handy, I am quite sure the locks would come off that bar very easily. Just give it to me and I shall see to it myself.'

'That won't be at all necessary, Sir,' the man with the cane says, and introduces himself to the driver. 'Henry Bushby, local magistrate. I am quite sure Mister Doyley, the church warden, will be along very shortly,' he says, trying to reassure the agitated man.

'Pardon me, but very shortly, Sir, is not short enough,' the coachman snorts, his nostrils flaring like an irate stallion.

'Keep your hair on, Mister. Here he is, a-comin' down the hill, see?' calls a voice from the side of the road.

All eyes turn to see a round old man with short stubby legs, come hurtling and huffing down towards the bridge. At the bottom of the hill, the puffed out Mister Doyley stops and bends over, puts his hands on his knees to catch his laboured and raspy breath.

'Someone get the man a drink,' calls the magistrate, 'he looks half dead.'

A pint of ale appears and Mister Doyley gratefully gulps it down. His face is pink and swollen, and one hand clasps his chest as if in enormous pain. He is clearly unused to moving at anything more than a snail's pace, and whispers among the crowd suggest he might keel over and return to the church in a box. Someone produces a small stool from the inn and the man is urged to sit down and gather himself together.

'Sir, please explain what the urgent business was that called you to the church. Pray do tell us. It must have been of the utmost importance to hold the Portsmouth Coach for so long,' the driver is compassionless and sour, his words scorch the air. He is not prepared even to wait for the man to catch his breath.

Mister Doyley winces, feeling coachman's wrath. 'I am ... so very sorry ... for the delay. I was ... waylaid by a ...,' he says, in short bursts between large gulps of air, and the last word he whispers, so that no one hears the pathetic reason for his delay, '... kitten.'

The coachman huffs, not really interested in his excuses at all. 'Well, do hurry yourself Sir, we must be on our way,' he says coldly, and begins to call out. 'Portsmouth passengers return to the coach, or we shall be away without you, make no mistake!'

There is uneasiness in the air. The horses are stamping and snorting, the coachman's brow is ever more furrowed. Henry keeps well clear of the carriage as he pushes his way gently through crowd towards the stables. He spots George with his *furriner* friends, readying their horses and about to depart. Hal is speaking to the enormous man who emerged from the inn first, a grey bear, dressed in such a heavy, dark coat as befits a cold and snowy February evening rather than a warm, humid June morning.

Henry turns his attention back to the coach and the hapless Mister Doyley, who has recovered enough to make his way in short, laboured steps towards the barred, decaying bridge. He wobbles slowly, wheezing, and his powdered wig slips on his sweaty head as he lurches from side to side.

The coachman has managed to round up his flock and they are assembled outside the inn, ready to re-board the coach. One by one they climb back up and settle down for the next leg of their pitiless journey. They are soon all in position, exactly where they had been ten minutes previously.

Henry has never ridden a coach and suspects that it is only slightly more comfortable than sitting on the hay waggon as it rumbles along the dusty farm tracks. This one looks top-heavy and unsound. He watches the fractious team of horses with a sense of impending doom. The elegant young lady sitting patiently inside, shows her face at the window again, a lavender posy held under her nose to soothe her delicate senses. Her distaste is evident and she looks in horror at the muddle of intoxicated commoners crowding both sides of the road around the coach. The noise and smell and the coarse language are making her as nervous as the horses. She retreats, her enormous violet wig almost catching on the door frame as she settles back on the cushioned seats, anxious to be moving away.

Mister Doyley is at the bridge, struggling with the oversized key jammed tight in his waistcoat pocket. It springs free of the cloth and in a few moments the bar is unlocked and moved aside. Now, the coach is free to cross the river and continue on its way to the south coast docks.

The coachman sighs under his breath, 'At last, at last.'

He releases the brake and holds the excited horses from taking off at speed. They stamp and snort and nod their heads, anxious to be far from this noisy, crowded place, their eyes surely too wild for a smooth ride. The bridge is long and narrow; the low parapet wall on either side less than three feet high and the medieval bricks are crumbling beneath its arches.

The driver eases the coach slowly forward. 'On now, come now, gently does it,' he urges caution as his team begins to move.

However, just as they are pulling away, there is a tremendous clattering of hooves. Storming out of the coaching yard comes one, then another horse, followed by two old mules, and then two more horses.

The *furriners* and their sidekicks are departing.

There is a flurry and rush as the horses with their menacing riders brush alongside the coach, almost touching it, with the two mules carrying Barehenger's lackeys following at a quick trot behind. Barehenger and his team head north, up Bridge Street, but the two sailors from the coast, rush down to the water's edge, along the side of the bridge and splash into the cool, shallow water. Their horses just manage to find their feet on the slippery flat stones laid out on the river bed as they ford the wide river. The air stirs like a whirlwind and grows cool as the riders surge past, and the horses pulling the Portsmouth coach panic. Agitated, they jostle each other for space and pull at the leather straps which hold them from dashing forward. The wild beasts with their nostrils flaring, are desperate to leave, but there is nowhere to go. Forward takes them over the narrow, low bridge and in their frenzy, the animals do not want to take that precarious path.

The only alternative is the slippery ford and they start to veer towards the river, following Oakheart and Gusst's route through the shallows. The uneven ford stones on the riverbed are not easy for a single horse and rider to cross at the best of times, farm carts with wide wheels have no trouble, but a carriage such as this, with its heavy load and thin metal rims – impossible! The driver knows this well, his eyes are full of angst as he senses the horses about to bolt. He tries to hold them, to steady them with his voice, but there is too much fear in it and they will not be calmed.

'Woah! Brandy, steady now! Come Coffee, steady,' he tries in vain but the horses have reached a state from which there is no way back. The passengers on top are being rocked to-and-fro as the horses pull the carriage jerkily down the uneven bank towards the water and the crowd on the ground moves quickly away from the treacherous scene. The widow is clinging to the rails of her perch next to the driver, her eyes widening as the danger increases, and the coach begins a dance towards disaster.

The sailors manage to jump down. The young scholars from the basket seats, not looking so jolly now, also climb off the coach, jumping clear of the wheels as it sways this way and that.

And then the inevitable happens. The coachman loses control and the horses rush towards the River Mole. The ground is soft and far from even, and as the they near the water, one wheel sinks into the earth and the coach sways too far to the right.

And then, over she goes. Luggage sprawls on the damp river earth along with the widow and the coachman, who could not leap clear in time.

An unearthly catastrophe is upon them.

RYE COTTAGE

MID-MORNING

While Annie is busy in the yard, batting the grimy washing, Molly goes inside to fetch some tea. Her heart is as battered as the laundry, her fear great and her resolve weaker for it. She considers reaching for what is left of the gin, but holds herself back. It remains undrunk. For the moment.

Back outside, the heat is growing.

'Bless you, Moll, I's gasping for a cuppa,' Annie says. 'Come, rest a while out the sun. You look like you's about to drop.'

However, Annie herself does not look so good. Her face is pale and beads of sweat grace her freckly brow. *Is she sick?* Her hand is resting on her belly and Molly, drowning in all consuming angst and perhaps the remnants of yesterday's gin, believes it to be the cursèd monthly bleed. She does not consider that her husband's sister has a lover who has already sown his seed.

They sit in the shade, with the bricks between the cottage's weather-blackened oak frame, laid more than two centuries before, cool against their backs. Little Joe is marching up and down the vegetable patch, still copying the Redcoats he saw trooping across The Common. His long stick-gun is almost taller than he, and Pudding is yapping at his heels. *Throw it, throw it, throw it!* He ignores her pleas and pushes the creature away roughly with his foot.

He is growing like his father. God help the woman he marries.

'Not long now, the babes,' Annie says.

'Suppose not. And I's had enough, cannot eat hardly a thing. 'Tis a most unjoyous feeling,' she says. 'Will all be over in a few days, if I ain't claimed by the Lord or the Devil.'

Death is all she can think of, as well as sleep. She wants to forget, to rest and dream. Of Jesse? *Oops, not him.* Not work, either, or perhaps only George's.

Annie wonders if she herself will ever be ready for what Molly is facing. With no husband, there is far more fear in Annie's position, but she cannot share her story with Molly, whose slack tongue would splatter it all over the village in a heartbeat. No, this is a secret which must be kept, for now.

'I cannot recall seein' no one as big as you,' she says.

''Tis truly a lump, ain't it? An' the bigger I gets, the more afeared I be. I don't understand how the good Lord made the most natural thing in the world so bleedin' frightening.'

'Why, 'tis the Curse of Eve,' Annie says.

Molly is silent for a moment.

The Curse of Eve, indeed. Why'd she have to go and take that bleeding apple? Could she not have turned away? Her thoughts turn to the little flask, and then to her husband's brother. *Easier said.*

'I's been here twice, what with the little blue baby girl what never tooked a breath, and then Joe, but I don't mind telling you I's more full o' fright this time. Truly, full to the brim,' and as she speaks these words, she hears that little flask calling again. *Come, Molly. I am here, come ease those fears a little.*

'And yet here we all are, and without our mothers' labours none of us would be. You must trust in God, Molly, 'tis dangerous to question his ways,' Annie declares, and Molly closes her eyes. There is always someone to tell her what she should or should not do. What comes next? A sermon on the Lord Almighty and his benevolence or wrath? She knows all about his wrath, for it has been instilled in her since birth, hence her copious crosses. Perhaps she will be told how she should not be so irreverent? But thank God, Annie is not so righteous and leads her along a different path.

'I suppose all women on this threshold have it. That fear of what's to come, I mean.'

'Cat Longhurst don't. Pops 'em out like peas and gets right back to her work. Hardly don't stop,' Molly says, and is in awe of her fearless neighbour.

'Well, she's a big woman, hips like a heifer. Maybe them babes just fall out,' Annie laughs, and tries to make sense of it herself, for she is slim like Molly, although somewhat taller. The ordeal could turn out to be an immense struggle, especially without a husband by her side. She is flooded by a wave of nausea as she considers that perhaps the baby's father will not stand by her.

There is always Eliza and her herbs. But could she take that path, should her lover let her down? She is not so sure.

They sit in silence, lamenting the absence of dear mothers, who, if they had not been lost to the very thing with which they are confronted now, would be here with words of encouragement and support.

Molly hauls herself up and begins to bat Joshua Reynolds' washing. 'Thank the Lord this ain't linen off the beds. I don't believe I could hold such a weight today.'

'Aye, these smalls be much easier to handle, but just look at that undershirt! What manner of stain be that, I wonder?'

'Do not ask, Sister, 'tis best not to know,' Molly laughs, then huffs and puffs as she pulls the washing out of the tub and wishes for the hundredth time that she had not agreed to it.

Annie looks up and calls out, 'Joe! Joe, where's you going?'

The boy is marching towards the Rye and The Common. 'I'll go,' she says, and Molly is grateful she does not have to fetch him herself. And look! Now she has an opportunity to check on Eliza and the flask. To test if her resolve is still strong.

It is not.

She looks over at Eliza in her chair. *Asleep!* She reaches up, unstoppers the bottle and swigs a little of the clear, astringent liquid. It burns as it goes down, but she gulps some more, then shakes the bottle. To her delight there is still a little left. *Just one more,* and then she replaces the flask.

However, Eliza is not asleep at all. As she reaches the door, Molly hears the click of her grandmother's tongue. *Caught. Shit.* She does not turn around, but returns to the back-breaking, grime-scrubbing work.

Annie is already steering Joe back towards the cottage. 'This boy's growing fast, Moll, look at him! How tall he is now!' she says.

'Aye, ain't he? Needs new clothses. See how his arms and legs stick out like fence posts!'

'Just like our Henry. Only this morn I asked Jesse to see if we had some old clothes of Ned's what he left behind. I do believe it be summer what does that. 'Tis sunshine what makes them grow quick, like corn and barley.'

Molly hears the name *Jesse*, and is surprised at the little flip her heart makes. How dangerous, how exciting. It must be the gin's doing, surely? She only had a sip, though. Or was it two? Perhaps a good slug? She shakes it off, the danger that is Jesse Hogtrough.

'I be sure you's right, 'tis summer indeed,' and she is skylarking, like her fickle husband, her mood now up with the gin and reality so quickly forgotten. However, the spin in her head and the flutter in her heart makes her question her choice of husband yet again. The wrong brother is persistent indeed, and Jesse appears before her with his table piled with produce, his arms strong from all his *hard work*. Several healthy children are running around their happy home. She pushes the man away, but alas, he does not go far, for she recalls a memory, from somewhere in yesterday's gin fuzz.

Walking along the Rye Brook on the edge of The Common, collectin' moss for the babes' rags. Jesse, clearin' ditches in the meadow on the other side. Workin' hard. Such a good man.

And then she looks at little barefoot Joe and remembers taking off his shoes so he could paddle in the stream. And she did not put them back on. Her heart squeezes as she realises they are likely lost, for she will not be able to go back to search for them for several days, if not weeks. The gin is not doing such a good job today, of taking her away from all the impossible realities which make up her life.

'Look Nannie, wormy,' Joe calls out.

Annie smiles as he holds up the pink creature for her to inspect. 'Yes, Joe, it be a right wriggly one that,' she tells him.

Joe puts it to his mouth ready to bite and a horrified Annie pulls his arm away just before it reaches his tiny teeth. Joe giggles, drops it on the ground, stamps on it with his bare foot. He picks up the squashed thing and shoves it in his aunt's face.

'Not wiggy now,' he declares.

'Lord above Joe, that be one of God's own creatures you's killed and for no good reason. Do be careful, for the Lord God be wrathful and vengeful when you cross him, you hear me?'

Molly glances over at her sister-in-law, who has raised her voice and scolded her son. Is that not her job? Perhaps she does not do it often enough. Madame Geneva is not motherly, she instils only carefree carelessness and Molly sees the source of the lackadaisical mothering she has adopted recently. It will surely not do for newborn babes.

'Just like his father,' Annie says. 'George were a terror when he were young, so Mother always sayed.'

'Still is,' Molly remarks before she realises what has passed her lips.

'Aye, I be sure of that,' Annie laughs. 'But after Ned left he were always good and kind to me, George were. Jesse's always been so serious and cold.'

Molly is amazed at this revelation. *George, kind?* But the woman does not have to live with his laziness, his stubborn nature, his lack of work. His skylarking. She cannot believe Annie has more good to say of George than Jesse. *Flip.* There it goes again, her heart, at the mention of his name.

'Tis a pity I see not so much of George nowadays,' Annie adds.

'Me neither. He's always with that bleedin' Hal Archer. Spends more time with him than at work, where he should be,' she half spits the words out in disgust at the man who steals away her husband from his rightful place. Oh! That gin is so quick to make her careless tongue speak her thoughts.

Smashing the washing dolly up and down, she directs all her anger at Mister Reynolds' smalls, but it is Hal's face which appears in the clouds reflected in the grimy water.

Had she been aware of anything other than her own fears and angst and anger, had she looked up, Molly Hogtrough could not have failed to notice Annie's reddening cheeks, a drop of moist escape the corner of her eyes and a deflated mood fall over the yard.

'Moll, let me do that heavy stuff. No need to bring on your increasement,' is all Annie says.

LETHERHED BRIDGE

MID-MORNING

There is silence amongst the dust, the scene frozen. People stare in disbelief at the mangle of wheels and metal, buckled and twisted on the underside of the Portsmouth Coach. Suddenly, the screams of trapped and injured, man and beast curdle the air. George rushes forward and breaks the crowd's ice.

'Ain't no one gonna help? You drunkards just gonna stand an' gawp? There be folk injured! And the horses! Unhook 'em! Don't just stand there, move your arses!'

The groom from The Running Horse rushes to the horses, tries to bring some calm to the squealing beasts, while others uncouple the heavy animals from their tangled leather trappings.

The undercarriage is twisted and the carriage torn, rocking and tipping precariously towards the river. Inside, the occupants are lying higgledy piggledy, crying in distress. George looks around and sees two strong lads, their mouths agape at the uneasy sight.

'Come on, lads, stop fishing for flies. Hold the carriage steady, real steady now, so it don't move.'

As they grab and pull down on the heavy contraption, George searches for the best way up.

'You ain't goin' up there, are you? The whole thing's headin' for the water,' shouts one of the men watching at the side.

'Someone's got to, ain't they? You could be useful and help these lads, could you not? Hold the thing still,' and without hesitation, George begins to climb.

The coach jolts and George almost loses his footing, grabs at the door handle. 'Hold it steady, I sayed,' he calls down.

''Tis too heavy, Mister,' one cries back.

'Lord God, ain't no one else gonna help? Lazy bleeders, the lot of you,' he shouts.

Two men push through the crowd and join the lads, and together they do their best to steady the coach.

George hauls open the heavy door and it crashes onto the side of the carriage with a clash. He peers down into the darkness of the velvet-lined coach. All he can see is a jumble of arms and legs, curtains and dress. In amongst the voluminous peach trappings of petticoat and silk skirt, is a young lady's face. She is white, not from powder but fear, and her terrified eyes are tearful. She is in a state of shock. Fortunately, she landed on top of the other passengers rather than underneath them, for the hefty bewigged gentlemen is in the tangle. George can see another male passenger, younger than the fat man, but nowhere to be seen is the fourth traveller.

'Miss, are you hurt?' George speaks gently to the young lady, whose legs are facing upwards, giving him a view he tries to ignore. Her fair hair is swept back tightly under a hairnet, her pastel-violet wig with its curls and ribbons, now graces the large gentleman's face. George isn't sure where to put his eyes to save the young lady's mortification.

She begins sobbing. Another pairs of hands is suddenly next to George. It is the shoemaker's son, Jack Garman.

'We'll have you out in no time, ma'am. Just stay calm,' George says, and turns to Jack. 'Mind the lady's dignity, if you will.'

They kneel down either side of the open door and George reaches in. 'Miss, take me hand. You'll be alright, we'll see you out. Just hold on, alright? Can you do that?' He isn't sure if she has heard, but then two limp, lilac-gloved hands appear. She is as light as a feather and together they pull her up. *Thank the Lord she don't have nothing trapped*, George thinks. As she emerges from the carriage, they straighten her petticoats to save her further embarrassment. However, her wig remains inside the carriage, atop the fat man, who is squealing like a pig. She collapses into George's arms in a faint.

'Someone get some drink for this lady, and salts, if you will,' George calls. More people have come forward and are waiting to help the young woman down from the carriage, which is still tilting towards the river. They lower her, but the lace from her enormous skirt catches on one of the metal steps. George calls out in the nick of time, and the dress is freed, her dignity intact. However, the missing wig will surely cause great embarrassment to her when she comes round.

The young gentleman, who was sitting opposite the lady, clambers out of the opening and George rushes to help him. He is also clearly very shaken.

'My cousin, is she alive?' he asks as he emerges, his voice quivering.

'Why yes, Sir, she most certainly is and with no serious harm, I believe.' George answers. 'Are you yourself hurt, Sir?'

'I think not, nothing broken anyway. But the old man who was in the carriage with us, he surely must be,' he pauses, takes a deep breath, 'injured badly, at the very least. He lies under an extra-ordinary weight. I cannot imagine anyone surviving such a crush.' The young gentleman's voice is trembling, and the colour is quickly draining from his face as he realises the lucky escape he and his cousin have just had.

There are more than enough hands helping now, and the opening around the door has become crowded as two more men jump up to help extract the remaining passengers, and they have a hard job of it, too.

As the pastel-violet wig emerges, George pulls it from the fat man's face and climbs down to the ground. 'Here, Sir,' he says, handing it to the young man, 'I believe your cousin will be needing this.'

George shakes his head as he walks away from the wreckage. He passes the coachman, now sitting on Mr Doyley's stool. The man looks dazed and bewildered, having been thrown clear of the carriage but mercifully landing the right way up. A sprained ankle but no other injury. The widow is sadly in a much worse condition. She landed awkwardly and is lying on the floor whimpering, surrounded by a crowd of dubiously helpful hands, for many only want a glance of something horrid. And a gruesome peep show it is, indeed.

'We need a doctor here, and quick. This lady's leg is destroyed,' calls Mister Bushby, who is closest and fanning the woman with his hat, avoiding the sight. Bone protrudes through fat and skin, and the wound is gushing deep red blood. 'Give the woman some space, for Lord's sake! Step back, I say,' and he pushes against the nosy, drunken onlookers, who hastily retreat. 'And get some brandy, too,' he adds. It is not clear if this is for the widow or himself.

George does not want to see the spectacle. He has had his fill of horrors today and makes his way to the inn, where he orders half a jar of cider and stands at a tall table, pondering the strange events of this fine summer's morning.

Henry, who has been watching his brother's heroic actions, joins him. 'Brother, what a mess,' he says, slapping George on the back. 'Is the lady alright, what you helped out?'

'You saw all what happened out there, lad?' George stutters. 'Mighty terrible, it were. Them poor horses, too. I hope none has to be shot.' He seems shaken, a state which Henry does not often see in his brother.

'Have not a care about the beasts, the horses be alright. I sees them led to the stables. I were outside when the coach come,' Henry says, 'just afore your friends left. I were looking for you.'

George looks at Henry, puzzled. *Friends? What friends?* And then he remembers. In all the kerfuffle, he had almost forgotten his meeting with Barehenger and Oakheart.

'They be no friends o' mine,' he says. 'Best you forget about 'em. Do not remember their faces. And mention to no one what you seen, neither,' he warns. 'Alright, brother? Are we clear?'

Henry nods, a little taken aback by George's tone.

'Clear about what?' comes a voice from behind.

George spins round. It is Hal and he has caught George unawares.

'Nothin',' George says, turning back to the table. 'Family stuff,' he mumbles and nearly downs his cider in one go.

'Yeah?' Hal sounds unconvinced. He turns to the younger brother. 'Henry, lad! How goes it at *Caen Farm*?' he says, in a mocking lilt. He has not been on good terms with Jim Caen since the farmer suspected him, correctly, of poaching rabbits on his land.

Henry shifts uneasily, fearing an interrogation about the fur-riners he has been told not to mention. 'Alright, Hal, goes good, I guess,' and he quickly steers the conversation to new waters. 'Look at this, a new pup, from the Chitty girls.'

'The Chitty girls, eh? That Liza, she be gettin' right flirty, got a wicked little sparkle about her last time I sees her. She be after you then, Henry? Temptin' you with puppies. Whatever will be next? I wonder,' and Hal winks at Henry.

Henry blushes but does not want to divulge it is the younger sister, Jane, who has captured his heart, lest they rib him for it.

Hal clicks his fingers in Florie's direction, trying to get her attention.

George takes no notice of the puppy. His mood is grim.

'After what happened with that coach, don't seem to me to be the right time to go a-cooing and all girly-gooey over a bleedin' dog. Some folk was injured, and badly, maybe killed even.'

He picks up his cider, finishes it off and slams the jug down. He was distracted by the coach fiasco, but not enough to have forgotten the enormous and dangerous task which lies ahead of him. He will face the noose or, at best, transportation to far away lands if they are caught mixed up with a gang of smugglers. What will become of Molly and his son, then? And the babes, if they survive. His gut wrenches, and an internal valve blows and screeches, with frustration at himself for agreeing to the work, for Hal's deception, with fear for Molly and a future without her.

Hal is getting impatient, for Florie is pointedly ignoring his signs for service. 'What's this place comin' to when you can't get a drink,' he says, shaking his head.

'I managed alright,' George declares. 'You's doing it all wrong, friend.'

George turns to the maid and catches her eye. 'Florie, darlin', could you refresh me jug and fill one each for me brother and Hal, here? There's a good heart.'

Florie smiles coyly as she brushes past. 'Anythin' fer you, Georgie,' she says, and bustles off to fulfil his request.

'See, Hal. You treat 'em right, they'll do yer biddin',' George looks away.

'Someone already treated her alright. You seen the state of her face, boy?' Hal says to Henry, grimacing. Florie hears, shoots a look at him, hurt and embarrassed, and quickly turns away.

'Ooh, looks bad. What is it? Pox?' Henry whispers.

'Aye, the French disease most probably. But no need to go hurtin' her feelings,' George says quietly. 'She gives good service to those in need. Like as she won't get much business now, eh? People has to take care where they spreads their love, would you not say Hal?' and he stares at his friend, a full on glare.

Hal only laughs, the meaning goes over Henry's head, but George knows that it could just as well happen to Hal as it could to Florie. After all, they are of the same cloth, are they not?

George has known the barmaid almost all her short life and it has been a hard one. Before the age of 10 she lost her mother and sisters, and was left at her father's beck and call, run ragged day and night. Hal, on the other hand? Well, he has a choice. He doesn't have to do what he does. It doesn't seem right that Florie has drawn the short straw. But who is he to say what God's plans are for her? Or for Hal Archer either, for that matter.

He looks at Florie again. 'She could'a been a lady, just like we could'a been gentlemen. Just a matter of luck,' he says. 'We can't choose where we's born, can we?'

Henry jumps at the word 'lady'.

'Oh Lord! Brother, I clean forgot why I's come looking for you,' he cries. George and Hal turn to face him.

'Well lad, spit it out now, do tell us,' George says.

They listen as Henry blurts out news of the eleven o' clock meet at the clock tower with Molly's well-to-do cousin, Mathilda Richardson.

'Well, we's missed that, then. Must be past eleven. What do she want, anyways?'

'To come and help Molly, and stay awhile after the babes is born, I think,' Henry announces, but he isn't exactly sure. 'Jesse did speak to her, he knows what was said. He went lookin' for you at the Bull.'

'Let him stay there, then,' Hal says, with a smirk.

'Oy,' George says, and prods Hal.

Any chance Hal gets to put Jesse down, he will take. George

will often ignore Hal's ribbing, but today Hal is on the other end of his anger. Blood is blood, after all, although it is a rare occasion when he will defend Jesse.

'We should go an' see what's up. Come, Henry, no doubt we shall find our brother at the clock tower, if that's where he said he'd meet the woman,' and for once he is glad to be away from his friend.

Outside, the untidy chaos of the upturned carriage is still in the process of being put right. Emptied of passengers, many hands are now trying to set it upright. The missing man proved to be beyond help, squashed by the weight of his three companions, including the enormous gentleman, who is now looking very pale and sipping brandy in the shade to help ease his shock.

The dead man is laid out on the ground, covered with a dirty linen sheet to stop the nosy drunks from taking a peek at the man's flattened, gory frame and the flies from laying their maggoty eggs in his barely cold flesh.

George pauses in the warm sunlight and shudders. How quickly things in life can change. One minute riding in a carriage, enjoying a sunny morning, and the next lying out cold, ready to be fitted for a wooden box. He sees himself stumbling up a set of crude steps towards a gallows rope, spies his own coffin awaiting him at the side of the platform.

It could so easily come to pass.

As they walk solemnly up Bridge Street towards the clock tower, George sees the young gentleman from the carriage striding down the hill towards them.

'My good man, you *are* still here!' the man exclaims, somewhat recovered from his ordeal.

'Good day again, Sir,' George says, politely. 'I trust you is well now, and your cousin, too.'

'I am, thank you, and my cousin is being cared for by Mistress Bushby. I have been looking for you all over and thought you lost. But here you are, finally! I wish to thank you properly for your kind actions in saving my dear cousin Emily from that wretched carriage.' The young man offers his hand with half a smile.

George looks rather shocked at this unusual show of intimacy from a member of the upper class. Henry nudges him and George starts to offer his hand, but as he extends it, he sees it is greasy and dirty, and withdraws it sharply. Instead he touches his non-existent cap, and the man claps George on the shoulder instead.

'I should introduce myself,' he announces. 'My name is William Fitzwilliam. My father is Lord Norton of Epsum, and my cousin Emily is Lord Norton's niece. We were travelling to Portsmouth to meet my brother, Captain of the Calais of the Royal Navy, due to arrive this week from the West Indies. Weather permitting, of course.'

Henry stands aghast. Royal ships and exotic places, nobility, respectability and captains. Captains, no less! It goes straight to his young head and he grins from ear to ear, overwhelmed by the impressive tale.

George, however, is not at all affected. In fact, his humility keeps his feet firmly rooted to the ground and he merely tips his forelock again. 'Pleased to meet you, Sir,' is all he says, in a quiet voice.

'And you, dear man, shall be rewarded for your kind assistance.

Pray do tell me who we should ask for and where you reside, that we may repay your kindness,' the young Fitzwilliam says.

'I don't need nothing from you, Sir. What was done was done freely and no more than what any man would do,' George declares.

Henry elbows his brother again, and seeing he has no intention of accepting anything, he blurts out, before George does himself out of a reward.

'This here's me brother, Sir,' he says, and makes the introduction on George's behalf. He stands up as tall as he possibly can and proudly announces, 'Mister George Hogtrough of Woodside in the parish of Ashted, Sir. He do reside in old Widow Greenfield's cottage, that be his wife's grandmother, Sir. Rye Cottage, down by the Rye Brook, near the old bridge by Caen Farm. That be where I live and work, Sir. Caen Farm, that is, Sir.'

Henry addresses Fitzwilliam enthusiastically, and then glances sideways at George and sees that angry spark in his brother's eye. To the untrained eye, nothing is amiss as George's expression seems one of indifference, but Henry knows to stop and gives no further information about the family to this complete stranger. However, he keeps smiling at Mister Fitzwilliam.

'Thank you, lad. Well, Mister Hogtrough, you will indeed hear something from us in due course,' William Fitzwilliam says. 'I thank you heartily again, you have done a great service to our family and it shall not be forgotten,' he smiles and lifts his hat.

'Please, 'twas nothin',' George replies.

They bid each other farewell, and as they move away from the young gentleman, George says, 'What the fuck d'you go and do that for, boy?'

'Dunno, was just answering the man.'

'Weren't your question to answer, were it? That gob of yours will get you into trouble one day if you ain't careful.'

Henry hangs his head, and the brothers continue up the street, towards the clock tower at the foot of Gravel Hill, in search of Jesse and Mathilda.

THE CLOCK TOWER

LATE MORNING

It takes Jesse over half an hour to make his way from The Bull Inn back to the clock tower. The riots and fires of London Town are forgotten. Instead, everyone stops him to gossip about the awful coach catastrophe. It sounds impossible to believe and Jesse ums and ahs about going to see it, but decides his appointment with Mathilda must take priority. However, with all the stoppages he is fifteen minutes late and Mathilda is already there, standing above the grime on her wooden heels, still clutching the basket with the kitten.

'Cousin Mathilda, I do be sorry for being so late.'

Mathilda twists around, so absorbed with the hubbub of activity around her she did not hear him approach.

'Oh! There you are at last, Jesse!'

'You did not manage to dispose of the cat, then?'

'The kitten? No! I first tried the church warden, whom I found at the door of the church on my way to the vicarage. I tried my best for at least a quarter of an hour to persuade Mister Doyley to accept the sweet little thing, but he seemed in such a terrible hurry to be away. I hoped not to delay him in vain, but he would not be swayed. So, on I went to the vicarage, only to find that the Rector's poor, motherless daughter has had three kittens gifted to her in the last week, and they will all have to be given away as the housekeeper will no longer have them in the house. The mess is causing some concern for their health, and apparently it has got quite out of hand. Not to mention the fleas. Mistress Saunders, the housekeeper, was adamant they will not take another and those they already have will be parted with as a matter of urgency,' she announces, pulling a very sad face.

'Drownded, I e'spect,' Jesse says, without thinking.

'Mister Hogtrough! How could you think that! And of the Rector, too!'

'Gracious me, I didn't mean to offend, nor sully the Rector's good name. I just meant 'tis difficult to give a cat away, there bein' so many to spare. Ain't easy, a cat. Should be outside, in my 'pinion, in the barns and outhouses, like,' he says.

'I cannot persuade you to take another then?' Mathilda coyly holds the tiny kitten out for Jesse to inspect.

Jesse's heart sinks. 'Well Cousin, Henry just tooked a pup, so we has quite enough animals now.'

'Oh! I am sure a dog is acceptable, but one small kitten, well, that is quite a different matter,' Mathilda smiles, but Jesse can see she is put out. Stuffing the kitten back into the basket, she lifts her nose in the air and looks around, as if for someone else she can latch onto.

Jesse blushes. He had not meant to upset her. 'Well, it ain't just one small kitten is it? She'll likely have several more, see?'

'I see, so you advocate drowning, is that the method you would use?'

'No! Oh, well, let me see what I can do,' he stammers, trying to save face.

Mathilda brightens. 'How wonderful! Thank you, Jesse.'

She thrusts her hand towards him and he finds he has acquired the basket with the kitten, while Mathilda skilfully diverts his confusion.

'Did you succeed in finding your brother? There is still the question of my helping cousin Molly to be resolved.'

'Sad to say I did not. But I's sure he will be down by the bridge at the coach accident, where everyone else seems to be headin'. Perhaps young Henry had more luck than I.'

'Well then, shall we walk together and see if we cannot locate them both?' It is a question, but she does not wait for an answer before she begins trip-trapping on her pattens, moving at speed towards Bridge Street and George's presumed location. 'I must make haste, for it is nearly midday and I hoped to travel back to Mickleham with Farmer Potter of Pondtail,' she calls over her shoulder.

'We shall walk down together, indeed, it seems,' Jesse says under his breath, and all he can do is follow.

As he hurries along behind her, the thought crosses his mind that this may not be as fortuitous a meeting as at first he had imagined. Help for Molly, yes, but at what cost? He had not realised the woman's character; *bossy and manip'lative,* come immediately to his mind. He does not relish being told what to do by a woman and begins to think of ways he can remove himself from the awkward situation, but if there are any, they do not come as easily to mind as his description of Mathilda Richardson. And what on earth will George think? He will get no thanks from his brother, of that he is certain. He finds himself trotting behind the widow like a little dog, holding the green-lined basket at arms length as if it contains a clutch of fragile eggs.

Having just come away from their discussion with Mister Fitzwilliam, George and Henry are heading up the hill, when Henry spots the unlikely pair flying down it.

He nudges George. 'Look out, Brother. Here comes Jesse now,' he says to George. 'What's he got there? Is that her, Molly's cousin?'

George nods. 'Aye, that's her alright,' he says, and chuckles at the sight of his brother in a state of flummox, holding the basket in front of him like it is on fire, his cheeks burning bright, his furrowed brow forming an angry frown as he chases after Mathilda, who seems hell bent on becoming another Portsmouth Coach. She will surely trip on her wooden stilts if she does not slow down.

'Well, now that ain't a sight we sees often,' George says. 'Brother Jesse bein' towed by the nose, and by a woman at that. Lord above, whatever next. Looks like he's met his match.' He laughs loud, his spirits lifted for the first time this morning.

George nods his head towards Mathilda as she tears on down the hill, but she hardly glances up, and carries on, holding her oversized black-laced hat with one hand and wobbling over the cobbles.

'Cousin Mathilda, Mathilda! Mistress Richardson! Wait up! Brother George be here,' Jesse calls after her and comes to a stop at the spot where his two brothers are grinning from cheek to cheek.

'You can take that look off yer faces, Brothers,' Jesse says out of the corner of his mouth. 'An' she'll be your problem, soon, if you ain't careful,' he adds, looking at George.

Before George can answer, Mathilda has wheeled around, limped back up the hill and is before them. 'Ah! There you are cousin! At last!' She holds out her hand for George.

'Cousin Mathilda. Heartily glad to see you,' George replies, ignoring the black glove.

'How is my dear cousin and her with-child condition,' Mathilda asks between breaths, even though she has already received much information from Jesse.

'Heavy, at the moment, real ripe. 'Tis making her tired, the great weight and I believe the babes will be here soon. Otherwise, she be in good spirits and no increasement yet, or weren't when I left her earlier,' he replies.

In good spirits? Aye, drownin' in gin, that be the only spirit she be in, and it be far from good, Jesse thinks.

Mathilda is still trying to catch her breath. 'I am at present,' she puffs, 'in need of something to occupy my time. So, I would be most grateful … if you would see your way … to allowing me stay and help dear cousin Molly … in her hour of need. Please do say that I would be welcome,' she says, looking very helpless and longingly at George, as if this invitation would mean the world.

George is sure his wife would appreciate another pair of hands, just not this pair. Molly's stories of Mathilda are as a rather stuck up, lazy girl, who was never easy to get along with, born on the other side of the river, and with airs and graces that were not at home unless they were waited on. But how can he put Mathilda off? He thinks for a second.

'Well, Cousin, please don't think that your offer is not at all welcome, because it most certainly is. But sadly, we has no room, the cottage bein' so small and all, and with old Widow Greenfield still living, and our son there, and what with the new ones comin' any day now. Moll could use the help that be true, but sorry to say, there just ain't a way to put up … erm, I mean to put you up.' *That gets us out of that hole,* he thinks.

Mathilda's face falls, her lips begin to pout and quiver, she stands there before them looking extremely dejected.

Henry has been listening intently to George's explanation, and once again his young and inexperienced mind misreads the situation completely.

'Why, Jesse, we has plenty of room, ain't we? Mistress Richardson could stay with us. I be sure Annie wouldn't mind to share her bed if it'd help Moll. Rye Cottage being just a stone's throw, 'tis perfect,' Henry smiles, pleased he has found a solution.

Jesse and George shoot a look at him, accompanied by a few daggers which slice through Henry's pride. Their younger brother realises his mistake at once. Too late.

'That will be absolutely perfect, thank you kindly, Jesse,' Mathilda says, looking at Jesse as if he is the one who suggested this arrangement. 'I shall make haste and be with you first thing the morrow,' she says, and before Jesse can say yay or nay, she has waved her goodbyes and is flouncing off in search of her transport home.

'Well I'm blowed,' Jesse gasps, and to his horror, he realises that he is still holding the kitten in the basket, while Mathilda is now hidden in the crowd walking back up Bridge Street.

George swings a kick at Henry, catching the back of his lanky legs. He nearly buckles under. The puppy, which has been asleep in his arms all this time, is rudely awakened, and begins to whine.

'Lord above, I do not know how the wife will take this news, for that woman will likely be more hindrance than help,' George says. 'Never open your mouth again in front of anyone when you does not know what you's lettin' others in for! First letting on me name and where I lives to Mister Fitzwhat's'isname, now this. Your tongue be looser than my wife's, and that's quite saying sommat!'

Henry looks even more dejected than Mathilda. 'I be right sorry, brother. Had no idea you wasn't warm to having her help for Moll. I thought…'

'Aye, you thinks too much, lad,' George interrupts him. 'Never done no one no good has thinkin'. Best stop now or I'll stop it for you,' he growls and throws a right fist at him. Henry manages to dodge it, but hangs his head in shame and turns away so his older brothers cannot not see the tears appearing in his eyes.

At that moment, he realises he has a lot to learn. It is not just books he must learn to read, but people, too, and he vows to set about doing it.

The only problem is, where to begin?

PART THREE

SATURDAY, JUNE 10

1780

Rose Cottage

Dawn

Jesse Hogtrough spent another restless night tossing and turning. He barely slept, and now, hot and sticky, the self inflicted welts on his back and chest are irritating like mad. But what point is there to penance if not to punish? During the short periods he did manage to doze, he spent what seemed an eternity cutting black corn with a black-bladed scythe, under a dark, stormy sky. He was waist-up naked and deep in The Common forest. Tasked with cutting a clearing, he knew not by whom, the sharp stems became thin blades of steel which ripped into his bare feet. A bright glow came from the centre of the glade, and he was drawn to it as if by an invisible force. He began at the foot of the King Oak, which stood at the edge of the crop, and worked his way in towards the light. Round and round he went, a perfect circle of mouldy-looking corn formed under his lacerated feet which oozed ebony blood. The diabolic crop fell away foot by foot until at last only a thin amphitheatre of sooty ears remained. A thousand black corn-eyes bobbed at him, then the crowd parted. There he found the source of the light, shining like a star, with eyes so green, like a freshly cut meadow in the bright July sunshine.

That damnded white kitten!

It looked up at him and mewed gently. He turned away, irritated, but the corn moved forwards, hemming him into the ever shrinking circle, preventing his escape. Their wispy long hairs were tiny black scythes, which scratched and clawed at his face and the already raw skin of his back and chest. And wherever he looked, the kitten was reflected in each and every one of their shiny eyes. He tried to brush it all away, for at that moment he knew it was not real, that it was just a dream, that he would soon awaken. But he could not move. The crowd kept coming, pushing and tearing into him. Lash. Lash. Lash. A rhythm which mimicked his tack room tool. He could only turn back to face the source of light.

As soon as he did, the relentless cutting stopped, the evil corn fell away and before him was the King Oak, now in the centre of the circle, and the kitten sitting in the small hollow of the tree's huge, knotty eye.

As he stared into its eyes, he saw it was no longer a cat, but a woman dressed all in white, and her eyes were bright, piercing green. And then he recognised her.

Oh! How he wished it were Elizabeth with her eyes of blue.

But it was not.

It was Mathilda Richardson.

He could feel her breath, perfumed and sweet, and she stroked his face with long, slender fingers, traced the shape of his eyebrows with her perfectly manicured nails, and came towards him until her lips were almost touching his. He felt himself stir where that feeling of lust always begins, that place which is the source of everything in him which must be punished. But it was too late, he was already hard, ready, needy, and although he wanted to pull away, he was paralysed. She had him in her grasp now, her willowy fingers and emerald eyes all over him, enveloping his being. And as she drew him in, she whispered to him.

'You can have me, Jesse Hogtrough. I am yours,' he heard. And then he was falling, tumbling into her eyes, rolling in amongst grass and flowers, a beautiful summer meadow, and deeper and deeper he went, falling, rolling, over and over. Her whispers became louder, then she was squawking, then screeching, as if he were a deaf old man. And her words were abhorrent and cut into his freedom, his easy life.

She said, 'But before you take me, you must promise not to drown the kitten, and then you must cut the corn, and build me a bed with golden drapes, lay my table with silver plate and fresh meat, and fill my cup with brandy, and I will have a new dress. No! Two new dresses, and three new petticoats and ....'

And now he is wide awake and somehow, to his horror, he finds his bedclothes are wet with his strange lust.

The grey sky is changing to blue.

Dawn has broken.

His day has begun, once again, very badly.

RYE COTTAGE

EARLY MORNING

Daylight sneaking through the ill-fitting wooden shutters and the tinkle of Little Joe pissing in the pail stir Molly from slumber.

The boy climbs in beside her, and as she shifts her weight around, she pulls the dark-haired tot to her bosom. Perhaps he will sleep again. Another hour in her dreams would be most welcome.

Where was I? Oh bliss! Jesse, at the King Oak.

A perilous place, for where on earth is her husband?

Where, indeed? Her hand searches the rough sheet where George should be. It is still warm, but he is missing and she cannot remember what he told her of his plans. Her head is like a pocket full of lint, a reminder that last evening she drank nearly a whole flask of gin.

Little Joe will not settle and she has no choice but to get up.

Downstairs, the fire is dead, the doors firmly shut. The room is sour, acidic. Meadowsweet and lady's bedstraw have worked their way into the corners and are stinking, like piles of forgotten laundry. She has neither time nor energy to gather more from The Common.

She sits Little Joe at the table and puts their last chunk of dry bread into his sticky hands. The fire is her first chore. She struggles to get down to her knees, to the cracked hearth. The lukewarm ashes she scoops into an old pail. She needs them to make lye and that laborious job must be done soon, for their stock of soap is dwindling fast. She adds it to the myriad of other tasks lining up to take her time, if childbirth does not steal it all away.

She really should take over Eliza's work or they will lose the business for good. Things given to the old woman in return for her remedies make life easier – cheese, eggs, butter, needles and thread and a hundred other things, all will be lost. Few come now to see her grandmother, worried perhaps that in her increasing blindness and senility they will be given poison rather than cure.

However, she is not Eliza. Her passion lies not with herbs but with beards, and this morning, she just cannot stop thinking about Jesse Hogtrough's. Far more enticing than the reality she has to deal with. Her eyes drift to the flask, high out of Little Joe's reach. But not hers. As soon as the fire is lit, she hauls herself up and stretches to get it.

Ouch!

A twinge between her legs, deep in her crotch and she holds her breath until the pain passes. It is a warning perhaps she should not ignore. She grabs the flask and quaffs a few sips before Eliza, with her disapproving, clicky tongue, emerges from her corner. As the liquid races through her, she begins to feel carefree once more, forgetting that carelessness always comes along for the ride.

Now, though, the bottle is empty. But not to worry, for standing next to it is another, an identical twin, and this one is full. A gift from George. Lord knows where he got the coin and anyway, she does not really want to know.

A groan comes from behind the heavy, dusty curtain.

'Gran? You all right in there?' she calls, and takes a draught of small ale to hide her gin-breath before she faces Eliza. 'Need a hand? I be just about ready to put the kettle on,' she continues, her head already light and loose. She could almost dance around their tiny home, but resists the temptation. No need to hasten the arrival of those babes.

Eliza moans, 'Darn it, Molly! Me bedding's all soaked.'

Shit!

'Oi's pissed meself agin. Just about had enough o' being old. When's it goin' to end?' the old woman grumbles.

Eliza's muffled sniffs and gentle sobbing worry Molly, for she has become quite crotchety and miserable recently. *Is her time near?* She tries not to dwell on this, just like she tries to stop her brother-in-law from penetrating her dreams and Hal Archer from angering her.

She tries also to hide the despair in her voice, but *damn, another bleedin' chore. No time even to give birth.* 'Come Gran, it ain't so bad. Won't take long to wash out. The weather be warm again, will all dry quick, like,' and she moves over to the cot, draws the heavy curtain gently aside.

A shrivelled face peers out at her from under its dusty black mob cap and the unmistakeable stench of urine assaults her nose.

'You's just finished all that darnded laundry, girl. Now you's got to be starting all over again, t'ain't roight. And you so near your toime. Pr'aps Oi can do it, eh? Come, Oi shall do it, yes.'

'No, Gran. Won't take long, 'tis just a couple o' things. George can fetch fresh straw, when he gets back.' *But where is he? Sommat about work?* 'Now, let's get you out of that wet stuff and washed. You'll feel better after a nice cup of tea,' she says, 'or how about a pipe, that always helps, don't it?'

However, on top of all the other things, her tobacco is also running short. Without it, her grandmother will be absolutely impossible.

After Eliza is clean and dressed, Molly whips up the soiled linen and heaves everything outside to the yard. Before she tackles it, they could do with that tea. Little Joe will be asking for milk, he can come with her to fetch some from the dairy. As she turns back to the house, another twinge pulls at her side, sharp, piercing.

Lord! Is it time? She prays it is not and the pain soon subsides.

As she enters the room, a cold shiver pulses through her.

Sommat missing! Good Lord, me boy!

'Joseph!' she calls. 'Lord God almighty, not again, not today. Joseph, Joseph,' she calls aloud. 'Where are you little one? Come to your mother!'

She realises she did not see him on her way out to the yard, and with her mind afloat with gin she is too easily distracted by other things, like Jesse Hogtrough and his beautiful beard.

She climbs carefully up the stairs to see if he has snuck back to his bed, but he has not. A little gin can certainly quell her angst, but she has not yet had enough to dispel her terror when the boy runs off. There are many possibilities for tragedy in those fears, the greatest that she will never find him, that he will be a wolf's breakfast. *Be there still wolves in the forest?* Possibly. Wild boar, more likely. They would not hesitate to eat a small child. An ugly cold creep grips her, for truly the boy might be stolen by gypsies or drown in the Oxmoor Pond, get wrapped and trapped in brambles and starve to death. So many dismays. They must be banished to the nether regions of her soul, but for that she needs more gin and looks across to the mantelpiece.

'Gran, I's goin' out after Joe. You's gonna have to wait for tea.'

'What? He gawn agin? Little devil,' Eliza squawks, 'he be more loike his father every day. Prob'ly down by them stepping stones.' Her mood has cheered a little after the pipe, or perhaps she has just forgotten about the wet bed.

Her memory goin', too?

God forbid she forgets how to make her cures.

'He be too young, I worry he'll fall in and drown,' Molly replies.

''Twill be but a trickle today,' and the old woman sits back, sucking, clicking, puffing, content, for the moment, to wait for her tea. No point filling up only for it to come streaming out the other end, unannounced, so shortly after. She is happy to stay dry, until she forgets why.

While her grandmother is busy arranging her cushions, Molly grabs the flask and stuffs it into one of her apron pockets, and picks up the little copper milk jug on her way out of the door. Might as well go to the farm on her search.

She will surely find Little Joe along the way.

Or Jesse.

She walks along the ditch at the end of the garden towards the stream, the air already heavy. She recalls her grandmother's words, *storms bring babies,* wonders if this is true, or whether the old woman was just being contrary towards George and his full moon theory. She certainly feels like she is about to burst.

When she arrives at the crude stones that cross the Rye Brook, there is no sign of Little Joe.

She steps over the shallows, trying to feel out the flat stones with her sandals, unable to see where her feet land. The brook is certainly not a trickle and one or two of the slippery stones are covered completely by the rippling water.

Half way across, she wobbles, nearly loses her balance and almost falls into the cold, babbling brook. Her belly pulls, the skin stretches, and she feels that twinge again. Somehow, she manages to reach the other side with only the hem of her skirt and her feet getting wet. Her hand reaches for the flask. To steady her nerves, she tells herself.

She continues to tipple as she follows the path along the meandering Rye stream, which glitters in the early morning light. The edge of The Common forest is on the far side of the meadow, and low hawthorn trees are dotted along the path, heavily entwined with honeysuckle. With Little Joe momentarily mislaid in the blur of gin, she sets the milk jug down, plucks a creamy honeysuckle flower away from its stalk and brings it to her nose, inhales its fragrance, then fills one of her apron pockets with the scented petals for a potpourri. She gathers some leaves, too, for Eliza makes a potion with them, a wash for the mouth. As she stuffs the leaves into her pocket, her fingers brush the cool ceramic bottle. She cannot resist another swig. Before long her pockets are packed with perfume and her mind a fuzz of fantasies.

She walks a little further. Where is she going? *Ah yes! Little Joe. Rose Cottage. Jesse. Oops.* She wobbles and sways, stumbles, and yet another sharp pain shoots between her legs. This one is far more painful than the others. Something has been stretched too far.

She puts her hands under her swollen belly, tries to ease the tender spot but it is too deep, too far out of reach and this time, the pain does not go away. Her hands start to shake, her head swims and she lets out a sob. *Not here babies! 'Tis too far from home and too far to Jesse's. Not yet, hold on.*

Her head is floating, her back aching, and now there is another pain, unfamiliar. A deep throbbing ache behind her hips. She looks around for a place to rest, sees a weeping willow, bent over the babbling stream like an old man leaning in for a drink, its trunk a natural seat. She sits and reaches into her pocket. One slug, then another. Then another. She breathes deeply, and feels herself calm as the pain eases. *Ah, yes, hold on, not here.* She closes her eyes and through the curtain of weeping willow leaves, sunbeams dance across her face. She relaxes, and as her fears dissolve, she dreams her fantasy again.

And there he is, her heart warmed by the sound of his name, *Jesse.* His full cupboards, his stability, his easy eye. The regularity of his work and the warmth of his bed. She lets herself drift into a dangerous desire. How quickly her problems are forgotten as she finds herself between his sheets.

That gin is a jeopardous liquid, indeed!

However, before it can take her to a place she really should not go, she is wrenched back to the present. Another sharp sting rips at her, this time it sears across her back, fires through every sinew. She is shocked and at once starts to panic.

The gin fails, for her predicament is sobering.

Not here babies, I sayed. Not yet, I needs to be home. She stands up, begins to breathe, deeply, slowly. The pain again, fiercer now, tugs hard at the deep muscles which need to stretch to extremes to set her infants free.

'Shite! Shite! Shite! Oh, Lord! Help me, please. This ain't happenin' now,' she says aloud, crosses herself, prays to her God, who must be listening to her every word, for if he does not listen today, then when does he? Another stab grabs at her. And then a rushing begins in her ears, at first a swirling stream, which she cannot tell from the babbling Rye Brook. It quickly grows, echoes like a deep ravine, coursing and crashing its way around her heavy panic. A wave of fear rises and begins to overtake her senses, but through all this, she manages to fumble and find that little brown bottle, hidden amongst the sweet honeysuckle leaves in her apron pocket. She unstoppers it, hands shaking, and raises it to her lips. The liquid scratches its way down, harsh and coarse. One gulp. Two. Three. Four.

She stops.

Not because her will is strong, but because the bottle, not long ago full to brimming, is now completely empty.

'Damn! Shite and damn again,' and she makes no cross, for both her hands are busy, one clasped to the source of her pain, and the other gripped around the bottle she had not meant to drink dry. She half hopes nobody is able to hear her cursing, and half that someone is near enough to come to her rescue. Anyone.

But this is a remote place, far from the cluster of Woodfield cottages, and not yet in sight of Caen Farm and Rose Cottage.

Even though it is early, the labourers are likely already in the fields, the women in the dairies or tending their young before they go out to gather on The Common. Her only companions are the birds, for some reason singing so hard, so furious this morning that they might lift the whole forest up to heaven. And if her ears were not so full of *whoosh* she would hear the tune of a solitary blackbird singing beautifully, high up in a nearby elm, the tree which lends its wood to coffins and caskets.

She sits on the willow seat, waiting for the shaking of her panic to stop, and lets out a loud sob, unsure which way to go. She would rather go back to the cottage and be at home, with her grandmother. But the old woman cannot call for help so easily, and with her shuffling gait it will take too long for her even to get to the next cottage up the lane, let alone all the way to midwife Eleanor Knocker's home near Barnett Wood. Why, it is almost halfway to Letherhed! If she goes back the way she came, how will she navigate the stepping stones? And what about Little Joe? He is nowhere, and now he must wait to be found, for she cannot look for him if her labour begins, can she? And where the hell is George? *Damn him!* The tears are flowing now, and the gin has not helped her panic to subside at all. It has only added to it.

Her head begins to swim, the *whooshing* increases.

She stands up, moves away from the water, for she does not want to end up in there. There is nothing for it, she must go to Annie at Rose Cottage. To Jesse's home. They will get the midwife. She bends to pick up the copper milk jug but it has gone. Where is it? She cannot remember where she left it, begins searching around the base of the tree. Silly, for she does not need it, but she is consumed with finding it. And as she creeps around the tree, bent over, holding her belly, she feels an uncomfortable *pop*, and a rush of warm spreads between her legs.

She cries out, 'Lord help me,' takes a few paces away from the leafy curtain towards the farm before darkness surrounds her and she collapses on the grassy path.

THE COMMON FOREST

EARLY MORNING

George snuck out of the house at first light, unusually early for him. Molly was dead to the world. He had to borrow yet more coins from Hal to buy her some gin so she didn't push him about his whereabouts today. *Let her sleep in, if she can.*

He lied and told her he was going to see that work with Farmer Trolter, but his destination is not the comforts of a well run farm. It is an old, dilapidated and long-forgotten barn, nestled in a glade, deep in The Common's forest.

Their hiding place, where they will repack Oakheart's tea for Mister Barehenger, tucked away from prying eyes, nosy neighbours, with only wild animals for company.

Hopefully, God willing.

However, he is uneasy and something is troubling him. He cannot say exactly what, for there are so many things on his mind. Money, Molly, tea, the noose. And a most disturbing, lucid dream which he cannot get out of his head.

Tied to the King Oak, arms and legs bound tight, he could not move. A group of women were dancing to a piper playing a mournful tune. They all looked like his wife, or Mathilda, or Florie, and one by one they danced past, blowing kisses, reaching out, touching him. He wanted to tell the Mathildas and the Flories to leave him be, to grab one of the Mollies, but he was held fast. A Florie came close, and as her lips touched his, he could smell the weeping, open sores on her face. Blood and pus, decaying skin. He turned his face away to avoid seeing how her flesh was being eaten to the bone by that awful disease. The dance soon took her away, but in whirled a Mathilda with her raven hair loose and flowing. 'Come here,' she demanded, close up and in his face.

'No!' he cried out. 'Not you! Where's Moll?'

'Here Husband, I am here,' he heard her calling, giggling. And there she was, dancing towards him, but not alone. She was with another man. He could not see the imposter's face as they moved nearer, and wanted to lash out, hit the fellow, bash him into the ground, but the tree held him fast.

The rogue led Molly away, the other dancers concealing their escape, then all the other women melted into the trees and suddenly, he had a clear view.

Molly was naked, tied to another King Oak and the imposter was having his way with her.

And she was enjoying it, moaning, groaning.

Shit! Molly, what the fuck are you doing? I am your husband,
you bitch!

He tried to shout, but the words only echoed in his head. The King
Oak laughed. 'Cuckold,' he heard the tree whisper in his ear, and then
he woke, a bad mood set in for the day.

He curses the old bat Eliza Greenfield for putting such a
dreadful idea into his head, *who will be bedding your wife then,*
eh? The words are scratching at his soul.

Once this work for Barehenger and Oakheart is done, he can
begin to put things right in his own house. He has had a long,
losing streak at cards and his debts are piling up, but once they
are cleared he will get an honest job. Less pay, but no risk.

He picks up his pace along a path lined with cow parsley,
nettles wound through with grandfather pop-out-of-bed, and
yellow flag irises, which wave him on as he scoots past.

Up ahead, at the edge of the ancient woodland, the dark figure
of a man is perched atop a gate. He waves and George glances
back to make sure it is not a signal that someone is following.
All is clear. The farm workers will be in the hot fields today, and
he thanks the Lord he will not be joining them, then curses the
Devil for the alternative he has chosen. An icy chill makes him
shudder and the cool morning air is not the cause.

'Morning Georgie,' Hal calls out cheerfully as he nears, and he
jumps down, scoops up an old billhook leaning against the gate
post. He rests the handle on his right shoulder with the blade
hanging precariously behind him.

Looks like a blonde grim. George grunts, 'Nothin' good about it, mate.' He leans his head on the gate, catching his breath. ''Tis too early, for one. Second time this week. 'Tis becoming a dreadful habit.'

'Aye, but early birds and worms, and all that. Will be quids in soon enough, will we not?'

'Aye, or dead.'

Hal pushes the gate open, and laughs as George falls forward.

George whacks him on the back, hard.

For being in a good mood.

For lying to him about the nature of their work.

For getting him involved in the first place.

He resists the temptation to give the man another hefty thump. *Breathe, man. Breathe. Don't lose it.*

'A little bit of prep, few hours' work and six weeks' wages, or more maybe. Easy money, Georgie boy,' Hal says as they begin their walk along the green ride.

'Yeah, easy for you to say, but that's about all. Still got to do it right, ain't we? And that Barehenger fella, he do make me more than a touch nervous. You seen the way he were looking at me yesterday? Jee-zus, I thought he was gonna kill me if I so much as sneezed.'

'Aw, come on, the gentleman were just eyeing you up for size! I reckon he swims on the other side of the pond,' Hal says, and winks at George, flutters his eyelashes, coy, like a maid.

George is not amused.

'You be joking, surely? A man like that? Nah! I ain't having it. And if he heard you say such a thing, he'd roast you alive. You may like to live dangerous, but I beg of you, leave us out. I will have no part.'

'What!? You's going all soft and gooey-girly in your old age, man!' Hal laughs. 'Anyways, I reckon you be just the right kind for him. What say you?'

George swings round to face Hal and as quick as lightning, thumps him sharply on the upper arm.

Damn! Lost it.

'I sayed leave me out, right?' and he holds up a thick, threatening finger. He is not playing today. 'I's warning you, Hal, less of that disgusting talk. You ain't got no idea where 'twill lead if it got back to the man. Cut it out,' and he quickens his pace, walks slightly ahead of his partner in crime.

They cannot afford to quarrel until their work is finished and Hal backs down. 'Sorry mate. Just havin' a laugh.'

'Yeah, well. Them criminals we's dealing with don't seem like they do *laughs*. Nothing feels good, just don't feel right. I's right uneasy about the whole bleedin' lot of it. And you don't have no wife nor child to be thinkin' of, and I's got two more coming any day now.' *If she lives.* 'Shite, Hal! Shite!' and he kicks a thick clump of grass growing at the side of the track.

'Well now, that's where you may be wrong,' Hal says, suddenly serious.

'What?' George stops in his tracks. 'You's proper gone and got yourself wed, without any of us knowing?'

Hal smiles, 'Might have! Then again, might just be planning a wedding on account of a truly special maid what's come along lately.'

'Yea? I'll believe that when I see apples on the King Oak!' George shakes his head in disbelief, for he cannot imagine Hal settling down to anything. 'Who be this fair maiden, then? I take it the Widow Meade ain't playing with your broom handle no more.'

'You are correct. The glorious Caroline Meade has gone and found herself a wealthy husband. I ain't been over Ockham way to clean out her yard for nigh on five months now. Not since it snowed.'

George mulls over this news as they walk through the woods.

'You sayin' you's going back to hard labour in them damp fields? I believe it not. Ain't you got another rich witch lined up, what will keep you in them silver buttons you likes to flash in our faces?'

'Nope, ain't no one else now, just this girl.'

'Well, I never thought that woman would ever let go. 'Tas been, what, two year now? Thought she had you for keeps.'

'Aye, same here. But you knows how them servant girls loves to gossip, 'twas all getting too risky.'

'And you ain't never going back, not even when her toff husband be away from home? Bit of extra coin on the side, like?'

'Nah, not this time. They says the gent's a mean fucker, worse than Barehenger even. Best stay well clear. Like I sayed, if them maids see me sneaking about again, we shall both be done for. I's made a clean break, like.'

George is not quite able to trust what Hal has told him, but if true, it is surely a good thing, for even if Hal had made a stack of money from the new world of mighty machines, love never crosses the social chasm, does it? They could never have a future together, the Widow Meade and Hal Archer, even if what began as a business arrangement, payment for his attentive services, turned eventually to true love. 'So, this girl what's got you all in a spin, she turned your head mighty quick, or was you a-courtin' afore the Widow Meade got fed up with you?'

'Fed up with me!? Hah! You doesn't know the length of me broom, boy! Nah, I been doin' it proper this time. Me heart's for this one, and for her alone. She be for keeps. Like your Molly, if you knows what I mean,' and at that very moment Hal Archer believes himself.

George thinks of Molly, how she grabbed his heart when he first saw her, took his breath away, captured him. And then he remembers his dream. *Fucking another up against that King Oak. Shit.* He reminds himself it was not real, but the image is difficult to erase.

'Aye, I do. Moll drives me bleedin' mad sometimes, but Lord, I know not what I'd do without her.' His heart tightens and thumps in his chest when he thinks of the trouble his unborn infants will cause his wife in the next few days. If he loses her, it will be half his doing. But then, if he loses this game and the hangman's noose finds its way around his neck, it will be a different outcome and no less dreadful. And what will become of Little Joe if they both die? He pushes the unwelcome thoughts away.

'Why all the secrecy though, mate? Why ain't you told us about this woman before, if she's so special, like?' he asks. 'Come to think of it, you never even mentioned you's stopped going to the Widow Meade, neither.' George is puzzled. It is unlike Hal not to tell him absolutely everything. His friend's silence leads him to believe there is something strange about the story.

Stuff and nonsense, maybe?

'Ain't no secret, mate,' Hal says. 'Suppose I di'n't want to curse it afore I was sure, like.'

'What be her name, then? At least tell us that.'

'Not yet, all in good time,' comes the reply. 'Soon, I will tell all, soon.'

The two men are very different and perhaps this is why they get on so well. George only ever wanted an easy life – ale, cricket, cards. Molly. But with Molly came children. He never really thought about how life would change once his family grew. It is certainly not easy. The responsibility, providing, protecting. However, Hal lives for excitement and George does not believe he will take to being a married man either.

'You's ready for a family, then? Won't be long afore your coin be spent not on shinies, but food and fuel and clothes,' he says.

'Aye, guess I's ready,' says Hal. 'Bout time, eh?' and he laughs, uneasily.

George studies his friend's face. He does not look at all comfortable. George thinks he might have hit a nerve, a truth his friend will not admit.

Settle down? Pft. He be kidding, right?

But that is not exactly what concerns Hal.

If he tells George the name of his lover, there is a chance they may no longer remain friends and he has to put off this revelation until their work for Barehenger is complete. He changes the subject. ''Tis said upwards of fifteen thousand Redcoats went up to Town.'

'Can't smell burning in the air this morn, so either the wind changed, or they got it under control,' George says.

'Aye, like as they have.

'Hope it don't mean they be heading back to their barracks, lurking along the roads out of London. Would be a terrible thing that, if Oakheart's waggons run into them,' George adds, quietly.

'Nah, they must have to hang around a bit, or 'twill all just rekindle,' and Hal tries to reassure himself as much as George.

'Barehenger,' he whispers, 'must know what the situation be. They could call the work off, if they feels 'tis too dangerous.'

George half prays they will, but he really could do with the money, now more than ever. He just doesn't want the work.

They discuss the tasks ahead, their voices low. They meet no one and nor do they expect to this early, but are cautious nonetheless. They veer left, away from the main ride and walk a narrow path, and a couple of hundred yards further, they turn again. The little-used trails get narrower as they go deeper into the forest, and are now wide enough only for a very small waggon. They begin to scan the undergrowth, watching for the secret, wild track through the dense trees, which will lead them to their hideaway.

'Look, there she be,' Hal says, and nods towards the entrance to the overgrown path. The trail is only just noticeable. If you didn't have your eyes on stalks, you would easily miss it. They push their way between clumps of tall bracken growing across the opening, not wanting to damage the ferns and expose the path just yet. The pack horses will do that later, when they transport the tea from the carts, which will have to be left on the wider path. For the moment, the way should remain concealed. As soon as they are three or four yards into the trees, Hal begins cutting away ivy and young saplings, nettles and brambles with the billhook, wherever they block the path. The woodland is dense here, but at times the trees are spread out, and where the sunlight manages to reach the ground, the forest floor is carpeted in green.

'This ain't part of The Common proper, is it? What with the barn here, an' all,' George asks.

'I believe 'tis part of Norton's Wood, but I ain't sure where the boundary is. Belongs to the Norton Estate, with Dukes Hall

Farm,' Hal replies. 'Good hunting ground this be, and fishing too, what with that lake not far away. Not that anyone from the Manor comes no more. Must have forgotten all about it, 'cause it ain't been worked for years.'

Norton? The name is familiar.

'Good timber gone to waste too, letting them trees bolt up like that, not pollarded or nothing. Can't see anyone hunting here now, 'tis too thick in places. Wouldn't be able to get a clear shot. Traps be good, though,' George adds.

The uppermost boughs of thin, gangly elm and beech reach straight up, and up again to find the light. Where sunshine squeezes through the thick canopy, the floor is carpeted with all manner of plants. Ramsons are rotting back into the earth, the air no longer heavy with their distinctive garlic smell. Remnants of bluebells, flowers long gone until next year when their riotous colour will once again brighten up the dull earth after a grey-white winter. There are moss covered logs, stones with fern clinging to the cracks, and bracken, in places as tall as a ten year old child.

Bramble and ivy creep about the trees, and would trip up even the most careful traveller, but as they make their way through the undergrowth, they disturb only what is necessary.

They soon reach their destination.

The path opens out to a small, almost circular clearing. At the edges, nettles and ferns hide in the shade of the trees, and tall spikes of pink foxglove grow where sunlight hits the ground. Branches stretch and nearly touch across the pale blue opening, leaving a hole to the heavens above like a pool of clear water.

This is their third visit. The men held back cutting the trail to keep it hidden, but have already trimmed back the grass and foliage around the barn. The half-derelict building stands to their right and will be in shadow until midday, when the sun will fill the place with its light, for an hour or two at least. Not quite a ruin, but without urgent repairs to the roof it will soon be lost. George thinks briefly of Rye Cottage and the work needed there, shakes his head to rid the thought of home.

One thing at a time, concentrate on this first.

He wonders whether the owners of the barn would think it worth the trouble to fix, for it is clearly a long forgotten relic. Almost beyond help. 'What it must be like to have so much you can forget about sommat so valuable,' he wonders aloud, and Hal nods in agreement.

'There's folk what live in worse.'

George can hardly imagine the world the aristocracy inhabits – his is very much a hand to mouth existence, uncertain at the best of times. At the beginning of every winter he is never sure if he will see another spring, yet here he is, already six-and-thirty. Some kind of miracle.

Norton! He remembers the name, the young woman he pulled from the Portsmouth Coach, wasn't she Lord Norton's niece? And the young man, his son? He wonders if they have recovered from the horror.

'Georgie,' Hal whispers suddenly, and grabs George's shirt sleeve. 'Reckon someone's been creeping about since we was here last.'

He looks worried.

George panics, scans the barn, the clearing and beyond into the darkness of the woods. The hairs on the back of his neck prickle and tingle at the thought their hideout has been discovered, their dealings unearthed. He can't see that anything is different, it all looks as it had when they left just a couple of days before. But would he notice if a pile of cut down tangly brambles had been moved? Or a rotten shutter on the barn left open? As he spins around to survey the scene, he hears a cry behind him and jumps, nearly out of his skin.

'HA!'

The cry is Hal, who slaps George hard on his broad back. 'Gotcha!' he says. Payback for George's earlier slap, and Hal begins clutching his sides with laughter at his friend's visibly shaken face. 'You's so easily frighted, Georgie boy!'

George is not at all amused and his fist finds that spot on his friend's upper arm which it has already visited today. This is no game, this work they have undertaken, and he wishes Hal weren't so dismissive of it.

'Fuck's sake, Hal, you are a right son of a bitch sometimes. This ain't no time for playin'. We got work to do, and if you don't take it serious, like, we might not live out the week.'

George's mood drops quickly. Skylarking, Molly would say, and he makes his way to the barn before he loses his temper completely and does something he might later regret. Like kill the man.

Hal begins to chicken walk and cluck, mocking and laughing, but one look at George's face tells him not to carry on with this mirth, although he is still sniggering to himself as George lifts the rusty latch and pushes open the top of the decaying stable door. It swings uneasily on its hinges, and with a creak and a groan it disappears into the darkness.

George reaches his hand in and unclips the bottom half, gives it a shove.

'We has much to do afore tonight, and it ain't long, eh? Tonight, Jesus Christ, midnight,' George says, as much to himself as to Hal, who brushes past and is soon hidden in the musty gloom.

'Don't you fret, we got time yet,' Hal replies. And then he adds jauntily, 'Hey, I's a poet and you di'n't know it!'

George shakes his head, but his demeanour has already softened at Hal's silly rhyme. He wants to stay angry, but Hal has a way of working him round. Yet another reason they have remained friends for so long. Anyone else would have been cut off and brushed aside. Hal? Somehow he is still here, testing sometimes, a bit too often these days, though still so easily forgiven. Like a brother. More than a brother, even. It is true that Jesse has certainly not been absolved so easily for his crimes. Perhaps he never will be. But Jesse's sins are unforgiveable, are they not? If Jesse's twin, Ned, were here, he would surely say the same.

George looks around. The interior of the barn is dingy, the light dim, but enough to see it is bare except for a rotten table in the corner, a three legged stool in no better state by its side. A couple of broken rake handles are strewn on the ground, their rusty heads lying close by, beheaded by time. There is a pile of old straw in another corner. It looks like a tramp may have taken a nap in it, the curved shape of a body still visible.

The upper barn is constructed of a heavy timber frame and rests on stone walls about two foot high. It is weatherboarded on the outside with time-worn oak, black as pitch, and inside open right up to the shingled half-hipped roof. There are two thick internal walls, old oak trunks laid one on the other, held in place by vertical beams.

'This thing is almost done for. Must'a been here a hundred

years, but dare say it won't last ten more, unless someone does sommat with that there roof,' Hal says.

'Reckon you's right there, mate. Lettin' sommat like this go all to ruin? What a damnded waste! Damn!'

'Best check the roof again,' Hal says, 'work out where we can do the job best. Won't have time now to mend them holes and there be a storm comin' up, too. I does hope 'tis over by the time the load gets here.'

'Aye, ain't got no time to patch up nothing,' George says.

There are three places where over hanging trees are visible through the gaps, and the early morning light which shines through makes them squint.

'Them holes up there are all west-facing, so we can use the other side, here, where 'tis dry. Should be alright, eh?' George suggests, and walks over to the pile of dented hay. It looks like someone has had some fun in it, for the hay is moulded to the shape of two bodies, not one. He wonders who would come here, and whether they will come again, slap bang in the middle of their work. His skin creeps at the thought. Just a crazy fear, his imagination working overtime today.

'We has room enough here, where we can store the stuff and keep it dry,' Hal says, standing near one of the walls.

Great arcs of cobwebs hang from the beams, with so much dust clinging to them they are as thick as rope. There are two windows, no glass but rotten wooden shutters closed across the openings. George unhooks one of the panels. Heavy, but the hinges still work. As he pulls it, something springs at him from outside.

'Shite!' He jumps back in time, avoids what would have been a nasty encounter with a coiled holly branch growing up against the shutters. It reaches into the barn like a spindly arm.

'Was not e'spectin' that! Shite! Give me quite a fright.' He turns to a grinning Hal.

'You's a poet, too,' Hal says and laughs. Always cheerful, his mood seems never to sway low or dip like George's skylark.

'Jus' get over here with that there billhook and cut that down, Hal. Could'a lost an eye! Jesus Christ.'

They set about discussing what they must to do, making mental notes of things which will have to be fetched. Light for working – a good stock of tallow candles, oil lamps would be better, safer. A little food and ale. Water from the pond nearby – they will need to cut a path to it for the ponies. There is much to do in the next few hours. They thought at first to do it slowly, bit by bit, but now their schedule has been rearranged, they will have to hurry.

'Hal, those babes are nearly upon us, I don't rightly know how I's goin' to be able to get all this stuff, or help at all,' George says, scratching his chin.

'Don't worry so, mate, I shall do it. Just come when you can, alright?' Hal is being unusually cooperative. But then comes the caveat, 'I'll call in a favour on you sometime.'

'Well now, what favour and when, is what I'd be worried about.' He hasn't yet told Hal that after their dreadful meeting yesterday, this is to be his last escapade. This kind of work just isn't for him. He cannot afford to hang, and Molly cannot afford to lose him.

Molly. Her name makes the hair on the back of his neck prickle and George suddenly wants to get back home. 'Hal, let's get a move on. I needs to be gettin' back, don't want to leave the wife long. She'll be at that gin if I ain't there to stop her. Don't want her drinkin' it all today, like.'

'What's got into her then? I mean, except your very own seed drill all them months back!' Hal chuckles.

'It ain't funny, Hal. She got the fear good and proper, what with her thinkin' it be twins, and she's prob'ly right. Poor thing got the memory of her mother dying so soon after she had a babe. Can't say 'tis pleasant, eh? Can you imagine it? Can you? Makes me shiver to me bones.'

'No point goin' there, mate. 'Tis makin' me knees go queer just thinkin'. Guess it ain't no wonder she's hitting the bottle,' And for once Hal is sympathetic to a woman's plight.

George wonders what on earth has got in to him.

Something has happened to change his perspective on a woman's lot, but what?

Rose Cottage

Early Morning

Annie Hogtrough has been helping Lucy Buttery fill pails and churns at the milking parlour since first light, and they have had quite a joyous start to their day. For Annie had good news and her lips were full of it, her heart bursting with a joy she could not contain.

Lucy took Annie in her arms and cried with her. 'So happy for you dear heart, what a blessèd relief the man will do right by you!'

As they held each other, Lucy inwardly sighed, for the man her friend has fallen for will not be an easy husband. However, Lucy did not divulge all she knows, did not want to be the one to break the spell. She wished she had been able to warn her friend, but news of Hal Archer's misdemeanours has only just reached her ears, and Annie was secretive about the affair until it was too late. She will have to be told soon, though.

'You must tell no one, Luce. None must hear afore Father and me brothers. Promise?'

'Of course Annie, I ain't gonna tell no one.'

Annie is half way across the yard, still smiling, when she spies a movement, something lurking outside the stable door. She stops in her tracks and peers into the shadows where the light has not yet ventured. *One of the lambs, strayed off the Common and separated from its mother?* A shape comes out of the dark corner and starts wandering towards the farmhouse.

It is not an animal at all, but Little Joe.

'Lord above! Run away again,' she whispers, and then calls aloud. 'Joe! Where's you going, child?'

The boy turns and begins running as fast as a three year old can. He totters and stumbles across the mucky yard, stamping in the wet dung puddles, clutching his breakfast of dry crust. He makes a beeline for Annie and she braces herself for a crash.

'No, Joe! Slow down! Slow down child! Watch the milk,' she cries, but he takes no notice.

'Nannie!' he shouts, as he slams into her skirt, giggles and wipes his grimy face and snotty nose on her apron. Annie gasps at the jolt, nearly drops the jug.

'Little Joe, what on earth you doin' here? You's a little pest! You look like you's just jumped out of bed, still in your smock and all. Where's your mama?'

'Where's your mama? Where's your mama?' he repeats. 'Mama busy. Joe 'ungry, vewy vewy,' and he holds up his bread and points at the jug. 'Nannie got milk, awroight?'

Annie laughs, her mood not diminished even a glimmer by grimy little boy stains on her clean apron. 'Sure, and you can have some indeed, but let's go inside so you can dunk your bread. Now, tell me, does your mother know you's here?'

Little Joe nods, clasps his dirty fingers around Annie's skirt and as they walk to the cottage door he tugs hard with every splash of his bare feet in the mucky puddles.

'Do not pull my dress so, Little Joe. Or there will be no milk left for your breakfast, see? And watch where you's putting your feet. Mind that slurry, won't you? You'll be treadin' it all in the cottage. You are a little beasty, Joseph Hogtrough, truly you are. Just like your Papa, ain't you?'

Joe laughs, 'No, not Papa. Lickle Joe, awroight?'

She shakes her head at his cheek and smiles, her heart still warm, her morning nausea not half as bad today. *Thank the Lord! Thank the blessèd Lord!*

However, she still has to break the news to Father William and Jesse. An uncomfortable and difficult task, for what on earth will they do with Father when she leaves for her marital home? With more than a little unease, Annie realises that she no longer cares. *The old devil can go to the Workhouse if he ain't called downstairs first. Likely 'tis the best place for him anyways.* She is a little dismayed by her ungodly lack of sympathy for the crooked old man, but his tyranny has worn her down. She is more than ready to make her escape, peace with God can come later.

Inside the cottage, Annie pours Joe a bowl of milk and he clambers onto the long, worn bench. His little arms cannot reach, so she pulls him onto her lap. He grabs at the milk, slopping it on the table.

'Goodness Joseph Hogtrough, what a mess you make,' she declares. 'How does Mama cope, eh?' And she smiles. *Mama! God willing, I shall be one soon.*

The boy begins dunking and sucking on the dry bread as if he has not eaten for days.

'Mama forget to give you supper yesterday?' she asks him.

Joe nods, his mouth stuffed full. Annie shakes her head in dismay. 'Poor Mama, she got a lot to do now, ain't she?' she remarks, and Joe's head bobs up and down. However, it really is unlike Molly to forget to feed her child. She wonders if Joe is listening, or even understands. Perhaps he is playing, like his father used to. She tests him.

'Has Mama got a new dress?' she asks.

His head nods, *yes.*

'And Granny Greenfield, too?' And again, *yes.*

'And what colour is Mama's dress? Is it blue?' *Yes.*

'Come now, they ain't got no new clothes, at all. You's a little beasty, Joe. Does you know that?'

He knows, *yes,* for is he not often told as much?

'I'll wager Mama ain't got no idea you's here.'

Joe grins, then giggles, spraying bits of bread and milk between his teeth and splattering the table.

'Why di'n't she come, too? To get your milk, like.'

'Mama busy. Lickle Joe milk for Mama, an' Papa, an' Grama moonbum,' he replies and begins stuffing more soggy bread into his mouth.

Annie laughs, *Moonbum?* But Molly would not send Joe alone, so something must surely be amiss. 'Alright Nevvy, when you's finished your breakfast, we shall take milk to Mama.'

'Yeah, yeah, yeah,' he replies, and punches the smoky air with a milky-wet hand. 'More firs, Nannie. Me wan more.'

'Mind your manners young man. Where's your pleases gone? Did they run off in the other direction to what you did this morning?'

'Peas, peas, peas,' and the boy thumps his fist on the table, grinning, showing all his little white milk teeth.

Suddenly, the back door creaks open and Jesse appears wearing a look like thunder. He has been with the horses, sorting out the stable boy's jobs for the day, but also looking for the white kitten, which last evening he had put there hoping it might die, eaten by rats or the other cats. However, he found it alive, and is almost grateful. After his terrible nightmare, he thought he should give it a chance, some water and a little milky bread for it is too small yet to catch a mouse. When Mathilda arrives, she will no doubt want to see it. No point upsetting her before she has her foot through the door, although the thought does cross his mind that it might put her off staying. But what about Molly? Who will help her, if not her bossy cousin?

'Mornin' Jesse.' Annie smiles, 'Look! Little Joe come to fetch some milk for his Mama.'

'So I sees,' he replies, glaring at the child. He has not noticed the change in Annie's lightened mood and does not greet his nephew, but turns back to the door, breathing in the morning air and finding it not cool and refreshing, but already humid and heavy.

'What has happened to Molly? The lad keeps runnin' away and I'll wager she ain't got no clue where he be,' Annie says.

'That will be the drink,' and as Jesse sits down, he shakes his head in disapproval at Molly's slide from God's grace. 'Smelled it on her two even back. Used to be such a sweet thing, but I reckon she's been at that dastardly bottle, supplied, no doubt, by our lazy and good for nothin' Brother. Where he gets the coin for it, Lord only knows,' he says, with a venomous hiss.

A shadow crosses his eyes when he speaks of George and Annie cannot fail to feel the rift, for it has been a part of their lives for such a long time.

When and where did it begin? It has something to do with Ned, she is sure. And Jesse is in as bad a mood this morning as she has ever seen. There is something wrong, but it surely cannot concern Molly and her drinking.

'I spent the best part of the day with Moll yesterday, and she were never at the bottle in all that time. I would never have thought it,' she says.

'You sure of that?' he asks, and throws her a quizzical look. 'I knows what I smelled, Sister, and it were gin alright. It were definitely gin.'

'Well now, if that be true, then I must talk with her, get her back to God's true ways.' She slips this in, for her brother's love of God and all things holy may warm him up. And since he started going to those Methodist meetings at Ashted, he has become ever more righteous, if that could be at all possible. 'Perchance you could speak to George, for he must also help put her straight,' she adds, although she guesses Jesse will not, for there will no doubt be violence in George's response at his brother's interference.

'Like as it was George what got the woman turned to drink in the first place. Or if weren't him what 'couraged her, then she be doin' it 'cause of him,' he growls and glowers, and again he lashes out the words.

What on earth has irked him so? Whatever it is, his eyes have that look of Father's about them and she would prefer not to be in his company for too long. Perhaps it is that coarse vest he likes to wear. Is it itching and scratching deeper into his wounds this morning? *He's been to the stable, did he visit the tack room?*

They look up as they hear Henry coming down the stairs. Once again the lad catches only the last sentence of his older siblings' conversation. 'Who be doin' what 'cause o' who?' he asks, ever curious.

Jesse and Annie look at each other and say nothing, for today's discussion about Molly's slide into ruin is not for him.

'Right then,' Jesse says, ignoring his younger brother's question. 'I shall say the Grace. We 'as a fair bit to be gettin' on with today, young Henery. Hay needs finishin', turnin' and gatherin' afore that storm what's brewing comes to the boil,' and his tone is brusque and cold, with none of the softness he is forever trying to cultivate to save him turning into a version of their vicious father, a transformation Annie believes is well under way.

'What be Little Joe doin' with us fer breakfast, then? Maybe you could answer me that?' Henry is miffed and disrespect is in his tone. Is he not old enough to know what is going on? He should be involved in family matters now he is no longer a little boy. He is nearly sixteen, for God's sake!

However, Henry has not read Jesse's mood at all well.

'Less o' your ins'ilence, boy,' Jesse grunts.

It seems Henry has already forgotten the issue of Mathilda's invitation and it has not yet been mentioned to Annie, in whose bed Mathilda will be sleeping. The situation is grumbling away in Jesse's mind. He draws a deep breath, and begins to say his

Grace. When he is finished they eat in frosty silence, in spite of the warmth already creeping through the door. There is no honey at the table this morning and Henry feels its absence. The quiet is broken only by Little Joe's slurping and William's usual stick-smashing on the floor above, his groans for Annie's attention. She ignores him. *Later, Father. Later.* Now Annie has a way out, she feels more courage than she has ever felt before. The old man is getting frailer as his bones grind the very life force from him and his threats of violence against her mean nothing now, for he cannot carry out his promises like he used to. No Annie, no food. Or drink. And now, at last, she can leave this place. *What a blessing!* Very soon, as quick as the banns can be read, so she has been promised.

As the last drops of milk are being sopped up, she cracks the silence. 'Jesse, please do not forget that old chest what you promised to release from Father's clutches. I could be getting' on with the mending today, if the rains come, like. Will be a perfect time to do it. Then Henry may have a new shirt, or two, even. And if there be nothin' fit for our brother, I could turn it to good use for Molly and the babes, or for this little'un, here,' and she gives Joe a squeeze.

Jesse has not forgotten, but rather he is reluctant to look over his twin's belongings. 'I do not believe I promised, Sister.' *The boy ain't deservin' of a new shirt, let him wear the old till threadbare,* he thinks, and the cilice pricks and irritates, reminding him why he wears it. Because of thoughts just like these. He turns to Henry.

'Lad, you has sommat what you needs to deluge to your sister. Maybe after she has heared it, she will not be so eager to help you out with them clothses.'

'Divulge, you mean, Jesse?' Annie corrects him. 'Ain't that the right word?'

Jesse glares at his sister, *Lord she begins to sound like that green-eyed Widow.* He tries to convince himself that he is more angry at his own ignorance than at being corrected, but that is a downright lie. *These women should know their place.*

'Divulge, then,' he says, trying to remain calm, but his annoyance at Mathilda's impending arrival is threatening to burst forth, like the storm, rumbling in the ever closing distance.

Henry now knows what is irking his brother, but stays silent.

Jesse will not let him off so easily. 'Go on, boy, speak,' he snarls, but still Henry does not utter a word.

'Spit it out, boy, afore I pulls it out of you,' and Jesse cannot hold it in any longer, his anger escapes and he slams his fist on the table.

Everyone jumps. Little Joe stops chewing, one last piece of soggy bread still in his mouth. He does not take his wide eyes off his grumpy uncle for a second, unsure of what is coming next.

There is no doubt at all that Father William's quick temper has been passed down to his oldest sons. Jesse mostly manages to keep it under control, unlike George, who lets fly at anyone who crosses him. However, today, the older brother is struggling with the devil in him which wants to lash out and strike Henry for his unbelievable stupidity.

Invitin' a stranger, a bossy woman at that, into our home without me permission. The cheek of him!

Jesse is incensed. Will the Widow Richardson pay her way, or will they have to support her during her stay? There will be extra food to find, for a start. George will not – cannot – contribute.

The man has nothing. Will she be of help to Annie around the house, or expect to be waited on hand and foot, like Father? From what he has learned, she is lazy and used to having servants who waited on her when she was young. And how long will she be here? Two days is too long in Jesse's mind, and perhaps it will be much longer if she plans to stay while Molly is lying-in. A month, at least. *Heavens above.* He is feeling most uncharitable and these are the questions he has been mulling over all through the night, in between cutting the never-ending field of black-eyed corn. He has not forgotten his wet sheets, either. He shudders and his questions remain unanswered while Henry remains silent.

'Speak, boy. SPEAK! Damn you,' and Jesse raises his hand high as if to strike out.

Henry flinches, holds his arm up to protect his head from the impending blow.

Little Joe bursts into tears. He had been frozen on Annie's lap, transfixed at the unfolding drama and watching Jesse as the demon uncoiled itself from his uncle's soul. But now the boy begins to struggle, to be free from this place, to make yet another escape. Annie holds onto him tightly and tries to calm him. Suddenly, he kicks back his feet onto her shins and sinks his little teeth into her forearm. She cries out and lets him go, and he slips onto the floor and runs out of the open door.

'You little tyrant, Joseph Hogtrough!' she calls and is left rubbing the red wheal his teeth have left. 'Thank goodness, his jaws ain't strong enough to break me skin,' she says, shocked at his actions. 'That boy's going feral, like a dog.'

'Like his father you mean,' Jesse growls, and then raises his voice and his hand. 'And now look what you's gone and done,' and he slams his palm onto the table and the blame squarely on Henry's shoulders. He struggles to bring his temper under control and continues to rant and rave about the boy's stupidity.

Annie gets up to go after the little boy, she wants to escape this anger, too, and has no idea what has provoked it. What could be so bad?

However, Jesse stops her. 'I'll go, Sister. And Henry here,' he splutters the words out and prods Henry hard on the top of his arm with a sharp finger. 'Young Henry here will tell you how he has rearranged our living quarters for the next goodness knows how long!'

Jesse grabs his hat and storms out of the cottage, slams the door behind him so hard that the walls shake and the old glass in the little window rattles in its frame.

Common Lane, Rye Brook

Early Morning

Outside, Jesse takes a few deep breaths, but finds no fresh air to cool his miserable rage. His demon rises whenever he suffers the slightest inconvenience to his stable, easy life, rears up at the merest provocation. Not to mention whenever anyone steps over the godly line he has created for them in the mud. He came very close to hitting Henry. Too close. Like father, like son. He needs to get that devil locked back up before it does any real damage. Those kind of injuries cannot be healed. He knows, for at the King Oak he damaged Elizabeth beyond repair, did he not?

After a few moments, he finds he is less angry at Henry than at himself for his lack of control. It is at times like these he feels the need of a woman, a soft and caring soul to ease his temper, for he is sure his aggression is somehow linked to a lack of tender love in his life. The memory of Elizabeth, her beautiful face, but then Ned's anger, is before him, as it always is when he considers moving on. The warning he was given, the consequences if he ever found someone to love, and he is reminded of why he is not married now and why he never can be.

He could not possibly put any woman in such danger.

He sticks his head in the wooden rain trough and the cool water slips right up to his neck. The cold brings him down to earth with a bump. When he can no longer hold his breath he comes up, shakes his head, the sharp drops of water spraying and shattering the still air around him. Only then does he feel sufficiently cooled off to chase after the little horror that is Joseph Hogtrough.

For a small child with stubby legs, the boy has made much headway. When Jesse turns into Common Lane, the boy is nowhere in sight, but as he rounds a gentle curve he spies him. The boy has forgotten his angst and is squatting near a half-dried puddle of mud, poking at something.

As Jesse draws next to him, Joe sees a long shadow loom up on the ground and stands up, points down at a large, black stag beetle. 'Beekle,' he says and only then does he look up. When he sees Jesse, his face falls.

''Tis alright Little Joe, I weren't angry at you. In fact, I ain't angry at all now. Di'n't mean to scare you, see? Come now, let's get you back to yer mother, shall we?' He stoops and picks him up, and Joe's bottom lip quivers. 'Now, Where be your mother?'

'Vere,' Joe points, across the meadow to the grassy path along the banks of the Rye Brook.

'Well now, that be the long way round to your back yard. What say you we go the short way, along the lane? By the front door, eh?' Jesse points down the lane towards the bridge, but Joe shakes his head.

'Vere, vere!' he shouts, and points again to the grassy path. 'Vat way, Mama vat way,' and he grabs Jesse by his straggly beard and pulls it hard.

'Ouch! You scoundrel! You's just like your father, boy!' Jesse drops him quickly to the ground and the boy scampers off towards the path, his way or no way. Jesse follows at a long pace, easily keeping up. The boy's legs are soon tired and he slows, begins marching like the soldiers he has been copying all week.

Ahead, Jesse can see what looks like a bundle of rags on the ground. 'What be that, there, Little Joe?' he strains to make out the shape, not fifty yards away. He squints, holds his hand over his brow, as if that will help bring the form into focus.

'Mama,' cries Joe and begins to run along the path.

Only then does Jesse realise it is not a bundle of rags at all, but the collapsed heap of a heavily pregnant woman.

'Lord above! Joseph, wait on me, boy. Wait!'

He is not sure what they will find, does not want the child to see something which might stay with him for the rest of his life. Jesse overtakes the boy and arrives at Molly's side first. She is pale and lifeless and he fears the worst.

'Molly, Molly, are you with us still? God help you, woman. Molly, wake up!' He kneels down on the ground next to her, picks up her hand and taps it, tries to wake her. He strokes her face, pats it gently, sees her pallor and feels the coolness of her brow, calls her name over and over.

Jesse holds his breath while he waits for a sign she is still alive. At last, she stirs.

'Thank the Lord! Praise be to God you live! How long has you been here like this?' He gets no answer, for although living, she is barely conscious. Jesse has no idea what to do next.

Little Joe begins to cry, lies on the floor on his back and sobs. 'Mama, Mama,' and he kicks his short legs in the air.

At that moment, Jesse sees the gin flask lying next to Molly. 'Oh! Lord! Water, she'll need water!'

He picks up the flask, tips out the last drop of gin. *Lord above how much 'as the woman drunk? This be an half pint bottle!* He slips down the shallow bank, pushing aside reeds and tall grass, holds the bottle under the surface until it is full, hopeful he can rescue her from what may only be a stupid drunken stupor and nothing worse.

'Come now, drink this,' he says, and tips the flask to her lips. The cool liquid dribbles into her mouth. She begins to cough and splutter. As she comes to, she opens her eyes.

Ah! There he is!

Not her husband.

Oh no! Not George. Rather, gazing down at her are the deep, brown eyes, and almost tickling her face is the russet beard of his ever present older brother.

Her perpetual saviour.

Jesse, oh Jesse! Always there for me, ain't you? Thankfully, the words do not escape her lips but remain floating in her head. It takes a few seconds before she is fully conscious.

'Sister, Good Lord! How long has you been here like this? What on earth happened?' he asks, helping her to sit up.

'I dunno, I's out lookin' f'little Joe, come over all queer, like. Where's he, me boy?' She is slurring, her words slow and blurred. She holds her hands to her head, rubs her eyes, her temples.

'Here. Right here, see? He come to the farm for milk, for dunkin' his stale bread,' he digs, at their poverty, their neglect.

'Ain't 'ungry now, Mama,' Joe says and stands in front of his mother, ready to pounce into her lap. 'Nannie gi'me milk.'

Jesse tries to stop him, pulls him to one side, but the boy kicks him and moves back to his mother. She smiles weakly at the sight of her little lost boy, now blessedly found, all thanks to Jesse Hogtrough. *Such a marvellous man, a good man.* She is sure he would make a truly perfect husband.

'Where's you bin, Joe? I's right worried. Let 'im come near, Jesse. I's feelin' a touch better.'

But she doesn't sound good. She sounds very drunk and looks extremely pale.

As white as the ghost of Elizabeth in his dreams.

Molly has forgotten her earlier twinges and tries to stand. With Jesse's help she manages to get to her feet. Once upright, a sharp pain pulls at her crotch. She grabs her belly and gasps, cries out in shock at the sudden discomfort. Jesse holds onto her as she nearly buckles under. He leads her to the willow tree seat and she sits uneasily on its rough bark, holding her head with one hand and stroking her bump with the other.

'Is that what made you fall? The birthing pains, has it begun, your increasement, like?' he asks. And then, before he can stop himself, 'Or were it the gin?'

Molly closes her eyes. He knows she is drunk, but how much did she drink, exactly? It is coming back to her, and in all probability it was not the birthing contractions, but gin which made her fall. Her head is spinning and she can see not one, but two Jesse Hogtroughs standing before her.

As if one foreign beard were not enough.

And something doesn't feel right. Another twinge catches her breath, and then she remembers. She is wet between her legs, her waters have burst. She is going to have the babies and nothing will stop them now.

That great threshold is before her.

Her greatest fear, Death, is beckoning.

'I come out lookin' for Joe, see? I had t' find him,' she slurs, clasping her belly. 'But them babes are a-comin', Jesse. I needs t' get home. Me waters have gone. What'm I gonna do? Where's George? You seen him? Left real early 'smornin' he did! Where's me husband?' And then she hiccups loudly, and then burps. ''Scuse me, dear Lord. Help me get home, I need to get back home, please. Jesse, do help me, please.'

'Can you walk, Molly?' he asks, hopes to God she can. *Lord above! She'll be as heavy as ten sacks of spuds.*

'Don't think I can. Things're all stretchy and pullin', I's scared if I walks, I'll 'ave 'em right here by the Rye! Lord help me! Jesse, don' leave me, please. Where's me husband? You seen 'im?' and she is in a right tizzle now, fractious and nervous, crying and unable to hold back her angst.

Jesse can hardly contain his anger at her stupidity for getting so drunk and walking out alone, but he does his best to restrain his righteous tongue.

'Now then, Little Joe, I needs you to lead the way back to the cottage. You go on ahead boy, I's gonna follow with your mother, back the way we come, see?'

Little Joe knows all is not well. He looks up at Jesse and nods, stomps a soldier's march back along the brook towards the stony Common Lane, while Jesse picks Molly up, with some difficulty. *Stone the crows, twenty sacks.* He manages to hold her, his muscles rippling and straining as he bears her weight and tries to walk with an air of calm security, but his back is breaking. She might well slip through his fingers at any moment. The sweat pours from Molly's pale face, and from Jesse's red one. Under his nose is the disgusting stench of alcohol, and the memory of Elizabeth's fear when faced by such a drunken fool comes rushing back to him.

They arrive at the cottage after what seems an eternity and Jesse sets Molly down on the long wooden bench. She looks very unwell.

Eliza is, as usual, by the hearth. Crumpled up and chewing on a cold, empty pipe.

'Back at last! Took yer toime, Moll. Loight this poipe up, be a dear. And where's me cuppa? Forgot t'make it afore you left, you did,' and she peers at Jesse. 'That ain't yer 'usband, choild! Too skinny by far. Who's you cavortin' with now? Lord above! What will your 'usband say!' She clicks her tongue and stares at Jesse as if she has never seen him before. However, she is playing, knows full well who Jesse Hogtrough is, and he is not a man with whom her granddaughter should be alone.

'Mistress Greenfield,' Jesse tips his forelock, not yet dry from the soaking he gave it earlier. 'I believe Molly's babies are coming,' he remarks, ignoring Eliza's dangerous insinuations. *She is surely losing her mind. She don't recognise me, or is she blind?*

Eliza just huffs. 'Well, where's me cuppa tea? Oi ain't had it yet this morn. Them babes can wait till tea's brewed, can't they? Tea first, babies a'ter. Get that kettle on won't'cha?'

Molly is sobbing. Whether it is the relief of being at home or the realisation that she is in labour, Little Joe tugging at her apron, her grandmother's demands, the effects of her tippling – whatever it is, it all comes out. Jesse doesn't know where to look, is very uncomfortable and cannot wait to leave.

'I'll go fetch Mistress Knocker,' he says, anxious to extract himself from the stuffy room.

He hears Eliza call after him. 'Ain't'cha gonna put on that kettle afore ye go?' she tut-tuts and clicks a disapproval. He shakes his head at the old woman's calls, but hasn't quite reached the garden gate when he remembers Mathilda's impending arrival.

He sticks his head back round the door. 'Don't forget, your cousin Mathilda's comin' this forenoon.'

'Oohh!' Molly cries out and he is not sure if it is with pain or dismay at the news. 'What, Silly Tilly? Wha'chya mean, she's comin'?' she splutters.

'Mathilda, aye. We did see her yesterday in Letherhed, at market. George ain't told you?'

'Lord no, he di'n't say nothin', did he? Where's he, anyways, me husband? Bastard. Oops,' she hiccups. ''Scuse me. Dunno how Silly Tilly can 'elp, she ain't never so much's cleaned out a fire. What good'll she be?'

Jesse explains Mathilda's intentions, her recent bereavement, her offer of help.

'I'd no idea,' Molly cries. 'None, 'ee di'n't tell me nuffin', see? Well, ain't nuffin' new, 'cause he never does tell me nuffin' ac'shally,' and she wipes her face with her muddy skirt, transfers the dirt from cloth to skin.

She looks like a wild animal, Jesse thinks.

'She can sleep in the ol' pigsty, best place. Would bring her down a peg, hah! Tha'tit would. Airs an' graces she got a-plenty, that woman.'

'That ain't no way to speak of someone who offers you help,' Jesse says, irritated by her lack of gratitude.

'Hah! You dunno her like I does. Growed up with her, I did. A right madam, she be.'

'Well, she ain't a child no more,' and then he remembers his dream of Mathilda's demands. Is it a sign she is not much changed? 'Anyways, 'tis all arranged. She'll share with Annie,' he says.

'Oh! Poor dear Annie! Sleepin' with miss Lah-di-dah.'

'Well, she did not exactly offer,' stammers Jesse.

'Ain't no one gonna put on that darnded kettle, Oi's still ain't had me tea. Lord, Oi's gonna do it meself,' Eliza says and hauls herself up from her chair, shuffles to the fireplace to swing the empty kettle over the flames, seemingly oblivious to the conversation going on around her.

'Gran, the kettle ain't filled, it'll burn!' Molly stumbles forward to save the kettle and almost trips face first into the iron arm.

Jesse catches her just in time. 'Sit down, and do not move, Sister,' he orders, then turns to Eliza. 'Mistress Greenfield, please wait for your tea. The midwife will be here soon enough. I be sure she'll make it. There ain't time fer me t'fill that kettle, I must be goin' for her, like.'

Suddenly, another contraction tears through Molly, she screws up her face in pain and cries out. Jesse turns away, embarrassed.

'Looks like them babies are a-comin',' Eliza says. 'Best you fetch the midwife, boy,' she says, pointing a gnarly finger at Jesse. 'Eleanor Knocker will make me tea, she will.'

But Jesse has already gone.

'Bout time, too,' Eliza mumbles after him.

After calling on the midwife, Jesse almost runs back to Rose Cottage. Many things begin to fester under his tricorn hat. That dreadful nightmare and Mathilda's screeches, his wet sheets, George's whereabouts, work, Father. That bloody fleabag kitten. A winged ant settles on his shirt. It is a sure sign a storm is coming when the ants take to the skies.

'Annie!' Jesse calls out as he thunders into Rose Cottage. The room is brighter, sunshine peeking through the rambling briar covering the tiny windows at the front, flung wide to dispel the woodsmoke, the stench of tallow and pissy Father William.

'What on earth has happened!? Did you find our little devil nevvy?'

'Aye, and more. Molly's labour is upon her,' he says, flustered, breathless.

Annie listens to his tale while she scrubs the kitchen table. 'Someone should go and find George and tell him. He'll want to be nearby,' she says.

'Aye, but where will the lazy sod be?' Indeed, where do work-shy men spend their time? The Inn? He does not know where to start looking. 'I take it Henry told you about his h'invitation to Mistress Richardson, that you will have to share your bed this night and for the coming ones, too?' he asks.

Annie stops scrubbing. 'Yes, Jesse, and I can't say it sits easy with me, what with Father like he is,' she says quietly, not wanting to disturb the beast from above. 'But if she can be of help, then it can only be a good thing, can it not? And Lord knows I ain't goin' to be much good to Moll, what with Father to be taken care of.' *But not for much longer shall I have to put up with his disgusting stench, his behaviour, his stick. Thank the Lord.*

'Where be the lad? Did you send him to the West Field, to be getting on with the hay?'

'Aye, that I did. And what about George?'

'Find him, I suppose. Lord knows where.'

'I'll go, Brother. You get on with that hay afore the storm, or you'll be fretting over it,' she says, and for this Jesse is grateful, but then adds, 'but I beg of you, Brother, do speak with him about Molly's drinking, and soon like, afore it gets too bad.'

His sister has the easy job.

NORTON BARN

MID-MORNING

Hal Archer holding a broom is not something George ever sees, but that is the sight which greets him as he looks back at the barn. They pulled straws for chores, Hal's was short, his job to sweep down the cobwebs.

'All you needs is a pointy black hat and you'll be right at home!' George says. He laughs as Hal puts the broom between his legs and begins rushing around the forgotten clearing, grips the handle and makes an evil face, his tongue hanging out of the side of his mouth. He begins mock humping the stalk, falls to the ground in ecstasy at the climax of his play.

Ever the joker. George shakes his head. He cannot not say he is not entertained, but his thoughts soon return to Molly.

'I must be heading back soon, see how Moll is.'

'You's right under the thumb, ain't you?' Hal grins.

'Cut it out, Hal, you knows why.'

'She'll be fine Georgie. Always is. Come to The Leg first, for an ale and a game of cards. What say you?'

'Nah, don't tempt me, mate. I has to be close by this time. And I shall owe you a leg if we don't get this work done right.'

As he busies himself raking into piles the undergrowth he has cut back, he shudders at the memory of the first time Molly gave birth. It is an evening he wants to forget, but which will forever be etched in his memory. And where was he? With Hal, of course, out drinking, playing cards at The Leg. However, that is not the whole story, and the bit he wishes to forget is what he remembers best.

They spent the evening at the table and he won a fair bit, a rare event. Instead of going home with a fist full of coins, he allowed them to burn right through his pocket and they fell straight into Joshua Reynolds' hands. George bought drinks all round for his friends, for Hal and Bobby Venn. For Moses King, who fired up his fiddle and played till the early hours. For Joshua and his wife, who danced with them in front of the fire. And for the maid, Gemma, the blacksmith's pretty charcoal-haired daughter, who thanked him most kindly for her cup of brandy by leading him outside to show him just how grateful she was. In the woodshed, behind the inn, she kissed him all over, then she lifted up her skirt and let him enjoy her. All of her. *Fuck! She was good.* The memory still moves him now, and it should not. He turns away from Hal, rearranges his breeches, tries to banish the thoughts which seem never to fade.

He strayed because his wife was out of bounds, because he could not enjoy his Molly-Mary, he tells himself. Had he known Molly's increasement had begun, he would have been home, would he not? Pacing and worrying, and drinking, just a little. But no one had come to fetch him, to tell him, and so he remained at The Leg. No worries or fears, and with a free flow of ale and brandy, because those hot coins burnt through his pocket all the way to his skin, as is their habit. Why can he never keep some by? For extras, like boots for his wife, or clothes for his boy, or patches of thatch for the roof. Is that not why he is mixed up with this bloody godawful work for undesirable rogues? Scoundrels like Barehenger and Oakheart. *Really?* He shakes his head at his own horsecrap. *Not because you are a lazy fucker, George Hogtrough?*

When he left the inn on that dreadful night, he stumbled home. Not blind drunk, but getting there. At the gate, he found a gaggle of women. They scoffed him, mocked him.

'Where have you been, George Hogtrough? Out whoring and drinking, as usual?'

The words cut him with their truth, but he laughed it off.

'You left your wife at the hearth, but how is she, your beloved woman? Do you even know whether she still lives? Do you even care?'

He became angry. Who were these women to question him on his whereabouts? What right did they have to demand he explain himself to them? Such things are private, between a husband and his wife, and he is his own man, makes his own decisions.

However, in their eyes, they had every right to call him to task. The women of Woodfield will look out for their own, band together and protect each other, wash and clean and cook when needed. Lend clothes, send round a pot of stew, a loaf of bread, a basket of vegetables, if they have any to spare. They have few rights, and this one they cherish.

He was so drunk he did not even question why they were gathered at his gate, and as he staggered up to the door, their admonishments washed him dirty like an oily rag. He went inside and walked into a cold hush.

Molly was by the fire, cradling a tiny infant.

It could not be! It was too soon, still weeks to go.

Something was not right, could not possibly be right.

He found himself almost sober and bent closer to take look at the tiny bundle. Even in the orange fire-glow he could see the perfect little face was pale blue.

Molly looked up, her face wet with tears, her eyes clouded with pain. The blood drained out of him and he could find no words of comfort. He backed away to the door, his throat tight, his head a mess.

This was his fault.

God's punishment, for stealing a moment in heaven while his wife was going through hell.

He panicked, rushed out of the cottage, pushed past the sneering women, ran and ran. When he finally stopped, he found himself at the King Oak, where they had first lain, where he had given Molly the babe who never lived, the child for whom they had married. He lay curled up in the King Oak's damp, mossy roots, trying to make sense of his nature. His infidelity, his reckless gambling and the ease at which his winnings had trickled through his fingers without a thought for the needs of his family. What kind of dreadful husband was he? Unable, unwilling, to provide, to give anything to the welfare of his wife and child. So easily distracted from the responsibilities of married life by a feckless friend, a skinful of ale, a game of cards and a beautiful young girl. A pathetic father he would make if he was ever given another chance. He was not worthy.

And then a vision of his brother's girl, Lizzie, flitted across the moonlit glade. She had come to this very same place to wrestle her own conscience, to weigh up her choices after another drunken idiot had spoiled her future.

She climbed up the King Oak, and for her, there was only one way down.

George's eyes settled on the branch above him, and swore he could hear the thick rope, squeaking as it rubbed against the King Oak's bark, swinging the girl's dead weight back and forth, until his brother Ned stumbled on the gruesome scene.

'No!' He screamed to the night sky. 'No!'

I ain't like that, that ain't me! To treat a woman so bad.

Afterwards, he became more serious, vowed he would change. Molly noticed, but he could not explain, for she must never know about the blacksmith's daughter. And look where he is now, dealing with criminals and contraband. *Out of the bleeding pot and into the boilin' kettle.* The refashioning of his self is not yet complete. In fact, he wonders if it ever began.

'George! Georgie, mate,' someone is calling. He spins round, sees Hal laughing. 'Where were you? Away with the ghosts or sommat?'

'Aye, like as I was. Let's get away from this place, we shall be spending enough time here soon enough.'

Hal flies the broom back to the barn, and then stops. 'Hark, you hear someone comin'?'

'Fuck off, Hal, don't play that game with me again,' George says.

'No, mate, I ain't playin' now. Listen,' and Hal is serious.

They stand still. There is a rustle, a swish and shuffle of dry leaves on the forest floor.

'Shit! Who the hell be that?' George spins around and sees, not the red coats of the soldiers he expects, but emerging from the trees and into the clearing comes his sister.

'Annie!' he calls. 'What the…?'

'George! Molly needs you, her increasement, 'tas begun,' Annie cries.

'Oh Lord! When?' George moves towards the path, back to the main forest byways.

'No time to explain now, Brother! Go! Quick! She be home and the midwife should be with her by now,' and Annie urges him on, pushes him out of the clearing.

George runs, darting along the narrow track, now thankfully clear of creeping obstacles. His thoughts for a moment only on being at home with his wife.

Until another thought crashes into his head.

An uneasiness. Something that should not be.

He slows his pace to a stop.

'What the…? How the hell…?' he asks himself aloud, questions unfinished, his voice low, growling and incredulous. How did his sister know where to find him? He could have been anywhere on The Common, or anywhere else come to think of it. He turns around and glares back into the bright clearing, but there is no sign of Hal or Annie. George burns with a need to quiz his sister and begins to retrace his steps towards the barn. He takes two or three paces, then remembers Molly.

How quickly he can become led away from her and her plight! He shakes his head in disbelief at his foolishness, turns once again towards the path home.

Annie has some explaining to do, alright, but his sister can wait. Molly comes first.

Rye Cottage

Mid-Morning

The scene which greets George as he bursts through the door of Rye Cottage is one of calm and order. He envisaged a terrible beast before him, the shape of Molly's fears, but it is not so. His wife is seated some distance from the fire. Someone has built it up well, for it is roaring strong and not smoking for once, two or three good logs on top of a bed of charcoal. Molly is perched anxiously on a well-used birthing chair, which the midwife carries around with her from birth to birth. Eleanor Knocker's daughter, Nell, is helping her. A small girl of about sixteen, she is busy folding cloths at the table. Eliza's chair has been pushed back against her cot, and Little Joe is dozing on her knee in the warm, sunny room, a rare occurrence, indeed. Their oak table has been shoved up against the cracks of the back wall, carving a space in the room for creation itself to fill. The bench is laid out with the tools of Eleanor's trade: cloths, two bowls, a pair of scissors, needle and thread, a razor, soap and a dish of butter.

'Ah, Mister Hogtrough, at last,' Eleanor says. She is a round, rosy, full woman with bright eyes and a good heart.

'Mistress Knocker, thank God you's here,' George says, and he appears nervous. This is not his territory. He must be near, *this time,* but not too close. This space is for the women.

'I come gladly, 'tis me work, after all. Now, I shall leave you here for a moment with your wife, while I go fetch a little water. Her increasement has begun, but it will likely be a while yet before the births, so don't you worry yourself if she gets a pain or two. Nell, come along now,' she says and shuffles off to the yard with her daughter.

'Georgie!' Molly calls out weakly as he kneels at her side. She is pale and sweating, and he can see that she is afraid, poised as she is, on the very edge of her fear.

'Molly, I be here now,' he says, stroking her clammy forehead. And so he is, this time. But Molly's angst is catching. *Jesus, she don't look good.* Molly lets out a cry as a contraction pulls her apart, and she begins to pant. *Stay strong, man,* and he says a silent prayer, holds her hand.

When the wave subsides, he moves away. He can smell gin on her breath and glances up at the mantle. The flask is gone. *Don't say she drunk the lot! Stupid mare!* Or is it he who is stupid for procuring it? *Damn!* Whatever he does is wrong.

'Molly, you be alright now, love. You's in good hands with Mistress Knocker, see?' Calming words do not come easy, but he knows Molly's belief is strong, so he adds, 'in God's hands, too.'

'I has to tell you sommat,' she blubbers. 'I ain't alright. Nothin's alright. I fell, see? I went lookin' for Joe. He ran off, and I had not a thing t'eat, and I went down by the Rye,' and Molly's eyes become bloodshot as hot tears spring from the corners and begin to flow once again down her pale cheeks. 'What if I's hurt 'em, the babes, when I fell? I shall never forgive meself.'

Another contraction is already building in her muscles. Her sobs give way to screams and she clings onto her husband's arm tighter than before.

He should not be mad at her, tells himself to direct his anger at his own idiocy for buying the gin as much as hers for drinking it.

As the pain passes, he whispers, 'Ain't no point thinkin' like that, Wife. Like as there's nothing wrong with them babes.' He cradles her head in his hands, kisses her forehead and his warmth brings a little calm to her turbulent soul. It is little wonder she looks pale. *A whole flask of gin on top of an empty belly? What was she thinking?* 'But you got back home, alright, see? So no harm done.'

'Blessèd be! But t'was your brother Jesse what brought me back, carried me all the way, he did.'

George goes cold and an image of Lizzie flits across the space before him, shaking her head. *No! No!*

'Little Joe went to the farm, see? Jesse were bringing him back,' Molly continues, 'and then he found me lyin' there, out cold on the ground. Thank the Lord he come when he did.'

For a brief moment, George is grateful that his brother exists.

However, Eliza, who has been silent till now, pipes up from the corner. 'Same as he brought her back not two noights ago.

Carried that stinky laundry, too. That man be where you ain't, George Hawgtrough, and that ain't a place he should be.'

He looks over at the old woman, and as Eliza glares at him it is Jesse he sees before him now, as clear as day.

His brother, standing under the King Oak. Lizzie, swinging from the branch above him.

No, Jesse should never be alone with me wife. God forbid.

Molly holds her breath, for she expects a barrage of ire and does not have the strength to respond or deal with her husband's dark moods. Her head is still spinning with gin, her fear immense, and her belly about to burst forth its contents.

Black clouds have shrouded his eyes, he is about to Skylark, and whoops! There he goes. Molly lets out a gasp as George's cold blood now runs hot with rage and he wishes Jesse had never been born, that Ned had finished the job he started.

He begins to piece together the last days. *Two nights back?* He was at the inn with Hal. *Damn! Should not have let her haul that laundry home alone.* It was wrong, but he had no choice, for they had that bloody business to arrange, and he could not let her hear or he would likely be hanging at the end of a noose, like Lizzie, for the gin gives his wife a mighty loose tongue. But was it not he himself, half-cut after a slow day at ale, who cajoled her into walking to the village, who promised to carry the laundry home and said he would soon catch her up? Gin might give Molly a loose tongue, but the very same poison leaves him with little resolve.

And now something else is niggling him. His dream, of Molly fucking another man. *Jesse?* His blood cools again, for he does not trust his brother as far as he could punch him. And then, all of a sudden, click! His mind twists away from the image of Molly up against the King Oak and locks onto Annie, how she found him so quickly at the clearing, as if she knew exactly where he would be. Someone must have told her of their work. That someone must be Hal, for who else knows?

And then it all makes sense.

He groans. *Not her, Hal, not our Annie.* Now it is clear why Hal was reluctant to name his maid, for George would never sanction a union between them. He knows too much of Hal's life, and he is sure Annie knows nothing. For what woman would take a man-whore for a husband? He groans again. *Were it them in the hay at the barn? Lord God no!*

He is still looking at Molly while these thoughts are buzzing around his head like angry, swarming wasps. His fists tighten and clench up, and Molly looks up at him with a fear a wife should never have in her eyes when she sees her husband looking at her.

He comes back to the here and now, and is shocked to see such dread in her eyes and realises that she believes his anger directed at her.

'Ah, sorry my love, sorry. Ain't you Moll, it ain't you,' he says, as he looks at her pale face, full of terror. He unclenches his fist, bends down and kisses her, strokes her hair, and feels her relax a little under him, as Eleanor and Nell return with pails of water. Molly is sobbing again, and he needs to get out. Away from the heat, away from his wife's trepidation. He needs to calm down.

He looks to Eleanor Knocker for a way out. She sees his discomfort and obliges.

'Mister Hogtrough, there are some things I needs you to take care of. First, close all the windows here and shutter them, and keep them doors closed. Find me some candles, too, the best you can. We shall need more water, hot and cold. If you would be good enough to fetch it from the well, for if it comes from the brook it may not be so clean. You can cook it up outside, can you not? I've knocked on the doors up at Woodfield, if you don't mind, so your neighbours will be along to help where they can. And take your son away, for this ain't no place for him. Mistress Greenfield is not able to watch him, and I shall need her help with herbs and such for your wife. And do stay nearby, Mister Hogtrough.'

Eleanor has taken charge and for once George is content to obey a woman's orders. When the windows have been shuttered, so no unwanted spirits can oversee Molly's plight, he leaves the house with Little Joe, and makes for the nearest well.

He is not used to spending time alone with his son, the boy is far too young yet to sit with him at the card table, or join him for a flagon of cider, to be his batsman or bowler. These are his joys, and God willing, the boy will live long enough that they can do these things together. He looks down at Little Joe, and feels the responsibilities piling up like a house of cards. The pressure of it all bends him, and his feet long to carry him away, past the Oxmoor Pond, up Woodfield Lane, all the way to The Leg, to the tankard which awaits him there. To this afternoon's game of cricket.

But this is no time to be weak, and besides, he will likely find Hal there, and at the moment, he could kill him. No, he has wife and child to care for and he pulls himself up.

'Right, little chap, let's go get water then, for your Mama,' he says.

Little Joe looks up at him, his brown eyes wide and inquisitive. 'Why?'

'Mistress Knocker needs it, that's why.'

'Why?'

'To keep Mama clean.'

'Why?'

'She be havin' a baby, or two p'raps. A brother or a sister for you, or maybe two brothers, or two sisters, or maybe one of each,' he says, aware that he cannot remember telling the boy why his mother has become so swollen. Has she explained it to him? He has no idea.

'Ano'ver Lickle Joe?'

'God help us, boy. No. Definitely not another you. One is enough, do you not think, eh? One is plenty. No. P'raps an Edward. Or a Sally.'

'A Nedward? Me wanna Nedward,' comes the reply. 'How old be Nedward?'

And so the questions keep coming.

It is going to be a long day. George can feel his patience, little that he has, already stretched. He needs someone to watch the boy. Little Joe needs to be out of the way till Molly is out of danger, if she ever escapes it, that is, and her fear is catching. He cannot forget her pale, cold face either, the dread in her eyes as she looked up at him. Will that be the last look she ever gives him? He scoops Joe up into his arms as a few words slip nervously from between his lips. 'God help her, please God, help me wife and babes.'

As they arrive at the well, George spies a horse plodding its way towards them, pulling a heavy cart. Farmer Caen is accompanied by a female figure, clothed in a darkness which even the sunlight cannot brighten. She is sitting next to the farmer, chatting away, her words carried easily to George on the gentle breeze. They get few visitors this far from the village, and he wonders who it can be.

Then he remembers. 'Lord, 'tis Cousin Mathilda. Completely forgot, what with all the other crap,' he says to Little Joe, who looks at him and grins.

'What crap?' his son asks.

George laughs. It will take a lifetime to give the boy an answer to that. 'Never you mind. But look here, see? Might just be our answer, little man, if we's lucky,' and he points at the cart and gives Joe a squeeze.

'Why?'

'You'll see, soon enough,' and George drops Joe to the ground, gripping his hand to prevent any sudden escape.

As the cart draws up, Jim Caen greets him, coldly. 'George,' he says and tips his hat.

George nods in polite response. Their harsh words a few weeks back have left a gaping chasm between the two men, and George will likely never be forgiven for refusing to do work he had at first agreed to take on. George turns to the black shadow sitting next to him, 'Good morning, Cousin.'

'Cousin? Oh! Is that you, Mister Hogtrough?' and Mathilda pers out from under her hat. 'Indeed, I see it is. A very good morning to you, too.'

'I sees you's found our visitor, Mister Caen. Thank you kindly for bringing the lady.'

Jim huffs and glares at George. He is prevented from saying

so by her presence, but Mathilda has been talking nonstop since she got on the cart. The farmer passed her at Barnett Farm, a mile and a half back along the track, and is more than happy that he can now offload her, for every sentence she utters makes him feel more miserable. She has complained about every ailment and wrong in the world and, most of all, her sorrowful life. A cloud of darkness is growing around the cart as she speaks and Jim is in a hurry to leave it behind. She looks uncomfortably hot with all her heavy, black clothes, and her hat sports an enormous brim and lacy veil.

She looks like the bride at the devil's wedding.

Jim is squashed over to the edge of his seat, slowly inching away, in a futile effort to escape the tendrils of ribbon blowing in the breeze, which brush his face like cobwebs.

George stifles a smile at Farmer Caen's obvious discomfort. 'Was your journey well, Cousin?' he asks.

'No, it was not. Not at all. I can tell you, Mister Hogtrough, that I am so very grateful to have arrived with everything intact,' Mathilda says. 'There were several places along the road from Mickleham, where Mister Potter's cart got stuck and I had to alight in order for his men to free it. Alas, he would only take me to Letherhed, and from thence, the only way forward was on foot. Thank goodness your kindly neighbour rescued me, otherwise I would likely already be extinguished at the side of the road from exhaustion. And Mister Can's cart is abominably uncomfortable, more so even than Mister Potter's.'

'Caen, mistress, the name is Caen,' and Jim Caen rolls his eyes. 'And indeed, ma'am, you are free to leave any time you choose. George, help the lady down, would you?'

George imagines Mathilda as a pile of black, smouldering ashes lying by the roadside and stifles a chuckle. 'Well now, Moll be at this very moment with the midwife, and so I hope 'twill not be long afore her ordeal is over. I'd say come to the cottage, but the room be so small, 'tis pretty full of help already, I's sure it will be too crowded for your comfort,' he lies.

There is room for one or two more at Rye Cottage, perhaps not that enormous hat, but at least he has saved Molly from her cousin's company, for the moment. And then he remembers that he has not yet warned Molly of Mathilda's offer to help, unaware that Jesse has already broken the news.

'We does need someone to care for young Joe here, that truly would be a weight off me mind,' he says.

Jim interrupts. 'Whilst I am sure you have much to arrange between yourselves, I, myself, do have work to be getting on with. George, kindly unload Madam's bags so I can get moving.'

The farmer is normally all hearts and flowers where women are concerned. She must have done a grand job of annoying him during the short trip.

'But where am I to sleep, Cousin?' Mathilda asks. 'I believe your brother mentioned sharing with your sister, and I should like to be shown straight to my room and settle my belongings, before taking charge of the boy. I am more than happy to take him, of course, just a little later this afternoon, when I am recovered from the journey. Such an ordeal it was and I have the headache coming.' She holds a limp, black-gloved hand up against her temples.

George is dismayed, but from what Molly has told him of Mathilda, he is not surprised. Jim sighs as he realises Mathilda will not be departing just yet.

'Right you are then,' George says, and smiles at Jim, who shoots him a sarcastic grimace. 'You might 'ave to wait for sister Annie. I know not if she be at home, but make yourself comfortable,' George adds, and this is almost true, because he is quite sure she will still be out with Hal, if his suspicions are right. The thought of them lying together in the hay and his anger at their liaison bubbles up again. He checks himself. *Later*.

Then he remembers William. He should perhaps warn her of the danger to be found inside Rose Cottage. 'Oh! But do avoid our Father, who art in bed. Disturb 'im not at any cost or you'll feel his wrath upon you, and more.'

George watches Mathilda's puzzled face, and he guesses she had not reckoned on sharing the house with a violent, wicked and crooked man. She will find out soon enough what the wretch William Hogtrough is about and for once he wishes he were a fly on Jesse's wall. He would like to see how she handles the old man.

'I really must fetch water for the midwife, and I's been gone long enough already. Good day to you both,' George says, and turns away before Mathilda can question him about William.

Joe does not respond to gentle tugs and has to be dragged towards the well. The boy is far more interested in Mathilda than are either Jim or his father, and cannot take his eyes off the mysterious and exotic black cloud, all lace and frills and ribbons, which has somehow found its way to their quiet corner of The Common.

ROSE COTTAGE

MID-MORNING

Jim Caen's cart rumbles down the stony lane and clatters over the wooden bridge. Mathilda jabbers on and on, about something and nothing. Jim shuts his ears. He's had a bellyful of her complaints, and his is a spacious one at that. They roll jerkily into the farmyard and as soon as the horse comes to a halt, Jim jumps down, amazingly quickly for a man of his weight and shape. He grabs her two enormous leather bags and dumps the heavy weights on the ground with a thud as Mathilda climbs down awkwardly, then he points to the cottage where she will be staying.

'Good day to you, ma'am,' he says, and makes a hasty retreat.

Mathilda stands in front of the tied farm cottage and looks over the modest building. It has seen better days. The blackened window frames are rotting and a few tiles are missing from its mossy roof. She had hoped for something more grand, but remembers Jesse Hogtrough from market yesterday, standing before her in worn, dusty clothes and a battered tricorn hat. A sure sign that his living was not going to be much. Glancing over at the elegant farmhouse she sees it is much more to her style. Three floors, tall windows, two huge chimney stacks and a red-tiled roof. There is potential there. She cannot recall if the farmer is married, whether he mentioned a wife on the journey. In any case, this small hovel, Rose Cottage, will have to do. For now.

Mathilda leaves her bags where Jim Caen dropped them, and thanks God it was not in one of the piles of horse dung dotted here and there. *Where is the farmhand responsible for this disgraceful mess?*

She turns back to the door of the Hogtroughs' cottage, lifts her hand, intending to rap the door loudly, and then remembers the old man in bed. Instead, she knocks softly.

No response.

She slides up the heavy iron latch and puts her ear to the crack. Just a few crackles and hisses from the fire, so she steps over the threshold and into an airless, dull space. Her dark cloud of billowing lace only adds to the gloom, and as she looks around the sparsely furnished room there appears to be no sign of life.

She scans, inspects, takes everything in.

The fire is burning low in the hearth at the other end of the room. If no one feeds it, it will soon be out. *Where on earth is the maid?* The tiled floor looks clean and recently swept, the table, also spotless, its only ornament a tall green jug with long stems of fresh, heavy-scented meadowsweet emerging from its throat. The flowers fill their corner of the room with the smell of summer, but there is a distinct stench of tallow hovering in the heavy air. *Oh dear, no beeswax. Pity.* There is one wide, leaded window beside her. At the front of the cottage on the opposite wall are two smaller ones, with a few nick-nacks perched on each of their sills – a shell, a broken ceramic pot, some candle stubs. The windows are closed, and a clambering pink rose has been left to grow wild outside, blocking much of the light. *That will have to be cut back,* she thinks.

A two-seater high-backed wooden chair faces the fireplace, its panelled back to Mathilda. A spinning wheel is pushed into one corner, and to her right an enormous dresser, its shelves sparsely furnished with green and white crockery. Herbs hang from the beams, together with pots, pans, and a few other kitchen implements. More stubby candles are lined up like pretty maids on the heavy oak mantelpiece, together with a jar containing rushlights – their holder next to it – and some thin, wooden spills. Mathilda sighs. It really is very much less than she had wished for. Even though she would have liked Jesse to be the farmer himself, it is clear he is a mere labourer, working fields and tending livestock. There is nothing of value here, except perhaps a bed, a warm hearth and a little food.

Mathilda pushes the door closed behind her and the ancient iron hinges let out a squeal. She steps off her pattens and as she walks slowly towards the fireplace, the hem of her skirt, now three inches lower, swish-swishes on the tiles. Her bright, curious eyes peer into all the corners. When she is half way across the room, she stops. An obnoxious smell hits her and she wrinkles up her nose in disgust. No amount of summer scented flowers could mask it, for it is all stale ale and vinegar, body odour, piss, musty old boots and sweaty feet.

At the side of the hearth she spies a kettle hanging from the pot crane. *Maybe there is tea. I wonder where the servant is,* she asks herself again and begins to unpin her enormous hat as she continues towards the kettle.

Suddenly, she catches a movement out of the corner of her eye and freezes. A deep animal snarl arises from the wooden seat and only now does she realise it is not at all empty, but indeed quite fully occupied.

The growl erupts into the angry voice of William Hogtrough.

'Well! Sonovabitch! Who the bleedin' hell are YOU?' he shouts, and cracks his stick down hard on the hearthstone. As it swoops through the stale air, the breeze it creates hits Mathilda's pale, shocked face.

She screams and steps backwards, nearly trips over her voluminous petticoats. She had not noticed the man at all! He who should be in bed is in fact hunched by the fire, completely hidden from her view by the back of his wide seat. As he leans further forward she can see the features of his gnarled and weathered face, shining red in fire glow, truly a demon if ever she saw one.

'Well, Mistress, what in bloody damnation are you doin', eh? Comin' into me home all sneaky and uninvited, like, and dressed up like the Angel o' Death an' all!'

His eyes are ablaze and he is brandishing his stick like a spear, poking and stabbing it towards Mathilda. She backs away just in time and begins to stammer an explanation, but for once, she is lost for words. It is clear this disgusting man is the source of the unearthly smell, for although his breath is heavy and sweet with alcohol, so strong she can smell it from where she stands, there is a noisome cloud surrounding him. His grey hair is matted and unkempt, his skin grimy, filthy. Lord only knows when it last saw soap.

'Sir, oh sir, I do apologise. If I had only known you were seated there,' she begins, but he does not let her continue.

'Well now you does, you may as well make yerself useful,' he growls. 'Fetch me a flagon o' cider, and quick, like. That wench of a daughter has it hidden somewhere, so make haste and find it afore I…'

But before his threat can be uttered, the old man begins coughing, a deep and rattling hack. It takes him a few moments to contain it. Mathilda watches in silence. He draws the phlegm from his throat and spits it into the fire. It hits the heat with a crack and a fizz. He sees her face looking aghast, and gives her a brown-stained toothy grin.

'Cider, woman! Where's me cider?' and William stamps his stick on the ground as he slurs the words out, and then laughs, which triggers another round of coughing, hawking, spitting.

This is certainly not what she had envisioned at all. Mathilda looks around, wonders where on earth she will find the secret stash to appease the disgusting man.

As she is contemplating this, the door opens and she is saved by the arrival of Annie, who bursts through, bringing a rush of fresh air with her. 'Mistress Richardson! Here already! We was e'specting you a little later. I's Annie, George's sister,' she says introducing herself. 'But you remember, do you not? Me brother's wedding. We met there I do believe.'

She grasps Mathilda's cold hands and gives her a warm, beaming smile.

'Annie Hogtrough! I do recall your face, yes. It must be five years since we met at my cousin's wedding. But you must call me Mathilda, please.'

'Aye, it must be that at least. How were your journey, Mathilda? I trust it went well.'

'Thank you for asking, dear. The journey was truly awful, but I will not bore you with it now.'

Mathilda's voice is shaking and her eyes are wide. Annie correctly assumes that an encounter with Father William is the cause of Mathilda's unnerve. 'I's so sorry I weren't here to greet you,' says Annie, and then turns to William, who is grinning from ear to ear. 'I see you's met Father.'

This is indeed the first time Mathilda and William have encountered one another, for William had been too drunk to attend his son's wedding, preferring instead to celebrate their marriage at The Leg of Mutton and Cauliflower, much to George and Molly's relief.

'We 'ave not yet been introduced proper like, daughter de-aar. Tell me, who is this charming lady what 'as stepped over our most modest threshold?' William's demeanour is now greatly changed and he is being as polite as ever he could be.

However, Annie knows too well what a trickster he is. Moreover, his outburst and call for cider reached her ears as she came across the yard. Mathilda, therefore, has already seen his ugly side and Annie feels guilty for not having softened their guest's first experience of William's beastly and duplicitous character. She continues her introduction and then says, 'Father, I did tell you this morning that Mistress Richardson is kindly come to aid Molly, and most welcome she is too.'

'Well, must'a forgot, di'n't I? Were thinkin' she was come to take me off downstairs, since she appeared so darkly, like. Well, anyways, pleased t'meet ye, Madam, I be sure,' William says. 'Ain't gonna get up, though. Bones ain't right, see?'

Mathilda does not see, for she has not yet witnessed the strange, contorted angle to which William's body has twisted over the last ten years or so.

'Mister Hogtrough, pleased to make your acquaintance,' Mathilda replies, a little nervously. She starts to extend her hand, but thinks better of it and gives him a small bob curtsey instead, to which he raises a wild eyebrow.

'No need to curtsey, Madam, for this ain't no bleedin' manor,' he chuckles, and he turns his head away, mumbles under his breath, 'Who the 'ell she think she is? Soon put that right.'

'Excuse me, did you say something, Mister Hogtrough?' Mathilda enquires, having caught only his whispers.

'Just saying nothin', 'tis all,' he replies, grinning, again exposing his disgusting teeth.

'I believe we got off to a very bad start. I hope we can put it behind us and begin afresh.'

William snorts. 'I s'pose we can alright. But that don't es'plain why YOU, Mistress Richardson, is come into my home all stealth, like a cat what's looking to steal me butter,' he stabs a finger at her, leans back in his seat and rests a hand on the top of his knotted walking stick, eyeing Mathilda suspiciously.

Annie is embarrassed. 'Father, please. Mistress Richardson will be no trouble to you at all,' she says and hopes rather that William will be no trouble to the widow.

And William is indeed thinking up mischief. 'Well now, what

if I wants trouble, daughter, de-ar?' he says and looks at Mathilda with a strange smile upon his face. 'If yer find me daughter's bed ain't big enough, there be room enough in…'

'Father! Kindly keep your thoughts pure,' Annie wants to tell him to hold his disgraceful tongue, but that would be a step too far. What to do? She wants Mathilda to believe that theirs is a good and godly home, which is far from the truth all the while their father inhabits it, but also to keep William from sending the woman running before she has been of any use to Molly at all. She turns to Mathilda with a mind to extract her from the situation, which, judging by her father's mood, looks like it could turn filthy dangerous at any moment.

Mathilda, meanwhile, although initially a little shocked, is a resourceful woman, and has already calculated how she can turn the situation to her advantage. She has quietly conjured up a plan even before Annie speaks.

'Come, Mathilda, let us fetch your bags from the yard and I shall show you to me room. I hope you will find it comfortable,' Annie says, and goes to fetch the brown leather cases from outside, assuming Mathilda will follow. She does not, and Annie is left to lug in the heavy beasts by herself.

At the top of the stairs there is a small landing. William Hogtrough sleeps, eats and mostly lives – apart from the rare occasions when his unwelcome and unholy presence haunts them downstairs – in the room to the left, which runs from front to back of the cottage, windows to east and west. To the right, Jesse and Henry's room is almost a mirror of Williams but slightly larger and contains the warm chimney breast. The third and smallest room, between the other two, is Annie's. It looks out onto the farmyard and catches the afternoon sun. A square room, it is furnished with a bed, barely big enough for two, pushed up into the corner away from the draughty window. A chest of drawers with a wash bowl and jug set out on it is next to the window. Two small shelves are attached to the wall and lined with various knick-knacks – a hag stone, a pine cone, a thimble – together with a brush and comb, and two or three bottles of homemade scent. There are heavy curtains at the tiny window but no bed hangings and no rug. More simple ornaments adorn the narrow windowsill, and a chair with an embroidered cushion is at the end of the bed. It is cosy and clean, but there is hardly any room for Mathilda's bags, let alone her hat.

Annie drops her voice, 'Mathilda, I must apologise for Father. He do get the drink in him sometimes and there just ain't no knowing what he'll say. I beg of you, do not be alarmed by him, his bark is worse than his bite now, like, and he do spend most of his time in bed lately, so he should not trouble you any. 'Tis terrible difficult for him to get up and down them stairs, see? But do steer clear of that stick.'

Mathilda is not particularly comforted by Annie's words, but there is little she can do or say. She is here now, so she will have to find a way to deal with him. She smiles weakly at Annie and looks around at the room as she removes her gloves.

'If you do not mind, Cousin, I should like to rest after my awful journey, it was terribly hot even at such an early hour, and dusty, too. My throat is so dry,' Mathilda's pale white hand comes up and touches her throat. Her eyes close for a second in a dramatic pose.

'Oh! Dear heart, I clean forgot to offer you sommat. I'll fetch tea, and some hot water so you can freshen yourself afore you go to Mistress Greenfield's. Molly's labour began this morn' and I be sure they'll be needing an extra pair o' hands, 'specially with Little Joe.'

Mathilda lets Annie leave the room none the wiser that she has already been informed of Molly's situation, and listens as she steps lightly down the steep stairs. Then, she finishes unpinning her hat.

There is not much in the room, but by the time Annie returns, Mathilda has silently fingered and inspected everything, and every nook and cranny of her new sleeping quarters has been explored.

RYE COTTAGE

LATE MORNING

It does not take Molly long to deliver her twins to the world. Having already been through the ordeal of labour twice before, her body knows exactly what to do. The muscles remember their arduous work and the process is mercifully quick, in part due to the babies being particularly small.

First comes a girl.

Eleanor Knocker wraps the infant in a linen cloth and passes the bundle to Molly, whose pallid, clammy face brightens a little when the baby suddenly screams for air. A healthy scream, and Molly lets out an excited gasp, laughs with joy for her living child. Prayers answered. One, at least.

Outside in the yard, George hears the cry. His heart leaps

out of his chest and comes to rest beside Molly's, but he makes no move to return to his wife's side, for he knows her work is not yet over.

Molly barely notices when a boy is delivered a few minutes later. A tiny thing, hardly bigger than Eleanor's busy hands, which hold him gently while Nell passes a cloth under his miniature form. Her joy turns to despair as Eleanor rests him against her breast. He is so tiny against the girl. She looks at the midwife with dismay.

'He be too weeny,' she cries.

Too small for the harsh world she inhabits, for the deathly cold of winter and the unearthly sicknesses which pass regularly from door to door.

'Don't you be thinkin' like that my dear or you'll have he gone afore he's had a proper chance. Now, he may be small, but perfectly formed is all he needs to be. So you just carry on like he's perfect and you sees what you can do. God willing he'll grow strong and live long. Do not give up, Molly.'

But Eleanor herself is not so sure the tiny boy will make it, and getting him to breathe is only the first hurdle. How his tiny lips will manage to grasp his mother's teat to feed is another matter. She instructs Molly to blow softly on the infant's face, but still there is no sign of life. Molly's hands are full holding both the infants, and her eyes so wet with tears she can hardly see. Nell steps forward and begins rubbing the babe gently, first his arms and legs, then she strokes his tiny back as Molly clasps him to her chest.

'Blow again, Molly, breathe your life into him,' Eleanor says. 'Pray he will come to us.'

Eliza whispers in the corner, *God have mercy on mother and choild, let your loight fill the babe with the gift of loife and bless he with a chance here on earth. Amen.*

The baby suddenly opens his eyes, looks straight up into Molly's. Her face lights up as the boy gasps for air. No cry comes, only a silent look of wonder at the first glimpse of his mother's face.

The whole room breathes with him, and Eliza crosses herself with thanks.

'Molly, you ain't finished, dear heart. The after burthen must come afore you can rest. Then we shall get them babes cleaned up.'

It is almost midday by the time Eleanor Knocker has finished and is as sure as she can be that Molly's body is free of the remnants of birthing. If any remain they will certainly cause her great harm, and the fate she fears will surely follow. A cruel twist that a mother's gift of life so often leads to her demise.

The midwife expertly cuts and ties the infants' life-giving cords at just the right time for each baby. 'Not too quick after, but not too long either, that they may have blood enough to give them a good start, see?' she tells Molly. Her knowledge is a blessing and Molly's heart overflows with admiration and thanks. She is still reeling after the morning's events, how everything rushed upon her so quickly. However, now she has survived the ordeal, fear and excitement abate, and the gin makes a comeback. Her stomach is grotty, drained, empty and her head is starting to spin again.

'I e'spect you's hungry Mistress Hogtrough. I shall fetch some bone broth, what your neighbours made for you,' Nell says, looking at her sickly pallor.

Yes, and yet no, Molly thinks, but she knows she must try to eat and at that moment, the waft of something cooking comes to her. Suddenly, she could eat a horse.

Two Woodfield women, Cat Longhurst and Hetty Archer, worked all morning in the yard. They washed out Eliza's soiled bedding, hung it over bushes to dry, watched over Little Joe, made a pot of bone and vegetable stew, and have now disappeared to prepare dinner for their own families, promising to return when they can.

Now they are no longer keeping their motherly eyes on him, Little Joe is barricaded like a wild animal in the old pigsty. George cannot trust the boy to stay put, and cannot bear the worry of the child running off or getting too near the open fire, contained as it is inside its low-walled circle of large stones. The tot occupied himself for a while, piling up a tower of flat pebbles gathered from the brook then knocking them down. When he got bored with that, he lifted a loose brick in the corner of his den, and to his great delight discovered a nest of woodlice. He prodded the miniature armadillos with a twig, watched them roll up into tiny grey cannonballs, flicked them around the den with his fingers. Now the child is standing at the gate, calling for his mother. On tiptoes, he can only just see over the top, but his father will not set him free until the women are back. 'Soon, son,' he says, and under his breath, 'God willing.'

But still he has only heard the cry of one babe.

He guards the pot of broth like a dragon would its precious eggs, turning the stew from time to time with a long wooden spoon, for it must not burn. It has given him something to do, taken his mind off Molly's plight, the work for Barehenger. *Annie and Hal.* He growls under his breath at the thought of the two of them together, still in the hay at the derelict barn, or anywhere else for that matter, and tries to dispel the unsettling image from his mind by bringing himself back to the task at hand.

The birds are hushed now, and leaves have stopped their rustling. A calm has descended on the land in readiness for the coming storm. George can smell rain in the air, it will not be long now. It seems Eliza was right about storms bringing babies, perhaps he should lend an ear to the old bat's wisdom more often.

And still only one babe has cried out. God forbid they lose another.

At last, he hears the latch on the door and turns to see Nell come out of the dim cottage and into the sunlight.

'All's well Mister Hogtrough, you can go in now. Take your wife some broth, please,' and Nell hands him a wooden bowl.

He releases the breath it seems he has been holding since he left Molly earlier that morning, and his whole body relaxes with an uneasy joy as he fills the bowl with steaming broth, unsure of what he will find inside.

The room is aglow. The babes, now washed and gently wrapped in soft cloths, are sleeping soundly, warm by the fire in a large wooden box which he had found some days before. Molly pleaded with him to find one big enough for two and he is glad he heeded her request. The bottom is lined with straw, and tiny sheets and covers, fashioned from bits of material given to Eliza by a seamstress from Ashted, traded for a lotion to heal a rash. A knitted blanket of coarse wool lies beside the box. A gift from Annie for Little Joe when he was born, now put to good use again.

As George enters the room, a slight draught zips across the floor and swirls around Eliza Greenfield's skinny ankles. She opens her sunken eyes. All the time Molly was in the midst of her labours on the birthing chair, the old woman was resting quietly in the corner, watching, feeling, helping her great-grandchildren to enter the world safely. Not able to see much in the darkened, shuttered room, scarcely lit by fire and weak candlelight, Eliza could make out only shapes and shadows. When the time came, she had disappeared into her cushions, let her head drop onto her chest, closed her eyes. They had thought her asleep, the others, but it was not so. She was working, side by side with the midwife and Molly, silently guiding the two new, innocent souls on their passage into the world. After both babes were safely delivered, and her prayer answered, she pulled out the afterbirth with long, unseen fingers, and Molly's body was left clean and wholesome.

Eliza can tell no one, trusts no one to keep her mysterious skills secret. Not even her own granddaughter with her loose, gin-addled tongue, lest the news escape and their little world be turned upside down, scarred with damnation which would surely be brought down upon her from the pulpit of St. Giles. This arcane knowledge will go with her to the grave, and she sighs sadly at the thought that there has been no opportunity in this lifetime to pass it on to anyone.

Time now, though, to leave the new parents be. Eliza gropes around for her tobacco pouch and finds it with its clay pipe mate on her little table. With some difficulty she hauls herself up, grabs her stick and hobbles towards the door.

'Bone broth, is there, Mistress Knocker?' she says, excitedly. 'Did Oi hear the girl say there be bone broth to be had? Fancy Oi could do with some of that.'

'There certainly is, Mistress Greenfield. Come, let me help you,' and Eleanor offers an arm.

After she has helped Eliza outside, Eleanor turns to George.

'Mister Hogtrough, your wife is well enough and everything has gone alright with the births, one of each you has. It was touch and go with your boy, and will be for a while, so small is he. But all in all was very clean indeed so there should be no childbed fever.'

'That's good news, indeed,' George murmurs, looking over at Molly who is staring blankly into the fire. 'Thank you most kindly, Mistress Knocker, for all you has done,' he continues. 'Please, you must let me have the bill for your work, like.'

'Oh, Mister Hogtrough, don't you worry none about that. The bill's settled already.'

George raises an eyebrow.

'Mistress Greenfield has offered to prepare some teas which help with pains and sooth a woman's troubles. I can sell them on. That will be enough to cover all my expenses,' Eleanor explains.

'Ah, I sees,' George nods, and for a brief moment he wonders why he is so harsh on the old woman, whether he has her wrong.

'But, now heed me, Mister Hogtrough. This was hard on your wife's body and her spirits, too. Making two infants, ain't for the faint hearted, and 'twill be harder still for a while to come. She must be lying in for a month at best.'

Eleanor looks over to Molly, who has now dropped to kneel on the hearth next to the box, gazing in wonder at the miracle of her sleeping newborns. She looks up and laughs, weakly.

'Rest, for a month? Oh, Mistress Knocker, that would be a real treat indeed! But I ain't got no time for that,' Molly shakes her head at the midwife's cuckoo-talk, the thought she can afford that luxury. She gets up and comes to the table, where hot food is waiting to fill her empty belly.

'Well, if there be no help nearby, I can lend you Nell for a week or so. But that's all I can spare her, and if she be needed for another birth, then I shall have to call her back.'

George remembers Mathilda. 'That be very kind of you, Mistress Knocker, but actually, we does have some help.' He would have been more than happy to accept the graceful, sweet Nell, but instead Molly's unearthly cousin is waiting in the wings, and he has not yet told his wife of her arrival. He puts a hand on her shoulder, to soften the news. 'Moll, yer cousin Tilly's here,' he says. To his surprise she has already been forewarned.

'Oh aye, I forgot. Jesse did tell me, but what help she'll be, I cannot say,' Molly says, between spoons of delicious broth.

George is stunned. Jesse, yet again where he himself should have been? He bites his tongue and feels his anger come to the boil, like the pot he has been watching all morning. He turns to Eleanor Knocker, and tries to sound calm.

'Well, I do believe my wife shall have her rest, Mistress Knocker,' and he looks over at Molly. Thank God the room is dark and she cannot see his face, for he does not want to spoil her joy, but damn that brother of his.

Bleedin' man, always sticking hisself where he shouldn't. First Lizzie, and now, bleedin' hell, not my wife, too!

Eleanor does not notice the change in his mood and continues cheerfully. 'Oh, that is good news, 'tis always better with family. Can she nurse?'

Molly laughs. 'No, she ain't had no child, not to my knowing, anyways,' she answers, cupping her fingers around the warm, smooth bowl. Then she stops. Those fears are beginning to stir again, another worry flits across her mind. *What if me milk ain't enough for two?* 'Lord help them,' she whispers, and looks over at the infants beside the hearth.

'Well, never mind. I be sure you'll do alright with just another pair of hands. But listen now, Molly, and you, too, Mister Hogtrough. There be one last thing and it be most important, see?' Eleanor says. 'No more gin, young lady. Not a drop, you hear me? It will do you no good. Now, I ain't no Methody and I's all for a bit o' brandy now and then to help with pains and problems and such, but I seen enough I tell you. That drink will lead you to ruin sooner or later. Lord only knows the women I seen up in London Town afore I come to Ashted,' Eleanor pauses, shaking her head and although George cannot clearly see her eyes in the dim light of the room, they have become moist with sadness at the memories of so many lost souls. 'I cannot tell you the horrors it brings.' She does not tell Molly she suspects small babies to be due to a mother's drinking. No point bringing any more guilt to the young woman's door, the church does enough of that. Anyway, she is not certain, it is just a hunch. And twins are always small, so perhaps it is not the cause in Molly's case, for the woman is not so big herself.

Molly turns away from the midwife, embarrassed and ashamed she was caught so drunk, and still not entirely sober.

'I will see to it that Molly don't have a drop more,' George says.

It is not clear whether George can hold to this promise, just as so many others which easily pass his lips are soon forgotten.

'Right, well do your best. And if you could get that birthing chair scrubbed with soap and hot water Mister Hogtrough, and bring it to me as soon as you can, I would be most grateful. Nell will stay with your boy for a while, give you a little quiet time here. I shall see meself out.'

When she has left, George looks up at the mantelpiece, to where the flask should be sitting. 'Moll, that gin was to last a week and you drank the lot. T'ain't no surprise you had a fall.'

Molly looks at him, her eyes filling up with hot tears. *Can't he just be pleased we has two living babes, and I live still?* He was right though, it was a foolish thing. 'I di'n't mean to drink it all,' she cries, 'I were just so scared. I di'n't think I'd live to see another day, truly I did not.'

She sits with her face to the hot fire, and all the angst and tension she has been holding, now comes out in waves of heaving sobs. She tries to release it all as quietly as possible, not wanting to alert anyone outside who might hear, or to wake the babes.

George holds her tight, strokes her hair, feels her anguish. This is not the time to berate her. 'Molly, love. Little darlin' Moll. 'Tis all done now, you's safe and so's the babes,' he whispers and looks down at the box where his two infants are sleeping, and shivers at what might have been.

Suddenly, she pulls away. She sits up and faces him square on, uncommonly angry. 'It ain't done, though, is it Husband? 'Tis only just begun,' she hisses through her tears. She wants to scream her fears at him, to shake him with reality, but does not want to disturb her peaceful infants. 'There be so much in life what ain't never finished. We has two more mouths and the burden for keepin' them fed falls solely on me for the next Lord knows how many months, and the boy be so weeny, you ain't properly seen how small yet. I just don't think he will make it! How am I goin' to get him to suckle, his mouth be no bigger than half a sixpence, ain't no way he's gonna get me teat in there. And Gran's getting older and more difficult, the cottage be fallin' down around our ears. Look at that crack in the hearthstone! I can nearly get me hand in it. The roof leaks so bad we's run out of pots to catch the drips. And you with no work and no money coming, and you ain't been up to the strip to tend the veg for ages, has you? And I ain't gonna be able to do no laundry for weeks! Now I's forbid from havin' the one thing what helps me through,' splutters Molly, through her sobs. 'And I know I should not drink so much, but Lord, I's tired and I likes the way it makes me feel. It makes me forget all this,' she throws her hands up in the air, 'all this shite.' She puts her head down, rocks backwards, forwards, palms pressed hard into her eyes.

Suddenly she stops and sits up straight. 'Lord forgive me, and then there's Little Joe! I almost forgot we had him then. Shame on me! He be a right terror at the moment and I can't stop him runnin' off! And why in hell's damnation is bloody cousin Tilly here? She be no good to no one, never was and never will be. Such a bossy, stuck up bitch she were when we was young. Who asked her? You ain't esplained that to me yet!' and Molly buries her head in her hands again, muffling her cries.

George does not know what to say. He is not used to comforting such an angry, weepy wife, or being confronted by one, either. And to lose another child will weigh heavy on them both. Molly was always strong and even-tempered, but she has changed. She is no longer playful and light. The dark circles creeping about her eyes are like the ghosts of mothers past, who faced the same fears as she and lost. Or perhaps it is the gin, playing with her youth. It certainly makes her brave, the drink, for she has never before spoken to him like this.

He slips back, to a time when life was easy.

He never liked to contract himself for a year, like other men. Tied to one farmer, the same piece of land. Paid once, on Old Michaelmas Day, having to eke out their coins through all the seasons, forever working today for next year's living. He preferred to do a bit here, a bit there, wherever he was needed. Day-work, paid when the work was done and then he was gone. He worked to live, for as soon as his fragile pockets were full he stopped toiling the fields and began enjoying life. No wife to keep, no child to feed, no crabby grandmother to keep at bay. No thatch to patch then, for he was still at Rose Cottage not at Rye. True, he had to put up with brother Jesse's weird habits and strange silences, lasting for days, sometimes. And Father's beatings, of course, although they got fewer as he himself got older and could skit faster out of reach of those iron fists and steely boots, while with age William grew only slower. Out of work, he spent his time at The Leg, at cards, at cricket. At women, if they came his way. And then Molly caught his eye. Instead of working the fields, he worked her. When she was ready he took her to the King Oak, lay her down on that mossy bed. He made her his, with his promises, with his seed. As soon as they were wed, well, back to the old pattern he went.

Toil, earn, spend, enjoy.

How life has changed since they lay together at the foot of the King Oak's twisty trunk. How he has not.

Something shifts in him, a stirring from deep in the murk of his soul, it rises, bubbles, bursts and before he knows it, there it is, staring at him in all its full glory.

It has a name.

Responsibility.

He shakes himself back to his wife, his newborn twins and growing boy, the leaky roof, their dwindling firewood and empty cupboards, the weedy strip. Even old Eliza Greenfield.

Shake off that bleedin' laziness and grow yerself up, idiot, he tells himself. *Or you's gonna lose the most important game of all.*

Indeed, never mind cricket or cards, if he is to win the game that is life itself, all he has been shirking will need to be dealt with, and soon. For if he loses, then so will Molly and his children. And then there is this work he has agreed to, Lord help them if it goes wrong. *Jee-zus Christ, what the fuck have I gotten myself into? This cannot be, I cannot put them through this with me.* And it is not Lizzie swinging from a rope in his mind now, but himself, from the gallows. He shivers at what might come to pass.

Time, now, to really put things right.

With his beloved wife's soul, with all her despair laid fully bare before him, and their two tiny infants lying at their feet, the playful squeals of his son coming from the yard, he believes he can do it. He has to, for if he does not believe it himself, how can he expect her to?

Molly is staring blankly into the fading fire now, calmer, perhaps resigned to her fate.

He takes her soft face in his hands, kisses her tenderly on each cheek, her lips, her temples, and presses his forehead to hers for a moment. Then he looks her deep in the eye, takes a deep breath.

'Things will be better, Moll, they will. I swear. I will do right by you and our children. Lord knows I ain't been a good bringer in of coin and food and such, but I sees now how that just ain't right,' he whispers, and Molly loses herself in his words as they slip and trip from his mouth. 'Things will get better. Say you believe me, let me take care of all your fears.'

She believes solidly in almighty God, but to believe in her husband's words and promises will take a mighty leap of faith indeed. She pulls away from him, gazes at his face, studies the frown he is wearing, etched so deeply that it laces his eyebrows firmly together, where usually they only meet when his moods turn dark.

But there is something in his eyes which is not darkness.

A glimmer of something else.

Is it hope?

Or truth?

'Promise?' she asks in a whisper, an uneasy echo of his pledge, and the word which only two days ago she no longer believed in, perhaps will become her friend again. She brings her hand up to his beard, curls her pale fingers gently through the wiry hair, pulls his face, his lips, his heart, very gently to hers.

'Promise,' he replies, and he is certain he will never become involved with such undesirable men again, that he will find a regular honest job, and tend their vegetables, chop wood, bring home cold coins.

He will become a good husband.

But Moll, just stay away from me brother, he thinks.

ROSE COTTAGE

DINNERTIME

Jesse and Henry return to Rose Cottage just after midday, with Henry still dragging his heels through the doghouse. A meal is waiting for them. Bread, a little crumbly cheese, some onion and chopped cabbage leaves. Radishes from the vegetable garden give Annie's platter a splash of colour. William is sitting by the fire, grumbling to himself and drinking steadily, like a foreign invasion force making itself unwelcome in their camp.

'Father, you's downstairs for a change. Your bones feeling better?' Jesse asks.

'Less o' yer sarcasm, Son. If you thinks I can't hear it in your bleedin' voice, you's wrong. Me bones will never be fuckin' better, you hear me? An' well you knows it. So quit asking, like any other answer will pass me lips,' he drawls. A dribble of spit runs down his chin. He doesn't bother to wipe it away and it joins the growing damp patch on his shirt which has been gathering all morning, like the rain in the storm clouds. 'An' if I could get up to kick you, I would. Remember that,' he says, as if anyone in the room could ever forget the violence William inflicted when he could move around with ease.

''Tis dinner time, Father,' Annie says, hoping to diffuse the situation and divert his attention. 'Here, 'twill fill your belly with sommat other than that there booze.' She passes a plate over his shoulder from behind, so his ever prodding stick cannot catch her.

As she sits down at the table, her eyes catch Jesse's, an under-standing between brother and sister of the unfolding situation. It will be a difficult day, and only end when Jesse and Henry haul William, comatose if they are lucky, back to his bed. Sometimes, when he is really bad, they leave him where he is, but they would rather he piss in his own room than the one they use the most. There is always a terrific mess after a day like today, and Annie resolves not to clear it till morning. *He can rot in his own shite,* she thinks, and at once regrets her harsh thoughts, but thanks the Lord the days when William Hogtrough feels well enough to creep backwards down the stairs are becoming less frequent.

The ungodly William does not wait for Jesse to say the Grace before he begins soaking bits of bread in his ale and stuffing them into his mouth, sucking out the liquid, his gums tender and what remain of his teeth as good as useless. These days he eats precious little of substance.

'Death come to visit us today,' he spits, through a mouth full of soggy bread. 'Death itself, I tell 'ee! Come sneaking through that door there, all stealth, like,' and he points a gnarly finger towards the open door. 'Wonder which one of us she come for, eh? T'ain't gonna be me, that's for sure. Must be one o' you lot,' and he begins laughing, then coughs and almost chokes on the bread.

'What's he mean, Sister?' Henry whispers across the table.

'He means Mathilda. She was all dressed in widow's black. Angel of Death, I heard him call her,' Annie whispers back.

'She be here then! That is good news, indeed, for Molly that is. Gone to help, has she?' Jesse asks in a low voice.

'No, brother, she ain't. She be upstairs resting and ain't comed down all morning. I tooked her up some hot water and a cup of tea, but I ain't heard nothing since. Di'n't like to disturb her.'

Jesse is surprised. 'Well now, an' I thought she were here to help. But Molly di'n't seem too 'thusiastic, like, when I mentioned her coming. Sayed she were right lazy,' he says. 'P'raps 'tis true.'

'She seems alright enough, come with a lot of baggage though, and packed full of airs and graces. Certainly walks and talks like she be a class above, that's for sure. But I reckon them airs will soon be blown out,' Annie declares.

'How come?' Henry asks, eager for information.

'Well, I weren't here when she arrived, but she had a right to do with Father. A few more conversations like that and any fanciful ideas she got will be away. He would not hold his tongue, and you knows how he can get. I quite thought she would hot tail it that instant.'

Lord, wish I were here to see that! Jesse thinks. He changes the subject and they stop whispering. 'Now, has we heard from brother George yet? How goes it for Molly and her travail?'

'Ain't heard nothin' yet. I were going up the cottage with

Mathilda, but she ain't put her face in and I di'n't want to leave her alone here,' Annie looks over at William, so engrossed in his meal he takes no notice of them. 'Well, I shall go along anyway, see how Moll is,' she says, smiling, as much at her own position as anything else. 'Exciting, ain't it?'

'Not sure I would call it exciting, Sister. Terrifying, more like,' and Jesse is puzzled at Annie's glee. 'Molly were scared out of her wits when I picked her up off the ground this morn, pale as anything. Looked like she'd seen a ghost, and sad to say, much the worse for drink. So blathered were she 'twill be a wonder she don't die from that alone. Poisonous stuff. 'Tis becoming more an' more a habit with her these days.'

'Like as to ease her fears then, Jesse. I been racking me brains and can't think why she would be so taken to it, unless she got good reason. She's always been so strong, ain't she?'

'Aye, well a few years married to that lazy sod, be enough to turn any to drink.'

'He's still your brother, do remember that,' says Annie. 'You's starting to sound a bit like the old man,' she says, lowering her voice, and she knows she is pushing the boundaries and his buttons, but will she not be soon out of here?

'Less of your disrespect, woman,' Jesse spits the words at her, cruelly. 'You remember whose table you's sitting at. I will not have you speak to me in such a way,' but Jesse regrets letting his mouth speak his thoughts.

As always.

ROSE COTTAGE

EARLY AFTERNOON

After the Hogtrough brothers return to their backbreaking task of cockling vetches in the March Field, Annie rinses their dinner plates and cups in a tub of water in the yard. There is still no sign of Mathilda, so she clanks around under the bedroom window hoping to stir the widow, to no avail. *What on earth is the woman doing, lazing around in that tiny room. Is she sick? Asleep?* Surely not, on a hot, sticky day like today. It is muggy with hardly a breeze, and the gathering clouds are almost upon them. *She must know Molly needs her help, or why else be she here?*

She goes back inside just as William is trying to get up from his fireside chair. 'You going back to your bed now, Father?' she asks, hoping, praying that he is.

'Yeah, I bleedin' well am. Had enough of sitting here, back's killing me. Where's that bottle o' gin, Daughter? I shall take it up with me,' he growls, as he hauls himself onto his unsteady feet. He cannot stand straight, his joints cemented by some awful condition he cannot name. His posture would be comical if it weren't evidently so painful. He stands bent forwards, almost at a right angle and looks somewhat like a tortoise as he waves his arms and stick for balance, turning his head this way and that to see where he is going.

Annie is in no mood to argue over his precious drink. She knows it is necessary to dull his pain, in lieu of expensive medicine they cannot afford to purchase from Doctor Scragg. It might well help, but they can ill afford even a drop of gin and certainly not the quantity William calls for. She retrieves a bottle, hidden behind a frayed curtain on the window sill.

'There ain't much left, Father,' she says, quite expecting the tirade of abuse and curses which follow.

William sneers, 'Well, get some bleedin' more then.' He lifts his head as far as he can and rolls his eyes at her.

'What with, Father? I ain't got no coin. Has you a penny spare anywhere, by chance?' A foolish question, but she is frustrated by his impossible demands.

'Oh! You's always so good at pathetic bloody ex'curses, ain't you? Always a reason why you can't help your poor old father,' he tuts and grumbles on. 'Course I ain't got no penny t'spare! Where d'you think I get's 'em from, eh? I don't see none raining down from our gracious bleedin' Lord in heaven. Or mebbe you thinks I keeps some hidden up me swollen fucking arse! Goddamn it! I's stuck in me bleedin' bed all day. Can't work, can't sleep, can't even have a decent shit without an agony from the depths of hell a-coursing through me. And you ask me, have I got a penny spare? Bloody hell girl, you must'a left your brains in your mother's…'

Blessèdly, this last sentence is not finished. William's outburst is interrupted by another rough, hacking cough which rises from deep within his chest. He nearly chokes on his miserable words and then begins the usual round of splutter and spit. The disgusting tobacco-brown phlegm lands in the embers of what is left of the morning's fire with a hiss.

As his insults cut her like a sharpened blade she fades out of the room. Her mind flips back to a time when this cottage was full to the brim with joy and love, so long ago, and yet it could be yesterday. However, she remembers that joy did not last and love quickly paled.

Mother hands her a package. 'For your lunch,' she says, smiling. 'Have fun,' she calls, as they skip into the forest. Sister Sally, three years taller, bossy mother duck, shrieks, 'Stay on the path.' Little siblings follow Sal along the narrow tracks, stomp in single file. She, Annie, ten years old; Will, a year behind; Maria, Susan, seven and six. They arrive at the King Oak, the mossy floor. Paced around, the enormous tree is seventeen child steps. Warm sunshine sneaks through holes in the leafy roof and dances on the floor. 'Sun Fairies,' Sally says. They make clothes from leaves, tear out shapes for breeches, shifts, petticoats and skirts, make piles of little stones, drape the tiny garments over. Make fences from twigs and long grass to enclose their magical garden. Leave crumbs of bread and cheese in acorn shells, collect flowers – forget-me-nots and daisies – and tuck the tiny bunches in the nooks and crannies of the old oak's roots. Offerings to the mystical creatures. Then the youngest, Susan, cries out. 'Too hot,' she hollers. ''Tis just the weather,' Sally says. 'July is hot. Come, take off your smock.' Gasps! 'What is it?' she, Annie, asks. 'Red rash,' Sal answers, 'we have to go, she needs Mother.' Scarlet fever takes all three: Will, Maria, Susan, all dead within the week. 'Fairies was angry – we upset their home,' Sal says. She believes her, goes back to the King Oak, tramples the flowers into the moss, spills out the uneaten crumbs, rips the leafy clothes to shreds. Mother cries and cries and does not stop. Father tries and tries but cannot close the hole the fairies left in Mother's broken heart. Joy begins to wane. The house is quiet, lifeless. A year or so passes by. She wakes one morn and brother Ned is gone, too. For the wide ocean, she is told. Of her brothers, only Jesse and George remain. George scowls all the time, and Jesse hangs his head. Why? Sally does not know, but something unsaid goes between the boys and Father. Mother does not see it through her tears. 'Where is my boy Ned? Run away to sea? It cannot be!' Surely he would not go without saying farewell to his beloved Mother, who cries out for him in the dead of night, hardly sleeps and looks for her firstborn all through the dark hours but cannot find him anywhere. Not at sea. Not with God. Vanished. Father drinks and does not stop. George glowers. Sometimes anger leaks out of his eyes and into his fists, and he punches Jesse. Ouch! He has a man's punch, her nineteen year old brother. No longer is he a boy. Jesse, older by a year, tries not to flinch, but she sees it hurts. And he never punches back. Why? She spies him sneaking into the barn. He spends hours in Ned's old tack room. Hours. Ned was good with horses, but Jesse cannot speak to them the same, so why has he gone to the tack room? She tiptoes in, finds a little knot-hole on the horses' side, watches what happens when he thinks no one is watching.

Lash, lash, lash.

She runs, cannot comprehend what she has seen, but never forgets. Tells George. 'Good,' he says. Still she does not understand and George will not give her any clues. Father drinks more and more. Henry is born. Mother dies. The babe is sent away – two years with Aunt Joan, nursed until he can eat their food. By the time Henry returns, Sally is a servant girl in Letherhed. She, Annie, does all the chores which Mother left behind. Father drinks all the time, shouts often, hits frequently, and his bones begin to twist. George never stops scowling and punching, but never at her. Jesse just sulks and scowls and lashes.

What the hell happened here?

Hell, that's what.

Hell happened.

Right here in this house.

Father is still throwing curses, but she lets them roll over her like a pin flattening soft dough, keeps her mouth buttoned and her eyes closed. An imaginary door stands in front of her and she hides behind it. Experience has taught her that any response is wasted and will only make things worse. Silence is her best protection.

She only watches. William Hogtrough's whiskery, wrinkled face is red and full of sweat and pain as he tries to walk towards the stairs. She makes no move to help, prefers instead to stay well out of reach of his wooden poker. He takes two steps, swears, gives in and steps back. He sits down heavily on the broad, hard seat of the fireside chair with a cry, his head on his chest, his breathing loud and laboured, and his face crumpled in agony.

'Ain't no good, I be stuck here, good and proper,' he snarls. 'Ain't no way I's a-gonna get up them bleedin' stairs. Shall have to get them boys to bring me bed down here for good.'

Annie shivers and closes her eyes. *No, Lord please not that.* It is bad enough him lying most of the day above, making demands by smashing his stick against the wooden boards. If he were downstairs all the time, life would become unbearable for everyone. She says nothing, for she is leaving. Soon.

'Gimme that drink, wench. Looks like I ain't got no choice but to wait on them lazy sons o' bitches.'

William Hogtrough is defeated.

Annie is stuck between pity and disgust. She can see the pain in her father's face, but he has inflicted so much on their family since Mother died that it seems to her God is now punishing him in return. Her sympathy is thin. She moves closer and stretches out her arm, offering the almost empty flask which he snatches with a grimace. The sudden movement increases his suffering.

'I'll see if I can't fetch some more, Father. Maybe Farmer Caen will see us good till I can sell some rushlights,' she says softly, hoping this will appease her father's mood.

'Oh, thank the bleedin' Lord, the idiot wench does have some sense at least. You do that, girl, and afore you go, fetch that feather pillow from me bed, so as to ease me aching back. This chair ain't no better than a bleeding stone slab. Might as well already be in me fuckin' coffin.'

Annie dashes up to his room, and as she passes her own she puts one ear to the door. Silence. She thinks of knocking to raise the Widow Richardson, but decides to let the woman be. She is still in mourning, after all.

Maybe that's it. A few weeks is not long to get over a beloved husband's passing.

She delivers the pillow to her father and then escapes the horrors of his poison tongue.

'Where you going now, Daughter?' he calls after her, as she is at the door.

'To Molly, see how she be doing. Then I'll be right back with your drink.'

'While ye's there, see if that old witch ain't got sommat what can ease me pain. Must be some potion or other what will relieve me suff'ring. 'Tis unnatural for any man to be living with so much hurt. And that quack Scraggs, he do be a useless son of a bitch, even when his pockets is lined with gold. He's took more blood out of me than is rightful, makes me feel worser, ever' time he do, and I ain't gonna owe him no more, so don't go calling on him again. You hear me?'

Annie does not hear, for she has already closed the door and is on her way to Rye Cottage.

Rose Cottage

Early Afternoon

From the tiny bedroom window, Mathilda watches Annie turn out of the yard, then makes her way carefully down the steep, narrow staircase. Contrary to Annie's imagination, Mathilda has been rather busy. With her ear pressed to the cool, worn floorboards, she listened to the family's lunchtime conversations and heard much to enrich her knowledge.

The miserable, crooked old man she met earlier will more than likely drink himself to death if he can ever get hold of enough to finish the job, and Annie, who must be nearing thirty, keeps house, for there is no other maid. Young Henry did not give much away, and lastly there is Jesse, rather handsome, she thinks, although too proud and dusty. It seems he is acting as head of the family, now that the old man is good for nothing except cursing, swearing, drinking. There is much she can accomplish here, but where to begin? Since she is alone in the house with the bent up father she will make a start on him.

At the bottom of the noisy stairs, she pauses, holding her bible tightly to her chest. She kisses the worn book and says a silent prayer, her black curls falling forward over her face. Then, as quietly as possible, she enters the downstairs room, where the repulsive smell she encountered earlier still lingers, just as strong and repugnant, if not more so. Before the old man has even noticed her presence, she has flung open the windows and the place is filling up with fresh air. She stands some distance away from the wretched man, who has not moved from his seat by the fire. *Is he deaf? Blind?* Blind drunk, perhaps, for he is wholly concerned with the now empty bottle of gin. The flask is tipped towards his lips, and with his eyes closed he is sucking at it, as if it were his mother's teat. In vain, for the jar is completely devoid of his beloved tipple.

Mathilda clears her throat. 'Ahem, good afternoon, Mister Hogtrough.'

William jumps in surprise. 'Mighty Lord above! Jesus, you gives me a bleedin' shock standing there all a-shadow,' he snarls. 'Still creeping about then, eh Mistress? A grim angel you surely is,' he snorts a disapproval at whatever it is in Mathilda he dislikes, and blinks in the bright sunlight now streaming into his normally dark hovel.

'Mister Hogtrough, I do not dress so from choice. My attire is out of respect for my dear departed husband. I am sure you must have heard of him. The wheeler Mister John Richardson of Mickleham. He passed out of this world on Holy Thursday, a fitting day for such a wonderful man to join his Maker,' and Mathilda hangs her head.

'Well, don't e'spect no symphony from me, woman. If he felt anything like what I does, he be lucky to be out of this damnded, *accursèd* world,' William replies, with a wail and a groan, like a ghost trying frighten anyone who cares to be afraid. He turns awkwardly and studies her with hollow eyes. He appears as gorged with agony as he is with the drink he uses to ease his pain.

She drags a stool across the floor to where William cannot reach her with his prodding stick and perches herself on it. Now she has removed her enormous hat, he can see her beauty. Her long, dark hair is swept up and pinned to the top of her crown, and a mass of tight curls cascades and frames her pale, oval face. However, beautiful though she may be, there is something to her which William cannot quite work out. *How long does this deathly creature plan on stayin' in me home? And how will she pay her way while she be under me roof?* These are the questions he plays with.

They have scarce enough coming in as it is, and there will certainly be less for him and his alcoholic remedy should they have to cough up for her keep.

'Do tell me, Mistress, what truly brings you to this lonely, God-forsaken one-eyed piece of Ashted Common? You don't strike me as a common sort o' woman, like. I believe your offer of help to be a ruse, Mistress. You doesn't look like you's done an h'ounce of work in your life,' he slurs.

'Mister Hogtrough, as you well know, I am come to help my cousin,' Mathilda says, her eyes far too green and bright.

Had William Hogtrough ever seen emeralds, sparkling their beauty in sunlight, he would say they were the same. However, from his limited perspective, the nearest he can equate them to is newly mown grass, glinting with early morning dew.

Bah! Too unnatural for any earthly creature. Witch?

Not satisfied with her answer, he says, 'Then why in God's name are you still here, Mistress, sitting at my fireside? Why ain't you with your cousin, drawing heat from hers?' and he raises an eyebrow, his twisted hands resting on his stick between his scrawny legs.

Mathilda says nothing. She stares back at him with a gentle smile on her face.

'Well!' he barks at her. 'Your ol'friend the Devil bit your tongue out, 'as he?'

Mathilda jumps as William lunges forwards, but her smile does not give way.

'This, Mister Hogtrough, is exactly why I am still here. I fear you have the Devil in *you,* Sir, and I offer myself as an aid to rid him, to cleanse your poor soul of his wicked influence and so to ease your suffering.'

William is stunned. Never in his life has he heard a woman talk to him in such a way, and with words best left to the pulpit rather than uttered by a creature who does not have the slightest idea of his suffering, let alone the nature of the beast which took up lodging in his soul many moons ago. He lets out an enormous guffaw at the absurdity of her words, which triggers yet another coughing fit.

Mathilda waits. Her words were spoken in all seriousness and she truly believes she can help.

William, although quite drunk, is not entirely incapable of thought, and the cogs and wheels of his agonised mind whirr and clank, trying to make sense of this woman. He scratches his bristly chin. *Straight out o' Bedlam, I reckon.* 'Mistress, unless you're a bloody witch, and I does suspect you is, for you surely looks like one, I can't bleedin' well see how you can possibly help me. Me! Of all people! I'll not deny your accusation, for God only knows 'twere a long time ago when I lost me soul to that ol' Devil, but do es'plain to me your wicked plans. I's a-curio to know just how you's gonna save me damnded soul,' William sniggers and slumps back on his pillow.

'There is nothing at all wicked about my plans, Mister Hog-trough, I can assure you. And please do not say such evil words about me. It is a most dangerous thing when you have no proof, nor will you ever have, for it is not at all true. A witch, indeed!' Mathilda is quite offended.

William snorts and strikes his stick against the floor with a hard crack. It gives Mathilda another jolt. 'Go on then, woman. I's eager to hear.'

She puts her bible at arms length, rests it on the edge of her knees, as if the word of God will give her some protection against this monster. She clears her throat and begins.

'First, let me tell you a little of my history, Mister Hogtrough. I was a posthumous child and never knew my own father, for he died too soon. But my mother soon found another, a man who stood admirably in his place. My stepfather was, shall we say, rather eccentric. Nevertheless, he was a kind and gentle man, and an adventurer where all things medicinal were concerned. He was an apothecary by trade and passionate about curing people's ailments. His life's work concerned the concoction of all manner of potions for healing, and most especially for the easement of pain. He made his living from these, which he sold to doctors and medical men far and wide. He made quite a name for himself in his field. And, he taught me how to make many of his miraculous cures before he sadly disappeared after a short spell of,' and here she pauses, clears her throat. 'Ahem, folly, I suppose you might say, brought on by the unfortunate testing of a new medicine, which proved to be somewhat less than useful. However, one of his more successful remedies I happen to have about my person at this very moment. It is tried and tested by many who gained much welcome relief after taking this miraculous tincture. I do believe it will also help you, Mister Hogtrough. It will certainly be a veritable start towards alleviating your awful suffering.'

William laughs, 'So, a quackess then, not a witch. Show me your wares, do.'

'Mister Hogtrough, please! Less of your name-calling. I am, after all, a child of God, not of the Devil, and I am no Quack, and neither was my well-respected stepfather.'

'Show me, woman,' he shouts, losing patience, and strikes the crooked stick again, hard down on the worn tiles.

Mathilda reaches deep into her skirt pocket and produces a small, ornate glass bottle with a silver-topped cork stopper, and lifts it up, so that William can see it. He leans forward and strains his neck as far as he can. He reaches out his hand, but before he can snatch it, she withdraws the tincture to her breast, with the bible.

'So that's it, eh, woman? I sees your game now. Poison, eh? More'n likely you did for your quacky stepfather, eh? Disappeared?

My arse, ha! And perhaps you even did for you 'usband, too!' William says, and raising his voice he begins shaking a crooked finger at her. 'I knowed you was the Devil's wench when you stepped over me threshold this morning, all creeping and a-nosing about like a spider at a fly.' The old man makes his hand into a spider, and scurries it across the air towards Mathilda, shooting her a dark look along with it, full of fear and pain.

'Mister Hogtrough, I really must insist you refrain from using such false words. I can assure you I am no murderess, no servant of the Devil, nor any witch. I will ask you for the last time, kindly do not speak in such a dangerous manner. And I can prove to you that this medicament is no poison by taking it myself, if you so wish, and I shall not perish in any way.'

'Then do it woman and prove yourself,' William hisses, eyeing her cautiously.

Mathilda unstoppers the bottle and takes a small, delicate sip of the clear liquid. 'There, Mister Hogtrough, is your proof. I assure you that I shall not die, rather I shall be free from all pain. That is, had I any in the first place,' she says, replacing the silver-topped stopper.

William reaches again for the bottle.

'Not so fast, Mister Hogtrough, we have not yet agreed the terms of my employment to rid you of your suffering,' Mathilda says, dangling the bottle in front of him. 'This is no cheap medicament.'

'Oh! So, now you means to make me pay, eh? You sees I ain't got so much as a pot to piss in. Look around, madam, see the poverty about me. Ain't nothing of no worth here.'

Mathilda smiles, but says nothing.

'Come on then, spit it out, witch-woman. What pray, be your price for this bottle of magical cure-all?'

'No names, Sir!' she says. 'Three weeks' board and lodging in your abode, that is all I ask. I believe it is a fair offer, for once you try this medicine, you will know I speak the truth.'

'Well now, three weeks, eh?' William scratches his chin. 'Seems rather a lot for a teeny tiny bottle.'

'Oh! You do not need much, I can attest to that. And this is not the end of it, I have plenty more, Mister Hogtrough. I can assure you that during my stay here, you shall not feel such pain as you do now, for it will be dulled and you will sleep, and dream wondrously, and feel much relieved.'

William sits back and studies her. How exactly she is going to rid him of his devil remains a mystery, and as he contemplates her offer, he pulls at a scab on his cheek and picks at his earlobe. The promise of relief from pain is too great a temptation, and after some moments he says, 'I thinks 'tis only fair that you lets me try this poison cure-all, then. And if it truly do relieve me suff'ring, well then you gets yourself a bed and food for one week, and one week only. And in that time, you gives me enough so I has no more pain. And if it don't work, well then you pays your way here, Mistress. D'you hear me? You pays!' William waves his stick to show he is serious.

'I believe that is quite a satisfactory agreement, for I know that after one week, you will know the power of this medicament and be open to extending our arrangement,' replies Mathilda. 'But you must also know that I will administer the medicine myself. For you cannot take it all at once. Too much of it will certainly do you harm, so it must be measured carefully.'

William snorts and begins a sarcastic outburst. 'Not a poison, she says! But you cannot take too much, for it will surely kill you, she says! Ha! You is a most curio and contrary beast if ever I sees one.'

Mathilda holds her nerve.

'Where do you keep the spoons, Mister Hogtrough,' she says. 'Then you may have your very first taste of heaven.'

Rye Cottage

Mid-Afternoon

At Eliza Greenfield's cottage, the yard is full. The women of Woodfield, upon hearing of the safe delivery of Molly's twins, arrived bearing gifts. Those who had nothing to spare came just with their good wishes.

For Annie, it is a most welcome change from the sad sight of her miserable father, and the afternoon is rapidly turning into a small celebration while they await the coming storm.

Eliza Greenfield is sitting like an ancient queen, grinning toothlessly under a black hat, delighted to see her yard filled once again with life and laughter, as it had been when she was a young mother, many moons ago. The Chitty girls are watching the fire, and Jenny Venn is presiding over a large pot of mutton stew, built from the remnants of the bone broth. Several small children are toasting chunks of bread on sticks over the hot embers at the edge of the fire pit with Hetty Archer, who is making sure neither child nor bread gets burnt.

As Annie crosses the yard, Emma Cobbett, the barmaid from The Leg, calls out, 'Annie! Your brother's askin' for you. Have you heard? Moll had twins, like she sayed she were. One of each, and the boy be so tiny, you cannot believe how sweet a thing he is. Prob'ly won't live the day out, though. They's already called for the Rector, just in case.'

Before Annie has had time to digest all this news, a hard, scolding voice comes across the yard.

'Emma Cobbett, shut that lazy trap of yours, girl. What a daft and silly thing you are. What d'you think you're doing inviting unwanted guests to our party? We shall keep that old devil Death away, so don't you go spoilin' nobody's day,' Hetty tuts, and wags a long finger at the maid, who blushes and mutters an apology. Hetty turns to Annie. 'She be right about one thing, though. The boy be so sweet. Makes me all broody, it do. I's feeling like an old cluck-hen meself!' she laughs.

Annie looks at Hetty, her future mother-in-law.

Has he already told her about me?

She wonders how much Hal has told anyone.

'Hetty Archer! Ain't you done enough? You's give us eight boys already!' Jenny declares. 'I certainly ain't wishing for more! This one's me last,' she says, as she cradles her full body.

'Come now, Jen, you's young still, there'll be more on the way after that one you's carryin' if Bob has anything to say about it,' Cat Longhurst chuckles, 'can't see him stopping in his prime, like!'

'Can't see me wanting him to, that's the trouble. Not the way he swings his plough about, anyways!' Jenny replies, and the women dissolve into laughter.

Annie crouches next to Eliza. 'Mistress Greenfield, how goes it? Father sends his regards,' she says, polishing up William's impolite sentiments.

'Goes well, my dee-ar, thank you koindly. And what about you, now?' Eliza says, holding out a crumpled hand.

Annie grasps it, and looks into the old woman's eyes, and Eliza raises an eyebrow. ''Tis alright now, and thank you for asking. I need do nothing, see?' Annie smiles, and whispers. 'The father, he'll do what is right by me, thank God.'

'Well, you's a good gal, very brave, Oi say, consid'ring.'

Annie is puzzled. What on earth does she mean? Brave? Considering what, exactly?

Eliza continues without giving Annie a chance to ask. 'But whatever comes, and no matter what anyone else moight say, there be plenty here about what will see you good, see?' Eliza nods towards the other women in the yard.

However, it is not joy in Eliza's eyes but something else. Pity? A small trickle of cold fear runs down Annie's spine, in spite of the warm sun, and she tries to shake off an uncomfortable feeling. She changes the subject.

'Mistress Greenfield, Father has asked if you might have summat for his pain. 'Tis right bad just now.'

'That'll be the storm rumblin', dear. Sure as bees make honey. It'll pass and ease a little in the coming hours, loike,' Eliza croaks. 'What say you? Shall we leave him to suffer, as the good Lord meant? After all, he's done so much wrong for you lot, ain't he?

Or would you rather see him free of hurt? P'raps that be easier for you. Roight miserable sod he's been these last years, a roight misery, indeed,' and Eliza clicks her tongue against the roof of her mouth. 'Where's me poipe, girl. Pass it t'me, do.'

Tempting as it is, Annie cannot have it on her conscience to leave William in pain. She tells Eliza as much, and once the pipe is lit and a few puffs have eased Eliza's mood, Annie helps her up from her chair and into the lean-to where all her precious herbal tonics are kept. Eliza picks out a jar of willow bark tincture and Annie decants some into a small bottle. After seeing Eliza safely back to the yard, she heads indoors, eager to meet her new niece and nephew, before it is too late.

The room is hushed. George is on the floor, staring into the fire, stroking Molly's hair. She is curled up next to the makeshift cot, sleeping soundly on a bed made from a straw-stuffed blanket. The windows are still shuttered and one candle is just about alight on the table.

George looks up. 'Sister,' he whispers, 'come, look at the babes, see how tiny they is.'

Annie peers into the box-bed. 'Oh my! I's never seen such perfect little faces,' she coos.

'Look at the boy, he be the smallest thing, ain't he?'

'Aye, so sweet Brother! My hearty congratulations to you, George. I be so glad all is well. And Molly, how is she?'

'Alright, I guess, but she needs rest. You must'a heard we's called the Rector, just in case,' he says.

'Aye, but that don't mean nothin', a quicker baptisement 'tis all.'

But they both know that a private baptism is only held for an infant not expected to make it to the church.

George looks at his sister as she fawns over the sleeping infants and he mulls over the day's uncoverings. He should be ecstatic that his wife and both infants are alive, and yet here he is, brooding over someone else's love affair, a nagging feeling gnawing at what should be a joyous mood. If he does not confront the issue soon, his anger will rise, violence will ensue and he has to work with Hal tonight. *Bleedin' hell, the time will soon be upon us.* He really should be there now, helping with the preparations.

'Where be that cousin of Moll's? She promised to take care of Joe. Lord knows Molly can do with him off her hands for a few days.'

'When I left she were still upstairs, sleeping after the journey, p'raps. She was only come from Mickelham, though. Ain't that far. Had a spat with Father, an' all, and it weren't pretty. Maybe she had second thoughts.'

'Lord, that's all we needs,' George says, dismayed he may not be able to get away any time soon.

'She don't seem like one to get her frock dirty, nor her hands. I would take Joe meself, but I am behind with me chores as it is, today.'

Yes, thinks George. *Behind 'cause you took time out to come and find me, and knew where I was, at that.* Rather than being grateful, his anger is brewing and festering in his guts, and Annie's words have brought up the issue again. He tries his best to stifle his fury, but it is no good. 'Annie, there be sommat I needs to ask. Come away from me wife. I wish not to stir her, nor the babes,' George whispers.

They sit opposite each other at the table, and George sets the tallow candle between them, its obnoxious mutton fat making the air slick as the wet wick fizzes and pops and spits. As George stares at his sister she sees a familiar frown grow across his forehead. He in turn, studies her worried face, not sure where to start, how best to ease the truth from her.

She has been the rock their family needed after Mother died and it is little wonder she never found a decent husband. There is no opportunity, never a moment when William doesn't have her at his fingertips. *Fetch this, carry that, clean my arse.* His demands on her are ever present and never ending.

Now he, himself, has a demand.

That she be honest with him.

'Annie,' he begins, his eyes locking firmly onto hers, holding her in his inquisitive grip. 'You has done much for our family, I knows you's given your own life for ours, and lookin' after the wretched old goat Father has become. Well, you's not had the chances you might to start a family of your own.'

'Come, Brother, why do you speak about this now?' Annie says, reaching across the table and taking George's huge, strong hand in hers. Something in her brother's tone and manner alarms her.

'I sees something earlier I cannot explain, and I wish to know the truth. For if I do not find it, 'twill be on my mind for the coming days, and I do not want my attention drawn away from Moll and the babes. Now, will you tell me?'

George squeezes her hand hard, and rather uncomfortable it is, too.

'Well if you asks me, Brother, then yes. But what is it?'

Annie is becoming uneasy, for George's moods can quickly change, and even though the light is dim, she can sense a darkness has come over him.

'Well, you were so quick to …,' but George does not have time to finish his inquisition, for at that moment there is a loud rap at the door and Annie is spared.

'Oh! That must surely be Mathilda come to help at last,' she says, rising from the bench.

At the sound of the door, Molly stirs from her slumber and looks up. But when Annie opens it, she finds not Mathilda, but the elderly Reverend Martindale in his powdered wig and starched collar, come to baptise the infants.

Just in case.

Rose Cottage
Late Afternoon

Henry and Jesse leave their work when black storm clouds begin to darken the sky. They arrive at Rose Cottage to find their father slumped against the arm of his chair. Although he looks most uncomfortable, he is sleeping soundly, snoring and snorting like a wild boar at truffles. It is a dreamful, wonderful sleep, too, something he has not had in a long time.

As Eliza Greenfield predicted, William Hogtrough's pain lessened as the afternoon progressed, but not at all due to a change in the weather. Rather, as Mathilda promised, the miraculous medicament she administered has taken hold and the odious man is now more or less pain free. His sons assume, however, that he is intoxicated by drink.

And things are different in their home. A change to the normally dark and stuffy room, kept so at Father's bidding whenever he ventures down the treacherous stairs. The windows are open, the air is fresh and although it is a little brighter, the clouds outside have dulled the light. And there is a voluminous black cloud of dark cloth and voile in the centre of the room, where Mathilda is struggling to arrange her enormous lace veil.

Still here then. Jesse grits his teeth, annoyed, but not surprised.

'Cousin Mathilda, I take it you's well rested,' he says and takes off his hat, holds it in front of him like a flimsy piece of armour. It pushes his linen shirt into the hair vest, which digs into his skin, prickling, itching. For once, he cannot ignore the urge to scratch and does so, fingers hidden behind his tricorn.

Mathilda spins around. 'Why Mister Jesse Hogtrough, how good it is to see you again. And young Henry, too. I must say I am so very grateful to you all for allowing me to stay. So convenient, being just a short stroll from my cousin's home.'

'You are most welcome,' Jesse says and hears his inner voice calling, mocking: *liar, liar!*

Henry can only smile. Like his nephew Little Joe, he is transfixed by the exotic creature before him, and cannot tear his eyes away from her beauty. Never before has he seen so grand a lady in their humble home.

Jesse looks over to William, slumped in slumber, his bony form untidy and dirty. *Good Lord, no!* It looks like he has pissed himself, and the empty gin flask is lying next to him on the seat. *Demon drink, ruins a man.* 'He be quiet today,' he says, embarrassed by William's condition. 'Finished that bottle by the looks of it. Most prob'ly need carrying up them stairs soon, is my guess.'

'Yes, but let us not disturb your father just yet,' Mathilda advises. 'I do believe he is far more,' she pauses, 'shall we say, innocuous, at sleep.'

'Aye, true,' Jesse says, although he has no idea what the word means, and his ignorance adds irritation upon irritation. 'Weren't plannin' on wakenin' him though. He be with us soon enough, I reckon.'

Mathilda only smiles. 'Perhaps he will,' she says, pulling her thick lace veil over her face. 'Now, I believe I am in order and ready to leave for my cousin's home. And who might accompany me? Young Henry, perhaps?'

Henry blushes now that her attention is on him rather than the other way around. 'Why yes, Mistress, I be glad to,' he splutters, looking at his feet.

'Bring news directly back, boy,' Jesse instructs. 'I will hear about Molly's condition, and the babes, after her fall, like.'

Mathilda gasps. 'She fell? Goodness! Why did no one think to tell me? Was she harmed? When did this happen?'

Jesse groans. He does not wish to explain Molly's drunken state, the shame of it. ''Twere nothing, really. She were out walking and her increasement began, lucky I found her, really. Carried her home, like,' he says, leaving out the worst.

'Why Mister Hogtrough, you are a hero! You must be rewarded for your quick thinking,' Mathilda declares.

'Don't want no fuss, that ain't the way we does things round here. Anyone would do the same.'

'Oh! But I disagree. You *must* be rewarded. I shall see to it myself if you are too modest to acknowledge your own brave actions.'

In all probability, this will expose Molly's condition, but before he can protest, the hem of Mathilda's dress is swishing against the cool tiles as she bustles towards the door where she slips into the tall wooden pattens.

Henry trots after her, like a doting puppy.

As his younger brother disappears outside behind Mathilda, Jesse notices, with dismay, that the white kitten has found its way inside.

It is now curled up in a small basket and has made itself very comfortable beside his hearth.

The Common Lane

Late Afternoon

Henry looks up at the sky, quite black now and the wind is getting up. The storm will break very soon.

'We should get a stroll on, Mistress. 'Tis going to storm bad, I fear,' he says.

'I believe you are right, young Henry,' Mathilda answers, looking up, with difficulty, from under her hat. 'Come, let us brisk it up.'

She begins interrogating Henry as they scurry up the lane. How old is he? Is he happy? Does his heart hold a maiden? What are his hopes for the future? The questions come thick and fast.

Henry is more than content to answer, for at last, someone is interested in his dreams. He is taken in by her charming nature, and his earlier shame at inviting her to stay is all but forgotten.

'Well, Mistress, as far as me future, I do be right grateful for all what I got at the farm, but I truly wants to do book learning. A life on the land, just ain't me, see? What it done to Father, bent over like a stick o' corn in the wind? No, I ain't gonna be all ampery, like he. I wants a trade, maybe go up London Town. Must be right int'restin' there, excitin', too. I dunno, but I sees how learnin' me letters will likely help an' all.'

He rushes out all his hopes and is highly animated.

'I think that an admirable idea, Henry. What a wonderful purpose you have set yourself. Now, have you got yourself a teacher?' Mathilda asks, hitching up her hems, forever worried her pattens are not lifting her high enough above the dirt. She wobbles as she tries to balance on the rough stones and is becoming more and more breathless as they race towards Rye Cottage.

'Well now that's just the problem, ain't it? Jesse don't think I should be doin' it, see? He don't want me going abroad or nothing, so he won't help. Won't even let me speak on it, actually. So, even if I finds me someone who can teach, I don't rightly know how I can learn nothin' without his knowing. Ain't got no money to pay for it, see? And I doesn't want to get all argy with him, he being so good to me and all, but I cannot bear the thought of *not* doing it. I dunno what to do for the best.'

Mathilda is quite out of breath now, and grasps Henry's sleeve, pulling him to a stop.

'Why hasn't your brother … a wife … or family of his own?' she pants.

'Well, he ain't. I mean,' Henry bites his cheek. It is one thing telling Mathilda about his own hopes and dreams, but Jesse would be mortified if he were gossiped about.

Having listened to Jesse moaning all morning about Mathilda coming to the cottage, them having neither space nor funds to support her, and still being in the doghouse for the invitation, he guesses that he may well end up *under* it if he says any more. He shuts up.

Mathilda begs him to continue, amazed at the change in the lad's manner.

'You must ask him yourself, Mistress. Ain't my place to be saying stuff what ain't my business.' In truth, he does not even have an answer to give.

Mathilda gathers her breath and they continue at a slower pace. After a few moments consideration, she says, 'I do understand. You are right to keep your brother's confidences. You are a good young man, you will go far.'

She wonders what secrets Jesse Hogtrough is hiding. A man of nearly forty, and a good, strong one at that, should be wedded by now with a horde of children around his table, not a spinster sister, a shackled brother and a miserable old father. She turns back to Henry. 'Now, as concerns your plans, I do believe you have found your teacher.'

'I have?' he answers. 'Where?'

'Come now Henry, you surely do not think that *I* attained my standing in life without an education? I was, indeed, most properly taught in many subjects. Moreover, I can do much more than just teach you to read and write. I can give you all kinds of advice and bring all sorts of connexions your way, in order to help you achieve your dreams.'

'You can? Oh my! I doesn't know what to say. Wait till I tell …,' he says, but Mathilda holds up her bible before he can finish.

'Jesse? No, you cannot tell your brother. In fact, you can tell no one. I shall find a way to tell him, in time. For now, it must be our little secret, for I do not wish to disturb your brother's peace by creating a storm in his own home. Those are my terms. What do you say?'

'I'll agree to anything in return for book learning. I cannot believe you would do that for me. 'Tis a dream come true!' His face is all joy, and it warms Mathilda to think that she can help the young lad.

'It is but a small step, for you will have far to go even after you have mastered your letters, and it will not be an easy journey. And London Town is not the exotic and exciting place you imagine it to be, for you may have heard that the streets are paved with gold, but in truth you will find there only mud and … oh well, much, much worse. But the least I can do is to help you begin. We shall find a secret place to study, and I am sure you will have it in no time.'

'Tip top! Thank you heartily, Mistress Richardson!'

Henry's elation escapes and he begins skipping the last few yards to Rye Cottage.

Jane Chitty and her sister, Liza step out from behind the rector's large dapple-grey horse, which is tethered to the garden fence.

Henry does not know where to put his face.

'What you looking so pleased about, Henry dear?' Liza flutters. 'You looks like a cat with a mouse, you does!'

'Oh! 'Tis nothin,' and Henry does his best to look composed.

'Henry, are you not going to introduce us?' Mathilda asks as she hobbles up.

'Aye, of course. Mistress Richardson, this be Liza Chitty, and her sister Jane,' he says. The girls curtsey in front of Mathilda.

'Pleased to meet you, I am sure,' she says. 'Young Henry, I shall leave you here, for my cousin will be waiting.'

Henry tries to save some face by calmly offering an arm to each of the girls. 'Best gets you girls home, 'tis gonna bucket down.' The girls giggle and Liza pulls Henry's arm tight to her breast as they make haste up the lane to avoid the impending downpour.

Mathilda calls after then, 'Do you girls know if the babes are yet safely born?'

'Aye Mistress, twins, one of each,' Liza calls over her shoulder.

Mathilda smiles.

Well, that's a good start on half the household, now for the rest.

She knocks the pink petals off Eliza's roses with her billowing dress as she swishes up the garden path, then stands before the door and straightens out her skirts.

Without knocking or waiting for an invitation, she bursts into Eliza Greenfield's tiny cottage.

RYE COTTAGE

LATE AFTERNOON

Mathilda finds Molly gazing at her newborn babes, sleeping soundly in their box-crib which has been set in the middle of the table. So exhausted is she that she does not hear her cousin enter, but all the other heads in the room turn to look. They see a large black shape and a hat so wide it skims each side of the door frame as it moves inside.

'Lord, 'tis the grim himself,' whispers Emma Cobbett, her eyes wide.

Cat Longhurst jabs her with a sharp elbow. 'Shush idiot, no more of your foolish words,' she hisses. 'How many times must you be told today?'

Molly looks round, and whispers, 'Ain't no grim, but not far off.' Then louder, 'Why, 'tis cousin Tilly, come to help.'

No one can mistake the hint of sarcasm in her voice, except perhaps Mathilda who only tenses at *'Tilly'*, her childhood name, and one she wishes to shed. Far too common.

'Cousin Molly! Why yes, it is I, *Mathilda*, come to help, indeed. How good it is to see you again after such a long time.'

She proceeds to address every stranger in the room - the Rector, readying himself to leave; Jenny Venn, Cat Longhurst, Emma Cobbett, sitting at the table, making a fuss of the babies - and introducing herself as 'Mistress Mathilda Richardson, wheelwright's widow of Mickleham' to each. No one can now be in any doubt that she should never again be referred to as *Tilly*. She acknowledges George and Annie, and lastly turns to Eliza, in her cushioned chair by the fireplace.

Eliza sees her, and at once knows her for what she is. The old woman nods and gives her a toothless grin, but says nothing.

Mathilda turns to Molly. 'You have produced twins, I hear. My goodness, what a clever girl you are, Cousin. I do believe congratulations are in order. And one of each! How thrilling,' she gushes.

Molly hardly has the strength to speak. After the day's events, she is feeling rather grim herself. But she is still here, and the babies, too. A miracle, indeed. However, she aches all over and all she wants is sleep, but her home is rather crowded. However, the Rector is about to leave, and she hopes the others will soon follow, so she can recover in peace.

Unpinning her gigantic hat, Mathilda looks around for some-where she can deposit it. There is little space, but she spies a loose hook beside the door. Then she steps off her pattens and shrinks.

She whips out a small, black painted fan from her pocket. The room is stifling and the approaching storm has done nothing yet to cool the temperature.

George is also uncomfortably hot. There are too many women in his home, and now Mathilda has arrived at last he can make his escape. His question to Annie is hanging in the air like another heavy storm cloud about to burst, and with the preparations for Barehenger's work to carry out, if Hal and his sister are … well, it will be difficult to keep his fists in his pockets tonight. It is drawing in fast and there is much to do. He really must be away.

'My work here is finished,' announces the Rector and turns to Molly and George and bows his head.

'Thank you kindly, Sir, for coming at such short notice, 'tis much 'preciated,' says George, ready to see him out.

'All in the line of duty, Mister Hogtrough. I wish you well with the infants. God is with them now.' He opens the door and looks up at the blackening sky. 'Well, I was hoping to arrive home before the heavens open but I fear the rain will be upon us sooner than anticipated. Good day to you,' he says, and is mounted upon his horse and trotting up the lane in no time.

While the women in the room are still cooing and aahing over the tiny infants, George sees his opportunity.

'Well, ladies, I must also be away. I needs to see a man about a rabbit. Sister, walk with me back to the farm, I's going that way,' he says, pulling Annie towards the door. She does not resist, but indeed has no choice, for George has her arm in his grip.

'Don't you mean a dog, George Hogtrough?' Cat calls out. 'Ain't that what you men usually see a man about?'

'No, Cat, I does mean a rabbit. 'Tis for our supper, like,' he answers. 'Wife's gonna to need more than bren'cheese and turnip now, ain't she?'

'True, that!' Cat wants to tell the man to pull his socks up and find work, for they all know how he lingers at the inn and slacks at his responsibilities. But she is in his home and it would never do to call him on his laziness here, nor anywhere in fact. After he has left, she bends close to Molly and whispers, 'Well, better late than never, but I do believe your husband be waking up at last.'

'Huh! You believe he's gone to find us a rabbit? I shall believe that when I sees it. A tankard, more like,' replies Molly, and she looks ghostly with her pale face and dark rings around her eyes.

Cat gives her a hug. It is time for them to depart and leave Molly to sleep. 'Come now ladies. What Moll needs is rest, till that rabbit turns up anyhow. And now Mistress Richardson is here to help, she can do without us under her feet.'

When everyone has gone, Mathilda asks, 'Now, how can I be of help, dear.'

She is a little shocked at the change in Molly, whom she last saw at her wedding five years ago. The woman has aged ten years in that time, her face sunken and her skin pale and pasty. Mathilda brushes off her concerns, for perhaps it is only the result of the ordeal she has just been through.

'I needs to sleep, Tilly,' Mathilda tenses at her name, but Molly continues, 'afore them babes wake and want to suckle. Won't be long, they's so small. You could see to me boy, that would be a great help. He be outside in the yard. Them Chitty girls was watching him, and watch him you must, for he needs a tight eye. Runs off at any chance,' Molly says.

She is slurring, sounds drunk, Mathilda thinks.

She must be very tired indeed, poor thing.

'I shall go and fetch him at once,' and she pats Molly's hand gently. 'I am here now, everything will be alright.'

Molly stifles a laugh. Mathilda is the last person who could make everything alright, unless her cousin has work for George, can nurse the twins, or is willing to smash a tub of laundry with a dolly. And then there is Eliza, who has nodded off in front of the fire, her pipe empty, lying in her lap. Will Mathilda change Eliza's bedding when it is soiled, help her wash and dress, fill and light her pipe? There are some things she is sure Eliza would not even let a stranger do. There are no answers, and if she weren't so tired she would call Mathilda out on her past laziness, but she does need her help with Little Joe and does not have the energy for a quarrel. The only thing she knows at this moment is that she must sleep. She rests her head on the hard oak table and is out of the world within seconds.

Mathilda eases her way through the narrow lean-to. Her dress hoops catch on the shelves and she is concerned that the fabric will pull all the little jars and bottles off and her dress will be ruined. She stops to read the labels and then sees that they are not words but pictures to signify what each contains. *What an interesting apothecary!* But no time to consider it now, she must get the boy indoors before the storm.

She is outside in the yard, just as the first spots of rain start to fall.

Suddenly, there is a huge flash and an almighty clap, and

Mathilda nearly jumps out of her dress. She clutches her hand to her chest, with the ever present bible.

The lightning struck very close by and she turns to look at the thatch. Thank God, the roof is intact. The only smoke to be seen is being pulled erratically from the chimney by the feisty wind. The trees' normal leafy whisperings have turned to frantic howls and screams, and the sky has turned a strange violet. The clouds are bubbling, and the wind is whipping itself up into an ever increasing frenzy. The heavens are about to pour down to earth.

She calls out for Little Joe.

'Joseph! Joseph! Where are you, boy?' There is no reply. 'Joseph? Come here, to your cousin Mathilda. I am to look after you while Mama is busy with your teeny tiny brother and sister. Come here, Joseph!' But the yard is empty, apart from Pudding, cowering under an old table, ignorant of the deadly power of lightning and terrified of the harmless thunder.

'Oh! Where are you, child? Come now, it is going to be terrific and you must come inside. Are you hiding? Now is not the time to play. Come here, Joseph. Where are you?' She is fractious now, the raindrops becoming fiercer by the second and her ringlets are starting to droop. 'Oh! My hair, my hair. Positively ruined.'

The storm has well and truly broken and enormous puddles are gathering all over the yard. The fire pit hisses and steams as the last embers are quenched by the icy downpour. Mathilda negotiates the return trek through the lean-to until she bursts through into the living room of the cottage, hair bedraggled and water dripping down her neck.

Molly is sound asleep, disturbed only in her dreams by the growing cacophony swirling around The Common. She has one hand drooped over the side of her babies' box, the cracks and grumbles making no dent in their slumber either.

'Molly, Molly,' Mathilda whispers, but just as she is about to shake Molly awake, a gruff demand comes from Eliza.

'Wake 'er not, Mistress. She needs sleep, see? Can't foind the little bugger, eh? Gone missing again, ain't he? Tch, tch. Should'a toid the little toike up, they should. Loike a dog, loike a dog,' and she clicks her tongue.

Mathilda is concerned. Keeping a boy tied up like a dog is not how she envisioned her cousin would treat any child, let alone her own. Do they do this as a matter of course? In any case, she must find the boy.

'Do you think he has gone with the women? Perhaps they took him. I am sure they must have taken him home with them,' Mathilda says, if only to quell her own angst.

'Naw, them shan't take he, not 'less they tell Moll first, loike, or she be worryin' summat rotten. He be down by the brook, or on The Common, most loikly. Him's always going off somewhere,' Eliza replies. She holds out her pipe, 'Now, fill this up, Mistress. Oi needs a puff or two, see? And re'glar loike, else Oi gets a lil'bit cranky.' She grins a toothless grimmace at Mathilda, her eyes asparkle with fire glow.

'But the weather, Mistress Greenfield, it is treacherous. We must find him!'

'Fill this up first, for Oi feels the crank settlin' in. Come, fill it Mistress, do, or Oi shall not be able to shift it so easy. 'Twill be there all even.'

Mathilda is a little shocked by Eliza's lack of concern, but the realisation that she is being asked, or rather *told*, to do something she has never before done takes her attention away from the boy for a moment.

Fill a pipe, indeed!

She does not know where to start.

''Ere's me baccy pouch. Oi don't see good no more, see? Me eyes be dim and hands so gnarly, see? Oi needs help with all the fiddly things, loike,' she mumbles, and pushes the little leather pouch into Mathilda's hand with her twisted fingers.

Mathilda does what is asked of her and hands back the pipe to Eliza.

'Loight it Mistress, loight it! Lord God Almoighty, ain't no good t'me loike that!' and Eliza shoves it back.

Mathilda is now completely at a loss. Eliza senses her confusion and is losing her patience.

'Get the spill there, see?' She points up above the fireplace. 'The spill, see? On the shelf. Then loight it and hold the flame to the bowl, see? Then you suck it like you's a baby. Easy peasy, ain't it?' she instructs, sounding more and more crotchety.

'Madam, I do not think I can do what you ask, but perhaps I can bring the flame to you, then you can do the sucking like a baby,' replies Mathilda.

'As you wish, Mistress, as you wish, but let no wax drip on me dress. Oi won't have no wax on it, see? Won't never git it out.'

The small pipe-bowl is soon lit and Eliza's crankiness averted, for the time being. Mathilda is relieved that at least one problem has been solved.

However, a bigger one looms before them. Where is the boy?

And how on earth will they find him in this weather?

THE COMMON LANE

LATE AFTERNOON

George and Annie hurry away from Rye Cottage, along Common Lane. The wind is picking up, and they can hear the forest beginning to come alive. It sounds furious. George's ire is simmering with it, for the more he thinks about Hal with Annie, the more it makes his blood boil. He stops at the bridge and grabs Annie's arm, preventing her from walking any further.

'Wait a moment, Sister,' he says. 'I will finish our conversation, what was interrupted by Mister Martindale.'

'Can it not wait, Brother. The storm be almost upon us. We should find shelter, and quick,' Annie replies. Her long auburn hair has come loose and the wind is whipping it around her neck like a hangman's noose. 'What have you to say that be so important?'

'Oh, 'tis important alright. Sommat what's bothered me since you come to fetch me earlier,' George glowers at her, and Annie sees the tempest in his eyes.

At once she is afraid of what he is about to ask, but there may be more to fear in his reaction when she gives her answer.

'Well, then dear Brother, do ask.'

She tries to sound calm, but her voice is unsteady.

George takes a deep breath, 'I wish to know, Sister, how you knew to find me at that clearing this morn? 'Tis so deep in the forest, so far from everything.'

'I,' she begins, but at that moment, that first bolt of lightning sears the sky.

It twists the very air apart and the tremendous crash gives them both a shock. They look over to where God's wrath has landed. A plume of smoke is rising above the canopy of The Common and they hear the crack of a heavy branch as it is torn from its tree.

'Holy crap, that were close,' George says, and for a moment he has forgotten his awkward interrogation.

'Aye, and thank the Lord it di'n't hit the houses,' says Annie, trying to pull her hair away from her neck and get it back under control.

George turns to his sister, intending to get his answer. But he must wait, for at that moment the heavens open and a vengeful rain falls from the sky, as if his anger is overflowing and threatens to drown them both.

They run the rest of the way and burst through the door of Rose Cottage, drenched to the skin.

Rose Cottage

Late Afternoon

Jesse has already closed the windows to the rain and is sitting on a stool beside the fire. The logs are spitting and wheezing as cold drops fall down the wide chimney. He appears calm, watching William sleep. However, his mind is in turmoil, mulling over the change to their living situation that Mathilda has brought, albeit temporarily, and what to do about his ailing father. That damned kitten is irritating him almost as much as his hair vest, and is batting a piece of dry bread around the floor between his feet. He resists the urge to kick it away. The clatter of the door turns his head, and can feel his disgust rising when he sees that it is not Annie returning alone, but that George is with her.

This is a man who has allowed his wife to become a drunkard, a danger to herself and her offspring. He is quite sure they bring news of all their deaths. He pushes his shirt against his skin, the discomfort reminding him that these are evil thoughts and his ungodly reaction should be tempered. Alas, if only he had remembered this before he formed the wicked image of Molly in her coffin, cradling her dead twins.

George nods a greeting.

Jesse only grunts a response, 'Any news on the infants, Brother?'

'Aye, twins, one of each.'

'And your wife?'

'Tired. Mistress Knocker says she should have no fever, 'twere a clean birth.'

'Well now, that be a relief indeed,' Jesse states, and wonders at that part of him which is disappointed that the news is not worse. He pushes the coarse shirt to his raw skin once more. *Wickedness, full of it you are, man. Wicked to the core.* 'Congratulations to you,' he says, grudgingly.

'Save them, Brother. The boy be small, ain't sure he will live long,' George says, and knows he should thank his brother for bringing Molly home after she collapsed, but cannot bring himself to utter the words.

'I shall pray for him, for all of you,' Jesse says, turns his face to the fire. 'Draw up a stool, dry yourselves.'

George and Annie sit between their brother and William. The thunder, lightning, and the fierce rain continue to roll around the cottage and The Common. Annie picks up the kitten, surprised that Jesse has allowed it into the house.

'Mathilda brought it in, while I weren't looking,' he says. 'Damnded fleabag.'

Jesse really is in a foul mood today, she notes.

'Perhaps Mistress Greenfield has sommat against the fleas, I will ask her,' and Annie lets the kitten curl up in her lap, grateful something has taken her attention away from George's questioning. It will likely not be avoided, he will demand an answer sooner or later. 'Seems quite clean to me, this kitten,' she says.

'Aye at the moment, but 'twill not stay that way, will it? They all has fleas soon enough, once they start catchin' rats.' It is a battle to keep vermin, lice and fleas from their homes, and the last thing he wants is to invite the enemy in.

George looks at Annie, catches her eye, but he remains silent, for in front of Jesse and William he can hardly expect his sister to reveal her secrets. His anger is no less, though, and he must be away from here as soon as the rain abates or he will explode. And the stench coming from Father is appalling. He wrinkles his nose up in disgust. *How'd they live with it?* He is glad he has found another home, albeit with another decrepit. At least she is clean, Molly sees to that. He does not blame Annie for not wanting, or being able, to keep their father in better condition, for the man has become a despicable wretch.

He licks his lips, his mouth dry. 'Annie, have you some ale in the house? Proper ale, or summat stronger if you has it,' George says. 'Wet the babies' heads an all,' he adds, looking over at Jesse, whose dark shadow is now growing, for George on a drinking spree in his home is his worst nightmare.

'Sure. We has an ale, and there be a drop of brandy somewhere,' Annie replies. She fetches a small flagon of ale from the black dresser and a bottle from a hidey hole, behind the jars of pickles. A place their father cannot possibly reach.

'I shall join you,' she says.

Jesse sits up, his face thunderous. 'Sister, did I not forbid you to drink that demon spirit?' he demands, incensed at her disobedience.

'Leave her be,' George says. 'If our sister wants to celebrate with me, why should she not?' he roars. 'Lord above, just cause it don't agree with you, and you's so damned bleedin' holy and Methody now, don't mean everyone else has to bow down to your fuckin' commands.'

'Do not speak to me so, Brother, and I will not have those curses spoke in me own home,' Jesse replies. 'And why ain't you with yer wife, eh?'

George bristles, remembering that in the last three days Jesse seems to have been with Molly more than he. At that moment there is a groan from the hard-backed chair as William stirs.

'Now look,' Annie says, alarmed at the growing tension. 'You've woken Father.'

They all know William was better left asleep, and watch as the pale, ghastly figure opens his eyes.

'Did I hear right,' William slurs. 'Brandy hid somewhere, has you Daughter, dee-ar? Or were I dreamin'? Bring some for your poor old Father, there's a good girl,' he says, groggily. As he becomes more aware of his surroundings, he sees George sitting next to him.

'George? Come to wet the babes' heads, did I hear? Means you's a father again,' he says. 'Your wife, does she live, after the awful ordeal, like?'

'Moll be fine, Father. Give me twins, too.'

George is surprised at William's concern, quite out of character these days. And with all the other things spinning in his mind, he is not yet ready to celebrate, but perhaps the brandy will mellow him, although if he overdoes it, he will surely spoil the tea-deal. A disaster, indeed. Jesse is right to be afraid of his drinking binges, another of his dreadful ways he should curb.

'Twins,' his father continues. 'I had twins once. And what a miracle it were, two babes for the price o' one. Double the bleedin' cost later. But you must be proud, Son. Yer Mother, she were proud, too.'

William's demeanour suddenly changes. His tone becomes aggressive and snarly, and he pokes his stick at Jesse. 'Pity one of 'em turned out to be such a damnded bleedin' bad egg, and drove the other away, eh?' and he spits at Jesse.

Jesse's face starts to burn.

'Father, what on earth do you mean?' Annie asks, a little shocked at this outburst, but enthralled at the hint of a dark revelation. *Drove the other away? How? Ned left because of … well, because of what, exactly?* As she got older, she heard hints that it was something to do with his girl Lizzie, but was that the only reason? She looks over and sees Jesse has become hot under the collar and is even beginning to scratch at his raw chest. She stifles a smile. *Perchance Father speaks the truth and now we shall find out what's behind my brother's disgusting evening ritual in the tack room.*

But George has other ideas. 'Best left unsayed, Sister,' he says, and catches Jesse's eye.

Jesse scowls, and Annie could cut the air between them with a scythe.

'Where's me drink, Daughter?' William asks. 'Fetch me a cup, summat strong, none o' that piss weak ale you gives me. Brandy will do nicely. I know not why you did not think to tell me you had it hid away.' His outburst forgotten, his only concern now is getting a drink between his lips, 'Come on, wench, hurry yourself.'

Wretched William has returned, in his voice the anger, ungratefulness, resentment, all those things which have twisted him over time into what he has now become. Annie hands him her own cup of brandy, and fetches another for herself.

An uneasy silence falls upon the room, broken by the fire spitting embers onto the hearth, the rain scratching at the glass, and loud cracks and rumbles from the passing storm.

George studies Jesse over the top of his cup. He knows exactly of what his father is speaking, but will not mention it, especially in front of Annie. It would break her heart. But then so will Hal. His head is bursting: family, work, secrets, life in general. He cannot rest a moment, enjoy his drink, nor celebrate his children's births, his wife's survival. He takes an enormous slug and drains the cup.

'Top it up, Sister, if you do not mind,' he says.

Jesse scowls even more fiercely, if that were at all possible.

Annie fills it, a little deeper this time. George is truly on edge and it has something to do with his earlier question, of that she is sure. He sits brooding into his brandy, his thick fingers gripping it so tightly, they turn white. Jesse is sulking, brows knitted together in a tight knot, eyes focused on a splash of tallow wax on the tiles, shaped like a devil's eye. Father has slipped back into a reverie, having hardly touched the drink. Most unusual. *What on earth is wrong with him today?* It is as if the storm has filled the room with memories and problems, thoughts and fears, none of which can be spoken aloud.

The house goes quiet and they are surrounded by a lull.

The fire has all but burned itself out, is no longer hissing, and the patter of rain has eased.

The storm has blown over.

George sets his empty cup on the mantelpiece and warms his wet breeches for a moment before readying himself to leave. 'We will speak later, Sister,' he says, putting a hot hand on Annie's shoulder, a warning that he will not let his question drop. 'I must be away to find Hal. You any idea where he might be?'

There is sarcasm in his voice.

Jesse hears it. 'Why the hell would our sister know where your friend be?' he asks.

George looks at him and shakes his head. 'Never mind,' he says. *Bleedin' hell!* He should not have asked her, that drink truly makes him lax. He glances over at William, once again snoring loudly, and without another word, George storms out of the stuffy room, slamming the door behind him.

However, Jesse is not going to let this go. 'What did he mean by that, Sister? Why would you know where Hal Archer lurks?' he asks. He knows George too well. The drink makes him sloppy, indeed, just like his wife.

Annie looks into her cup. She wants to tell him everything and also to say nothing. At some point she will have to come clean with her news, because she is growing and will not be able to hide it. Perhaps the time has come to let it out. She puts the cold metal to her lips and takes a sip of the harsh liquid. She has not yet had enough to make her brave, and decides to say, 'Nothing'.

But like George, when Jesse has a bee in his bonnet, he will stop at nothing to get it out, even if it stings him in the process, and this one will do just that.

'Sister, I asked you a question,' he says, and she hears the maliciousness inherited from their father. But there is that other tone, the one which demands, probes, needs to know, to have total dominion over this, his own household. How she wishes he would find himself a wife. *Why hasn't he?* She takes another sip, then a large swig. She needs a lot of courage to come out with her news.

Before she can say more, Jesse jumps up and snatches the cup out of her hand, throwing the remaining spirit onto the fire. The flames flare up like a fire-devil. Annie cowers, puts her hands up to protect her head, expecting a clump from her brother's heavy fist. It doesn't come. Instead he sits back down on his stool, leans towards her, his face close to hers, hands on knees, and he repeats his words, calmly, slowly, 'I asked you a question. Now answer me.'

Annie sobs. There is no way out now. He will not hit her if he knows about her pregnancy, of that she is sure. She can use it as a shield.

'I am with child,' she hears herself say through her tears.

Was it her?

Surely not!

It must have come from another's lips. She could not have said that, so straightforwardly.

But she did, for she hears Jesse laugh, a strange and twisted sound.

'Do not jest, Sister,' he says, like he has heard an impossible joke. 'That drink has got to you quick, like. Two sips is all it takes to make you play the fool. 'Tis exactly the reason why I forbid you to partake.'

Annie's eyes well up with tears, her face turns red.

And then he realises that his sister has spoken the truth.

'No! Good Lord, 'tis true?' he says, bringing his hands to his head. 'Lord Almighty. Who be the father?' he screams at her.

She can say nothing through her tears.

'No! Please do not tell me it is that good for nothing, Hal Archer!'

Annie sobs.

'Good God, help us! You stupid girl. How thick can you be? Do you not know of his reputation? From where it is rumoured he gets his money to pay for them silver buttons and buckles he loves to parade on his clothes and shoes?' Jesse says, shaking his fists at her. 'His smooth hands what never seen a spade nor tilled the earth? His dandy breeches, his silken bows?'

Of course his sister does not know. That kind of talk does not reach young women's ears, it is whispered in the dark corners of alehouses, at the edge of card tables. It is seedy, disgusting, devilish. How could his innocent sister have heard tales of Hal Archer's disgraceful business? She hardly ever leaves the farm. However, she must be as bad as he, for she let him take away her innocence.

Now she must pay for her ungodly behaviour.

Annie is weeping loudly, her head in her lap. A cold snake of fear has coiled around her spine and is squeezing her breath, suffocating her. She has missed something. What is it that she does not know about her beloved Hal? What horrors will her brother now tell her about her intended?

But Jesse has no intention of telling her.

He is only concerned with making her pay for her dishonour.

'May the Lord God strike you down for your whoring! You Jezebel! The shame you bring on our family. You are no longer welcome in this house, no longer fit to be called a sister of mine. Get out! Get out now, and do not come back,' he bellows, screeching in her face.

He hears an animal, his own voice rising and swelling from groan to howl, a fierce disgust at the deflowering of his sister by that rake, Hal Archer, and he is sure the union has his brother George's blessing, which makes it all the more despicable.

Annie rushes out, and on the doorstep she crashes into Mathilda, puzzled by shouts coming from the cottage.

'Annie, Annie, you must come and help!' cries Mathilda, with panic in her eyes. 'The boy Joseph has disappeared!'

However, Annie cannot see through her tears, cannot hear through the howl of Jesse's words still ringing in her ears. She does not stop to answer, and Mathilda watches as the troubled woman splashes across the sodden yard.

Mathilda turns now to the source of the howling.

It is not one of the farm's dogs as she first suspected, but human, although barely. She steps gingerly over the threshold to a dismal scene.

Father William, awoken by the uproar, has somehow managed to get up and just as Mathilda enters, he raises his stick, and with an enormous *thwack* he brings it down on Jesse's head.

'You're a bleeding burnt pot, callin' out the kettle for being too black. Scoundrel, you is!' he shouts at his son. 'Bleedin' plank stuck so far in yer fuckin' eye, you cannot see your own devil.'

Jesse raises his fist to strike his father, but at the last moment he spins around and strikes the mantelpiece instead. His clenched hand jars, as skin and bone smash into solid oak. At once, he wishes it had struck William, a softer landing, although perhaps more painful for everyone in the long run.

'Mister Hogtrough, what on earth are you doing?' Jesse hears Mathilda shriek from the door. It is not clear which Hogtrough she is addressing.

'Well, if it ain't the Angel of Death come to fix up this broken wreck of an 'ome. Welcome back, Mistress,' William snarls, and crashes back down onto the harsh bench with a curse and a howl.

'Did you not sleep well, Sir? The medicine, did it help?' she asks, her eyes wild and confused, trying to make sense of it all.

'Sleep? If you can call it that, then aye. Had a dream so vivid, I's sure I were dead and in God's arms. Took me to heaven's garden, he did. And then was revealed to me such things as I had blinded meself to, truths what were best left unsayed. Buried and forgotten. And then I wakes, and finds me pains and agony returned. And *this*,' and he pokes his stick again at Jesse. 'This poor excuse for a son, so righteous and full o' God, and yet so evil to the very core. All these years, I drunk to forget what he truly were, but all was remembered to me in that dream. Nay, 'twas more a vision, so clear it were. All comed back like a damnded rotten penny,' and William breaks down in a sob, rare tears rolling down his grimy cheeks, and he buries his head in his cup of brandy.

Jesse glares at him and is silent, for the old man speaks the truth. He is evil to the core, indeed. But why has this affair, for so long left alone, now come up for air?

Mathilda could answer that question if she chose.

She knows full well the kind of dream about which William is talking, for hers are similar: luxurious and comforting, but also, sometimes, far too revealing.

The answer is in that bottle with the little silver stopper.

Left to run free, the turmoil in the room will transmute to

immense upheaval. However, she remembers why she has returned and pushes aside what she has just witnessed in order to deal with the altogether more pressing concern of the missing boy.

'Gentlemen, this is not a time for arguments and revelations. Save your troubles for later, for we have a potential catastrophe upon our heads. Young Joseph has run away, disappeared. We must hurry to find him.'

Jesse huffs, and rubs his head, which is beginning to swell from William's clump. 'The boy's always running off. Why, only this morn he were here beggin' breakfast. Bit Annie, too, like a wild dog. Likely he's gone to sniff out food, the child be half starved. Neglect ain't nothing new to him. Don't see why we must help search, yet again. Find his father, if you want help finding the child,' he scoffs.

His head is throbbing now, and he is feeling a little dizzy. He slumps back down onto his stool.

'I am wholly disappointed in you Mister Hogtrough, a man who only a short while ago was in my praises for an act of benevolence in saving my dear cousin after an atrocious and treacherous fall. I insist that you re-think your decision and join me in the search. You have a deep knowledge of the land, The Common hereabouts, whereas I do not. Come, the child disappeared before the storm, he must be frightened and soaked through. We must get to him before he catches his death and return him to his mother before she realises he is gone.'

'Molly ain't been told, then?'

Mathilda shakes her head. 'No, she certainly has not. My cousin is in a most fragile state after her ordeal and is sleeping. The news would cause her great distress. I have left instructions with Mistress Greenfield to tell her the child is with her friends along Woodfield Lane when she wakes.'

Jesse recalls his own dream that morning, the ever decreasing circle of black corn and Mathilda screeching demands at him.

But this is hardly a demand, is it?

He is being asked to look for a lost child, his very own nephew. In spite of his feelings towards George, he knows he should help. It is not the boy's fault that his parents are useless, and it would certainly look bad on him if he did not join the search. As if things could look any worse. The shirt is pricking his skin, and he realises that he has been absentmindedly rubbing and irritating his open sores.

'S'pose there ain't nothing to do but look for the little bleeder. You go gather help from Woodfield, I'll search around the farm,' he says, and before Mathilda has time to thank him, he has stomped outside.

He makes for the trough, dunks his head in the cold rain water right up to his neck.

For the second time today.

THE COMMON FOREST

LATE AFTERNOON

George sprints through the wet forest to the clearing and finds Hal has been busy at work around the old barn. A couple of oil lamps, three stools, a supply of bread and cheese, and some flagons of ale have appeared. The floor is swept, the cobwebs gone and a fire is ready to be lit in the centre of the glade. However, there is little chance it will ever catch a flame, sodden as it is after the storm. It will have to be rebuilt with dry wood if they can find any. In any case it will only be needed after their work is complete, so as not to draw attention to the place.

'Ahoy, Georgie. Weren't e'specting you so soon,' Hal says.

George is gloomy and Hal fears the worst for Molly and the babies. 'Lord, don't tell me summat bad has happened,' he says, a look of concern on his face, which George wants to pummel. Instead he shakes his head and keeps his clenched fists in his pockets. 'Nope, Moll's good. Twins, boy and girl.'

'Well! Congratulations are in order then! Come, I have a bottle of rum stashed in the barn, let us celebrate,' he says, cheerfully.

'Nah, not in the mood.' George had thought a sprint through the trees might shift his bad frame of mind, but is still feeling as miserable as ever.

'You still worried about this night?' Hal asks. ''Twill all go as planned, you'll see.'

George looks at Hal and his eyes grow even darker, for the more he thinks about his friend and his sister, the more it disgusts him. He can hardly bring himself to speak to the man, who two days ago was closer to him than a brother. How things can quickly change. He turns away, walks towards the barn.

'Georgie, what has got into you, mate?' Hal says, grabbing George by the shoulder.

George shrugs him off, and the urge to bash him is almost overwhelming. He grips his fists into rocks by his side. Tomorrow he can have it out with Hal, but the twisting and burning inside, the pain of keeping it locked up is unbearable.

And the brandy is working it all loose.

He turns round. Hal at once sees the anger in his looks, and backs away with a frown.

'Lord Almighty, you looks like you's got the devil in you.'

'Maybe I has,' George replies. It is no good. Unless he finds out the truth he will not be able to concentrate. On the other hand, if he hears the news he is dreading, what will he do then? He is caught between the devil and the bottle.

'Get it out, brother, for whatever it is, it ain't doing you no good.'

'T's afeared that if I unleash this menace, it will cause untold havoc, but there ain't no other way, for it be burning away at me soul. I has no wish to argue with you Hal, but there be something I wish to know.'

'Ask, and I shall tell,' Hal says, still moving away.

'That woman you plan to wed, that special maid, what you told me about this morn but would not name. Do not tell me 'tis me very own sister.'

Hal is silent.

'So, 'tis true then?' George's fists clench tighter and Hal sees their danger.

He says nothing, better to wait until George has calmed a little until he speaks.

'Damn you, Hal Archer, damn you. Why d'you have to spoil everything?' George curses him. 'We was brothers, closer than me very own. But I cannot, will not, allow no communion between you and Annie. I knows too much about the way you lives your life, your whoring with all them rich women, and God knows it ain't pretty. If you marry Annie you puts me in a God awful place. She must be told everything, or she will be shocked and broke when another comes along and tells her, and you can be sure someone round here will spill your secrets, sure as night follows day. You sayed yourself the maids are already talkin'. Would break her, see? She be so innocent, so good and sweet, she don't deserve that,' and George is full of rage.

'If that's what's bothering you, brother, I shall tell her. She can make up her own mind,' Hal replies, still moving slowly away from George, who is stepping ever closer.

'Do not call me brother, for we ain't and never will be now,' growls George, with a look like thunder and he prods Hal on the shoulder with a rocky finger, pushes him backwards. Now the man is almost atop the unlit fire. 'Not by law, nor by friendship. Can you not see your past has catched up with you now? I always sayed it were a dangerous game you played. You think Annie will forgive you that? To know you's bedded dozens of wealthy mistresses, for their money? You are nothing but a whore, Hal Archer, and I will not see me sister wedded to the common rake that you are,' and George spits on Hal's feet.

'I told you I's stopped all that, been months now I ain't been at that game. Ever since I got with Annie, I's a changed man. I'll do good by her, you'll see.'

'And this other game? What we's mixed up in here? You think that be good enough for me sister? Answer me that, Rake,' and George comes at Hal, grips him by the shirt, shakes him hard so his un-tied blonde hair thrashes about wildly. He pushes him, Hal stumbles but does not fall. He is far slimmer than George and if George went for him, he could never hope to fight the bigger man and win. His only defence is retreat, so he skits around the pile of wet logs and moves towards the barn, as George grips his head in frustration.

'If it ain't good enough for your sister, how comes it be good enough for your own wife, eh? Do not pull that one on me, George.'

'It ain't good enough for Moll, though, is it? I sees that yesterday, in that hell hole at the inn, full o' demons it were. What danger has I put my family in by agreeing to this damnded work? Easy money for a few hours' work you says, but what be the price if it all goes wrong? From all sides we has trouble. Redcoats and magistrates and the noose on one, and them two devilish gangs on the other. Ain't no winners, see? This be the last time. Ain't my kind o' work.'

'Well, to be honest, I agree. I sees that if I want to do good by Annie then I has to stop. But this job were planned long afore she come along, so here I am, seeing it through. I shall go labouring in the fields after,' Hal says.

George does not believe for a moment that Hal would ever get his fine hands dirty, digging shit into the earth for a local farmer. He himself has a hard enough time getting down to it, but Hal!? *Pft.* He thinks for a moment, and then says, 'Call it off, Hal. Call it off with Annie. It ain't goin' to work, and she will never have you after you tell her about them weepin' widows anyway. Never. She would be too ashamed.'

It is Hal who is silent now, thinking about how to tell George that calling it off is not an option. There is no beating about the bush, he must tell George that she is with child.

'That, I cannot do. 'Tis too late.'

'What do you mean? Ain't never too late to do the right thing,' replies George, and looks at Hal, who stands with his arms out, palms up.

And then George realises, and he knows, like Jesse, that his sister is well and truly lost.

At the edge of the clearing, out of sight of the two men she loves most in the world, the rough bark of the thick oak pushes into Annie's spine. She wishes it would open up and swallow her whole, take her away from the despicable revelations she has just heard. But she is still here, and the pain creeping across her heart is making it hard to breathe.

She curls up on the damp moss around the roots of the tree and howls silently to the earth.

WOODFIELD

LATE AFTERNOON

Before Mathilda begins her search, she gives William another careful measure of her cure-all. He is soon quiet, in a kind of sleep, except for the occasional pig-like snort. The man was clearly unnerved by his disturbing dream, but Mathilda has no idea what it means. There is certainly more trouble in this family than at first she realised. It may take longer to fix. Three weeks may have to stretch to six, or more.

She searches the barn for Annie, calls through the open stalls, but does not go inside. One look at the floor, thick with flies and dung and piss, sends her scurrying. She tries the kitchen at the back of the farmhouse, in vain, for no one has seen the woman.

Annie is nowhere to be found.

Henry is ambling up the lane just as Mathilda arrives back at Rye Cottage. His dark hair flops across his face with every stride and he is chewing on a piece of straw, trying to whistle and grin at the same time.

'Henry, how pleased I am to see you,' Mathilda says, in quite a fluster. She lowers her voice lest Molly should hear, for the gap between the cottage door and its frame is so big she could pass her bible through it. 'Come, help me round up a search party, for young Joseph has disappeared,' she whispers, grabbing onto the lad's arm, and pulling him towards the forest before he can protest.

She is somewhat dishevelled compared to her earlier pristine appearance, and outside, without her enormous hat, she seems to have shrunk by half. He tries to calm her. 'Little Joe's always running off, Mistress. Chances are he be by the brook, at the stepping stones, like. Have you looked?'

Henry is as nonchalant as his older brother and not taking the situation at all seriously. However, Mathilda is convinced it is a lot more worrying than anyone will so far acknowledge.

'The brook? What brook? I know not where the brook is.'

Henry turns around and points at the bridge. 'That one there, what goes under the bridge. The Rye Brook. This be Rye Cottage, see?'

'Oh! I see now. But the boy has been missing since before the storm. Is there anywhere to shelter by the stepping stones?'

Henry shakes his head, 'I don't believe there ain't.'

'Oh! The poor little thing. Where is his father? He should be found, I am sure he will help.' Mathilda is now hissing more than whispering, in her haste to get the words out.

'Aye, that he would, Mistress, but I has no idea where he be.'

'Does he not work for a farmer around here? Could you not go to the fields and seek him out? Or the forest, perhaps? Would he be chopping wood?'

'Brother Georgie? Nope, he don't work for no one round here,' Henry laughs.

'Well, where does he work, then?'

Once again, Henry is in danger of letting things spill out which he is sure should be contained. He shrugs his shoulders and chews hard on the straw.

Mathilda throws her hands up in despair. 'Well, what are we to do then?'

'Come, I'll take you to the stepping stones, see if he be there. If not, well, then I shall go fetch some of the folk from Woodfield and you shall have your search party, if that makes you feel better.'

She seems a little calmer, for now they are actively looking.

However, when there is no sign of Little Joe at the stones, Mathilda instructs Henry to run as fast as he can to gather as many people as possible. He returns in a quarter of an hour to find Mathilda standing on the bridge, scanning The Common's scrubland for signs of the toddler and Jesse. She can see neither. Henry has brought with him the Chitty sisters and the two youngest boys from the Longhurst family, Rob and Will. It is hardly the posse Mathilda had in mind.

'Is this all, Henry? Is there no one else?' she enquires.

'They's all back at work now the rain's stopped, or busy doing summat else.'

Liza Chitty sidles up to Henry's side and claims him. 'Do not worry, Mistress, I be sure we shall find the boy, will we not,

Henry?' she says and pulls him away up the lane towards The Common. 'Come, us will check the forest, up by the King Oak,' she instructs, and turning to her younger sister with a sly smile, she bosses her in the other direction. 'Jane, you take the lady to the Wishing Tree, and Rob and Will, you can go up the Oxmoor Pond, see he ain't falled in, like.'

Liza has taken over and before Mathilda can protest, the girl has organised them all to her liking and is marching away towards the King Oak, arm in arm with Henry, who glances over his shoulder longingly at Jane.

He is with the wrong sister, but it seems there is nothing he can do about it, at least not without hurting Liza's feelings.

'How will we know if you are successful?' calls Mathilda after them.

'Takes about an hour to get to the Wishing Tree and back. We shall meet here when you's done,' Liza answers, clearly in her element now she has Henry all to herself.

THE KING OAK

LATE AFTERNOON

Henry and Liza wander along the track, navigating puddles which lie like cracked mirrors in the clay crevices. They soon reach the edge of The Common's forest. The trees here are evenly spaced, an area of long-fingered oaks,which have not been pollarded for some years. Nothing much grows under their dense canopy, but the path soon opens out to a more wild and natural woodland. In places, where trees have fallen, it is quite open to the sky. Some of Woodfield's livestock are grazed hereabouts, and as well as a few sheep, Henry catches a glimpse of a wild deer darting between the trees.

As they travel deeper into the forest, the path narrows. It is lined with tall, stooping grasses, wild flowers and herbs which are dripping water droplets onto the soft earth. Liza walks ahead, chatting on and on about her friends, all of whom, Henry notices, seem to have found themselves lovers and certain proposals of marriage, while she herself is still waiting. She is clearly not looking for Little Joe, and keeps turning round, smiling at Henry over her shoulder.

At first, Henry only wishes he were with Jane, but he is soon mesmerised by Liza's behind as it sways this way and that in front of him, and before long he is gripped with desire for the older sister. At least he remembers to scan the trees for signs of the boy, and stops to call out for him occasionally.

The breeze whispers and skits through the branches, lazy raindrops drip off the summer leaves, and the constant whirring of crickets and cheerful birdsong has resumed now the skies are clear again. It is a pleasant enough afternoon, the air cooler but no less humid. The wet grass soon makes the hem of Liza's dress sodden and she begs Henry to stop. She ties it up high above her knees, wantonly, Jesse would say, but Henry cannot take his eyes off her. They carry on until the trees begin to close in on them, and then all of a sudden the path tumbles out into a clearing.

They have reached the King Oak.

The ancient tree is standing tall in its court, a large glade which opens to the blue above.

Henry stops dead as they walk into the bright space, his mouth open at the sight before him. 'Bleedin' hell, will you look at that!' he cries, in amazement.

Liza has hardly stopped talking, but is now lost for words at a sight which shocks her.

The ancient King Oak has lost one of its arms. The dismembered limb is smouldering, and lies twisted and broken on the ground.

''Tis broke almost in two, the poor old King Oak.'

'That ain't a good sign, Henry,' Liza wails. 'Mother sayed that when the King Oak dies, so will The Common and all the folk hereabouts.'

'That be just old wives talk, Liza. You doesn't want to believe all that horsecrap.'

'Well, Mother got that from her mother, who got it from hers, goin' right back to whenever. That ain't old wives talk, that be truth.'

'Well if all them grandmothers ain't old wives, I know not who is. 'Tis drivel, Liza. Shouldn't listen to none of it. Still, that tree looks right lopsided now, like it's gonna fall over. And look at the size of that branch what's come down. Look! See there, 'tis burning.'

Coils of smoke escape from the torn end of the branch, which seems ablaze from the inside. Henry looks up at the tree. Lightning has ripped a strip of bark from the top to the bottom. A pale sore of smouldering, exposed wood, winds around the trunk like a snake. He follows it up into the highest branches where it eventually disappears.

'I don't hold out much hope,' he says, whistling, 'the bark all gone, like that. Me brother told me if the bark don't join up all the way round, the tree will die. For sure, 'twill be lost.'

Liza begins to sob. 'See!? 'Tis gonna die, and with it so will we,' she says, and falls onto Henry, burying her head in his chest.

''Tis alright Liza, you'll see. Nothing bad's gonna happen,' Henry says, wrapping his arms around her.

Liza tilts her head up and gazes at him with her large, blue eyes. 'Promise?' she says.

'Promise,' Henry replies, smiling.

Then their innocent lips meet and Henry Hogtrough finds himself kissing the wrong sister and making promises he may not be able to keep, under the ancient, torn King Oak.

THE COMMON FOREST

LATE AFTERNOON

Mathilda and Jane trudge through the forest towards the Wishing Tree. The ground has quickly become muddy underfoot, Mathilda's pattens are useless and only make the going heavy. She is in danger of toppling over, but instead of slipping them off and risking her hem in the mud, she totters on slowly. They call out for Little Joe, looking for signs the boy has passed this way, but their search is fruitless.

They do, however, find Annie.

As the track rounds a curve, she is walking towards them, carrying a stick and whacking at the tall bracken alongside the path. Her hair is loose and matted, and her cheeks are streaked with moss and dirt.

Mathilda is puzzled at the change from the clean and seemingly stable woman she met that morning, to the tearful one rushing out of Rose Cottage, and now this dishevelled wreck. And she is to share a bed with her this very evening. It troubles her not a little. This place is becoming ever more strange and she is beginning to wonder why she ever thought it a good idea to come. Then she remembers Molly and her pledge to help the cousin with whom she spent so much time as a child.

They must find her boy.

'Oh! Dear Annie, what on earth has happened? Did you fall?'

'That be a good question,' Annie replies. 'Yes, I did. And right royally too,' she says, holding back her tears. No point crying any more, the damage is done and she might as well accept her fate. 'What you doing, so far from Molly? I thought you was here to help?' she asks. 'And Jane with you, too?'

'We's looking for Little Joe,' Jane answers, staring at Annie, whom she has never before seen in such an awful state. 'You seen him?'

'Nope. Could be anywhere, that child. Always running off.'

'Yes, yes, so everyone says, but the boy has been gone since before the storm. Come, help us search for him,' Mathilda begs.

Annie sighs. She is exhausted, but perhaps it will take her mind off her troubles. 'Alright.'

'Do you know where we might find his father? I am sure he would join us, for it would be a hard man who could leave his child lost in this dismal forest.'

'This place ain't dismal, Mathilda. It breathes life into us folk, gives us so much. You just ain't got to know it yet, give it time, and you'll see,' Annie snaps. She did not mean to sound so harsh, but that is how she feels after the revelations she heard at the clearing.

My intended a rake who sells himself to rich women and, together with my brother, planning some skulduggery at this very moment which no wife deserves to be a part of.

The words echo in the depths of her heart. She has no idea what it is her menfolk are up to, and does not wish to find out. What she has heard already is quite enough.

Mathilda huffs and straightens her dress, then sees it has been ripped by brambles along the path. 'Gracious me, look at that! My beautiful dress. Torn, and almost beyond repair,' she complains, and fusses over the fabric.

'Me, too,' Annie mumbles.

'I beg your pardon?'

'Nothing.' Annie searches her pockets for a handkerchief and not finding one, she wipes her nose on her sleeve.

Jane looks at her, aghast.

Mathilda shakes her head, and turns back to her task. 'Now, where do we begin to find the boy's father? Annie, where does your brother work?' she asks.

However, Annie is no more forthcoming than Henry and ignores Mathilda's question. In any case, it is one she is sure she will never be able to answer. Hal told her they were repairing the barn for the landlord, obviously a lie. *Dark work is what they be up to.* Then she finds herself in a dilemma. If she reveals where George is, then she must either lead them to him or she must go back herself. If she takes Mathilda and Jane there, then whatever the men are up to might be compromised. As much as she hates Hal at this very moment, she has no wish to put him in danger. The only solution is to go herself, for whatever she is feeling now,

Mathilda is right. George should be told, and Little Joe must be found. And once George knows Little Joe has gone, he will not bother himself with her. Will he?

'I shall find him,' Annie says.

'Ah! That is so good of you Annie, dear,' and Mathilda is thankful that at least one responsibility has been lifted from her. 'We shall continue to the Wishing Tree. If the boy has not been found by then, we shall return to Woodfield and muster up some more hands,' she says, laying a hand on Annie's arm. 'Good luck, dear heart.'

Annie ignores her, and twists away. She returns along the muddy path she has already trodden today, unlike Mathilda, not caring where her feet land.

Mathilda stares after her. *Something is truly amiss.*

Annie picks up her skirt and rubs her face. She must look a mess. How will she tidy herself up before she reaches her brother and Hal? An impossible task. *As is finding Little Joe*, she thinks. The boy will no doubt appear when he is ready. But something is niggling her, an uneasy feeling, an impending something.

And then she remembers.

In the confusion, after learning of Hal's dirty secrets, she forgot that Jesse has thrown her out of Rose Cottage and she is now homeless. There can be no doubt that Jesse knows about Hal's work, from where he got his silver buckles. But how had *she* missed it?

The pieces are all falling into place, and with them, her future is crumbling.

RYE COTTAGE

DUSK

Someone is grumbling. Moaning, groaning. It must be George, and he's in a shocking mood, bashing and crashing around. She ignores him, walks out of the cottage door. She cannot be doing with his temper today. She has more important things to think about. Something has been lost and she must find it.

She is walking in The Common forest, knows well the path, for it leads directly to the King Oak. She tries to run, but needle-like brambles catch her ankles, hold her back. Finally, she stumbles into the clearing. What she seeks will be here, she knows it, feels it.

She looks up, the King Oak stands before her, arms spread wide, welcoming as usual, and that one giant knotty eye winks at her.

And there it is, what she has lost.

She knew it would be here. It is hanging from a branch, swinging back and forth.

Her precious flask!

Who put it up there, out of reach? She moves closer, stands underneath and looks up.

Wait! The flask of sweet gin is gone!

Instead, there is a tiny wooden box, a cradle. She hears crying, but it's so small, the box, surely not big enough to hold a baby. The crying continues. Oh! It must be her boy-twin, her newborn, the one so minute he fits easily in her husband's palms.

She calls out, 'Mama's here, I's coming.' But no sound comes.

She stretches up, on tiptoe, holds her hands high above her, pushing towards the precious box. Why isn't she taller? It is no use, the cradle swings on and on, out of reach, and the crying does not stop.

She begins to scream and cry, she is fierce, desperate. Still no sound comes.

All of a sudden, the wind begins to whip around her skirt and in moments a tempest is upon the clearing. A flash, and she turns away as a bright spark of lightning tumbles from the sky and hits the King Oak on the huge, gnarly knot-eye. She hears a thud.

What was swinging has come crashing down to earth.

She opens her eyes, rushes forward, ready to bring her infant to her breast.

But to her horror, what lies on the soft moss is no baby.

Splayed out before her is the decaying corpse of a once beautiful girl. Naked, bloated and blue-black, her pale legs are twisted and buckled. A thick rope encircles her once slender neck. The girl's blonde hair is twisted and plaited around the rope and her once rosy lips are as black as the deepest bruise.

She stares in horror at the body. All she can think is, 'But where is my baby? What have you done with my beloved child?'

She hears a rough howl, a groan. An animal? No, it is human, although barely. She turns around.

Is that the King Oak, crying? The twisted knot-eye is oozing yellow sap-tears. And kneeling on the moss, entangled in the roots of the ancient tree, is Jesse Hogtrough. He is weeping, too, and his tears are slow and black, like the darkest, thickest treacle.

But what on earth has he done to his beard?

Good grief! He has cut it off!

The light is starting to fade and Little Joe has still not been found. No one has yet told Molly, who is unaware that the boy has been gone for nearly five hours. She slept long, awoke from that disturbing dream to find the babies grizzling, fractious for her bosom, and her head still throbbing with remnants of gin. If only she could tipple up, it would stop. However, there is no flask on the mantle. It has gone, as has George. And Mathilda. She is alone in the cottage with the babes and her grandmother. Eliza is scrunched up, huddled in her chair. The clay pipe has fallen onto her lap, its ashy contents adding to her dusty skirt. Suddenly, one of the babies lets out a wail, and the old woman opens her eyes.

'You awake, Gran?'

'Not by choice,' Eliza replies, grumpily. 'She found 'im yet?' she says, still half asleep.

'Found who?' Molly asks.

Eliza quickly realises her mistake. 'Nothin, Oi's dreamin', tha's all.'

'Found who, Gran?' Molly repeats. 'Where be Mathilda? Has she been here all the time I were asleep?'

Eliza shrugs. 'How should Oi know, carn't see, carn't 'ear. Don't know nuffin,' she says and pulls her shoulders up around her ears, protecting herself from the barrage of Molly's questions.

'And George? Has he been back?' Molly asks, continuing the onslaught.

'Told ya, Oi knows nothing. Loight me poipe, Moll dear, there's a good gal.'

Molly is now suspicious and increasingly nervous. She lights the pipe, then opens the front door and stands in the garden, surrounded by Eliza's summer herbs and flowers, petals already curled up tight for the night.

She ignores the babies' cries as she looks around for signs of life.

North to Caen Farm, and south to Woodfield, and out over the dusky, damp scrubland. *Where is everyone?* She could not go to find them, for the babies need feeding, and often at that, and she has no energy to walk, with her head beating like a drum, and a dull ache between her legs where birth has left its scars. For some reason, a tight knot is building in her stomach, like there is something bad she should know but cannot remember. The babies are still crying, but she blots out the sound, for she can hear something else in the distance.

A shout coming from The Common.

Someone is calling.

A name.

She strains her ears, and even though there is hardly a breeze after the storm, The Common brings the words to her.

'Joseph! Little Joe! Where are you?'

And then everything slows down. As if the clock of time needs winding, the seconds drag by and come to a stop. Bats flit so slowly in the sky above her, that perhaps they will fall to the ground. Leaves are frozen mid-flutter, the grass stops swaying, crickets stop rubbing their legs, and smoke hangs motionless above the chimney. The landscape becomes a painting.

And Molly Hogtrough stops breathing.

Nothing moves.

Because now she knows.

Little Joe has gone.

THE CLEARING

LATE EVENING

They search The Common until the light fades. Even Jesse, with his sore head, stomps the little-trodden paths, calls and peers between the trees. When they cannot tell the difference between a thick log and the body of a small boy, they return to their homes. Not much to be done until morning's first light, but the night will thankfully be short, for the longest day of the year is nearly upon them.

George is in pieces. He could not sit still long enough, nor find the right words of comfort, so he left Molly in Cat Longhurst's care. If it were not for the threat of Barehenger's wrath, he would go to the Inn and drink, and begin the search again at sunrise. As it is, he has arranged to meet Hal near the path to the barn.

Hal is relieved the search party has broken up, for it will soon be time for their rendezvous with Captain Oakheart's men. He had envisioned it going on long into the night. Of course, the boy must be found, but what can possibly be done after dark except skulduggery? He patrolled the paths around the clearing, concerned that the forgotten barn would be stumbled upon, their work rumbled. He needn't have worried, for no one thought to go that far into the forest. However, he is still unnerved by George's earlier mood and cutting words, and now the work they must do together will no doubt be done with George in a sulk.

When Annie came to tell George that Little Joe had disappeared, he could see she had been crying, but there was no chance to ask her why as she turned away from him and ran with George back to Woodfield. Perhaps Jesse was hard on her, for did Annie not promise she would soon tell him about the two of them? He shrugs off his concerns, they will have to wait till this job is out of the way. His thoughts are interrupted by the dark shape of a man approaching, and he ducks behind a tree.

He hears George whisper, 'You there, Rake?'

'Aye, here,' he replies, ignoring the slur, and steps out into the low beam of George's oil lantern. George pushes past him without another word and trudges towards the edge of the clearing. They stand in silence, with Hal mentally checking that everything is in place.

George is still churning over the day's events, he cannot focus on what is to come. His fear for Little Joe's well-being consumes him, and then his tiny baby boy, who Molly tells him will not likely last the weekend. His heart hangs heavy. *Hal with his rich fucking widow's silver buckles, and Annie carrying his child!* The words have roosted in his mind this evening, with Barehenger's grizzly eye and the hangman's noose. His stomach gurgles, and he realises he has hardly eaten anything. He has no appetite now, anyway.

St Giles cuts a call through the darkness and he strains to hear the distant bell. The air seems to tremble as each count arrives. Or perhaps it is his knees. He counts eleven, one more hour and the dreadful work will be upon them.

'Best make our way back up to the main path, wait for the waggons,' George says, officious and stern.

'Aye,' his erstwhile friend replies. 'Guess there ain't no going back now, eh?'

'Nope, no going back,' and George pushes past him. *Not a fucking chance, Rake.*

Suddenly, to his right there is a crack of twigs breaking underfoot.

'What's that?' George whispers. And then, 'Lord! 'Tis me boy. Little Joe! You there, son?' he calls quietly, and then he is gone, dashing through the shadows, the weak light of his lantern swinging ahead, throwing ghostly shapes against the dark trees.

'Wait up, George,' Hal hisses. 'Don't be rash, mate. 'Tis probably a badger or a fox, a deer maybe.'

But George does not hear over the crackle and snap as he tramples through the undergrowth, and Hal quickly loses sight of the lantern.

As George disappears into the darkness, Hal shakes his head. No point going after him. He turns around, one last look at the barn before he goes to meet the pack horses and takes charge of the tea, alone if need be. He holds up his own lantern, and it spills pathetic light a couple of yards ahead of him. He walks towards the barn, takes three paces, and then sees with a chill exactly what crackled the undergrowth.

Not a small child at all, but a pair of black boots, which now stands before him, and as he lifts his lantern it illuminates the unmistakeable red coat of a soldier. A man about his own age is grinning at him like a devil, eyes sparkling with the reflection of Hal's oil lamp. The Redcoat pokes a pistol at Hal, who takes a step backwards.

Shite! What to do?

Throw the lantern at the man, blind him with oil, then if the man fires a bullet it may miss, give Hal time to skit into the darkness of the forest. Risky, but what is the alternative?

The gallows!

As Hal's blood turns cold there is no chance to do anything, for a hood is slipped over his head from behind and his lantern is wrenched from his hands. A grim voice whispers, 'Keep quiet, right?' Hal has no choice but to let the men bind his arms by his sides.

Meanwhile, George is still stumbling through the forest. There is no path and the dismal light from his lantern does little to show fallen logs and bramble wire on the forest floor. In his desperation to find Little Joe he has forgotten the meeting, the pack horses, the work. Barehenger's menace.

Suddenly, he stops. *Idiot!* The sound he heard could not possibly have come from a three year old's tiny feet, and the boy would be crying after so long away from home, would he not? He curses his stupidity and spins around to head back to the clearing. He is too far away to see Hal's light, and the hairs on the back of George's neck bristle and twitch.

That feeling again, that something is wrong.

Nothing feels right.

He turns and takes a step back the way he came.

Suddenly, a hand from behind grips his face, tight across his mouth, and a strong arm jerks his head backwards. His body comes to rest against the warmth of another's. He cannot move.

'Say not a word,' whispers a gruff voice into his ear. 'Not a word, you hear? And do not struggle.'

George feels the cold muzzle of a pistol against his temple and freezes. He cannot speak even if he wants to, his head tipped uncomfortably backwards, his mouth jammed shut, rough fingers grasped firmly against his lips. One twist and the man could break his neck. Or shoot out his brains. His mind is a-whirr.

What is this?

Who the hell has him captive? What side is he dealing with, Barehenger or Oakheart's? *Traitors!* Or the Kings' men, excise men? *Fuck.* The hangman's noose appears before him more vividly than ever. *Damn and fuck!* He tries to pull free of the tight grip around his neck and mouth.

'Do not struggle, I said,' comes the whispered voice again. 'And make not a sound, you hear me?' The voice is deep and grizzly but muffled, as if the face is hidden behind a scarf or kerchief.

George tries to think. He is a big man, and strong, surely he could break free, even though this other also has power in his body, for he feels strength in the man's fingers. But his assailant has the advantage of a pistol. And how many others are there in the forest? Without his lamp, how could he see who else is thereabouts? He may run into them. No, the only thing he can do is to relax and gather himself, ready to explode and push away from whoever is holding him should the opportunity present itself.

But his captor senses his plan and tightens his hold.

'I said not to struggle, do not try and get away, right? Just wait, you will be free soon enough. For now, just wait, and be silent.'

He is confused. What does the man mean, *free soon enough*?

There is a familiarity in the voice, but he cannot place it. One of the smuggling gang? Hellish faces flash before him: Barehenger, the Vice Admiral, Crivins, the other, with the wayward eye, Trayling? *No, none of them.* The voice not west enough for Oakheart, not well-bred enough for Mister Gusst. The only other person who knew where they were working is Hal, and perhaps he told Annie, but if either of them gave this game away it would mean certain death for their loved ones. *Hal!* All of a sudden his anger at his friend dissipates and in its place grows an immense fear for the man's safety. He lets out a groan.

'Still, I said, stay still and quiet,' the man whispers again. 'Damn you, boy! You's still as bloody minded and rebellious as ever.'

And all of a sudden George realises who has him, the voice as familiar to him as the sun rising in the east, and the moon in the night sky.

It is one he has not heard for many years, but indeed, he knows it very well.

THE CLEARING

BEFORE MIDNIGHT

Hal's nostrils are full of the smell of mouldy timber and rancid oil. The soldiers pulled the hood from his head as soon as they had him tied up, but replaced it with a filthy gag, likely used by someone to wipe their hands after filling a lantern with fish oil. The taste of it is making him queasy. If he vomits, he will surely choke to death. He cannot move his legs, bound as he is with hemp twine to one of his own three-legged stools. It is wound round his calves, his wrists, his ankles, and he is propped against the cool, damp barn wall. He is a fly caught in a spider's trap. But where is the spider? More to the point, who is it?

He watches the Redcoats in the centre of the clearing. They have lit the fire, which is now smouldering, the wet logs throwing off more smoke than flame. The men are standing around, silent. They seem to be waiting for something, or someone. The only sounds are flames hissing out hot air from wet wood, and the scuff of the men's heavy boots on the damp grass as they shift their weight around. The clouds have rolled back in and he can hear the soft patter of raindrops.

His mind races as he tries to distract himself from the taste of the disgusting rag.

The job of controlling and accosting smugglers falls to excisemen, but these devils here are Redcoats, soldiers tasked with fighting wars or quelling riots. So why the hell are they here? Did they just chance upon the clearing on their march out of London? *Impossible, too far off the main path.* They must know about the tea, or why would they have captured him, bound him, gagged him? Who informed on them? One of Barehenger's gang or Oakheart's? He despairs, turns first this way, then that, forming answers to a thousand questions and not finding even one which makes sense.

His thoughts turn to Annie, his unborn child, and then the gallows, for he does not believe he will come out of this unscathed. If he is lucky, perhaps a respite to his certain death sentence and transportation to a far flung land. If Lady Luck takes him to America, he will enjoy many years of hard, hard labour, will probably never see England again. His child will surely be born a bastard. And then Hal Archer does something he has not done since he was a young child. He begins to weep. As waves of fear and sorrow roll over him, he feels his bowels begin to move and suddenly he needs to shit. *Nerves. Pull yourself together, man.* He does not want to be taken to goal with crap in his pants, for he is certain he will find no change of clothes waiting for him. He will take the stains and the smell to the gallows. What a thought! Hanging there with the contents of his lily-livered guts smeared down his breeches. He is embarrassed for his dead self, shudders and manages to bring his body and his tears under control. His self-pity soon passes.

What's the hour? And where the hell is George? Stupid idiot, running off into the forest. It weren't his boy, 'twere these men in red, more like!

Perhaps George saw the soldiers before they saw him, has gone to meet the waggons, to warn them. Then, Oakheart's men will help get him out of here. A glimmer of hope! And what then? *Kill the soldiers?* He shivers. Killing was never part of the plan, he did not sign up for that. He is not a killer, and not a smuggler, either. Like George, he has realised far too late in the game that he is not cut out for it. He prefers a woman's bedroom to the damp forest floor and dark byways, and the Widow Meade with her silk and lace, and enormous velvet-draped bed is too easily remembered. The feel of her fur and the weight of her purse. Oh! To explore the warmth of her once more. *No! Bleedin' hell, no.*

Annie already growing ripe with his child and still he has thoughts for Caroline Meade!? He stifles a sob, a groan. His bowels make a move to escape again and he squirms on his seat. The sound and movement alerts his captors.

'Ah! See there? I believe the *prisoner* is restless,' whispers one of the men, nodding towards Hal.

'Well, so he is,' laughs another, looking over, but quickly turning back to push a log closer to the fire with his boot, so it may catch the damp flame. They murmur quietly together and pay him no more attention.

He counts them. Five. They could easily be taken down by George and Oakheart's crew. He relaxes a little, for surely he will get out of this predicament and he grasps at belief in escape. And then he goes cold again, for George is right.

He is no good for Annie.

How can he be when the Widow Meade slipped so easily into his thoughts?

But Annie, dear Annie, she is such fun, and his equal. He can be himself with her. If he gets out of this place, she will give him a child, something he will never have with the glorious Widow Meade. He sees now that perhaps a family of his own is just what is missing in his life.

He finds himself saying a rare prayer.

God willing, I live, and I will make you my wife, darling Annie, as soon as can be.

And God willing, I will forget about Caroline Meade.

THE COMMON FOREST

BEFORE MIDNIGHT

As George relaxes, the cold pistol is taken away from his head. 'So now you know me, eh? Brother!' the man whispers. *Brother!*

Yes, for it is indeed his older brother, Ned Hogtrough, returned from the sea, from the grave. From where, exactly? George nods, it is all he can do, for Ned's fingers are still tight across his mouth.

'I needs you to listen, and listen good, afore I sets you free, alright?'

George nods again. He isn't going anywhere.

'That man, Windy Gusst, scum he be. Scum, see? He planned to kill you both, you and your friend Hal there. Ain't never were no tea comin' up from the coast, not from his side anyways. 'Twas all a ruse to steal money from us, see? And you was caught right up in the middle,' Ned hisses in his ear.

Us? His mind whirrs, confused. A cold dart of fear shoots through him. *Ned must be mixed up with Barehenger! Never!* He has a million questions, but Ned continues, and what he says sends more chills deep into George's bones.

'Gusst had men hereabouts, planted in the wood. They was watchin' the clearin', plannin' to pounce and do you in after Oakheart's waggons turned up and the crates was unloaded. I believe they's gone now, but we shall stay quiet, just in case any's still about. Weren't e'specting you to go running into the dark, see? You should'a been at the clearin' with your mate.'

Bleedin' hell! Hal! Perhaps they have they already killed him! He squirms, wants to run back to the barn.

Ned allays his fears. 'Calm yourself. Have no fear for your friend, neither. We's one step ahead of them nasty, crook't old bastards,' Ned says, with venom in his whispers. 'We has a gang at the barn, see? They be *ours*, but dressed as soldiers, all in red. Gusst's men seen 'em, and believed 'em to be true Redcoats and that's when they scarpered, see? There was only three of Gusst's men, and we outnumber them by far. Ain't nothin' they can do to you now. They'll be shittin' themselves, proper, like. They only e'spected to see the two of you, not a bunch o' robin redbreasts. And we shall let them run away, and follow them a while, cause we wants them to be well away from here afore we eat, drink and get merry. And we will be merry, you mark my words, Brother.'

George is still bewildered, cannot see the plan. There are so many things rushing through his head, Ned's return, his involvement, Hal's safety, Barehenger! Soldiers? But Ned has not finished.

'Now listen, and remember good, here's what we will do, right? We shall go back to the clearing, and when you get there you will see them Redcoats.'

George stiffens.

'They ain't real, are they, remember? They's our fellas, see? Made to look like the King's men, so them double-crossing crooks will run away like little girls, all the way back to Windy Fart's skirt tails.' Ned releases his grip a little, but his fingers remain across George's mouth, for he cannot risk him crying out. 'Now here's your part in this plan. I be dressed in Red, too, and you are to play my prisoner. I shall escort you back to the rest of our men, and when you get there, you play along, see? Your friend most likely be bound and gagged by now, but by us, mind, not by them crooks. 'Tis all a play, see? He don't know what the fuck this is all about, yet, so he's prob'ly shit hisself already, afeared o' the hangman! Poor sod,' Ned laughs quietly.

Poor Hal. Indeed, he must be terrified for his life.

'Now, you ready to move? Remember, we needs to be sure Gusst's men have scarpered afore we can rest easy, so play along nicely now. And whatever you do, do not give our game away.'

THE CLEARING

JUST AFTER MIDNIGHT

Hal's skin is stinging, the hemp rope cutting into his wrists as he twists and tries to loosen the knots.

No good. He cannot escape.

The spatters of rain have stopped and the clouds have moved on, and now the wet logs have shed their damp they are burning brighter. Hal peers into the semi-darkness, where the blood-red of the soldiers' coats is made sharper by firelight, and watches the men take turns to prowl around the perimeter of the clearing, poking ahead their rifles armed with bayonets. He prays George managed to get away and find help.

Suddenly, there is a soft, owl-like whistle from the other side of the clearing.

'Ahoy, 'tis only I, with the other man,' comes a soft voice. 'Don't shoot.'

And there is George, *the other man*. Hal's heart sinks, for it looks like he has been captured, too. George is brought into the circle by another Redcoat. *That makes six, but perhaps there are more in the trees,* Hal thinks. And then, as the reality of their situation hits home, *Jesus Christ, we are truly fucked.*

'Make no sudden movement, or you will be shot, you hear me?' the soldier instructs George, who remains silent but looks around and sees Hal tied up near the barn. He makes no gesture towards him.

'Stay there,' the soldier says to George, and he obeys. *Nothing he can do,* thinks Hal, as George is flanked by two bayonets pointing at his ribs.

However, this new Redcoat comes over to Hal, holds a lantern up to his face, bends close and grins. He brings his finger up to his mouth, 'Ssshhh. And you stay quiet, too, right?' And he winks. Winks!

Hal is puzzled, for he sees a familiar face. For a moment he wonders where he has seen him before, and then he twigs. *Bleedin' hell! Looks just like Jesse!* The nose, eyes, identical. Hair shorter and no long beard neither, for it has been cropped. But how can that be? He is utterly astounded, completely bemused. The man is Jesse's double, they could be twins! *Twins? Son of a bitch, the missing brother, Ned Hogtrough! Well, stone the bleedin' crows!* And he cannot imagine for a moment how this came to pass.

There is movement in the trees, another hoot and two more Redcoats appear.

George recognises the unmistakable shapes of Barehenger

and the Vice Admiral as they slouch over to Ned and speak in low voices.

'Untie the man,' Ned calls, nodding over to Hal. 'For they are all gone, the petty scoundrels.'

Ned, Barehenger and the others change out of their phoney red jackets and are soon in their normal drab colours. They draw up the remaining stools from inside the barn and a couple of fallen logs from the edge of the clearing, and sit around the fire, drinking Hal's ale and devouring the bread and cheese he had provided for their work.

The plan has worked and Ned begins to explain exactly how they stumbled upon the treacherous plot to kill George and Hal in order to extort payment from Barehenger's gang.

'That Windy Gusst, he got a most terrible reputation for double crossing, and so we was suspicious of him from the out. We turned one of his men to our side, to get information of his doings.'

'A spy?' George says.

'Aye, and weren't hard to find someone willing to snitch, for Gusst don't treat his friends no better than he do his enemies, see? Oakheart ain't so bad, but since he got involved with Gusst, or Windy Farts, as I like to call him, his reputation be heading out to sea. Ain't no one likely to deal with him no more. Least, not till he gets rid of that upper-class snoot.'

Hal rubs his wrists where the rope has left red welts.

Barehenger sees his discomfort. 'Boys did a good job, eh? Had to make it look good, see?' he drawls. 'Gusst's men was all about, in them trees. Watchin', waitin' to kill you. Had to make 'em believe we was real, that Redcoats truly had you by the short'n curlies. Them pussies wouldn't mess with the Kings men, see?'

'Kill us!?' Hal says. It is the first he has heard of the nasty plan.

'Yeah, they was gonna snuff you out,' the Vice Admiral chuckles, like it is all one big joke, but George is still in shock and Hal now joins him.

'Wouldn't kill a soldier. Gutless, they is,' the Vice Admiral adds, then lets out a loud belch. The man is swigging on a flask of spirits in between stuffing chunks of bread into his mouth. He is well on the way to being blind drunk.

George studies him, no longer afraid of the man he so recently believed was a danger, for this undesirable wretch has just saved his life. He turns to Ned, who is now filling in the rest of the story.

'Oakheart's men left their base with tea alright, but unbeknown to them, two of the gang were workin' secretly for Gusst. Along the way, they switched the tea for boxes o' worthless leaves, without Oakheart's men knowin' nothing about it. Gusst's boys was gonna wait till the waggons had made the delivery and turned for home, so Oakheart would have been told in all honesty that the tea was delivered as planned. Then Gusst's fellas was gonna jump in here, kill you, and bury you hereabouts. Then, all they had to do was unload the crates in the woods and cart the empties away, or burn 'em p'raps. When you di'n't turn up to meet us with the repackaged tea, Oakheart insists it were all delivered, and as far as he knew, it was. Then Windy Gusst tells us, "Your two men must'a stole the load and had it away on their heels." And we'd have to pay up, for you was our men, brought in to the deal by our side, see?'

'Villain!' the Vice Admiral slurs. 'We's gentlemen, see? But that Windy Farts don't know how to behave with honour. He got it coming to him now. Ain't too long for this world, me thinks.'

'Why di'n't you just call off the deal when you found out about the plot?' George asks. 'A far easier task, eh?'

Barehenger laughs. 'Aye, true that, but now Gusst's got a few problems, ain't he?'

'That's right. Our spy warned Oakheart's men there was Redcoats in the clearing before they got here, so they hot-tailed it away with their stash of travish afore it were delivered. Now Oakheart's goin' to be askin', "where's the tea?" He's only got a load of leaves,' Ned explains. 'We couldn't let Windy Farts get away with it, could we? An' it ain't gonna be pretty, I can tell you. Unless Gusst's men manage to switch the crates back, that is.'

'Jesus, Brother, so we was worms danglin' on the end of hooks!' George cries.

'Yeah, that about sums it up,' Ned laughs.

'How can you be sure they's all gone, though?' Hal asks.

Barehenger explains, 'We knows just how many men come up with the waggons, and how many extras for protection, see? We knowed where they all was. They's all accounted for, but we's got a few men still followin', just to be sure.'

'How's you gonna explain that the Redcoats just let us go? When word gets out we ain't been arrested, awaiting a hangin' for our crimes, like?' George asks, not sure this plan is quite as secure as they are making out.

'What crimes?' Ned asks. 'You ain't done nothin, have you? No tea, no contraband, just two men moochin' about in the forest. Trappin' rabbits or summat. Even if Gusst smells a rat, ain't nothin' he can do now. Deal's off. You live, we keeps our silver, and Windy Fart's in it up to his arsehole. One way or another, we'll make sure Oakheart gets to know which of his gang is really working for Gusst.'

George is relieved, it all seems watertight. And now it is over he can relax a little, although in his relief he has forgotten that there will be no pay for the work he has not done, and his debts are going to have to be paid one way or another. He stares at Ned, can't quite believe that his brother has turned up, more than a little astonished at the circumstances, but dismayed that his brother is working for Barehenger. Indeed, Ned seems to be an integral part of the gang. While the other men are talking amongst themselves, he turns to him.

'How d'you get to work for the likes of Barehenger,' he asks.

Ned laughs, and puts an arm around George's shoulder, brings him close and whispers in his ear. 'Brother, I don't work for no one. See this lot here?' and he sweeps his flagon around the circle of men. 'Well now, they all work for me, see? All of 'em.'

George's astonishment grows.

'So, Barehenger ain't the boss of this outfit?' he whispers.

'Not at all! I am.'

'Lord Jesus Christ, the way he were lookin' at me yesterday, I thought he were gonna kill me if I put a foot wrong!'

Ned chuckles. 'Nah, he were watchin' you for me. I wanted to know you was alright, see? Not havin' seed you for so long, and I couldn't exactly come to the meet yesterday, could I? Too many faces in Letherhed would know me, or mistake me for me brother, start askin' silly questions, talkin' about beans and barley and horseshit.'

'Well, I never. Bless my stupid soul. I thought the man had it in fer me, truly I did!'

'This ain't your game, Georgie, is it?' Ned asks, still laughing.

'No, brother, it really ain't for me. Ain't got the balls for it. This be the last time. I's going back to digging that horseshit. Safer, muckier an' smellier, but safer.'

Hal joins in their conversation. 'Same here, Georgie.' And he looks at George, hazards a smile, hoping for forgiveness.

George is not ready, and under his breath says, 'I'll believe that when I sees it.' Forgiveness and acceptance are a long way off yet. He looks at Ned, and wonders whether he should tell him that the man sitting next to him is hoping to become their brother-in-law. He says nothing. It can wait.

But perhaps with Ned's eyes and ears, he already knows.

They sit in silence for a moment, as the other men chat and drink and become merry, indeed.

Their reverie is disturbed by a noise from behind, coming from the barn.

'What was that?' asks Hal. 'Rats?'

It comes again. 'Why! Sounds more like a child, to me,' Ned says.

George jumps up. 'Jeez, 'tis me boy!' and he rushes into the barn.

He comes out moments later with Little Joe in his arms, the boy rubbing sleep out of his eyes, grizzling.

George is grinning from ear to ear.

'Sleeping in that bundle o' hay in the corner, all covered over he were, hidden good and proper! How he got all the way over this side o' the Common, I'll never know. How'd he miss Gusst's men? And how in God's name did *we* miss him!? Thank the Lord he be safe!' and he kisses him on the forehead, tucks his jacket around Little Joe and holds him tight to his chest.

PART FOUR

SUNDAY, JUNE 11

1780

Rye Cottage

The Early Hours

George crouches next to Molly and whispers, 'Moll, Moll, wake up! Wake up, sweetheart.'

She is curled up on the makeshift straw bed in front of the fire's dying embers. The twins are lying quietly nearby in their drawer-cot, and Eliza is sleeping, hidden behind the curtain in the corner. Little Joe is fast asleep too, still in his father's arms, and as Molly sits up and rubs her own sleep from her worried eyes, he passes the child to her.

'Oh! Georgie!' she squeals, her relief evident. 'Thank the Lord! Where were he? Is he alright?' she whispers.

George strokes her hair, a warmth flowing from his heart to hers, and he is thankful that they are all safe.

'I shall tell you all about it in the morning. For now, just know that he be alright, yes. He had some bren'cheese, drank a little ale, so likely he'll sleep till morn. He be tired out, I reckon.'

Molly holds her son close, squeezes him and breathes again in what seems like the first time in weeks. And as George's hands brush her cheek, that love she once felt for him surges back. She looks up. Even by the soft light in the room, she can see something has lifted from his eyes. There are so many questions. Where was Joe found, and how? She will not sleep without answers, but her heart is peaceful at last, with all her children safe, and with her husband's love and comfort by her side once more.

As she looks around, the room seems full somehow. Something is making the space around them seem smaller, more enclosed.

'Georgie,' she begins, and then gasps. It is now clear what has filled their home, for she sees they are not alone.

Sitting at the table is the shadow of a man.

'Good grief, Husband, you has brought a stranger to our house at this time o' night, and with me here like this, only half dressed!' she cries, pulling the blanket over her legs.

'Hush Wife, have no fear, for that ain't no stranger,' replies George. He looks over at the table to the man sitting there, who looks back at them and nods his head.

'That be my brother Ned.'

Molly is puzzled for a moment, and then whispers, 'The twin!? What disappeared all them years ago?'

'Aye, the twin,' Ned says softly across the room, with a smile, his voice the same as Jesse's, although perhaps a little rougher.

'Oh! My lord, but I must offer you an ale or sommat. Let me see to it. There be gruel, too. I made it from what was left of the bone broth, and …'

'Hush, woman. Stay there, you ain't got no need to get up for nothing. I shall see to Ned, like. We has much to discuss anyhows. Now all you needs do is sleep, for them babes will surely be awake and wanting your breast soon enough. Now, you let us be and go back to your slumbers.'

Sleep!? How on earth can she sleep with no answers, a strange man, *a strange brother* in her home. However, she lies back down on the blanket with Little Joe nestled in her arms and watches the fire burn ever lower, the embers twisting into strange shapes - devil eyes, oak trees, and *Good grief, is that a beard?* Although she makes out she is drifting off, she keeps one eye open and both ears, which strain to hear her husband and his long-lost brother's whispers as they discuss their much.

And much does she learn, too.

'You want an ale, Brother?' George asks, sitting down opposite the man he has not looked at eye to eye for seventeen years. 'Ain't got nothing stronger.'

'Ale be good, Georgie,' Ned replies. 'Ain't one for strong booze, best to keep a clear head in my line.'

George cannot stop staring at him.

The last four-and-twenty hours have been a dream and nightmare all mashed into one gigantic pulp of mess. The nightmare, well, he does not want to think about what might have been, but the dream is in this room, all around him. Molly alive with the newborn twins, Little Joe, safe and well. His family all together.

And then there is this man, not three feet away. He cannot believe his brother has turned up, and in a manner totally unforeseen.

He passes a cup to Ned, 'To your good health.'

Ned returns the toast, 'To yours brother! And your family's. Looks like you got yourself a good nest.'

'Ain't bad. Thatch needs some work. Leaks. A lot. Got pots and pails upstairs catching rain. Hope they ain't too full after that downpour or 'twill be drippin' on us soon enough,' he laughs.

'Well, why ain't you mended it, brother?' Ned asks, with a chuckle. 'Hah, you don't have to answer that! You ain't changed at all, have you? Never was one to do what you should.'

George smiles. 'True, that. But 'tis about time I mended me ways. The roof may follow. Actually, 'tis Moll's grandmother's cottage. You remember old Eliza Greenfield what lived here?'

'Aye, the Garden Witch?'

George laughs, 'Yeah, we called her that when we was children, di'n't we? Well, she be sleepin' behind that curtain,' and he points over to the dark corner.

'Well, I'll be blowed! Still alive? She must be goin' on ninety.'

'Comin' up eighty, actually, and she don't let no one forget, neither.'

The tallow candle spits between them as their smiling eyes meet across the table. George holds out his hand and Ned grasps it. Fingers lock and seventeen years of lost brotherly love passes silently between them.

'Where you been, Ned? You was sorely missed, left a hole as big as an ocean, you did, just weren't e'spectin' you to be away this long. We just about give you up for dead.'

'Ah! Not dead George, far from it. Come close a few times. And where ain't I been is more the question. 'Tis a long an' twisty tale, Brother, too long for tonight,' he pauses, and sees George is eager for his news. 'Some of it, you truly does not want to hear, neither,' and he grins, showing a black hole where once two teeth were anchored.

George wonders how they were uprooted. Like his own? A drunken brawl, a clump in the face for looking at a man the wrong way. A heavy price, losing a tooth for a look. He does not ask, instead he says, 'Aye, reckon you's right, 'specially after what I sees of your acquaintances at The Running Horse yesterday. Unlikely lot they is.'

'Unlikely, perchance. But the Vice Admiral is right. Gentlemen they truly is. When they wants to be. Honest and hard working when they have to be. Not like ol' Windy Farts, eh?'

George laughs, nervously. 'Truth, I be happy never to hear that name again, nor meet his kind.'

He wonders how a man from the backwater of The Common came to be involved in such matters. He looks over his shoulder. Is Molly sleeping? He cannot be sure, but he certainly does not want her ears to bear witness to the names of villains and ruffians, even though there is a gentleman one sitting in her own home, at her grandmother's table. She does not need to know. To his wife, Ned must remain a brother, once lost, now returned. He drops his voice, hopes she cannot hear him.

'That Vice Admiral, how'd he get his name? Don't look none like a navy man,' he says.

'No, he ain't! Never did set a foot on the wavy boards. His full and splendid title is Vice Admiral of the Narrow Seas,' Ned whispers. 'See, when he's been at drink, the man fills the boots of the unlucky sod sat next to him with an ocean of piss. Terrible habit.'

'Jeez, glad I were the other end of the room at that meet, then,' George laughs, shaking his head.

The room falls silent and a question hangs on Ned's lips. It seems he cannot voice it, but George hears it in the tallowy air between them, knows at once the subject that must be broached.

A name not yet spoken, but which cannot be avoided.

'Jesse?' George asks.

Ned's fists tighten and his eyes cloud. 'Aye,' and he takes a deep breath. 'What to do about Jesse, eh?'

'Will you see him, now you's here?' George asks.

Ned closes his eyes. He has already made up his mind.

'Yeah,' he says finally, and lets out years of pain with his breath. George waits for him to continue, as Ned takes a swig of ale. After a few moments seemingly lost in the grim past, he speaks.

''Tis only recent, like, that I's allowed meself to remember. See, when your friend Hal were brought in by Barehenger and then you come along with him, it all come back to me. 'Twas then I realised I cannot just walk away, cause me soul, it ain't goin' nowhere. 'Tis right where this dreadful journey began. Never left the spot. I's gotta forgive Jesse or I's trapped there, at the King Oak,' and he looks up at George, a deep sadness in his face. 'Won't never forget though. And we won't never be like the brothers we once was. But forgiveness? Well, that be on me mind, 'tis necessary, or I ain't never gonna rest.'

George nods, for it is something he wrestles with every day. And yet he is no nearer forgiving Jesse than he is to repairing the roof, although, at least he is starting to think about the thatch. George lends an uncomfortable ear, for it is painful to hear the story again after so long trying to forget it.

'After I walked out that day, I jus' kept on goin'. Di'n't care to turn back, couldn't bare to look and recall that dreadful sight. My lovely Lizzie, hanging from the branch. When I cut her down, to see her lying all blue and swollen at the foot of the King Oak. God, forgive me, I nearly killed him. I thrashed him with that cat o'nine tails till his skin was raw. Di'n't want to stop, an' I don't know how I did. But summat made me throw down that ol' flail and just walk away. And walk? Bleedin' hell, did I walk!'

Ned shifts on the hard wooden bench. 'Did Father never speak of it after? What Jesse did, like?'

'No, he never did.'

'I heard he lives still,' says Ned.

'If you can call it that. He stuck his nose in a bottle when you left and he's had it there ever since. His bones are all crook't and crumpled. He ain't hardly able to walk nowadays, spends most of his time in his pit. Wretched, he is. Gives them all much grief in that there house. I reckon knowin' the truth of what happened turned him inside out,' George says, and then looks at Ned, puzzled. 'How the hell d'you hear he were still alive?'

Ned shrugs. 'From time to time I gets information from hereabouts, like. In this business you has hears everywhere,' he grins.

In this business, thinks George. *Good Lord! Me very own brother a smuggler, and a top one, at that!* It is all just beginning to sink in.

'I heared Mother passed.'

'Aye, two year after you left. She died thinkin' you'd run off to sea. Called for you on her deathbed. Oh, man, did she wail.'

'Probably best she didn't know the truth. I hoped Father would not tell her,' says Ned.

'No, he never did. She'd lost one son when you walked out and he didn't want her to lose Jesse too, so he invented the high seas for you. Even though …,' George hesitates.

'Even though he thought she'd lost the wrong twin, eh?' Ned finishes his brother's sentence.

'Yeah, that's about it.' George stares at him for a moment. While Ned's face is certainly more scarred, has seen more life, the twins are still incredibly alike. The same eyes, the way the eyebrows turn down at the ends, the dark red hair and whiskers, Ned's shorter but also flecked with grey. Everything identical, from the shape of the nose to the hang of the ears. They come from the same stock, had the same upbringing. So, why did Jesse's soul turn out so bad, so nasty?

'I'd forgotten how much you look alike,' he says.

'That's all, though. Skin deep is as far as it goes. We's oceans apart, hearts apart,' says Ned. 'Prob'ly always have been. I's done some things I ain't proud of, that be true. But I's always had respect and kindness for a woman.'

'Do you never ask yourself why he did it?'

'Christ, I did, at the beginning, like. Was the only thing what went round and bleedin' round in me head. Nearly sent me mad, so I stopped. Blocked it off, shut it up.'

George nods. He, too had asked, why, why, why? But got no answers. 'First I reckoned it were the drink, but then I got to thinkin'. I mean, look, I get drunk. A lot. Done some wrong things, too. But ain't never … Lord, could never even think o' doing what he did.'

'Nah, that ain't it. The drink got him all fired up, but I believe it were there in his rotten soul all along. There were clues, when we was growin' up, I just chose to ignore 'em. I always knew he had a jealous streak, but to go so far. I mean, I only tasked him with givin' Lizzie a message, to tell her I was called over to Mickleham to see that sickly horse and so I couldn't meet her. Didn't want her waiting ages at the King Oak, thinkin' I'd forgotten. Just never e'spected the bastard to put on me best jacket and pretend he were me,' and Ned's eyes fade, the light in them dimming as he recalls in words what he has never before been able to speak aloud.

George thinks of Molly, how he would feel if Jesse had done the same to her. He feels sick to his stomach at the thought that it was Jesse who carried his wife back after her fall. It should have been him, she should have been in his own arms, safer there, not the arms of that damned wicked man.

Ned continues, 'At first, I couldn't understand why she jumped. It di'n't make no sense. We was so happy, had so many plans. It were all perfect. We was walkin' on clouds every day, could not bear to be apart. So, why? Why would she tie a noose around her neck and end it all, so sudden, like? And then her sister come to me, and explained.' Ned looks up at George, shakes his head, disbelief still haunting him. 'Lizzie told her sister she knew at once it were Jesse when he turned up at the tree, trying to pass hisself off as me. He had not a chance in hell of foolin' her, for she knew me so well. But p'raps the drink made him think otherwise. Anyways, she went along with his game for a bit, like. She saw he were drunk, and at first he were playful. Then he started getting frisky with her, up too close, tried to kiss her, touch her where he shouldn't. So then she tells him, "Look, I knows you ain't Ned."

Says to him to step back or she would tell. But he kept saying she had it wrong, it was Ned in front of her, and why didn't she believe him? She started crying. I suppose his demon rose up then, when she wouldn't give in. Up it came from the depths of his soul. For that's when he pinned her up against that tree and took everything away from her. From us. Forever,' Ned's fists are clenched again with the tragic memory. 'She could not live with it, he broke her. For she knew that every time our eyes met, she would see him, too. Every time we lay together, she would remember him violatin' her. So, she jumped.'

George says nothing. What is there to say? The story is not new. He has known it seventeen years, although not in so much detail. He has held it uneasily in his memory, tried to wipe it out and failed. Never spoke about it to another soul. Not Molly. Not Hal. Not even Father, who also kept it to himself and tried to drink the memory away.

It has been an awful burden for them both.

'Did you never regret not going for the constable? To get justice for Lizzie?'

'No! Fuck! What justice would a court give a dead girl from the edge o' The Common? A man's word against hers? And six foot under she di'n't have nothing to say. Lizzie told only her sister, asked her to explain everything to me. And to protect her parents, the sister were sworn to secrecy. Was bad enough she died by her own hand, but knowing the real cause would have made it even harder. Both families left in tatters, too. What good could come o' that? Her family believed Lizzie unwell, unstable, and I punished Jesse in me own way. No magistrate would have dealt him as many lashes as I.'

'You know, I ain't sure he ever let them sores heal. Annie tells me he flails himself two or three times a week, in secret, like,' George says. 'He goes to your old tack room in the barn, locks the door. Once, she got curious and spied on him through an 'ole in the wall. And she sees the flecks o' blood on his shirts when she washes 'em. He wears a rough hair vest, too. Must irritate the fuck out of him, on them open wounds.'

'Well now, is that so? See? There's a little bit more justice for you,' says Ned, almost smiling. 'What about women? I heared he never wed. Is that true?'

'Aye, 'tis so. I ain't never seen him with a woman. Not once.'

'Seems he heeded me warning, then,' Ned says.

'What warnin'?'

Ned is quiet for a moment, as if trying to recall his exact words, for perhaps he has long forgotten them. But when he speaks, it takes him right back and they roll off his tongue as clear as if he were speaking them on that very day.

'I told him, "If I ever hears you has a woman you love, or a wife with a child in her belly, I will come back and inflict on her what you did to my Lizzie. But I will not leave her to die by her own hand, I will finish her off meself. And I will make it look like you's done the deed, and you will hang, just like Lizzie and my unborn, but from the gallows in front of a jeering crowd, and not all alone from one of the King Oak's arms." That was me promise to him.'

George is shocked, his mouth drops open. 'Good Lord, you really meant to do that?'

'Nah, it were just a warning, weren't it? But I give it to him along with the lashes. I suppose he thought I meant it. Perhaps I did at the time. I were so bleeding furious, in so much pain, like I never felt before nor since, and them devilish words, well they come from somewhere real deep. When I look back, I cannot believe I made such a threat.'

And then George realises what Ned has told him. 'Brother, you never sayed that Lizzie was with child.'

'No, that I never did say. She was going to tell me that day, at the King Oak. It was her sister what told me instead.'

Rye Cottage

Well After Dawn

Molly stirs. She finally fell into a short but deep and dreamless sleep after giving the twins a quick feed. The babes suckle and nibble like little fishes, and then are quickly satiated, their tiny bodies unable to cope with hardly more than a spoonful of her first milk. The tiny boy struggles to latch on, so she dribbles the warm liquid into his mouth in the hope it will sustain him.

Little Joe is still curled up in front of the fire, sound asleep, exhausted from his trek through The Common. *Thank God, he be safe.* These words repeat in her head, she crosses herself at every prayer, and her arm is getting tired. She looks around at the dusky room, sunlight trying to enter through cracks in the shutters.

Eliza has not yet woken, and at the table her husband and his brother are sleeping, heads on hands. They were talking quietly together until first light, then finally fell silent. Only then had she slept.

She has much to do. The babes will be wet, their bedding soiled. Their dirty linen must be washed and the infants swaddled in fresh cloth, lined with clean moss. She must fetch water from the Rye Brook, although perhaps the rain tub is full after the storm, and wood from the The Common, for the fire needs cleaning, re-building, and she is sure there are no decent logs in the wood shed. If she can find some dry enough to burn it will be a miracle. Then she can make tea. Gran will not be happy until that is done. They will have the last of that bone broth for breakfast, for she has nothing else. She will have to get to the farm, somehow, for bread and a little milk from Mistress Caen. Perhaps Eliza has something she can exchange for it, and some cheese, too. She needs a piss first. There are a few beans ready to pick from the vegetable plot she has been trying desperately to cultivate over the last few weeks, and she can dig up a few early potatoes, so she will make a soup for dinner. Perhaps she can stretch it and they will have enough to offer the returned twin.

And then there is a beard to forget, some very dark fantasies to dispel and a husband's love to rekindle. Where to begin?

She does not move, cannot take her eyes off the two sleeping brothers.

She begins at the end, with George and Jesse and Ned.

Good grief! What she learned about Jesse Hogtrough in the early hours, while she was pretending to sleep, has shocked her and left an empty, sinking feeling in her belly on top of the gin's aftermath. No wonder George has been so troubled, having kept that grim secret close to his chest all these years, and no surprise William is so bitter and twisted. She can hardly believe they were talking about the man she thought would make a better husband than her own. She feels extremely foolish. And more than a little sick.

Yesterday's dream of the King Oak comes floating back, the strangest parts of it now make sense: the man she thought was Jesse-no-beard was really Ned; the dead woman with the rope entwined through her hair, Lizzie; and that old King Oak, once again the centre of it all.

Molly shudders when she recalls the image of the young corpse, and her grandmother's words echo in her ears, *jus' cause the man goes t' church, don't mean he be a good 'un.*

Eliza knew, perhaps she heard a hint of it all those years ago, but from what she learned from George and Ned, the secret was well kept. More likely, her grandmother saw right through to Jesse's dark soul, while she herself could not see further than his damned bloody red whiskers. She will never be able to look him in the eye again.

She will, however, look at her husband differently, far more softly, and neither eye nor thought will she ever allow to stray again. *I promise,* the word becoming familiar and friendly again.

She is roused from her thoughts by a weak cry coming from the cradle-box. One of her twins is calling. She must be busy now, there is much to do.

While Molly is feeding the baby there is a sharp knock at the door. George looks up from his sleep and stumbles across the floor. 'Tis too early, who the hell's that.'

It is Annie, carrying a basket of bread, cheese, eggs and a flagon of milk, and her arms are full of freshly picked meadowsweet for strewing. She looks at her brother, sheepishly. Her eyes are bloodshot, her hair dishevelled. She looks like she has slept in the barn. And so she has.

'Sister,' George says, and in all the excitement and discussions with Ned, his return, catching up, reminiscing, he had forgotten about all about Annie and Hal.

'May I come in?'

He opens the door wide, and as she steps over the threshold she hands him the basket. 'I come with food. Di'n't think Moll would be fit to get to the farm and that you'd need something in your belly for when you return from your searching,' she says. 'I's surprised you ain't gone already. 'Tas been light for hours.'

'Annie, dear Annie, thank you for your kindness. But thank the good Lord, Little Joe were found late last evening. Look, he be sleepin' soundly still.'

'Ah! Bless the Lord Almighty for his safe return,' Annie says when she sees Joe curled up near the hearth. And as her eyes adjust to the shuttered darkness of Eliza's cottage, she realises they have company. 'Oh, I do beg your pardon, I did not know you had visitors.'

A familiar voice comes out of the darkness. 'Sister Annie, good God! How you have grown!' The man at the table stands up and comes towards her.

Annie is confused and her face falls. She knows the deep tones well, but she was not expecting Jesse to be here, and speaking to her on such friendly terms after yesterday's expulsion from their home. And saying such strange things, too. Why, she saw Jesse only yesterday, he should not be surprised that she has grown. Her belly cannot have swelled so much in a few hours. And if it had, he would certainly not sound so pleased.

Ned steps forward into the early sunlight streaming through the open door, and he smiles at the first sight of his little sister after seventeen years.

At once, she sees her mistake. The voice almost identical, but the face! Its adornments very different; the same colour hair, not long and free, but cut short; no bushy red whiskers but a tidy, cropped beard; an earring in one earlobe; a scar across the left eyebrow. A softness in the eyes.

She squeals with delight, 'Good Lord! Am I looking at a ghost, risen from the ocean floor? Or is it really our long lost brother Ned, returned safely home to us?'

'Ah! Little Sister! You can call me Neptune if you wish, but Ned is much more to my liking,' and he scoops her up, kisses her cheeks and holds her tight to him, as if she were still the eleven year old girl he left behind all those years ago.

Annie buries her head in his neck and weeps.

RYE COTTAGE

MID-MORNING

Eliza rose soon after Annie arrived, and the two brothers took themselves outside to the yard to smoke pipe and talk again about old times, while Annie helped the old woman to dress, emptied her piss pot, filled up Eliza's own pipe. Now the old woman is settled in her chair by the fire. The shutters have been pulled back and the room is light and warm. The place is brighter, lighter, happier. Far less fearful.

Ned fetched water from the brook, Annie made tea. Little Joe is under strict orders not to go further than the garden, and after his frightful journey, everyone hopes he has learnt a hard lesson and will stay close to his mother. He keeps asking to be taken to see the *Bwack Wady* – Mathilda he means – but he is told, *All in good time, boy.*

George went along the lane to Caen Farm to cadge firewood, for what he will be able to gather from the forest today will be wet and burn only smoke. He stopped at Rose Cottage to collect Henry, with the excuse he needed the lad to help him with the wood. Jesse did not question him, still bruised and sulking after Father William's attack. He was readying himself for church and instructed Henry to meet him there, but after learning he was to meet his brother Ned for the very first time, Henry has no intention of attending a Sunday service. He was overjoyed to hear Ned is not dead and has finally returned. There will be time later for Ned to see his father. For now, he wants to get to know the little brother he has never seen.

To her relief, Molly has been told she must spend her time caring only for the babies. Annie has assumed all her other duties: providing food and refreshment, seeing to Eliza and Little Joe, washing the babes' bedding, sweeping. Everything. It has taken her mind off Hal and her predicament, and for that she is most grateful. As is Molly, for she much prefers helpful Annie to lazy Mathilda, who Henry tells her was still in bed when he left. Molly is not at all surprised. Did she not tell everyone that her cousin had too many airs and graces, did not like to get dirt under her fingernails and would be of no use at all? It will be expected of Mathilda, now she is now the only female at Rose Cottage, to care for Father William. Chances are she will not stick around for too long.

The baby girl is doing well. They named her Sarah, after George's mother. The boy, Thomas, has already earned the nickname Thumb on account of his size. He is struggling, but his mother gently encourages him with her soothing, coaxing words. Somehow, the tiny babe is still breathing, and drinking dribbles from her teat. Molly counts every minute as a blessing. Although her fear has subsided, Thumb will need a lot of care if he is to thrive.

Eliza may well have more than a hand in his survival, too. She is quiet in her corner while the babe is trying to suckle, seemingly asleep, but ever watchful with her unseen all-seeing eye. She opens his mouth, wide, guides his miniature lips, and tells him, *now, toiny boy, pull with all your little moight.* And so he does.

The men and Henry, sit at the table, drink ale, talk about everything and nothing. Henry is in awe of his older brother, who, although identical in looks, is the absolute opposite of Jesse in character. The man is friendly, charming, interesting, cheerful, playful - everything his twin is not.

Suddenly, there is another rap at the door.

'Why 'tis right busy today,' George says, as he twists himself off the bench.

It is Hal who greets him, half smiling, half grimacing, catching George off guard. Still full of cheer from his talk with Ned and Henry, George has all but forgotten the harsh words which passed between them and he has not yet had a chance to talk to Annie about the child she is carrying.

'Alright, Georgie?' Hal says, testing the water. What reaction will he get? He is not sure.

'Hal,' George replies, and his smile falls away, his eyebrows draw together and that sullen, frowny face he wears so often is upon him, skylark that he is. However, he cannot be truly angry today with anyone, although perhaps he will have ire to spare for Jesse, as always.

'I be looking for Annie. Lucy told me she were helpin' Moll, seein' as she's been throwed out the house.'

Throwed out!? George steps out of the cottage and pulls the door to, lest anyone inside should hear, but Annie has already heard Hal's voice and stands at the crack, listening.

'That son of a bitch throwed her out?' George says quietly. 'Jeezus that bleedin' man gets worser the older he gets. I guess he found out about you?' he asks, and goes cold as he remembers it was likely because he himself put the suspicion in Jesse's head.

'Aye, and the child,' Hal replies, sheepishly.

'Bleedin' hell, Hal. You better come in, talk to her, if you can.'

'Best not, mate. Lucy told me Annie heard us arguing at the clearing yesterday. She knows everything, about … well, you know, about me past an' that. She were right upset, an' I know not if she will see me. I just wants to get a message to her, if you don't mind to pass it on. An' I know it ain't what you wants to hear, but I will make her me wife. You know me better than most. 'Tis not my way to leave her to the mercy of the Parish nor the Workhouse, nor Jesse. I wants her to understand I'll always be here. I loves her. If she decides 'tis me she wants, that is. Warts an' all.'

George grunts. He hopes warts is the least Annie might have to deal with, for he has no idea what Hal might have brought back from his travels across lavish Turkish carpets and under silk counterpanes, and if he can keep his breeches from wiping clean the Widow Meade's floorboards again it will be a miracle. Hal will also have to make an honest living from now on if he wants to keep his head on his shoulders should they marry.

Annie peeks through the open crack as Hal tells George of his plans. However, as much as she is dismayed at learning of his disgraceful antics, she cannot keep her eyes off him, her heart is aching for his love, and she feels his child inside her, yearning for a father. That hunger pulls her through the door and she steps outside into the warm sunshine.

Hal sees her first, over George's shoulder, and his eyes light up. Maybe she will give him an audience after all.

'Annie, darlin' Annie,' he says. 'Come, walk with me a bit in the forest. 'Tis a fine morn.'

'Do not darlin' me with your sweet talkin' horsecrap, Hal Archer.' she replies. As she steps around George she pushes Hal out of the way and stomps out of the garden towards The Common. 'I ain't got much time, Moll be needin' me.' She is going to make him work hard.

'Right,' says Hal with a grin. 'That's as good a start as any,' and he turns and follows, skipping to catch her up. 'Wait for us, sweetheart.'

'You have no right to sweetheart me, Hal Archer,' she says, and to herself, *yet*.

George shakes his head, God knows what will become of his sister now. He returns to the cottage but leaves the door wide open, for the morning light and fresh air are welcome visitors.

As George sits back at the table, he glances at Molly, dozing next to the sleeping babies. At the table, Joe is sucking on a piece of bread, telling Henry the few bits of his long adventure through the forest he can remember. With his uncle's help, his fantastical 3-year-old mind conjures up encounters with ferocious bears and hungry wolves.

Eliza shuffles over to the table. 'Ned Hawgtrough, well now, Oi remembers you. Roight little toike you was. Called me all sorts o'names you did when you was young. Don't you think Oi's forgot. No! Indeed, Oi has not,' she mumbles. 'Jus' cause you's been gawn for so long, Oi ain't forgotten, see?' and she waggles a crooked finger at him.

'No, Mistress Greenfield, I be sure you ain't forgot,' says Ned, smiling. They were good times, back then, before Jesse's demon showed up. Good times, indeed.

'So, now you's back, 'tis toime to pay up, loike,' Eliza continues. 'And pay up, you must, cause Oi ain't forgot nothing, loike. Garden Witch, you called me. And 'twere a dangerous thing to be saying about an innocent old woman what just loikes t'grow 'erbs and whatnot, do you not think, Mister Hawgtrough? Oi moight'a been burnt for it, or ducked in the Oxmoor Pond, or sommat.'

'Oh, I don't think you was in any danger, for had they not stopped all that witch huntin' by then?' Ned laughs. *Pay up? What will she think of next?*

'Well, nothing ain't never sure. Could'a turned roight around and begun agin, loike. You never knows. Fickle lot, them what's in charge, fickle, see? They moight blame a Garden Witch for anything at all. Moon don't shine roight, baby come along with one gammy leg, or crop what grows bent. Anything at all, see?'

'Well, then I must apologise sincerely for what we done then, for we di'n't mean nothing by it but a bit o'fun,' and he smiles at Eliza. 'I hope you will forgive us, Madam.'

'Oi forgives you, Ned Hawgtrough,' and she pauses. 'Still toime to pay up, though,' she says, and she edges closer to him on the bench, puts her gummy lips to his ear. 'My hears tells me you comes across a bit o' noice tea from toime to toime. And my hears also tells me you has baccy,' And she sits back and looks at him from under her black mob cap, with her beady, black eyes all a-twinkle. 'An' brandy, too. Roight?' she adds.

Ned laughs, and raises an eyebrow at George across the table. George shrugs. He makes a pointy hat above his head with his hands while she is not looking. *Yup, a witch, Brother. Garden or otherwise,* he thinks.

'You got some very special hears there, Mistress Greenfield, that be true enough, even if you ain't no Garden Witch,' Ned says. 'I will pay up, if that's all it will take to wipe away the sins of me childhood. I shall bear your ask in mind, if I come across these things at all on me travels, that is,' and he makes a mental note to have a couple of bags of tea, and baccy, and some brandy, too, delivered to her cottage when he gets back to his base near the river. Perhaps he will even bring her the parcel himself, for he has missed this place on the edge of The Common, even if he has not missed the memories of Lizzie and her fate, for they are always with him.

The sound of horses coming down the lane reaches their ears, but instead continuing towards the farm, the trap pulls up outside the cottage.

'You waitin' on anyone, Georgie?' Ned asks.

'Nope, not at all,' and he drops his voice. 'Maybe someone for the Garden Witch's potions,' and he nods over at Eliza who is already hobbling back to her chair. 'People used to come all the time, not so often now she can't see too well.'

'Don't look like this geezer's dressed for a visit to a witch, but he's certainly coming this way,' and Ned nods his head towards a gentleman coming up the path through Eliza's precious garden.

George turns to see a well dressed young man, a familiar face, and behind him, two lads carrying an enormous hamper. 'Good Lord, 'tis the man from the Portsmouth Coach, ain't it?' he says to Henry, who immediately recognises the gentleman who introduced himself as William Fitzwilliam.

'Aye, brother, that be him alright,' Henry says. 'He remembered where you live!'

Mister Fitzwilliam reaches the door and calls out, 'Good day! Anyone at home?'

The stranger's voice wakes Molly, who sits up, 'Lord we 'as visitors, what must I look like,' she mumbles. She gets up, pulls her hair straight, ties it back with a piece of ribbon she finds stuffed in her pocket, smooths down the creases of her apron. Thank God Annie found a clean one for her, at least she looks half presentable.

As George greets Mister Fitzwilliam, Molly comes to stand next to him, surprised that such a visitor is standing on their doorstep.

'Good morning, Sir,' George says and tips his non-existent hat.

'Ah, Mister Hogtrough himself! I am very pleased to find you at home this morning. And this is your wife, I take it?'

'Aye, this be she,' says George, and he puts an arm around her shoulder, pulls her close. 'Me wife, Molly.'

'Delighted to meet you Mistress Hogtrough,' and he tips his hat to Molly, who bobs a curtsey. 'I am very happy to find you both here, for I come with gifts from my cousin Emily,' he says, and then turns to George. 'If you remember, Mister Hogtrough, you helped her out of that awful situation two days ago, by the bridge in Letherhed, the overturned coach.'

Molly looks up at George. *Overturned coach? What is he talking about?*

This is the first she has heard of it. Perhaps her husband told her when her mind was full of gin-fuzz. She cannot recall.

The young gentleman continues, 'I feel sure you cannot have forgotten, it was such a terrible shock.'

'No, I could not forget that in a hurry,' George replies.

'Well now, my cousin Emily understands that you have been blessed with twins. Congratulations to you both, I do hope they are well!'

Molly nods, 'Yes Sir, very well indeed, although a little small.' *Lord above, news travels fast.*

'Well, it is good to hear that they are alright, for she has sent some swaddling and clothes for the infants, and linen for their cradle. And I do believe she has included some items for you Mistress Hogtrough, and your young son, too. Shoes, boots, dresses, shirts, and breeches for when the boy is ready, I believe. I am not sure exactly what she instructed to be packed up. But you will find it all in this hamper,' and he points to the large wicker basket now blocking the garden path.

'Goodness me,' Molly says. She knows nothing of George's good deed and looks up at him, amazed. She turns back to the young man in very fine clothes, 'Why thank you kindly, Sir, and to your cousin,' she says, and the man steps aside to reveal the size of the basket which, should they bring it into the house, will take up all the space. Molly is speechless, but cannot wait to open it and see what it contains.

'Sir, you did not need to do this, as I sayed, what I did was only what anyone else would do,' George says, but is also curious to see what is inside the treasure trove.

'Yes, yes, Mister Hogtrough, that's as may be, but I did say you would be rewarded, and so you are. My dear cousin Emily was keen to show her appreciation. I think you will also find some cured ham and preserves for your larder,' says Fitzwilliam, smiling. 'For if your wife is nursing twins she will need additional sustenance.'

George is dumbstruck for a moment, and then remembers his manners. 'Thank you Sir, 'tis very kind of your cousin, most generous. And how is the lady, Sir? Has she recovered?'

'Cousin Emily is well, thank you. I would not say she is completely recovered, but she is resting and being well looked after. I am sure in a few days she will be feeling much better. However, I believe the shock of being trapped in that coach with the unfortunate man who was crushed, well, it will take some time to leave her memory, if ever,' he says, and his eyes cloud at the recollection.

'Ah 'tis good to hear she is on the mend. But yes, that be an awful happ'ning what none should never have to see,' George adds. ''Specially not for a young lady, like.'

'No, indeed,' Fitzwilliam says, and then pulls himself up, as if shaking the memory momentarily from his mind. 'Now, where shall we put this basket for you? Should we bring it inside?'

George looks at the size of it, and turns to Molly, who is still aghast.

She pinches herself to see if she is really awake.

'Well, I think it be alright there, Sir, for we has a house full at the moment, what with fam'ly visitors and the newborn babes, like.' George is also aware that he has not invited the man in, which he sees would be appropriate and yet not, for he is sure that Fitzwilliam has never before seen the interior of such a lowly, run-down cottage.

'Of course, of course,' and he turns to the two lads with him. 'You can leave it there, boys. Take the trap to the farm and turn it around in the yard, I wish to speak to Mister Hogtrough alone.'

The two lads are quickly atop the front of the small open carriage and move it off towards Caen Farm.

'Now Mister Hogtrough, may I call you George?' he asks, but does not wait for an answer. 'So, George, this is from me personally, a gift in thanks for all you did for us,' and Fitzwilliam reaches into his coat pocket and pulls out a little brown leather pouch, which jingles as he hands it to George.

'Good Lord, I mean, thank you kindly, Sir. I don't rightly know what to say, how to give thanks enough for all the generous gifts you's delivered to our door today. I be quite overcome,' and he takes the bag. It feels weighty. Perchance it holds a few copper pennies, certainly not silver which would be lighter, and anyway, hard to come by. Or perhaps it contains some tokens, issued by local traders in Letherhed to fill the gaps in the coinage which the King does not seem to be able to correct. *Might fill me tankard at The Leg a couple of times,* he thinks, with joy.

It seems Fitzwilliam has not quite finished. 'There is one more thing,' he says. 'My father, Lord Norton, understands you are looking for work, and he is in need of a labourer for a garden project at the Lodge. He wonders, if you are free from other obligations, whether you would present yourself to his steward tomorrow at ten o' the clock to discuss the details. Shall I say to him that you will come?'

George wonders at how the man has managed to find out so much about him and his life. Then he remembers that Lord Noton owns the barn where he and Hal had been preparing to repackage contraband. The gentleman might possibly not be so forthcoming with an offer of work if he knew what they had planned to do there.

Molly nudges him from his fish-like speechless pose. 'Dear Husband, do answer the gentleman,' she says, smiling broadly. It seems their world has suddenly turned around on its head since yesterday, and what a relief that is.

'Yes, yes! I am able, for I'm under no contract to another. I will be there, definitely, at ten,' George says, and now he is smiling, too.

Fitzwilliam says farewell to the family as the horses draw up, and he is soon heading back across The Common to his family's estate. As they watch him trot off, Annie comes walking up the Common Lane, smiling. She is alone, but seems happier.

'All good, sister?' George asks.

'Aye, all good, brother,' she replies. 'I've decided to take me chances with the rascally rake, for I loves him, and I has no other way out of this, does I?'

Molly, having been asleep when Hal called earlier and missed all the fuss, looks at Annie, puzzled. 'What rascal be that, sister?' she asks.

'You may as well know, Moll,' Annie says, and pauses, takes a deep breath. 'I's with child and Hal Archer is the father,' she says.

'Oh!' Molly is speechless. She has been so hard on the man in recent weeks for poaching her husband, but now it seems George has been offered an opportunity away from whatever he and Hal were cooking up together, and suddenly, Hal does not seem so bad after all. 'Well, you kept that a bit quiet, girl,' she says.

'Aye, Moll. I daren't say nothing. I were so worried what Jesse would say, you know what he be like. Anyway, he found out yesterday and has throwed me out of the cottage. But Hal's gone off to see the Rector, to get the banns called, and then to find us a home, quick, like,' Annie smiles, a little sheepishly. 'There's Spindle Cottage, that new home up the top of the lane, near his mother's. 'Tis empty now old Mister Spedding upped and went to stay with his daughter.'

'Well, then! 'Tas turned out alright, blessèd be, you must be very relieved,' Molly says. 'Now, come! Do help me open this here ginormous basket, for I cannot wait to see what be inside, and I's gonna be pinchin' meself for a month with all today's wondrous news!'

'With gladness,' Annie replies, and they get to work on the hamper.

George leaves them to it and goes back to the table.

'Well brother, Henry here's been telling me of your good deed after the coach upturned, like. Well, I'm blowed, looks like the man's give you a good reward. But come now, spill out the bag. How much have you there?' Ned asks, grinning.

'Most prob'ly enough for a couple of ales. I hopes, anyways,' George says, and his face, for once, is cheerful and carefree. He pulls the strings of the pouch apart and tips the coins out. They roll onto the table, glinting in the sunlight.

'Good God,' George says, astounded. 'I ain't never saw so much gold in me life! Look at that! Five bleedin' guineas! Stone the crows.'

And as long as he can stop those fire-coloured coins from burning holes in his pockets, it looks like he will be able to keep his promises to Molly.

Their future is already looking better.

Epilogue

After church, Jesse avoids Rye Cottage, where he is sure his sister has taken shelter. He stomps a different route homewards, continuing the trace of Woodfield Lane when it stops being a worn road and turns to little-used grassy track. He crosses the brook by the narrow bridge near Dukes Hall Farm and glances over at the buildings. The pond in front of the dilapidated farmhouse is now green with pernicious weeds and tall bullrushes. It has been allowed to become far too overgrown since the last good farmer left.

Wasters, lazy good for nothings have taken up residence and now it is going to ruin.

Like me bleedin' family.

Father lying buckled and broken in his pit. Sister Annie, who let her flower be plucked too soon and by a worthless rake at that. Brother George, the workshy fool, and his drunken, licentious wife.

And Henry-head-in-the-clouds, dreaming of gold-paved streets, pies in the sky, did not even turn up at church as he was instructed.

What a bleedin' useless lot they are, his righteous self says.

And then he recalls William's words. They chasten and spank him again, and he reddens. Sadly, no one is near to see his discomfort. That plank stuck so deeply in his eye, which his father pointed out to him, was surely cut from the King Oak's ancient woody hoard, for that is where he, himself, was lost to his own demon.

And to drink, to lust.

To Elizabeth. Or rather, where she was lost to him.

Finally, the lane peters out, and he cuts across the open grazing land following a scrubby path. He beheads the sad, drooping bonnets of pretty wild flowers as he passes, crushes them with his angry fist and throws them to the ground. When he reaches Caen Farm he does not stop, but continues on, eyes down, walking between the trees along the twisty forest paths.

Before long he has arrived at the beginning of his failure.

The King Oak stands before him in the centre of its court, now dismembered, torn almost in two. One enormous, thick and twisted arm is lying next to the squat, wounded trunk. Faint wisps of smoke coil up from the still smouldering branch.

Elizabeth comes again to mind. That was her branch, where deep cracks split the tree on the day she climbed up the Oak's gnarly body and out along the limb, and then slipped uneasily off. The fissures were hidden, the branch only waiting to crash to the ground and follow the young girl's body to the earth.

Now it has fallen, the King Oak is finally rid of her tragedy.

He walks towards the ancient tree, torn asunder by heavenly light, ripped apart by earthly dark.

His dark.

Images come flooding back, washing over his sores like the cat o'nine tails, scratching at his mind and unsettling his soul. He resists, but they insist, and appear to him as clear as day.

The quart of brandy he picked from Father's stash and drank till it was empty. *Idiot.*

His brother's jacket, snug around his shoulders, a perfect fit.

His mummery, tom-foolery, pretence at being his twin.

His malicious jealousy.

Elizabeth, her blonde locks tumbling over her slender shoulders, down around her delightful bosom. *Her temptation.*

No! His weakness.

The brimful of envy, which rose up and took what was not his to take, the devil moving in him, uninvited and unwanted, used despicable force against a beautiful soul.

Her tears, her wails, her fear.

Later, the rope around her red, burned neck. Her face, contorted, puffy, blue, swinging from the branch.

His brother's fists, his brother's grief, the punches, cuts and lashes. The open wounds which never heal.

Afterwards, the Oxmoor Pond, where he held his blackened, swollen face under the murky water to wash away his sins. So foolish to think that any amount of clear water could ever reach the depth of them.

His eternal shame. His disgrace. His punishment.

He drops to his knees in a rooty, mossy hollow before the King Oak.

A confession squeezes out from between his quivering lips.

'Dear Lord, forgive me for I have sinned, and mightily,' he stutters. 'Sins of greed, of lust and gluttony. Sins of the flesh, of envy,' the words ooze like treacle, thick, sticky, heavy and dark, they slither from his soul, through the prison bars of wiry, red beard, which has held them back for so long.

Finally, they have escaped and, now liberated, they present themselves to the King Oak and to Jesse's God.

A raw offering, indeed.

Tears come. Seventeen years of pathetic, salty shame rolls down his cheeks and puddle at his knees. The mossy hollow fills with his dishonour and he sinks into the horror he became on that awful afternoon. His cold lips mumble on and on, praying for forgiveness, as he wallows in repentance.

He falls silent and then…

'Forgiven,' says his own voice back to him.

So clear it was, as if from without, and not within.

Too real.

Snap. A crack of twig.

He is not alone. He looks up, and there stands his reflection.

'Forgiven,' it says again. 'And I release you from the threat I uttered, too. You are free to move on, if you can. But we shall never speak of this again. Understand, Brother?'

And Ned Hogtrough leaves his twin kneeling before the broken King Oak, and heads for a place far away from the past.

ACKNOWLEDGEMENTS

King Oak has been a long time in the writing, so firstly, I wish to give thanks to everyone who has put up with me harping on about it.

In Switzerland, thanks especially go to Esther, without whom I would have floundered.

My thanks also to Bea, Eveline and Conny, who go above and beyond with their generosity; as well as to a great ambassador, Luzia; to Roli and Jürg for their laughter; to Stee for buying the first copy, and more. To everyone else who has helped and supported me since I have lived in their wonderful land – the list is too long to mention all here, but you are certainly not forgotten.

Many, many thanks to readers Liz and Sandy, for their patience in ploughing through a very hefty, pre-edited version, and for their enthusiasm and encouraging words.

Also thanks to Scott Pack for his invaluable editorial assessment and other welcome advice; to Nell Wood for her amazing design; to Beth for her technical skills and help with the website.

Thanks go to John Rowley at the Leatherhead & District Local History Society who provided information regarding Lord North.

And thank you from my heart to my great friend Angie, for her critical eye, sage advice, and so much more.

AUTHOR'S NOTES

Firstly, a note about place names. Ashtead, as it is now called, has gone through many spelling variants. Samuel Pepys, writing in 1663, referred to it as 'Ashsted'; in 1773 it was recorded on a map as 'Asted'; by 1820 it had become 'Ashsted' again. I chose Ashted, for no other reason than I wanted it to be a little different from the current spelling. Similarly, for Letherhed and Epsum – these are my spellings and may not have any historical provenance.

Research for this book lead me to many places. The genealogical sites ancestry.co.uk, findmypast.co.uk and familysearch.org were a real inspiration. Whilst growing a family tree, I came across the tight-knit community of Woodfield on the edge of Ashtead Common. The discovery of half stories about the inhabitants' escapades piqued my interest and ultimately gave me the idea for a series of books, the first of which is King Oak.

When I picked the date of Thursday, June 8, 1780 as a starting point, I had no idea that the Gordon Riots were in full swing in London. The fascinating history reveals an unsettling time which could quite easily have led to another civil war in England, and the upheaval caused considerable cost to life and property. The riots were ultimately quashed before the mob got too far out of hand. Susanna Elizabeth Phillips (nee Burney, 1755–1800) wrote a contemporary account through letters to her sister, the novelist Fanny Burney. A few years later, Susanna was living at Juniper Hall, Mickleham. Most famously, Charles Dickens wrote a 'posthumous' history of the troubled times in Barnaby Rudge, and BBC Radio 4's 'In Our Time' presented by Melvyn Bragg has an episode dedicated to the riots. There are numerous online resources detailing the event, for which I am grateful.

Frederick North, 2nd Earl of Guilford, (1732–1792) was prime minister of Great Britain from 1770 to 1782. He was better known by his courtesy title of Lord North. He may or may not have lived in Ashtead, but he certainly had connections to the surrounding area, having once owned the property 'Durdens' (long a famous stables) in nearby Epsom. His stepbrother was William Legge, 2nd Earl of Dartmouth, the grandfather of William Legge, who was rector of St. Giles, Ashtead between 1826–1872. Thomas Martindale was rector between 1777 and 1782.

The details of the Portsmouth Coach episode is entirely fictional. However, in the 'Journal of the House of Commons 1782', a petition by several 'Noblemen, Gentlemen, Clergy, and Freeholders of the County of Surrey' was presented to the House. The petition concerned numerous bridges in the county which were 'narrow and incommodious for Carriages and Passengers (whereby much mischief has been done)'. In order to ensure good communication between London and Portsmouth, which the petitioners considered as being 'of the utmost National Consequence', no doubt due to the importance of the naval docks, they called for private bridges to be transferred to the County in order that they could be properly rebuilt, widened and kept in good repair. As evidence of the dangerous nature of the bridges, they cited an accident with the Portsmouth Coach attempting to cross the bridge at Leatherhead, which occurred around 1780.

The Leg of Mutton and Cauliflower in Ashtead, and The

Running Horse in Leatherhead still exist. John Skelton wrote a poem (c. 1545) called 'The Tunnyng of Elynour Rummyng', about an infamous landlady at The Running Horse who watered down her beer with … well, I shall say no more, but she certainly paid for her sins, according to Skelton. A little before the King Oak's time, but an interesting story, nonetheless.

I chose the midwife Eleanor Knocker's name in recognition of Elsie Knocker. Born Elizabeth Blackall Shapter in 1884, in Exeter, she was a British nurse and ambulance driver in World War I. Together with her friend Mairi Chisholm, they 'saved the lives of thousands of soldiers on the Western Front in Belgium' (source: Wikipedia). Elsie Knocker died in Ashtead on 26th April 1978 at the age of 93.

There is a trove of old ordnance survey maps dating from the mid 19th century at The National Library of Scotland's website (maps.nls.uk).

Local history groups also provided a wealth of information. Leatherhead and District Local History Society (leatherheadhistory.org) and Epsom and Ewell History Explorer (eehe.org.uk) were particularly useful.

Ashtead Common is now owned and maintained by City of London. (cityoflondon.gov.uk)

The veteran tree known locally as 'King Oak' still stands in a leafy glade, deep in Ashtead Common's forest.

Whether anyone ever made any promises to anyone there, I cannot truly say.

A NOTE ON THE DIALECT

There are a few Surrey words included in the book, which I learned from Graeme Davis' book 'Dictionary of Surrey English, a New Edition of A Glossary of Surrey Words by Granville Leveson Gower', published by Peter Lang.

Dialogue in King Oak, particularly for the older characters, perhaps reflects some of the old Surrey dialect, but for ease of reading, I have kept it to a minimum. Mr Davis' book mentions malapropisms being common in the old dialect. I have included some, just for fun – ex'curse for excuse, for example. Any other misspellings are intentional where they appear within dialogue.

Another source of 18th century English, particularly for the smugglers, is the wonderful 'Cant – A Gentleman's Guide to the Language of Rogues in Georgian London' by Stephen Hart. I unashamedly stole the Vice Admiral's name and explanation for it from there, along with some other terms, so thank you, Stephen.

Although born in Surrey, I grew up in East Sussex, where there is a definite crossover of dialect words from its Surrey neighbour. I was not sure what terms would be strange to readers from other parts of the English-speaking world, or speakers of other languages who may come across the book. Therefore, I have listed in the glossary only those which were new to me.

GLOSSARY

ampery	decaying, rotten
bevers	eleven o'clock meal
cockling	weeding, 'cockling the vetches' (This comes from 'Farming in Dorset - Diary of James Warne, 1758', but perhaps they also used it in Surrey. Included because it is a wonderful expression.)
dorling	runt of a pig's litter
increasement	labour pains
one-eyed	as in 'a one-eyed piece of Ashted', out of the way, neglected
purl	ale with a dash of wormwood
runagate	tramp, someone 'running from the law'
swells	gentry
travish	refuse, rubbish
wasp	an infected prostitute

Printed in Great Britain
by Amazon

24602800R00233